Dear Reader,

I'm delighted to share my new novel, *The Stolen Child*, with you and introduce you to a brand new set of characters! I loved creating the story for Stella, Tom and Grace and hope you'll be intrigued by the mystery of what happens to baby William!

It's wonderful to hear from my lovely readers, so please do get in touch via Facebook www.facebook.comJennieFeltonAuthor or follow me on Twitter @Jennie_Felton for my latest news!

Love,
Jennie x

**Praise for The Families of Fairley Terrace sagas:**

'Believable characters, a vivid sense of time and place,
thoroughly enjoyable' Rosie Goodwin

'Fans of Katie Flynn will love this' *Peterborough Evening Telegraph*

'Enthralling . . . Jennie Felton . . . writes her stories straight
from the heart . . . evokes time and place with compelling authenticity,
and conjures up a feisty heroine and a cast of engaging characters'
*Lancashire Evening Post*

'Sweeps us back to a time of struggle and hardship in a story packed
with high emotion, dramatic landscapes and the harsh realities of
living and working in a mining community' *Blackpool Gazette*

'Has everything a family saga should have – happiness, extreme sadness,
love, death, births, etc. but above all it was a real page turner . . .
Thank you, Jennie, for writing such a wonderful book' *Boon's Bookcase*

'If you like the style of Catherine Cookson, Josephine Cox
or Katie Flynn then you'll enjoy this'
*Books With Wine And Chocolate*

'A great read with a cast of believable characters' *The People's Friend*

## By Jennie Felton

*The Families of Fairley Terrace Sagas*
All The Dark Secrets
The Birthday Surprise (short story featured in the anthology
*A Mother's Joy*)
The Miner's Daughter
The Girl Below Stairs
The Widow's Promise
The Sister's Secret

*Standalone*
The Stolen Child

# The
# Stolen
# Child

## JENNIE
## FELTON

HEADLINE

First published in Great Britain in 2019 by
HEADLINE PUBLISHING GROUP

First published in paperback in 2020 by
HEADLINE PUBLISHING GROUP

1

Cataloguing in Publication Data is available from the British Library

ISBN 978 1 4722 5644 7

Typeset in Calisto by Avon DataSet Ltd, Bidford-on-Avon, Warwickshire

Printed and bound in Great Britain by Clays Ltd, Elcograf S.p.A.

HEADLINE PUBLISHING GROUP
An Hachette UK Company
Carmelite House
50 Victoria Embankment
London EC4Y 0DZ

www.headline.co.uk
www.hachette.co.uk

For Kate and Becky,

with love and thanks for all your support.

It's about time I dedicated a book to you two!

# *Acknowledgements*

First – a huge thank-you to all my readers! If you didn't continue to buy my books none of the other acknowledgements would be necessary, because I'd be out of a job! I hope you continue to enjoy them as much as I enjoy writing them.

I am so lucky in having a fantastic team supporting me. I am eternally grateful to Kate Byrne, my wonderful editor at Headline, and my equally wonderful agent, Rebecca Ritchie, at AM Heath, who are always there when I need them and work so hard on my behalf. I am in total awe of Jane Selley, my copy editor – how on earth does she manage to keep tabs on everything with a cast of so many characters so as to be able to point out that a character or place in the early chapters has changed its name towards the end?

I'd also like to mention the team at Headline, especially Rhea Kurien, Phoebe Swinburn, Rebecca Bader, Olivia Allen, Caroline Young and Martin Kerans – who beaver away behind the scenes.

Thank you, all! I'm having a ball and I hope you are too!

# Chapter One

## February 1911

The mewling whimpers roused Stella Swift from the light doze she had fallen into in the fireside chair. Automatically she reached out for the handle of the perambulator, which was drawn up beside her, rocking it gently though she knew it would do no good. It never did. The whimpers grew louder, hiccuping sobs escalating into anguished cries.

Leaden with exhaustion, Stella levered herself up, lifted the baby from the pram and sank down again, unbuttoning her nightgown, exposing one heavy, milk-filled breast, and guiding the gasping mouth towards her nipple.

To her immense relief, he was latching on, sucking, and Stella prayed that he would get a proper feed this time. For a full minute she held her breath as the sharp tingles ran little rivers through her breast and into the deepest parts of her; then, as they lessened, despair flooded in, obliterating hope.

Oh no. Not again. By the light of the moon streaming in through the gap in the curtains, she could see that the rosebud mouth had gone slack, the baby's head was lolling against her chest. She jiggled him, trying to wake him enough to get him to latch back on, but he only grumbled a little, his downy head still heavy against her.

Why? Why did he yell hungrily every time she laid him down, only to fall asleep the moment he was cradled in her arms? He was tired, she supposed – he never slept properly in his cot or his pram – but she was tired too, to the point where she could scarcely think straight any more, let alone struggle through the days caring for him and her three other children.

Six weeks it had been going on now, almost from the moment he was born. Six weeks of stressful days and broken nights while the black cloud of depression that surrounded her grew ever thicker. She could feel it now, weighing her down, suffocating her as if a feather pillow was being pressed over her face so that she struggled to breathe.

She'd experienced something similar after the birth of each of her children, often on the verge of tears, forcing herself to do the things that had to be done, feeling useless, utterly worthless. It wasn't unusual, her neighbour, Francie Newman, had said. A lot of women felt that way after having a baby, and it soon passed. She'd been right; gradually Stella had recovered, getting back to her normal chirpy self. But it had been nothing like as bad as it was this time.

None of the others had been this much trouble, of course. Oliver, who was six now, had been a contented baby who'd always slept well, and he hadn't changed much, Stella thought ruefully. She still had a job to wake him in the mornings – sometimes she had to stuff him into his school clothes while he stood beside his bed, eyelids drooping, still half asleep. Alec, a year younger, might be a little monkey, but he tired himself out with his antics and fell asleep as soon as his head touched the pillow. As for Emily, a year younger again, she was usually a good girl. Being so close in age, they were a tight little unit, looking out for and amusing one another, and Stella had almost forgotten the dark days that had dogged her after each birth.

And then, to her dismay, she'd found herself pregnant again, the last thing she had wanted.

'Four's a good number,' Tom had said, seemingly quite pleased. 'And the others are at school now and off your hands all day. It'll be easier for you to manage.'

Stella had bitten her lip and said nothing. It was easy for him to say that. It wasn't him who had to cook and clean, wash clothes and bedding, take the children to school and collect them each day, feed them, put them to bed. During the week he was at work in the pit from dawn till dusk – dark, even, in the long winter months – and all for a pittance that she had to make stretch somehow to keep body and soul together. Another baby wouldn't just be more work; it would mean extra expense too. She'd long since got rid of the layette that had served the first three children – most of it was matted and shrunken from countless washes anyway, and she had hoped their family was complete. Now, from somewhere, she'd have to magic up a new set, and clothes for a toddler too as the baby grew. Not to mention that there would be another mouth to feed.

No, she hadn't been best pleased, but since there was nothing to be done about it, she'd put on a brave face and hoped for the best. And when William had been placed in her arms, she had been so suffused with love that all her misgivings had been forgotten. She couldn't imagine how she could not have wanted him. Tom had been right. Four *was* a good number. They *would* manage.

But then the problems had begun – the constant crying when he should be sleeping, the dozing-off the minute she began to feed him. And the depression she'd suffered with each previous birth returned with a vengeance. She was weighed down by exhaustion. Tears were never far away. Her temper was frayed like the old binders she'd dumped four years ago. Sometimes she felt locked away inside herself, so that speaking required enormous effort; sometimes she heard herself snapping at Tom, shouting at the children over the slightest misdemeanour. She'd even slapped Emily across the back of her legs for laughing when Alec had scribbled his name in crayon on the scullery wall and Stella had flown into a rage, hitting out blindly. 'It's not funny!' she'd screamed at the little girl.

Almost at once she'd been horrified and ashamed at what she had done, gathering a sobbing Emily into her arms and weeping herself into her daughter's soft golden curls. Giving the boys a clip round the ear when they deserved it was one thing; slapping Emily hard enough to raise red finger marks on her plump little thighs was something else entirely.

The blackness had descended again then. She was a terrible mother. She was making life miserable for all of them. They'd be better off without her. She wished she could end it all. Go to sleep and never wake up. But she couldn't. They needed her. She was trapped in a haze of exhaustion and despair, an endless round of chores and trying to cope. And all the while the baby crying . . .

She'd managed to get some nourishment into him tonight at bedtime by expressing some milk from her throbbing breasts into a pap boat and drip-feeding it to him. Tom, who was getting more worried about her by the day, had suggested they move the crib to his side of the bed, and he'd rocked it with an outstretched arm until Will settled. Grateful and tired out, Stella had fallen asleep the moment her head touched the pillow, but a couple of hours later, the thin mewling cries had wakened her. She'd struggled up and out of bed, anxious to get to Will before he woke Tom too. He had work tomorrow and another long day hewing coal in the depths of the earth. He needed his sleep.

She'd grabbed her dressing gown from the hook on the back of the bedroom door and taken Will downstairs. She managed to get a little more milk into him, then laid him in his pram and settled herself in the fireside chair. She did that sometimes to avoid disturbing Tom, and she prayed she could snatch a couple more hours of much-needed sleep herself.

But now Will was awake again. And once more refusing to feed. Stella could feel the tension rising inside her like a kettle coming to the boil.

She'd try the pap boat. It had worked earlier. Please God it would work again.

She went to the scullery, fetched it, and expressed some more warm milk. Then she lifted Will out of his pram and went to sit down again. But disorientated and heavy with exhaustion, she landed heavily against the arm of the chair, bumping down into the seat, and the pap boat slipped from her grasp and smashed on the tiled fire surround. Shards of glass and a couple of larger fragments swam in a sea of milk, and Fluffy, their cat, who had been curled up in front of the fire, shot up and streaked out of the room.

'Oh no!' It came out as an anguished scream. 'No! No! No!'

Frightened by the sudden eruption, Will began to cry again with all the strength of his little lungs. Tucking him roughly under one arm, Stella reached down to right the remains of the pap boat before more milk spilled out, but it broke apart beneath her searching hand, one large jagged shard piercing her palm and cutting into her finger. Instinctively she jerked her hand up into her lap. Blood was gushing from her cut finger, though as yet none was seeping from the spot where the piece of glass had embedded itself in her palm, erect as a well-aimed dart on a dartboard. Instinctively she grasped it with her other hand, yanking it out and staring at it for a moment as if transfixed.

Blood was dripping down on to Will's white nightgown, but she barely noticed. She was aware of nothing but the sharp pain throbbing in her finger and the black despair that was closing in on her as if the broken glass had cut not only her hand but the fragile thread of her control. Her head drooped; tears ran unchecked down her face and mingled with the blood.

'I can't stand it!' she cried brokenly. 'I can't stand it any more!'

'Stella? What . . . ? Oh my God, Stella!'

She barely heard Tom's voice, didn't register that he was there. She simply sat rocking herself and sobbing, the piece of glass still clutched in one hand while the other dripped blood on to Will's gown.

Tom was across the room in a few quick strides, horrified at the scene that had met his eyes.

He'd already been half awake when the commotion had begun; he hadn't been back to sleep properly since Stella had taken Will downstairs to feed him. He was desperately worried about her, and anxious about Will too. The doctor hadn't been able to find anything wrong with him, saying he was just a colicky baby and he'd grow out of it, but though Tom wanted to believe him, a niggling doubt remained.

His overriding concern, however, was Stella, who he knew was barely coping. She'd gone through a worrying stage after the other children had been born, but nothing like this. He remembered a woman who had lived nearby when he was a boy; she had 'gone funny', as his mother had described it, after she'd had a baby, and had smothered it while it slept. Though he'd never seen the woman again – she'd been taken away to the lunatic asylum, his mother had said – the horror of it had cast a long shadow and he'd scuttled hurriedly past the house for years as if it was haunted. These past weeks he'd watched Stella becoming less and less like herself, and found himself thinking about his former neighbour for the first time in years. God forbid that Stella would do anything to harm Will, but he hurried home from work each day, never knowing how he'd find her and increasingly anxious.

The minute he'd heard her screaming, he'd leapt out of bed and rushed downstairs, breath tight in his chest. As he'd gone into the living room, he'd turned cold at the sight that greeted him.

The sharp fragment of glass in her raised hand, hovering above Will's tiny form. The blood. The glazed look in her eyes. And most chilling of all, her anguished words: 'I can't stand it! I can't stand it any more!'

'For God's sake, Stella, what have you done?'

His hand shot out, grabbing her wrist. The piece of glass fell from her grasp and he reached for Will, lifting him out of her unprotesting arms. The baby was yelling lustily, but mercifully he seemed unharmed. Tom laid him in his pram and turned his attention to his wife.

He could see now that the blood had come from her hand; it was running down her wrist and soaking the sleeve of her nightgown. There was a pile of clean binders on the kitchen table; he fetched one, using it to catch the drips while he examined the wound, which looked to be fairly superficial, then wrapped it tightly round her hand. He knew from past experience that fingers could bleed heavily, but hopefully that would stop the worst of it. And to be honest, he was more concerned about her mental state than a couple of cuts.

He dropped to his knees beside her chair, holding her bandaged hand and looking into her face.

'What happened, Stella?'

She shook her head, still rocking, still gazing unseeingly into space. Tears were rolling unchecked down her cheeks. He wiped them away with his fingers.

'Talk to me, Stella, please.'

Still nothing. Her mouth worked a little, but only to chew at her bottom lip. Her flooded eyes flicked towards the pram; her free hand went up to cover her ear, as if to shut out the sound of the baby's crying. She whispered something. He leaned closer.

'What?'

'I . . . can't . . . stand it . . . any more . . .'

The same words she'd sobbed out earlier. Tom's heart dropped into the pit of his stomach. His worst nightmare was becoming reality. She *had* been going to harm Will. Thank God he'd come downstairs when he had. But what the hell was he going to do now? There was no way she could be left alone with the baby again. She needed help. He'd have to get the doctor to her. But it was the middle of the night. And Will needed feeding. First things first. Somehow he had to try to get some milk into him, get him to sleep, so that at least he could think straight.

In her present state he wasn't sure it was a good idea to ask Stella to try and feed him, but with the pap boat in pieces he didn't know what option he had. He lifted Will out of the pram, laid him in Stella's lap and pulled the neck of her nightgown open.

'He's hungry. Try him again.'

'It's no use,' she whimpered.

'Just try.' His tone was stern now and she seemed to respond to it, lifting the baby's head to her breast.

To his relief, Will latched on, and with Tom's hand resting against the back of his neck to keep him steady, he sucked desperately for perhaps five minutes. Then his head lolled again.

'See?' Stella's eyes rose to meet Tom's, challenging, as if to say 'I told you so'.

'He's had some at least.' Tom laid Will back in the pram,

pulling the lacy blanket up to cover him. 'Now, you're going back to bed.'

'He'll be awake again soon . . .' Her voice was tearful, but at least she was talking.

'I'm fetching the gravy boat.' He'd thought of it as he sat silently watching the baby feed. 'Squeeze some milk into that. If he does wake, I can try to get some into him.'

'But—'

'I'll stay down here with him. You need some sleep, Stella.'

'So do you.' Her voice was flat, expressionless.

'I'll be all right.'

Wordlessly she expressed some milk into the gravy boat. Tom set it on the table and urged her towards the stairs. She was moving like a woman in a dream, limbs awkward and heavy, and as he pulled the covers over her he saw that her eyes were still staring, haunted.

He turned off the oil lamp, kissed her forehead.

'Just rest, my love, and don't worry about anything.'

She didn't reply, but as he pulled the bedroom door shut behind him, he thought he heard a muffled sob.

He went back downstairs and settled himself in the chair she had vacated. There was nothing more he could do tonight. But first thing in the morning he was going to call the doctor. They couldn't go on like this. Stella had reached breaking point and she was a danger to both herself and Will, and perhaps to the other children too.

Tom closed his eyes and tried to get what rest he could. But the anxiety was a cold, hard knot in his stomach. He had no idea what anyone could do for Stella, how they were going to manage or what was going to happen next. But he had a terrible feeling that they had reached a turning point in their lives and nothing would ever be the same again.

# *Chapter Two*

Dr Alistair Mackay drove his motor up the long, curving hill out of Hillsbridge and along the straight stretch that was Dunderwick Road. He passed a row of terraced houses – miners' cottages – on his left-hand side, with open fields on his right, then slowed as he approached more rows of tied cottages beyond them, coming to a stop outside number 21.

No pony and trap for him now – he'd treated himself to the Model T Ford two years ago and had never regretted it for a second. The motor saved him so much time; he was able to make home visits to even the most distant villages much more easily, and it was immeasurably easier to get it going than to have to persuade a sometimes reluctant pony into the shafts of the trap.

This morning, damp and bitterly cold, with the cloud so heavy it was still not properly light, was a case in point. He'd not long been out of bed when there had been a knock at the door. He'd hastily buttoned his waistcoat and shrugged into his tweed suit jacket as he hurried downstairs.

By the time he reached the hallway, his wife, Jessica, had already opened the door and was speaking to a young lad he didn't recognise, but who looked to be about twelve or thirteen years old. As she heard Alistair behind her, she stepped to one side, making room for him on the doorstep.

'This is Ferdie Newman – he lives next door to the Swift family in Dunderwick Road. Mr Swift asked him to come for you. It seems it's urgent.'

'Is it the baby?' Alistair asked, anxious. He'd attended Stella in her confinement just a few weeks ago, and the child hadn't appeared to be suffering any complications. But infants were horribly vulnerable, and nothing caused him more distress than a new little life cut short.

The lad twisted his cap between his hands. 'He didn't say – just to fetch you quick sharp. But I could hear the babby crying.'

'I see,' Alistair said, relieved. If the baby was crying, at least he was alive. But it wasn't like the Swifts to call him out for no reason. 'Very well. I'll come now.' A thought struck him. 'How did you get here? Would you like a ride back?'

'It's all right. I got me bike.' The lad jerked his head in the direction of the road, and Alistair saw a bicycle propped up against the low wall beside the gate.

'I could put it on the back seat.'

'No, you're all right.'

Alistair was surprised at him turning down the chance of a ride in a motor, but he guessed from the lad's body language that he wasn't completely comfortable. Because Alistair was 'the doctor', he supposed. Though he never put on airs and graces, always treated his patients as equals, many of them were in awe of him.

'Do you want a cup of tea before you go?' Jessica asked as the lad scampered away down the path.

'Is there one in the pot?'

'Yes – it should be brewed by now. And what about something to eat?'

'No, just a quick cup of tea. I'll have breakfast when I get back.'

Jessica poured it, adding milk and two sugars the way he liked it, and he drank half a cup in between buttoning his jacket and fetching his medical bag and overcoat, then headed for the door. Jessica followed him into the hallway and reached up to give him a kiss on the cheek.

'Take care.'

He grinned. 'You still don't trust me to drive Lizzie safely, do you?' It had been Jessica's idea to give the motor a name.

'Of course I do! It's just that . . . well, accidents happen.'

'Don't worry. I'll be careful. And I'll probably be hungry enough for bacon and eggs when I get back.'

But telling Jessica not to worry was a pointless exercise. She'd worried about him when he'd been driving the pony and trap, afraid a wheel might come off or the pony bolt or slip when the roads were icy. She'd always had a vivid imagination, and since becoming a doctor's wife she seemed more aware than ever of all the misfortunes that could suddenly disrupt, or even end, a life.

But he loved her for it, just as he loved everything about her. Until he'd met Jessica, he'd been a confirmed bachelor in his thirties, considered very eligible by more than one mother seeking a good marriage for her daughter, but his demanding profession had been more than enough for him. And then, five years ago, he'd fallen in love.

How lucky could one man be? he sometimes asked himself. Happily married, in a profession he loved, and the proud owner of a smart Model T Ford – black, with red leather seats – that usually started first time when he turned the starting handle. No more having to harness up the pony on filthy mornings like today. And the motor would be there outside the house in Dunderwick Road when he finished his visit to the Swift household, not halfway down the lane as the trap had sometimes been when the pony had gone off in search of fresh grass to munch.

Collecting his medical bag from the back seat, he opened the gate to number 21, walked down the path between tidy lawns and neat flower borders, bare now for winter, and rapped on the door with the brass knocker fashioned in the shape of a fox's head.

Almost at once he heard footsteps running across the tiled entrance hall, and the door was opened by a small boy wearing a solemn expression. Close behind him were his younger brother and sister, looking equally solemn. Somewhere in the house, the baby was crying.

'Oliver, isn't it?' Alistair's voice still carried a soft Scottish burr, which was less thick now than when he had first come to Hillsbridge some sixteen years ago, but which he had never lost completely. 'Can you tell your daddy the doctor is here?'

Tom Swift appeared in the doorway of the living room and joined them in the little hall. 'Come in, Doctor. And you three,' he said to the children, 'make yourselves scarce. Go and play in the front room – I've got the fire going in there, so it should be warm by now.'

'What about school, Daddy?' Oliver asked.

'We'll worry about that later.' Tom turned to Alistair, who was closing the front door after him, and lowered his voice. 'Can we have a word out here before we go in? It's Stella, Doctor. I'm worried to death about her.'

'Of course. What seems to be the trouble?'

'I don't know, and that's the truth. But she hasn't been herself since William was born, and last night . . .'

He went on to relate the events of the previous night in an urgent whisper.

'I don't know what she meant to do,' he finished. 'I'm just glad I came downstairs when I did, or . . . well, it doesn't bear thinking about. I can't leave her on her own with the baby – I should be at work now, but . . .' He spread his hands helplessly. 'All I could think of was to send for you. I don't know what you can do for her, but she's got to have some help or I dread to think what might happen.'

'You did the right thing.' Alistair's heart had sunk. It sounded to him as if Stella was suffering from puerperal fever, which was not uncommon, and if memory served him right he thought she had had it before. But if she really had intended to harm young William then it must be far more serious, and really there was very little he could do to help her.

One look at her was enough to confirm his worst suspicions. She was seated in the fireside chair, rocking back and forth, her hands working ceaselessly in her lap. But her eyes were glazed, her expression vacant, and she was completely ignoring the baby crying in his pram.

'Stella?' he said, pulling an upright dining chair beside her and sitting down so that he was more or less eye level with her.

For a moment she did not respond at all; it was as if she was locked away inside herself. Then her lips moved and she mumbled something too softly for him to hear.

'I didn't catch that, Stella . . .'

Her head swivelled towards him with startling abruptness and the dead eyes were suddenly alive and blazing.

'I can't stand it any more!' It was an angry shriek, as if she was blaming him for not hearing her the first time. 'He won't stop crying, and I can't bear it.'

Then she turned away, the dazed expression back on her face.

'He does cry an awful lot,' Tom interjected. 'And it's a hell of a job to get any feed into him. We did mention it to you, if you remember, and you said it was most likely colic.'

'It probably is,' Alistair said. 'I don't expect it's anything to worry about, but I'll take another look at him later to be sure. At the moment, though, my major concern is Stella. I think the best thing would be for her to be taken into hospital, for the time being anyway.'

'You mean the cottage hospital at High Compton?' Tom was looking more worried than ever, wondering, no doubt, how he was going to manage.

'No,' Alistair said evenly. 'They wouldn't be able to help her there. I think she should go to Catcombe.'

'Catcombe?' Tom repeated, horrified. 'You mean . . . the asylum?'

'The mental hospital, yes.' Alistair didn't like the old term, still commonly used locally. It carried a terrible stigma, as well as invoking horror and dread. 'They have the facilities to keep her safe, hopefully help her back to her old self, and take care of the baby too.'

'William would go with her?' Tom asked. He was still reeling from the shock of what the doctor had said, but struggling to remain calm.

'While she's still breast-feeding, yes. But that would be supervised, and he'd be looked after in the nursery at other times. It may well be that it's her nervous state that's been upsetting him, and in calm surroundings the feeding problems will be solved.'

Tom ran his hand through his thick thatch of fair hair. 'Oh Doctor, I don't know . . .'

'I don't think we have any choice, Mr Swift,' Alistair said sympathetically. 'As you've said yourself, she can't be left here with a baby to care for while she is so poorly. And hopefully it won't be for long. As soon as she recovers, she and William can come home.'

'I suppose so . . .' Tom clearly didn't like it one little bit, but what choice was there? 'When . . . ?'

'I'll make the arrangements at once. Then, if you can pack a bag for her and the baby, I'll come back as soon as my morning surgery is finished and take her myself.'

'Thank you, Doctor. I'm sorry to cause you all this trouble.'

'No trouble at all. And none of this is your fault. I'm just sorry it's happened. But don't worry. I'm sure she'll recover before long and be back here with you and the children.'

But for all his comforting words, as he left the warmth of the little house for the clammy cold of the February morning, Alistair Mackay was not feeling overly optimistic.

He'd come across something similar when a patient had insisted on having the bedroom window locked because she was terrified that she would throw her baby out, but Stella's case seemed to be much more serious. He only hoped that a stay at Catcombe would put her right, but he had heard of cases where the patient never made a full recovery.

He was concerned about the baby too. Was it possible he'd missed something? Once they were in the hospital, he'd do some further investigation. For the past six years he had been one of the medical officers who dealt with any physical ailments among the patients there, and he would make little William a priority. Get the baby right, and hopefully Stella would improve too.

He tossed his medical bag on to the back seat of the Ford and cranked the starting handle to bring the engine to life. Then he set out to drive home, where he might just have time for some breakfast before taking his morning surgery.

The asylum at Catcombe had been built some sixty years earlier, in response to the new legislation that required each county to provide for the mentally ill: two three-storey wings either side of a central block with an archway in the centre, all constructed from locally quarried stone. Surrounded as it was by acres of land it was more or less self-sufficient, with its own farm and kitchen garden, a smithy and workshops. In the intervening years, as overcrowding had become a problem, extra accommodation had been added – a cottage ward near to the farm for the men who were fit to work it, and a villa to provide accommodation for thirty women. It was approached by way of a driveway with an iron-gated entrance flanked by stone lions mounted on pillars of the same local stone.

It was just after noon as Alistair turned into the drive, William in a Moses basket on the front seat of the Ford, Stella sitting behind. Tom had asked if he should accompany them, but Alistair had thought it would be better if he didn't. From previous experience, he knew there could be upsetting scenes when a patient realised they were about to be incarcerated.

Stella, however, still seemed lost in a trance. He'd kept an eye on her during the half-hour drive and seen nothing to indicate she had any real understanding of what was happening. Hopefully it would last until she'd been admitted and he could leave her in the care of the nurses.

Baby William had been quiet too for the whole of the journey: the motion of the motor seemed to have lulled him into a much-needed sleep.

Alistair drew up as close as he could to the main entrance and left Stella and William in the motor whilst he rang the bell. Then he helped a still catatonic Stella down and gently lifted the Moses basket and placed it on the top step so that he would be ready to grab her should she suddenly come alive and try to run away.

Moments later, the door was opened by a fresh-faced junior nurse. As a frequent visitor, Alistair had no need to introduce himself.

'I have a patient for admittance,' he said. 'Mrs Stella Swift. I telephoned earlier to let you know I'd be bringing her in.'

'Oh yes, Doctor – come in.'

The nurse opened the door wide, then took Stella by the arm and led her inside while Alistair followed with William.

'I'll fetch someone to attend to you.'

She hurried off, her shoes squeaking on the gleaming tiled floor. From somewhere deep inside the building came the muffled screams of one of the more demented patients.

Alistair glanced at Stella. A slightly confused look had replaced her previously blank expression, and as the asylum's matron bustled into the entrance hall, which smelled of antiseptic with overtones of boiled cabbage, it became one of alarm. He placed a hand on her arm.

'It's all right, Stella. Nothing to be afraid of.'

'Dr Mackay . . .' The matron's smile of welcome softened her pudgy – and rather forbidding – features. Alistair knew that a kind heart beat beneath the stern exterior she showed to the world, but also that she ran a tight ship and would stand for no nonsense.

When he'd first been appointed as one of the asylum's medical officers, it had been a grim place. The physician superintendent and the matron were a married couple nearing retirement who were impatient of the new liberal and far more humane practices that some asylums were introducing. They believed in straitjackets and cold baths, locked cells and ankle chains and handcuffs if necessary. Inmates had been subjected to a living hell, with little hope of ever being released.

Alistair had been amongst those who had campaigned vigorously for the much-needed reform, urging the committee who oversaw the administration of the asylum to ensure the establishment moved with the times and the barbaric treatment of the inmates ceased. It hadn't been easy – the superintendent and his wife had been running Catcombe for so long that they seemed part of the bricks and mortar of the place. But eventually Alistair and his allies had their way. The unpleasant pair were pensioned off, and a new superintendent, Dr Hubert Kirkwood, had taken charge.

Horrified by the conditions he had found, Dr Kirkwood had called the staff together and told them things would be changing from now on. A pleasant environment, rest, work and rewards for good behaviour would be far more likely to yield results and improve the mental health of the patients, and restraints were only to be used in the most extreme cases. To this end he had appointed Matron Carey, and she in turn had instilled the importance of the new regime in her nurses, most of whom were only too happy to comply.

Whereas previously patients had often been confined in dark cells and dormitories, there was now plenty to occupy them. As well as working in the gardens and on the farm, the men sometimes played cricket or boules, though football was not allowed for fear of violence. The women were set to sewing clothes, sheets and bath towels, and there was even a piano in their recreation room so that they could enjoy a sing-song when there was someone who could tinkle out a tune.

No, although it still pained him to have to resort to having a patient committed, Alistair no longer worried that their condition could only worsen under the inhumane treatment meted out to them, and he hoped that in this calm environment Stella would soon regain full health and be able to return to her family.

Now that there was no longer the motion of the car to soothe him, William had begun to grizzle. Matron Carey turned to the fresh-faced junior nurse who had opened the door to them, and who was still hovering.

'Take the baby up to the nursery, if you please, Sheldon.'

As the girl took the Moses basket from Alistair and started towards the staircase, Stella suddenly came to life.

'No! No! My baby . . .' Her voice was panic-stricken, her eyes wild. 'Bring him back!'

Alistair laid a restraining hand on her arm. 'He's in good hands. You'll see him again soon, I'm sure.'

'But he'll be hungry . . . I have to feed him.'

That, Alistair thought, was a good sign. According to Tom Swift, it was trying to feed the baby that had brought all this to a head.

'And so you shall. Just as soon as you've had a nice bath,' Matron Carey said soothingly. 'Now come along like a good girl . . .'

Tears were streaming down Stella's face, and it was all Alistair could do to prevent her from running after the nurse, who had now reached the first landing.

'There's been a bit of a problem with his feeding,' he said, still holding firmly to Stella's arm. 'It appears he falls asleep at the breast before he's had enough to satisfy him.'

'Don't worry, Doctor, we'll soon sort that out,' Matron assured him.

Alistair nodded, hoping she was right. 'I'd be grateful if you could get him weighed and keep a record for me so that I can assess whether he's developing as he should.'

'We can do that, Doctor. If he's been a difficult feeder, it's more than likely because Mother hasn't been relaxed with him. I feel sure our nursery nurses will be able to help. And now . . .'

'I'll leave you to it, then.'

'I'm sure that's for the best.'

Alistair squeezed Stella's arm. 'Now don't worry about a thing, Stella. I'll be back to see you soon, and in the meantime, both you and William are in very good hands.'

But her eyes had glazed over again and she didn't reply. He wasn't even sure she was aware of what was happening.

In the doorway, he turned back, asking the question he always asked when he visited the asylum.

'How is Florrie, Matron?'

'She's been doing well since I allowed her to work in the nursery. As we both know, she loves babies. Too much, unfortunately.' She sighed. 'I think it's very unlikely she'll ever be allowed to go back to her old life.'

Alistair nodded. Sadly, given Florrie's history, he was of much the same opinion. Resigned to what seemed the inevitable, he said his goodbyes and left.

Florrie Carter. Jessica's sister. His sister-in-law.

One of the reasons he'd been so determined to get the regime at the asylum changed. But also the person responsible for him finding Jessica.

It was not long after he was first appointed as a medical officer that he was called in to treat Florrie, who was suffering from a nasty chest infection – not uncommon, given the cold, damp conditions the patients had been forced to endure.

Before going up to the infirmary, he had checked her records to find out why she had been committed, and was saddened by her story.

Florrie hailed from Easterton, a village some four miles from Catcombe, where she had lived with her husband, Bert, a quarryman who worked in one of the many quarries that scarred the Mendip Hills. Five years earlier, she had been devastated when her first baby had been stillborn. Some weeks later, when she was up and about again, she had begun wandering the streets, and more than one mother had discovered her staring into perambulators left outside shops, and even stroking the face of the baby inside, or rearranging the covers.

When a baby eventually went missing, the finger had immediately been pointed at Florrie. The local policeman had gone to her home and found the house empty; her husband was, of course, at work, and of Florrie and the baby there was no sign. But there was irrefutable evidence that they had been there. The shawl that the missing baby had been wrapped in and his little bonnet were on the bed, and when Bert was contacted and asked to check the layette that had been bought in readiness for his and Florrie's own baby, he confirmed that certain items were missing, as was their perambulator.

A frantic search had ensued, and to everyone's enormous relief, Florrie and the baby were found some hours later on a bench at the edge of a copse that overlooked the valley. The baby was unharmed and was soon back in the arms of his mother. But clearly Florrie was in no fit state to be allowed home, even if she had not had criminal charges hanging over her. Two doctors had certified her insane, and she had been taken to Catcombe, where she had been ever since.

What the notes did not say was that Bert had long since given up visiting her and, according to local gossip, had taken up with a pretty young lady from the next village. But mention was made that since she had become seriously ill, her younger sister, Jessica, had been given leave to spend unlimited time with her – a privilege indeed given the strict regime at Catcombe at that time.

One day, a young woman Alistair assumed must be the sister was sitting beside Florrie's bed when he went up to the infirmary, holding Florrie's hand and sponging her forehead with a damp cloth. His first impression was of a heart-shaped face framed by tendrils of nut-brown hair, and anxious brown eyes, but he was too concerned about the state of the patient to take more than a fleeting glance.

Florrie was clearly very ill, her breathing laboured, her skin clammy yet burning hot to the touch, and when he listened to her chest, his suspicion that she was suffering from pneumonia was more or less confirmed.

'What can you do for her, Doctor?' The anxious brown eyes sought his.

Alistair considered. 'Oxygen is a possibility. It would make her more comfortable, but I'm not convinced how much good it does. Then there's antiserum therapy. It's known to be helpful, but it's a lengthy treatment, and rather costly.'

'Oh, don't worry about the cost. Whatever it is, we'll find the money somehow. We've got to get her through this, Doctor. She's only twenty-five, and she's had no life at all.'

Privately Alistair couldn't help thinking that death might come as a happy release, given that he could see no hope of Florrie ever being allowed to leave this hellhole. But perhaps he was wrong. Perhaps she would one day be well enough to return to some sort of normal life, and the justices would consider she had paid for her crime with some of the best years of her life. And whatever their situation, he didn't like losing a patient.

But Florrie, it seemed, was made of sterner stuff than he had first thought. She was a farmer's daughter, and until she married, she had worked on the farm. Even afterwards she had gone back to help out, and years of heaving heavy bales of hay at harvest time and caring for livestock in all winds and weathers had made her physically strong. To his enormous relief, she had turned the corner that night, and it wasn't long before she was making a miraculous recovery.

In those first worrying days, however, he had kept a close eye on her and got to know the sister who was constantly at her bedside well. She still lived at home on the farm, he learned, though she didn't do any of the heavy work Florrie had done, instead looking after a flock of hens and making butter and cheese. But somehow she was finding the time to sit with Florrie every day, and he was impressed by her devotion to the sister who had been locked away for five long years. All too often, the inmates' very existence was brushed under the carpet by their loved ones – there was a dreadful stigma attached to being 'in Catcombe'.

'She's still my sister,' Jessica had said, almost angrily, when he had complimented her on it. 'Whatever she'd done, I'd still be there for her. And I want to be sure she's being looked after properly when she's ill. Goodness knows, the conditions here are just too awful to be believed.'

'They're certainly far from ideal,' Alistair agreed. 'I've only recently been appointed, but as soon as I find my feet, I intend to try to do something about it, I assure you.'

'And not before time,' Jessica had said passionately. 'My father wouldn't let his animals be treated the way they treat the poor souls here.'

Alistair had insisted Florrie remain in the infirmary until she was completely recovered, but the day came when he could no longer find an excuse to delay her return to her old quarters, and he realised that it hadn't only been Florrie's welfare that had been behind him continuing to visit daily. He'd looked forward to seeing Jessica, and now the prospect of not seeing her again was not something he wanted to contemplate.

Usually Jessica was still beside Florrie's bed when he left, but on the last day, after Florrie had been collected by one of the nurses in charge of the mentally ill and whisked away, they had walked down the stairs together. Jessica was visibly upset, and his heart ached for her.

'Can I give you a lift home?' he asked as the asylum door closed behind them.

'Oh, I don't want to take you out of your way,' Jessica protested.

'You won't be. I'm heading back to Hillsbridge and I go through Easterton.'

'Well, in that case, thank you.' She tried to smile, but her big brown eyes were liquid with tears.

He wasn't at all sure that this was the right time to ask her out, but he did anyway, and to his delight, she accepted. Six weeks later, he had asked her to marry him, and she had accepted his proposal too. That day, he thought, had been the happiest of his life.

Looking back, he thought he had known from the first moment he laid eyes on her that this was the girl he wanted to spend the rest of his life with. After so many years of bachelorhood, he'd fallen in love – and in the most inauspicious of circumstances.

So much had happened since then. They'd had a little girl, Constance, who was now three years old, and there was another baby on the way. His efforts to reform the asylum had borne fruit, and conditions were now so much better for the unfortunate inmates. But poor Florrie was still locked away, and likely to be for the rest of her life. And now he'd had to commit another poor suffering soul. He'd hated having to do it. But what choice was there? If Stella Swift was a danger to her baby and to herself, there really was no alternative.

With a deep sigh, he started the Ford and headed back to Hillsbridge and the patients who were waiting for him to call on them. He loved his job and almost everything about it. But sometimes, just sometimes, he wished there were parts of it that he could delegate to someone else.

# Chapter Three

The house was quiet – too quiet. No clatter of pans as Stella prepared or cleared up a meal. No squeals or chatter as the children played. No baby crying. Nothing but the occasional soft clunk or fizzle from the fire as the coals burned through and settled, sounding louder than usual in the otherwise silent living room. Even Fluffy, the cat, was nowhere to be seen. He'd slunk out when the doctor had arrived and not yet come home.

Tom sat at the dining table staring unseeingly at a cup of tea gone cold before him. He could scarcely believe Dr Mackay had taken Stella to Catcombe; worried though he'd been about her, irrationally as she'd been behaving lately, he hadn't thought for a moment it would come to this.

But he supposed it had been inevitable. He couldn't get the picture out of his head – Stella with the sharp shard of glass in her hand hovering over baby William, and both of them splattered with blood. Couldn't forget her words: 'I can't stand it any more.' Kept seeing her terrifyingly blank expression, the desperation in her eyes the only sign of any emotion or awareness. He'd known something had to be done, for her safety and William's. He just hadn't foreseen anything quite so drastic.

Now he had to decide what he was going to do. He'd missed a day's work today, but he couldn't stay home indefinitely. They couldn't manage without his pittance of a wage, and the house went with the job. The bosses would hopefully overlook a day's absence, given the circumstances, but they'd soon lose patience if it continued. His position would be filled by one of the carting boys, eager for promotion to collier so as to earn more money and not have to spend his days dragging putts of coal along the narrow, faulted seams from the coal face to the bottom of the shaft that connected to the pit head. Then it wouldn't only be his income that was lost; it could be their home too.

But if he was to return to work, he had to sort something out regarding the care of the children. The three of them were all now at school during the day, but they weren't old enough to take themselves there and back, or at least the two boys weren't old enough to be trusted to look after Emily as well as themselves. Besides which they were usually still in bed and asleep when he left for work and had already been home again for hours before he got back himself. They needed help with getting washed and dressed, and someone had to prepare their breakfast and cook their tea when they got home again. Whilst he might be able to arrange for them to walk to and from school with one or other of the neighbours' children, he couldn't expect anyone else to care for them and feed them day after day, maybe even week after week, for he had no idea how long it would be before Stella was fit to come home again.

And for all he knew, there might be Will to consider too. They wouldn't keep him in the asylum once he was weaned, and if Stella was still too ill to be released, they'd send him home without her. But he wasn't going to worry about that yet. For the moment, the most important thing was to get help from somebody who could be here all the time to look after the children's needs. And he could think of only one person: Stella's sister Grace. He was reluctant to ask it of her; she had a job of her own, working in the little general store in their home village of Shillingford, and who knew if they would keep the position open for her?

Besides which, he and Grace had shared history. They'd walked out together for the best part of three years before Grace had ended it with words that had cut him to the quick. He'd known it was his own stupid fault and he'd treated her badly, but he hadn't realised just how much he cared for her until he lost her.

But that was all in the past now, and what choice did he have? His own mother would never be able to cope with three small children – she had a heart condition that meant she had to be very careful not to overdo things – and Stella's mother was fully occupied caring for her husband, who suffered badly from silicosis, the miner's lung disease that came from breathing in coal dust day after day for the whole of their working lives.

Grace, on the other hand, had no ties. She had been widowed just two years after she had married, and before she and her husband had had a chance to start a family. Cliff Baker had been a coal miner too and had been killed in a roof fall at his pit. After his death, Grace had been forced to leave their tied cottage and had moved back in with her parents. It suited Annie, her mother, to have some help about the house, fully occupied as she was with caring for Amos, but Stella had once intimated that her sister found it difficult sharing a kitchen again when she'd been used to running a home of her own. 'Much as I love my mam and dad, I wouldn't want to have to do it,' she had said.

That didn't mean, of course, that Grace would be any happier taking Stella's place here. But Tom couldn't see that he had any option other than to ask.

He glanced at the mantel clock. He had just about enough time to get to Shillingford and back before the children came out of school – if he put a step on it.

Making up his mind, he fetched his overcoat and gloves, fixed bicycle clips around his ankles to keep the legs of his trousers out of the way of the chain, and set out.

The moment the bell jingled over the door of the general store and she glanced up from cutting a wedge of cheese to see Tom coming in, Grace Baker knew something must be wrong. Why else would he be here in the early afternoon when he should be at work? And as he approached the counter, weaving his way between the sacks of flour and potatoes that were stacked up against the shelving that lined the walls, the serious expression on his ruggedly handsome face seemed to confirm it.

'Tom?' she said anxiously, the wire still poised over the cheese. 'What are you doing here?'

He hesitated. Mercifully the shop was empty of customers at the moment, but one could come in at any minute. Having grown up in the village, Stella was well known, and if anyone overheard what he had to say, the news would spread like wildfire.

'I need to talk to you, Grace. But . . .'

Grace read his mind. 'In private, you mean?' she asked. He nodded. 'Just let me pack this up.'

She finished cutting the cheese, then weighed and wrapped it, part of an order she was making up for delivery to Shillingford Manor, the home of the Wilton family, local gentry who also owned a very successful brewery. Then she wiped her hands on her apron and lifted part of the counter to form a gateway through to the business side of the shop.

'Come through.'

Tom followed her into a small storeroom, where Mr Lines, her employer, was unpacking a box of biscuits and putting some into a large glass display jar.

'I'm sorry to disturb you, Mr Lines, but could you mind the shop for a minute?' Grace said apologetically. 'My brother-in-law has cycled over from Hillsbridge because he needs to speak to me urgently.'

Mr Lines's eyes narrowed behind his wire-rimmed spectacles, but he put another handful of biscuits into the jar and snapped on the lid before nodding abruptly. Grace was a good worker, efficient and totally trustworthy, which was more than he could have said for her predecessor, and it wasn't like her to ask favours or take things for granted.

'Well, don't be too long,' he said tersely. 'There's a lot of these biscuits broken and I want to get in touch with the whole-saler about it. I can't afford to sell all that lot off at half-price.'

'We won't be, I promise.'

Grace caught a glossy golden-brown curl that had escaped its pins and tucked it back into the neat coil at the nape of her neck. Then, as Mr Lines left them alone, closing the door behind him, she turned anxiously to Tom.

'What is it? What's wrong?'

He told her, and she listened with growing dismay.

'Oh Tom, that's dreadful! I knew she wasn't herself, but I never for one moment imagined . . .' She broke off, biting her lip.

'Me neither,' Tom agreed. 'It really took me aback when the doctor said he would have to commit her. I almost wish I hadn't called him, but when I saw her with the broken glass, the baby in her arms, and blood everywhere . . . well, I couldn't see that I had any option.' He looked up, the anguish written clearly in his eyes. 'You don't blame me, do you?'

'Oh Tom, of course not! If she'd harmed Will . . .' Grace shook her head, and the curl escaped once more. 'No, you did the right thing. But it's just too awful for words. Whatever are you going to do?'

'Well, to tell the truth, that's why I'm here,' Tom said. 'I was wondering if you could help me out. It's a lot to ask, I know, but . . .'

'You mean . . . ?'

'Come and stay for a bit. Just until I can sort myself out. Or they let Stella come home. I'm in hopes that they'll be able to put her right pretty sharpish, and sort out Will's feeding problems too. But there's your job here to think about, I know. Do you think your boss would give you the time off?'

'I don't know, but let's not worry about that. It's the children's welfare that's the most important thing.'

'I'd give you what I can, to make up for being short of your wage packet . . .'

'Don't be so silly!' Grace said emphatically. 'Of course I'll help out. No question about it. But I don't want paying. It's a bad job if I can't step in when my sister's children need me.'

'Well, we'll see about that. But I really am at my wits' end, Grace. I'd be so grateful.'

'That's settled then. When do you need me?'

'I'm all right for today, but . . .'

'Give me a chance to explain to Mr Lines, then I'll go home and pack a bag. I could come over later this evening so I'd be there to get the children off to school in the morning, and you'd be able to go to work tomorrow without worrying about them,' Grace said decisively. 'How about that?'

'It would be a weight off my mind. But I don't know how I can ever thank you.'

'You don't need to,' she said shortly. 'The thing that's

worrying me most is telling Mam what's happened. She's going to be in an awful way to know Stella is in Catcombe.'

'Just tell her she's in the best place, and it won't be for long.'

It was the second time he'd implied this was short term only. But Grace wasn't sure she shared his optimism – wasn't even sure he believed it himself. He knew as well as she did that once incarcerated behind the locked gates and high walls of the asylum, patients didn't come out again, or at least not for a very long time, and then they were often taken back in soon after. As for the stigma attached – that remained for ever.

'Go on, Tom, you'd better make haste if you're going to be back in time to meet the children out of school,' she said, trying to push the awful thoughts to the back of her mind.

'How will you . . . ?'

'I'll get a cab. Would you believe we have one now in the village? A motor, not a pony and trap.'

'Promise you'll let me pay him.'

'Oh go on with you.'

But his insistence warmed her heart. That was the Tom she knew, generous and with a moral compass firmly fixed in the right direction. There might have been times when he'd sowed his wild oats, but he'd been young then, and that was what young men did. Not any more. Now he was scarcely recognisable as the young blade who had broken her heart.

Once Tom had left, Grace prepared herself to break the news to Mr Lines that he would have to manage without her for a while. He wasn't going to be very pleased, though it shouldn't be too difficult for him to find a replacement. There were plenty of local girls who would be only too glad to have what was, after all, a very pleasant job, and only last week a miner's wife had come in asking if there was any chance she could work a few hours a week while her children were at school.

She couldn't expect him to keep the job open for her, she knew. But she wasn't going to think about that. Tom, Stella and the children needed her, and family came first.

She'd find something else when the time came. If it ever did . . .

Again her heart contracted at the thought of her sister locked up in that awful place, and she prayed for Stella's sake that Tom was right when he said he didn't think it would be for long.

As she expected, Mr Lines was not best pleased to hear her news.

'I'm really sorry to leave you in the lurch,' she said, 'but Mrs Coles was in the other day asking about a job, and I'm sure she'd be only too happy to step in at short notice. I could call in on her on my way home, ask her to come and see you, if you like. She worked in a shop before she got married, I understand, so it wouldn't take her long to get back in the swing of things.'

'Hmm. I'll think about it.' Mr Lines looked meaningfully at the box of groceries Grace had been packing up for delivery to the Manor when Tom had arrived. 'You're not proposing to leave until you've finished making up Mr Wilton's order, I hope? His housekeeper is expecting her groceries this afternoon, and young Reggie Evans will be here soon to take them out to her.'

Reggie Evans, though still at school, was their errand boy, delivering orders on his specially adapted bicycle as a way to earn a bit of pocket money.

'Of course not!' Grace said indignantly. 'I'll stay until my usual time, and make sure everything is up together before I leave.'

'That's all right then,' Mr Lines said shortly, heading back to the stock room. He turned in the doorway. 'If I'm not in the shop when school turns out and all the nippers come in, be sure to keep a sharp eye on them. You know what they're like – can't be trusted any further than you can throw them.'

'Don't worry, I will.'

Though it was true there were a couple of young varmints who weren't above stealing an apple or stuffing some biscuits into their pockets, most of the children who came into the shop to spend a few pennies on sweets were honest and well behaved, in Grace's experience. But she wasn't going to argue with Mr Lines just now. She was anxious to remain in his good books in the light of the bombshell she'd just dropped. She liked working in the shop, and hoped she'd be able to return when all this was over. Besides which, she did feel dreadfully guilty.

But she'd have felt far worse if she'd refused Tom, she thought. The children – really still little more than babies – needed her. They would be bound to be unsettled by Stella's sudden absence from their lives, and Grace was the closest thing to their mother, a much-loved aunt who spent as much time with them as she was able. Hopefully Stella would recover more quickly if she knew they were being cared for by someone she trusted. And Tom . . . Her heart bled for him, faced so unexpectedly with this dreadful situation. He wasn't one to show his emotions; like most men, he took a pride in being strong, the rock on which the family relied. But that didn't mean he couldn't be overwhelmed by the enormity of his responsibilities. It didn't mean that beneath that stoical exterior he wasn't shocked and devastated by the turn of events, desperately worried for Stella and not knowing which way to turn. And just because he'd once broken Grace's heart didn't mean she didn't care for him now, as a brother-in-law and a friend.

Sometimes, though, she remembered the way she'd once felt

about him, the handsome young man she'd been crazy about, so crazy that she'd been prepared to put up with the humiliation of knowing he was seeing other girls behind her back. How stupid she'd been, wasting the best years of her life on a dream! How lacking in pride! But she'd said nothing, so afraid was she that she would lose him altogether if she made a fuss about it.

But all the unhappiness he'd caused her must have been building up inside her, like the steam in a kettle on the hot coals, slowly but surely reaching boiling point.

It was the evening preceding her birthday. There was always a special tea with bottled fruit and birthday cake, and Grace had expected Tom to be there to share the celebrations. He spent a lot of time at their house. Mam, who could be very opinionated when it came to anyone other than family, had taken a shine to him and always made him welcome. When they'd been out for a walk, he often came in for his supper. Sometimes he'd still be there when Stella and her parents went to bed, and the two of them would have a cuddle on the sofa until Grace's mother called down the stairs: 'It's time you were in bed, my girl! And you too, Tom Swift, or you'll be good for nothing in the morning!'

So for all his infidelities, it never crossed Grace's mind that he wouldn't be there to share her special tea. But when he walked her home on the eve of her birthday, he told her he wouldn't be able to make it.

They'd reached the gate leading to the path to Grace's front door. It was a cold, frosty night, the moon and stars bright in a black velvet sky. At his words, Grace spun round to face him.

'I won't see you tomorrow? But it's my birthday!'

'Sorry,' he muttered. 'I've got things to do.'

And the spark that would light her fuse was struck.

Grace had a pretty good idea just what Tom meant by 'things

to do'. He'd been cheating on her with Dorrie Humphries – a very pretty girl who also lived in Shillingford. Dorrie had told her so. 'He won't leave me alone,' she had said slyly. 'I thought you ought to know, Grace.' Then she'd suggested that if the two of them put their heads together, they could hatch a plan to get their own back, though she hadn't specified what that might be.

Grace had been dreadfully upset, of course, but she'd still allowed things to go on in the same old way, hoping that Tom would tire of Dorrie as quickly as he'd tired of all the other girls he'd had a fling with. She was the constant in his life. One of these days he'd get over his wild ways and settle down, and when he did, it would be with her.

That night, however, something snapped in her. She'd had enough. She wouldn't be made a fool of any longer.

She tore her hand away from his and the furious words seemed to come from nowhere.

'I know where you're going, Tom. You're going to see Dorrie Humphries, aren't you? Well, let me tell you this. If you go out with her tomorrow – my birthday! – you needn't bother coming back here. You're nothing but a rotten cheat, and she's welcome to you!'

Tom had gaped open-mouthed at the tirade, but she hadn't finished yet.

'I've just about had enough of it – you going off with any girl who takes your fancy and thinking I don't know. Thinking that you can still wind me round your little finger. Well, you can't. Not any more. Go on – go! Get lost!'

'Well, if that's the way you feel . . .' Tom sounded affronted rather than guilty or apologetic.

'It is.' She'd turned her back on him then and flounced up the garden path. With her hand on the doorknob she'd looked round, just once. Tom was still standing there, stunned, and she

felt a moment's ecstatic triumph. That had told him! She should
have done it long ago.

'Where's Tom?' her mother asked when Grace came in
alone.

'I've finished with him. He's been cheating on me for ages
and I've had enough,' she blazed.

For the moment, she was too angry to cry. The tears had
come later, and plenty of them. Her dreams were in tatters, her
heart broken, yet she remained resolute. She wouldn't go back
to him and have it all begin again. No, she wouldn't have him
back now if his hair was dripping with diamonds . . .

A year or more had gone by. In all that time, she and Tom
had never spoken. She'd begun going out with Cliff Baker; she
didn't feel about him the way she'd felt about Tom, but that
could only be a good thing. Cliff was a nice boy, kind,
considerate, and he treated her well, buying her little gifts,
bringing her flowers, certainly never cheating on her. He'd even
given her a ring that he said had belonged to his grandmother,
and though he put it on the third finger of her right hand, she
had the feeling that what he was really hoping was that one day
she would wear it on her left.

And then, to Grace's shock and dismay, Stella confided that
Tom had asked her out. The younger sister he had used to tease
had blossomed into an attractive young woman, and he had
actually asked her out!

'You don't mind, do you, Grace?' Stella had said anxiously.

'Stella, you can't go out with him!' Grace had been horrified.
'You know what he's like.'

'He's changed,' Stella had said stoutly.

'Huh! A likely story! Leopards don't change their spots.'

'He has,' Stella insisted. 'And I really like him. I always have.
But I won't go out with him if it's going to upset you.'

'It won't upset me,' Grace said tartly. 'I'm well over Tom Swift. I just don't want to see you hurt.'

'I'm a big girl now, Grace. I can take care of myself.'

'Oh, do what you like,' Grace sighed. 'Just don't say you haven't been warned.'

And so Tom was once more back in the house, his feet firmly under the table. It was awkward to begin with; Grace avoided him whenever she could. But to her surprise and relief, it seemed he *had* changed. He was treating Stella the same way Cliff treated Grace, and there was never so much as a hint of gossip about him and other girls.

When Cliff finally asked Grace to marry him, she had agreed, and not so long afterwards, Tom and Stella got engaged too. Gradually the tensions between Grace and Tom had eased, and the attraction that had once sparked between them mutated into friendship, the warm, comfortable, easy relationship that came from knowing each other so well. She had long since got over the almost obsessive way she had once felt about him, and she was full of admiration for the man he had become, a wonderful father, a considerate and loving husband. It was hard now to believe he had been the wild young Lothario who had caused her so much unhappiness.

Quite honestly, she had no one but herself to blame for that, Grace sometimes thought. She should never have allowed him to treat her that way. If she'd been more outspoken earlier, things might have been different.

But that was all a long time ago, in another lifetime. Now Tom was part of the family, Stella's husband and the father of Grace's nephews and niece. Old scores had long been settled and forgotten. All that mattered now was that she could help out when he and Stella needed her most.

\* \* \*

It was just after seven when the taxi deposited Grace outside the cottage in Dunderwick Road. The cloud and misty rain had cleared now; the moon and stars were already bright in a clear sky, and a chill breeze made her face tingle. Usually she enjoyed breathing in the cold, crisp air; it made her feel alive and cleansed, but tonight it only heightened the feeling of sadness that had hung over her ever since Tom had told her what had happened. She didn't suppose Stella would be able to go out and feel the delicious freshness, perhaps not even see the moon and stars. She'd be shut away behind the forbidding walls of the asylum. No wonder their parents had been so upset when she'd broken the news to them.

How had it come to this? she wondered. Stella had everything she had ever wanted: a loving husband, three lovely children and a new baby, a home she took pride in. She was fortunate – so fortunate – and she'd been grateful for it.

'I can't believe how lucky I've been,' she had said to Grace not so long ago. 'I just wish you could be as happy as I am. It isn't fair that you should have lost Cliff the way you did. And I pray every night that you'll meet someone else, fall in love, get married again and have children. They are such a blessing. Until you have one of your own, you can't know how wonderful being a mother is.'

'Don't worry about me. I'm fine as I am,' Grace had reassured her, but it wasn't quite true. Sometimes she couldn't help but envy Stella, though she never entertained a moment's resentment. She loved her sister and was glad she'd found happiness.

She'd been touched, too, that Stella should remember her in her prayers, though she doubted it would make the slightest difference. Stella had always been the one with a strong religious belief. In their youth, when they'd shared a bedroom, Grace used to tease her for spending a few minutes on her knees each evening before getting into bed, and Stella would respond that she'd do well to do the same.

Was she praying now? Grace wondered. If so, she could only hope that those prayers would be answered. The thought of her lovely, sweet-natured sister locked away in that awful place was more than she could bear.

But there was no time for dwelling on that now. With a heavy heart, Grace walked up the path to the house, gave a perfunctory knock on the door and opened it – as was the custom, it was on the latch.

'It's only me!' she called out.

Usually when she visited, the children came running to greet her, full of exuberance. Not today. She found them in the living room, still sitting around the dining table with their father, the remains of a meal in front of them. Tom had clearly done his best to make them a decent tea, but it must have been late by the time he finished preparing it, and she could imagine how hungry they would have been by the time he put it on the table. Unless of course they'd filled up on biscuits or hunks of bread and jam while they were waiting, which would go some way to explaining the leftovers on their plates. Or perhaps they were just too upset to eat.

'Hello, you lot!' she said in a tone of forced cheerfulness.

Three sets of eyes regarded her unsmiling, and their return of her greeting was uncharacteristically subdued.

'Any news?' she asked Tom.

He shook his head. 'No, but I wasn't expecting any.'

'I suppose not.'

'Have you come to stay?' Oliver asked, looking at the carpet bag Grace had packed with a change of clothes and some toiletries – enough to last her for the next few days at least.

'If you want to be helpful, Oliver, you can show Auntie Grace to her room so she can unpack,' Tom said.

'It's my room really,' Emily piped up. 'But you can have it. I don't mind.'

'I've put her in with the boys for the time being,' Tom explained. 'She's going to enjoy that, aren't you, Emily? Though I'm not sure they are quite as pleased.'

'I could have made do down here on the sofa,' Grace protested.

'And wake up with a stiff neck and backache? After you've been so good as to come and help us out?' Tom managed a shadow of a smile. 'I'd have slept down here myself and let you have our room, but I thought . . .'

Grace nodded. She knew what he had been going to say. She would have felt dreadfully uncomfortable sleeping in the bed her sister and her husband shared. But it had made work for him, having to change the bedding in readiness for her, she thought. No wonder he'd been so late getting tea.

'Let me just take my things up, then I'll get stuck in to clearing up and getting the children ready for bed,' she said.

'Oh Grace – I don't know how I can ever thank you . . .'

'No thanks needed.' She hoisted up her carpet bag and let Oliver, now bursting with self-importance, lead her along the hall and up the stairs.

# Chapter Four

'Come along now, Stella. Let's go and find your baby.'

Ivy Gill, the nurse, was plump and rosy-cheeked, with a relentlessly cheerful manner.

Stella got up from the settle where she had been sitting staring into space, and began to follow the nurse, then stopped suddenly, looking round, puzzled and anxious.

'But where are the children?'

'In the nursery,' Ivy replied patiently.

'What are they doing there? They're too old to be in a nursery. And they'll want their tea.'

'No, dear, not *your* children. The babies.'

'But . . .'

'Your baby is in the nursery. But not your other children. They're at home with your husband, and I'm sure he'll have seen to it that they don't go hungry. So you can stop worrying about that.'

'I don't understand. Where am I?'

'You're in hospital, dear, because you're not well. Come on now.' She put a hand under Stella's elbow, urging her towards the stairs.

The nursery was in a converted roof space above one wing of the hospital. When he had taken over as superintendent, Dr

Kirkwood had wanted to locate it elsewhere, to a lighter, more accessible room, but the logistics had made that impossible. The asylum was full to bursting with patients from all over the county. But Matron Carey had had the room repainted in eggshell blue – so much more cheerful than the previous depressing sludge colour, as she had said at the time.

There were seven babies there at the moment, their cribs lined up against the walls. When it was time for their offspring to be fed, the mothers would be escorted upstairs by a member of staff. Between whiles the little ones were cared for by Cissie Whitcombe, the nursery nurse, assisted by Alistair Mackay's sister-in-law, Florrie.

As Stella and Nurse Gill entered the attic room, Cissie came bustling over. She was older than most of the other nurses, a big-boned, capable-looking woman who had been a midwife in a previous life. Now she ruled the nursery with a rod of iron.

'Ah! William's mother, isn't it? Good! He's more than ready for his feed – and you are too, by the look of it,' she added, glancing at the wet patches darkening the front of Stella's asylum-issue smock. 'Come with me.'

She urged a bewildered Stella towards a crib on the end of the row.

For once, William was not crying. He lay tightly swaddled, his eyes wide and alert. His pursed rosebud lips were crusted with dried milk, evidence that he had been fed earlier from the supply that was kept on the cold slab in the kitchens in case any of the mothers were unable to nurse their baby.

For just a moment, as recognition dawned, Stella's face softened with love. But as Cissie tried to place William in her arms, she shrank back. Whereas earlier she had been distraught when he had been taken from her, and worried that he might be hungry, now she could think only of the desperation that consumed her when he refused to feed.

Cissie gave her a little push towards a low chair set at the foot of the crib. As the back of Stella's knees connected with the edge of the seat, she sat down abruptly, and before she could protest, Cissie had propped William in her lap. Another moment of maternal instinct kicked in as Stella's arms went round him, one hand supporting his head, the other preventing him from slipping off her lap, then, as Cissie began to unbutton her smock, her eyes went dark with panic.

'No . . . no . . . I can't!'

'Of course you can,' Cissie said firmly. 'Some babies suckle more easily than others, but I'm here to help you.'

'No!'

Stella was flailing wildly now, trying to push William back into Cissie's arms. Upset by the rough handling, he began to cry, at which Stella only struggled the harder.

'Florrie!' Cissie called over her shoulder. 'Can you help me here?'

Florrie was sitting with one of the other mothers, a young girl who had been committed for no other reason than she was unmarried. Her baby had been born prematurely a couple of months ago, and his development was still causing concern. Now Florrie leapt to her feet and hurried over.

'Take the baby, please,' Cissie instructed.

Florrie did as she was told. William was yelling lustily now. His swaddling had come loose in the tussle, he was kicking furiously, and his little legs, one ankle encircled with the identity band that all the babies wore, pounded the air in time with his cries.

Meanwhile Cissie had turned her full attention back to Stella.

'What's the matter with you, my lady? How can you be so selfish? Do you want your baby to starve?'

'I can't do it! I've tried and tried, and I can't!' Stella was almost hysterical, and tears were streaming down her cheeks. 'He'll just fall asleep on me, and I can't bear it!'

Cissie shook her head, sighing heavily. With the mother in this state, they'd get nowhere. Hopefully in a day or two she would settle down a bit and they'd try again. For the moment, the best she could do was persuade Stella to express some milk to make her more comfortable and provide some sustenance so that either she or Florrie could feed the baby.

'It's all right,' she said, adopting the most soothing tone she could muster. 'I won't make you feed him if you don't want to, but we do need some of that milk. Just calm down and sit there quietly while I fetch the pap boat.'

Stella's eyes were still wild, but the shudders that had shaken her body were less violent, and by the time Cissie returned with the pap boat, she had slipped back into an almost catatonic state. She didn't resist as Cissie did what she had to. And when Ivy Gill arrived to escort her back downstairs, she went unprotestingly, moving like a woman in a trance, and without a single backward glance at William, quiet again and cradled in Florrie's arms.

'Right then. That's done, and the little one's fast asleep. I don't know what the problem with him is, though the way the mother was carrying on, it's hardly surprising he's all upset.'

Florrie had fed baby William, swaddled him tightly again and returned him to his crib. She'd rocked him for a little while and he'd soon fallen asleep. Now she went back to sit beside Rose Gooding, the young mother of the premature baby, with whom she was very friendly.

In the beginning, when it had been thought he would not survive, Rose had been allowed to spend most of the day in the nursery with him, and somehow, though he was now growing and gaining weight, the arrangement had continued, with Matron Carey turning a blind eye to it, though really it was against regulations. She couldn't see that Rose was doing any harm by being there, nor likely to. She wasn't mad, and in Matron's opinion shouldn't be in the asylum at all, but that was what happened to some unfortunate girls who got themselves into trouble. If they were a cause of embarrassment to their family or employer, getting them certified with 'moral insanity', or 'erotomania', was a convenient diagnosis that would keep them out of the public eye. When the baby was weaned, adoptive parents would be found for him, with any money that changed hands going into the asylum coffers, and the mother would be discharged back into the community to fend for herself, so long as the whole experience hadn't unhinged her. So why not let Rose enjoy her baby while she could? Even if it did make it harder for her to part with him when the time came. At least she'd have her memories.

Today, though little Wallace, as she had called him, had long since finished feeding, Rose hadn't returned him to his crib, but was still nursing him, fast asleep, in her arms. She looked up, shaking her head as Florrie took the chair beside her once more.

'Well, that was a to-do and no mistake! What in the world is wrong with that woman? How can she not want to feed her own baby?'

'It's the fever,' Florrie said, pleased to be able to show off some of the many things she'd learned since being allowed to work in the nursery. 'Awful thing. Can send a woman right off her head. I reckon it had something to do with what I did – that and the grief, of course. Mostly they get over it in time, though,

46

come to their senses, and then they can go home and carry on as normal. I've seen it happen a few times. Though I must say I've never seen anybody quite that bad,' she added.

'But you're better, and they haven't let you go home,' Rose said, shifting Wallace's position slightly.

'Well, the ones that get out haven't done anything wrong, have they? Just gone a bit funny. I stole a baby. Just walked off with it as if it belonged to me. If I hadn't been sent here, I'd be in jail. And if they ever let me out, I might still have the law after me.'

'But at least you'd get out of jail when you'd done your time,' Rose argued, stroking her baby's downy cheek gently. 'As it is . . .'

'I'm happy enough.' Florrie smoothed down her big white apron over her patient's smock. She was proud of the apron; it made her feel like a proper nurse and not an inmate. 'I've got my own room in the new villa, I don't have to worry about getting my own food – I was never much of a cook – and I love working with the babies.'

'But wouldn't you like one of your own?'

'I had one, and I lost her. I never even got to hold the little mite. Only ever saw her in the nurse's arms. Like a tiny waxworks, she was . . .' For a moment her eyes misted, and she blinked hard. 'Dolly, I called her. That's what she was like. A china doll. My little Dolly.'

'But you're still young enough to have another.'

Florrie shook her head. 'No chance of that. Dolly saw to it. They say I nearly died myself, and I was too messed up to ever get in the family way again. Anyway, it takes two to make a baby, and I don't suppose Bert – my old man – is waiting for me. Not that I'd want him to. Too fond of his drink, Bert, and handy with his fists when he'd had a few too many. I always reckoned it was his fault that Dolly was born dead, but that's another story.'

'You mean he punched you in the stomach?' Rose asked, horrified.

Florrie let out her breath sharply. 'I don't want to talk about it, Rose. And it doesn't matter any more. It's a long time ago now. No, one way or another I'm better off where I am. There's nothing for me out there. But you . . . that's quite a different kettle of fish. They'd no business putting you away.'

Rose's pretty face hardened, her full lips tightening, dark eyes sparking with anger. 'That's what money can do,' she said bitterly. 'Money – and being in with the right people.'

'Wicked, that's what it is. Wicked! I don't know how he can get away with it.'

'If your name is Whittingly Challis,' Rose said, her voice still low and bitter, 'you can get away with anything.'

There was no arguing with that.

Sir Oswald Whittingly Challis was local gentry and owned great swathes of the land surrounding Catcombe and far beyond, which included several highly profitable quarries. His father, Sir Hugh, had been a good landlord and employer, well liked and highly respected, but Sir Oswald was known amongst his tenants and his workforce for a bully who rode roughshod over anyone who dared to cross him.

But for all that, he had friends in high places. A justice of the peace himself, he hunted with the local member of Parliament and the county high sheriff, and served on the committee that oversaw the running of the asylum. Hardly surprising, since his father had been one of the magistrates responsible for the building of the place back in the 1840s.

Now his elder son, Rupert, was following in his footsteps,

learning the quarrying business in readiness for the day when he would take over the helm, while George, younger by two years, had been accepted as a gentleman cadet at Sandhurst. His wife, Lady Cecelia, meanwhile, busied herself with working for the community. She chaired committees of ladies who raised money for good causes and donated their cast-offs to the poor and needy. Many a local family spoke highly of her generosity and the help she had arranged for them when they had been suffering hard times, unaware that her apparent altruism masked a heart almost as cold as that of her husband. Cecelia Whittingly Challis liked being seen as Lady Bountiful; it gave her the satisfaction lacking in her marriage.

When Rose had left school and been taken on as a scullery maid at Easterton Manor, the Challises' stately home, she'd thought she'd done well for herself, and when she was promoted out of the kitchen to be a parlour maid, she was both delighted and proud. As a scullery maid she had been up at half past four each morning, creeping into the family's bedrooms to light their fires, blacking the kitchen stove and laying the breakfast table in the servants' hall. Now she had an extra hour in bed before beginning her duties. The day was still long, and the work hard, but she much preferred dusting, plumping cushions and changing bed linen to the hours she'd used to spend with her hands immersed in greasy washing-up water.

It never occurred to her for a moment that her step up in life would end in disaster, and she'd blithely dismissed Cook's words of warning on her last day in the kitchen.

'Just you watch yourself, my girl,' Cook had said, waving her rolling pin for emphasis. 'The Challis men can't resist a pretty face, and you're a sight too nice-looking for your own good.'

It was true – she was, with her oval face, her thick hair so dark it was almost black and her dark brown eyes. But she'd only laughed, too delighted with her promotion to listen. She'd fended off advances before – when Cyril, one of the footmen, had trapped her in the larder and tried to kiss her, she'd given him a good hard slap across his face. Neither he nor any of the other male staff members had bothered her again.

'Don't worry, I can take care of myself,' she'd said airily.

Cook had pulled a face. 'It's a different world up there. If you go slapping the gentry, you'll get your marching orders. And then where will you be?'

The irony of it was that when the very situation Cook had warned her about had arisen, Rose hadn't wanted to put up a fight. She'd been swept off her feet. Flattered. Infatuated. She knew that now, though at the time she'd thought she was in love, and dared to dream impossible dreams.

Which had all turned to ashes. Now, locked away in this terrible place and knowing that as soon as he was weaned, her baby son would be taken away for adoption and she would never see him again, never even know where he was, she felt nothing but bitterness and a burning hatred for the family who had brought her to this. The power they wielded was absolute. It had been explained to her in no uncertain terms that if she ever told anyone who had fathered her baby, her father, Frank, would lose his job in Sir Oswald's quarry, and where would he ever find another one? The family would have lost their home too since it was a tied cottage, and Rose had known she had no choice but to keep silent.

She knew that although tongues might wag and people might speculate, with no evidence it would soon be forgotten.

But Rose wouldn't forget. Her heart had already been broken once, and soon it would be broken all over again. She didn't know how she could bear it. Life was so unfair! She cradled little Wallace close to her heart and vowed she would never, ever let him go. But even as she made the promise, she knew it was one she would be powerless to keep.

In the big communal dining hall where the men and women now took their meals together, Stella sat at the long deal table, her food untouched in front of her. Opposite her a young lad drooled as he spooned food awkwardly into his mouth; beside her a sad-faced elderly woman muttered constantly to herself, while on her other side a girl of perhaps nineteen or twenty surreptitiously stabbed at her wrist with the prongs of her fork whenever she thought the attendants on duty were looking the other way.

Stella barely noticed them. She was in a world of her own, confused and frightened and lost. Her whole body was rigid with tension, her breasts felt heavy and uncomfortable and a great yawning hole seemed to have opened up inside of her. She ached with longing for her children, even baby William, though the thought of feeding him again filled her with terror. It just wasn't right without them. It was as if she'd lost an arm or a leg, still able to feel it though it was no longer there. But more than anything in the world she wanted Tom, wanted his arms around her, wanted to hear him telling her that everything was going to be all right. A tear rolled down her cheek and splashed on the back of her clenched hand. Please! she whispered silently. Please, I want to go home . . .

'Come along now, Mrs Swift, eat up! We can't see good food go to waste.'

Stella glanced round, startled, at the brisk voice coming from behind her. The nurse who had spoken had a face like a suet pudding, pasty pale with small dark pinpricks of eyes that might have been the currants. She was one of the old brigade, used to treating the patients harshly, though she had learned to temper her ways when the superintendent or matron were around.

Stella shook her head wordlessly. She thought that if she took so much as a mouthful of the mutton stew on her plate she'd be sick. But Mabel Cummings was having none of it.

'You will eat it, Mrs Swift, or you'll have no pudding.'

I don't want pudding, Stella wanted to say, but no words would come.

'Well, we'll see about that,' Mabel Cummings said briskly when it was clear Stella had no intention of doing as she was told.

She prodded the old woman on Stella's left, who had now finished her meal and was wiping up the remains of the gravy with a hunk of bread.

'Go and sit over there, Ethel,' she instructed her, pointing to a vacant place at the end of the table.

Ethel gave her a resentful look, but got up and moved away, still chuntering to herself, and Mabel plonked herself down heavily on the wooden bench.

'If you won't eat, I'll just have to do it for you.' She forked up a lump of stewed lamb, aiming it at Stella's mouth. 'Come on now, stop acting up and eat this.'

Stella pursed her lips tightly, like a stubborn child.

'Open your mouth!'

With a sudden and abrupt movement, Stella pushed Mabel's hand away.

Startled, Mabel dropped the fork, which clattered on to the plate of food. A chunk or two of carrot flew off on to the table, along with splashes of gravy, which also splattered the bib of Mabel's starched white apron.

The nurse's face darkened with fury. 'Now look what you've done, you bad, wicked girl! You *will* eat this, or it's a cold bath and the straitjacket for you!'

'No!' Stella attempted to get up, but the bench was too close to the table to allow it. Frustrated, she shoved the plate away from her, and more stew spilled over, pooling on the scrubbed deal.

'That's it!' The nurse had had enough. She grabbed Stella's arm roughly, pulling her back down on to the bench.

'What is going on here?'

The man's voice was stern yet concerned. Intent on getting her charge to eat her dinner, Mabel hadn't noticed the superintendent coming into the dining hall and standing quietly just inside the door to make one of his regular inspection visits. Now, flustered and anxious, she attempted to explain herself.

'I'm afraid we have a difficult patient here, sir.'

'She's clearly upset, Nurse. Bullying will do no good at all.'

Dr Kirkwood was not a big man; in fact he was slightly built and considerably shorter than the buxom Mabel. Balding, and with a pair of wire-rimmed spectacles perched on his aquiline nose, he might have been dismissed by some as the last person to control a large staff and an even larger number of difficult and sometimes disruptive patients. But for all his small stature and unprepossessing appearance, Dr Kirkwood exuded authority.

Now he turned his attention to Stella. 'Can you tell me what's wrong, my dear?' he asked, his tone gentle and friendly.

Stella regarded him mutely, her eyes wide and anguished.

'Are you missing your baby?'

She nodded.

'Would you like to go up to the nursery and see him?'

A flash of panic skittered across her face. 'Not . . . feed him . . .' she whispered.

'Very well. But you would like to see him?' She nodded again. 'Then so you shall. I'll take you there myself.' He turned to Mabel. 'Can we move this bench, please, so that she can get out?'

Inwardly Mabel was fuming, but she knew better than to argue. She stomped along the line, motioned to the patients sitting on the bench to get up, and hoisted the end of it, sliding it back at an angle to enable Stella to clamber out. Then she moved it back again and indicated to the patients that they should retake their seats.

The superintendent was already ushering Stella towards the door.

'Too soft!' Mabel muttered to one of the other attendants, who had been watching the altercation with interest. 'No good will come of it.'

The attendant, a burly middle-aged man, said nothing, and Mabel's lips tightened.

So he was another one who favoured these new-fangled ideas. Couldn't they see Stella Swift was going to be trouble if she wasn't kept in check? One way or another, Mabel was going to make sure she *was*.

'It's Stella, isn't it?' Dr Kirkwood said as he led her up the stairs.

'Yes.' Her voice was so soft as to be barely audible.

'And you only arrived today. You must be finding it all very strange. But don't worry, you'll soon settle in. Nothing will seem quite as bad tomorrow, nor the day after that. I shall see you myself, and I'm sure that together we can find a solution to all your problems. When you're feeling better, your baby will behave better too. And you'll be able to go home to your family before you know it.'

'Thank you, Doctor,' Stella said meekly.

'No thanks necessary, my dear. It's what I'm here for. And the nurses too. Some might seem a little intimidating at times, but they all have kind hearts, and they do what they think is best for your own good.'

At this time of evening the nursery was dimly lit, with the oil lamps turned low and only a little of the remains of the daylight creeping in at the small high windows.

A different nurse, not much more than a girl, was sitting at the central station, a halfpenny periodical, *The Union Jack*, open on the table in front of her.

'You'll strain your eyes reading in this light,' Dr Kirkwood cautioned her.

'Oh – I'm not reading, sir. It's not mine . . .'

But colour had risen in her cheeks and all the way down her neck to the collar of her uniform frock.

Dr Kirkwood bit back a smile. All was quiet in the nursery. If none of the babies needed attention, Nurse Dando was welcome to take a few minutes' rest. Though he wasn't convinced she was old enough to be left in charge on her own throughout the night. He'd ask Matron to take a look at the duty rosters and see if she could arrange for one of the more experienced nurses to take over the night duty in future.

'Stella would like to spend some time with her baby,' he said now. 'Can you tell me which crib he is in?'

'Oh . . .' Nurse Dando's flush deepened. 'I'm not sure. I haven't been on duty long.'

Dr Kirkwood glanced meaningfully at the periodical.

'I can soon tell you, sir.' She hurried to the row of cribs. Besides the tags on their ankles, each crib had a notice bearing the name of the occupant taped to the wall above it.

'This one,' she announced triumphantly, pointing to the end crib.

'Put a chair out for Stella, please.'

'Does she mean to feed him?' Nurse Dando asked. 'Only

Cissie – Nurse Whitcombe – fed him just before she went off duty. She said—'

'No.' Dr Kirkwood cut her off before she could make reference to Stella's unwillingness to feed her baby. 'She just wants to sit with him for a little while.'

Stella was gazing in wonder at William. He was sleeping soundly, more soundly than she'd ever seen him in all of his short life. She could scarcely believe it. He looked like a cherub, she thought, his eyes closed so that long lashes lay on his downy cheeks, his lips pursed. There was little enough of him to see above the tight swaddling, but she wasn't going to disturb him. She reached through the bars of the crib, laying a hand gently on the firm mound of his small body, feeling the warmth of him spread from her fingers through her veins.

'Stay as long as you like, Stella,' Dr Kirkwood said, patting her shoulder. 'At least, until lights out. I'll have one of the nurses come up and fetch you when it's time.'

She glanced up at him and he was greatly encouraged by the change in her. Her eyes, previously wild and frightened, were now soft with love.

'You see, my dear? I told you everything was going to be all right, didn't I?'

With a nod to Nurse Dando, he turned for the door. When he glanced back, Stella was still sitting motionless with her hand on her baby and a look of contentment on her face.

# Chapter Five

Grace had just filled the kettle and set it on the hob to make a much-needed cup of tea when there was a knock at the back door. Surprised, she smoothed down her apron and went to answer it.

The clock on the scullery wall, a heavy, oak-framed piece too large for the space it occupied, was showing just after ten. After taking the children to school and watching them line up in the playground under the supervision of a teacher, she'd returned to the house and cleared away the breakfast things, fed Fluffy, then made the beds and tidied the living room, all with a heavy heart. She couldn't stop thinking about Stella, wondering how she was, whether there was any improvement in her condition, and worrying about what the future held. This whole business was a living nightmare, and she was drowning in a sense of unreality.

With the immediate chores finished, she'd felt lost and aimless, the day stretching before her bleak and purposeless. She would have to collect the children from school at three, but somehow she had to fill the hours until then. It was far too early to begin thinking about preparing the evening meal, and in any case the thought of food and the smell of it cooking turned her stomach. There must be jobs that needed doing about the house that would keep her occupied, but somehow it felt wrong to look for them. This wasn't her home, it was Stella's, and the very idea of checking for cupboard shelves that needed cleaning, even investigating the laundry basket for dirty washing, made her uncomfortable, as if she was trespassing, meddling with things that weren't her business.

If only it wasn't so far from Hillsbridge to Shillingford she could have done a few hours in the shop, which would have given her less time to worry about Stella, besides easing her conscience for leaving Mr Lines in the lurch. But the distance made that impossible. If she owned a bicycle, she might just about have time to do it, but she didn't, and to walk . . . By the time she got there, she'd have to turn around and come back again.

Now, though she could have done with the comfort of a friendly face, she cringed at the thought of having to talk to a stranger who would no doubt be wanting to ask a whole lot of questions that she didn't feel up to answering.

Dreading the inquisition to come, she opened the door to see a plump, rosy-cheeked woman of about her own age, with a coat pulled on but not buttoned over a wraparound apron.

'I hope I'm not poking my nose in where it's not wanted, but . . .' The woman on the doorstep hesitated. 'I'm so sorry Stella's been taken ill, and I wondered if there was anything I could do to help. I'm Francie Newman, by the way. I live next door,' she added.

'Oh, that's kind,' Grace said awkwardly, 'but I think we're managing, thank you.'

'That's all right then. But you know where I am if you need anything.' Francie turned to go, obviously worried she might be intruding, and as she did so, Grace remembered what Tom had told her.

'It was your boy who fetched the doctor, wasn't it?' she said.

'I don't know what Tom would have done without him. There was no way he could leave Stella.'

'My Ferdie, yes. He's a good boy.'

'And you're good friends with Stella, Tom said.'

'We get on well, yes. We've been neighbours a long time now, ever since she and Tom got the house. Before Oliver was born, that was. Her and me were expecting at more or less the same time, though it was her first and my youngest – our Reg.'

Grace made up her mind. Obviously Stella and Francie were close.

'Would you like to come in for a cup of tea?' she asked.

'That would be nice. As long as I won't be in the way . . .'

'Not at all. I'm all on my own and feeling a bit like a fish out of water.' She opened the door wide and stood aside. 'I expect you know the way through.'

Francie smiled. 'You could say that.'

'And where everything is kept. I've wasted so much time looking for things. But at least I know where the teapot is, and the cups, and the kettle should be coming up to the boil. Do sit down, and I'll make the tea.'

Francie sat on one of the dining chairs and opened her coat. 'It's nice and warm in here, I must say. It's as cold as Christmas outside.'

'It is, isn't it? I see the snowdrops are out, though, and a few crocuses, so I suppose it won't be long before spring is on the way.'

They were running out of small talk. When Stella had made the tea, she set the pot on a table mat, fetched cups, milk and sugar and sat down herself.

'I'll just let it brew for a minute . . .'

Francie, who had been tearing at a hangnail, took the bull by the horns. 'Have you heard how Stella is?'

Grace shook her head. 'Tom's going to ring the hospital from the pit manager's office, if he'll let him.' She hesitated. 'You do know where she is, do you?'

'Well . . . I'm guessing. Catcombe, is it?'

'Yes.' In spite of herself, Grace felt a wave of shame.

'I'm not surprised,' Francie said grimly. 'She's been going downhill ever since she had Will. And that's not to be wondered at either. I know she's been at her wits' end with him not feeding, and crying all the time. It's enough to drive anybody crackers.' She winced, colouring a little at the unfortunate turn of phrase, and hurried on. 'They don't seem to think there's anything to worry about, but you can't help wondering.'

'Tom said the doctor is going to give him a thorough checking-over if it goes on.' Grace poured the tea and pushed the sugar bowl in Francie's direction. 'Do you . . . ?'

'Couldn't drink it without.' Francie stirred three heaped spoonfuls of sugar into her cup, and Grace thought it was unsurprising she was so plump.

'So how many children have you got?' she asked, eager to change the subject away from Stella.

'Five – and don't I know it! Ferdie's eleven now, the twins, Gillie and Beattie, are nine, Ned's eight, and then there's Reg, the same age as Stella's Oliver, like I said. But there won't be any more if I've got anything to do with it.'

Grace smiled and nodded sympathetically, but she couldn't help thinking Francie didn't know how lucky she was. They might be hard work now, but they were all growing up and things would get easier. Grace would have given anything to have a family of her own, but it hadn't been meant to be and she didn't suppose the chance would ever come again. She was almost thirty years old, and a widow. Most men of her age were married with children, and the ones who weren't were not, in her experience, the kind to settle down. There were only two single men in Shillingford; one still lived with his mother and was a big softie, while the other spent all his free time – and his money – at the races or in the pub with his close friend the local bookmaker.

'You lost your husband, I understand,' Francie said now, almost as if she had read Grace's mind.

'Yes. He was killed in an accident underground,' she said. She didn't want to elaborate, and in any case she guessed there was no need. If they were close friends, Stella would have told Francie all about it at the time.

'I'm sorry,' Francie said, her rosy face sombre. 'It's what we all dread, isn't it? A knock at the door and the colliery manager or the deputy standing there.'

Grace couldn't answer. It was just as Francie said, and even now, five years later, it was still as fresh in her mind as if it were yesterday.

It hadn't been a knock at the door, though. She had been in the garden, getting in the washing, and as soon as she'd seen Cuthbert Wilkinson, the colliery manager, rounding the corner of the rank of cottages, she'd known something terrible had happened. But for some reason she'd never understood, she'd finished folding a pillowcase, placed it on top of the laundry basket and unpegged another. Had she been holding on to normality as long as possible, trying to delay the inevitable? In denial? She didn't know. Then Cuthbert had called to her and she could ignore him no longer. She'd walked slowly towards him, still holding the pillowcase.

'Mrs Baker . . .'

His voice was grave, and every line, every wrinkle in his face – she could see it now – was a deep chasm in his leathery skin. Funny, she'd thought. She'd never noticed before how old he looked, as if he should be retired, not managing a busy pit.

'Mr Wilkinson . . .'

Her stomach was turning over, she felt sick with dread, yet her voice came out sounding perfectly normal.

'Can we go inside?'

Another painful twist in her chest, as if a vice was tightening around her heart. She crossed the path to the house, her legs seeming not to belong to her but moving of their own accord. Pushed the door open. 'Please go in,' she tried to say, but now there was a lump in her throat and the words could not squeeze past it.

'I think you should sit down.'

They were in the living room now; she had no recollection of getting there. She wheeled around to face the manager and found her voice again, though it was tight and breathy.

'What is it? What's happened? Is it Cliff?'

He told her. There'd been a roof fall; Cliff had been crushed beneath it. They'd done their best to get him out, but it was too late. He was dead.

At the time, she'd been too much in shock to take in the enormity of it. The loss of her husband – and inevitably, eventually, her home. The loss of all their hopes, dreams and plans. The children they would never now have. All that had come later, along with the overwhelming grief, and a sense of guilt she couldn't shake off, that it was somehow her fault for not loving him enough. That there had been times when she'd looked at Stella, so happy with Tom, and wished that it was her, not her sister, with the man who had been her first love, the man she had felt so passionately about that she'd ignored his infidelities until at last she'd been unable to ignore them any longer and had snapped. This was her punishment – like the man in the parable whose seed fell on stony ground, even the little she had had been taken away because she hadn't valued it enough. Hadn't been grateful. And she'd wept bitter tears for a good husband lost in the thunderous crack of falling stone and a cloud of choking dust, never again to see the sunlight, feel its warmth on his face, smell the fresh pungent scent of new-mown grass . . .

'Well, I suppose I should be going.' Francie pushed back her chair and stood up. 'I've got a thousand and one things to do, but it's been nice to meet you, and you know where I am if you want anything – even just to talk.'

'That's really kind.' Once again, Grace felt awkward, though she couldn't be sure why. For a while, they'd been just two young women chatting over a cup of tea. Now . . .

As Francie picked up her cup, carried it through into the scullery and set it down on the linolcum-topped cupboard as if she was quite used to doing so, Grace realised what it was. Francie was at home here; she was the interloper. Then, again out of long habit, Francie opened the door to let herself out.

'Don't forget now, any time—'

She broke off mid-sentence, interrupted by a shrill and tremulous voice calling: 'Joey! Where are you? Joey!'

A tiny, wizened elderly woman came into view from behind the fence screening one of the neighbouring paths, carrying a gilded birdcage, the door open, held high.

'Oh, have you seen my Joey?' she called as she neared Francie and Grace.

'Sorry, Mrs Plumley. Not today.' Francie seemed quite unfazed.

'Has she lost her bird?' Grace asked, concerned, as the woman hurried off along the backs of the houses and up another path, still calling his name.

'Her canary? I doubt it,' Francie said. 'He'll be somewhere in the house. She lets him fly free, and a tidy mess he makes too. But she won't have had the door or windows open on a cold day like this. He's flown upstairs, I expect.'

'But all the same . . .' Grace's soft heart was touched by the old woman's distress.

'It happens all the time,' Francie reassured her. 'Once a week, at least. If she can't see him, she gets in a panic. When she gets tired of looking, she'll go home, and there he'll be, mark my words. Trouble is, she's a bit touched.' She tapped her forehead to emphasise her meaning, and this time it didn't seem to strike her that her words were not the most tactful, given Stella's circumstances. To Grace, however, they were like salt in an open wound. Was that how people would talk about her sister when it got out where she was? 'A bit touched', or 'gone funny'? Would they ever look at her in the same way again, or would the stigma hang over her for ever?

'Right, I must get on. Let me know, won't you, if there's any news.' Francie was heading back towards her own back door. As she reached it, she raised a hand in farewell and disappeared inside.

Grace went back into the scullery and closed the door after her, trying to push aside the unwelcome thoughts of the gossip Stella's incarceration would arouse. Francie hadn't meant anything by her tactless words; if she had, she'd never have said what she did. She was clearly a good friend of Stella's, and would be there for her when she was allowed to come home. In the meantime, Grace herself had found a neighbour who had gone out of her way to be friendly. Perhaps in a day or two she wouldn't feel quite so much a fish out of water. But all the same, she couldn't wait for the day when her sister was well again and she, Grace, could return to her old life.

For both their sakes, and for the sake of Tom and the children, she prayed Stella would soon begin to recover.

That afternoon Grace left the house in good time to collect the children from school. She'd noticed there was only half a loaf of bread left in the larder and she wanted to call in at the bakery in town before meeting them. Stella used to bake her own bread before William had come along and she'd had to spend her days trying to get him to feed or stop him crying, but Grace didn't feel competent to attempt it in an unfamiliar kitchen with an oven she wasn't used to.

She found the place without too much trouble, a little tea room that was also a shop, with loaves of bread and trays of rolls and cakes on display on a glass counter. From the delicious aroma that met her as she opened the door and went inside, she guessed it fronted the bakery, while the baker's living quarters would be upstairs, on the first floor and in the attic rooms above.

A couple of customers were seated at one of the tables with a pot of tea and a plate of toasted teacakes. They gave Grace curious glances before returning to their conversation, as did the girl behind the counter when Grace reached the head of the short queue. Everyone knew everyone else in Hillsbridge, she guessed, and a stranger was bound to attract attention. But to her relief no one questioned her and she bought a loaf of bread and half a dozen jam tarts and beat a hasty retreat, feeling terribly conspicuous.

The mothers waiting in twos and threes at the top of the incline that led to the school gates were less reticent, however. When they noticed Grace standing alone a little way off, there was a hiatus in their chatter as they took a good look at her, and one in the nearest group to her asked the question that was on all their minds.

'We haven't seen you here before, have we? Are you new to the area?'

Grace turned to see a woman with a thin face and pinched features whose eyes, small and mean, were bright with curiosity.

'I've come to collect my nephews and niece,' Grace said, trying to edge further away.

The woman was not to be put off. 'Who's that then?'

Grace wished heartily that she could tell the nosy woman to mind her own business. But these were acquaintances of her sister; when this was all over, Stella had to live with them.

'The Swift children,' she said, still trying to put some distance between her and her inquisitor.

'Oh! So where's Stella?'

'She's not well.' Grace had no intention of going into details, but there was no stopping the wretched woman.

'Oh dear. What's wrong with her?'

Grace was saved from answering by the clanging of the bell. As one, the mothers surged forward into the playground, making for the cloakrooms on one wing of the building. Etched in stone above the one to the right was the word 'Boys'; to the left the stonework bore the legend 'Girls'.

Grace headed towards that one. Oliver and Alec were quite big enough to find their own coats, but at only four years old, Emily was a different matter. She followed the other mothers into the cloakroom with its rows of pegs and a stand of four washbasins, and was horrified to see that the plastered walls were running with water – condensation, she presumed; there had been no really heavy rain for the last couple of days. So that was the reason some of the mothers had been carrying their children's coats – they took them home and brought them back again rather than leave them here to hang against the wet walls. Grace resolved to do the same tomorrow; she only hoped

Emily's coat had been hung with the inside out, otherwise it would be uncomfortably damp for her to put on. The last thing she wanted was for the little girl to get a chill.

The same was probably true of the boys' cloakroom, she thought, but at least they were older and hopefully hardier. There wasn't much you could do to protect small boys; if you fussed, they would most likely be bullied for being sissies.

The cloakroom was now a heaving mass of small bodies erupting down the two stone steps that led from the classrooms, and the noise of their chatter as they escaped to freedom was ear-splitting. Grace spotted Emily at the foot of the steps and waved to her, but the little girl remained where she was. Grace could see she was reluctant to push her way through the throng, so she went to her instead.

'Emily, my love. Come on, let's find your coat.'

A pair of troubled brown eyes looked up into hers.

'Where's Mammy?'

'She's not well, remember? But I'm here instead.'

Emily's lips quivered as if she was about to cry, and Grace's heart ached for her. But what could she say to make it right? She was no more used to coping with an unhappy little girl than Emily was to coming out of school without her mother there to meet her. Usually, when Grace visited, the children were excited to see her, running to her, eager for the treats she invariably brought for them – sweets, biscuits, a small toy. This was entirely different.

'Where's your peg?' she asked Emily.

'Over there. But Mammy . . .'

Grace fetched Emily's coat. Mercifully it was hanging with the outside against the streaming wall, so the lining hadn't got wet. She set her basket down, then helped Emily into the coat and fastened the buttons.

'Let's go and find the boys.'

Oliver and Alec were waiting outside in the playground. They too were more subdued than usual.

'All right, you two?' Grace asked in a determinedly cheerful tone.

'Yeah.' Oliver said it almost defiantly, as if his pride would not allow him to show his true feelings. Alec kicked a small stone so that it skittered across the yard, refusing to look at her.

'Let's go home then,' Grace said. She pointed to her basket. 'I've got jam tarts here. Do you like jam tarts?'

Instantly, as if by magic, both boys brightened up.

'You bet!'

'Course we do!'

Grace smiled to herself and took Emily by the hand, and the quartet set out up the long hill that led to Dunderwick Road.

After Francie had left that morning, Grace had made a stew, which was now simmering on the hob in readiness for the evening meal. To keep the children going until then, she set the jam tarts on a plate, made cups of sweet tea for the boys and poured a glass of milk for Emily. Oliver and Alec tucked in with gusto, but Emily was still glum, taking one bite of her tart and chewing it over and over as though she was finding it difficult to swallow.

'Come on, my love, eat up,' Grace urged her.

Emily shook her head wordlessly.

'I'll have it if she doesn't want it,' Oliver said, reaching across the table.

'No, Oliver. It's Emily's. If she doesn't want it now, she can have it later.'

'Can I have another one anyway?'

'Share it with Alec. I don't want you spoiling your appetite for your supper, and we have to leave one for your dad, in any case.'

Emily was still staring down at her plate, crumbling a bit of pastry between finger and thumb and looking on the verge of tears. The sight of her forlorn face tore at Grace's heartstrings.

'Cheer up, my love. Try to be a brave girl,' she said.

Emily raised her head. Her lip was trembling, her eyes brimming with tears. She pushed her plate away so violently it collided with her glass of milk, also untouched.

'Careful!' Grace warned. 'You almost knocked that over.'

With a small choking gasp, Emily jumped down from her chair and ran from the room.

'Oh . . .' Grace could have wept herself. 'Just behave yourselves, you two,' she told the boys, and followed Emily upstairs.

She found the little girl curled up on her bed, sobbing as if her heart would break.

'Oh sweetheart, don't, please.' She sat down on the bed beside Emily, stroking her niece's hair away from her wet face. 'Mammy will be home again soon, I promise, and everything will be all right.'

'It's not just Mammy.' The words came out all of a rush, but so thick with tears that Grace had to lean closer to make them out.

'What then?' she asked.

'Miss Slocombe . . .' A pause for more gulps and sobs. 'She's going to be so cross with me.'

'Miss Slocombe? Your teacher?' A nod of confirmation. 'But why? Why would she be cross with you?'

'I broke my ruler. I didn't mean to. I was just playing with it and it snapped.' It was all tumbling out now in a rush.

'I'm sure she knows it was an accident,' Grace tried to console her niece.

'Suppose. She gave me another. But she told me I had to take care of it, not play with it again. But I was putting it away in the desk and the lid came down and . . .' More sniffs. 'And . . . oh . . . I broke that one too . . .'

'Oh, Emily, darling, it's not the end of the world. It's only a ruler.'

'No . . . *another* ruler . . .'

'Just explain to her, my love.'

Emily began crying harder. 'I daren't tell her. I'm so ashamed. And she's going to be so cross.'

'She's going to have to know, Emily,' Grace said reasonably. 'Do you want me to speak to her? Tell her what's happened, and that you are really very sorry?'

Emily looked up at her with pleading tear-filled eyes.

'I'll go and see her in the morning when I take you to school,' Grace promised. 'She might tell you to take more care with things, but she won't be cross with you, I'm sure, so you can stop worrying about it. Now, are you going to come down and eat that jam tart before your brother does?'

Emily scrubbed her eyes with her hand and nodded.

'Come on then.' Grace gave her a hug, took her by the hand and led her to the top of the stairs.

If only all their problems could be solved so easily! she thought.

By the time Tom got home from work, Grace had the water ready for his bath, simmering in the copper. His face was black with coal dust, hiding the worry lines she'd noticed yesterday, but there was a heaviness in his step, as if he had all the cares of the world on his shoulders, and a bleakness in his eyes.

'Any news?' she asked when he had greeted the children.

'Just the same. And they think it would be better if I didn't visit for a day or two. They want to try to get her settled.'

'There's a stew for supper when you've had your bath,' she said. There would be time to talk more about Stella when the children were in bed. 'And I've put clean clothes and towels out for you.'

'Bless you, Grace.'

Something twisted deep inside her.

Tom would, she knew, usually have his bath in front of the living room fire at this time of year. But with her here he would have it in the freezing outhouse.

'Don't be long. It's like an icebox out there,' she said.

'Don't worry. I won't be.'

He ruffled both boys' hair and chucked Emily under the chin, striving for a normality that Grace was afraid would be a very long time in returning, then went out into the cold, dark evening.

# Chapter Six

'Right then – are we ready? It's a bit foggy out there, so it might take us longer than usual, and we don't want to be late for the service.' Alistair Mackay picked up his little daughter, settling her on his hip. 'You're ready, aren't you, Constance?'

'Are you sure it's safe to go if it's foggy?' Jessica asked anxiously.

The weather had changed abruptly again from bright and icy to clammy cold, and a thick mist had descended overnight, obscuring the valley beneath the hill on which their house stood.

'There'll be no problem as long as we take it carefully,' Alistair reassured her. 'There's never much on the roads on a Sunday. And you want to see Florrie, don't you?'

'Of course I do. But . . .' Jessica still sounded doubtful.

'Put your hat on then, and let's get going,' Alistair urged her.

Jessica fetched her hat and settled it on her head in front of the living room mirror, but her hands shook a little as she thrust the hatpin through the moss-green felt so that she missed the thick twist of nut-brown hair and instead grazed her scalp.

'Ouch!' she exclaimed.

'Calm down, hinnie.' Alistair often resorted to his native Scottish endearment, especially if Jessica was upset about something. Usually it would make her smile. Not this morning, though. She merely jabbed the pin in at a more forgiving angle and turned away from the mirror still looking anxious.

'There's nothing to get yourself in a state about,' Alistair said, trying to soothe her, but managing to sound faintly irritated.

'I know, I know. It's just that I can't help worrying with Constance in the car and this blinking fog.'

'Come on. We'll be fine.'

He headed out into the hall and towards the front door, and Jessica picked up her gloves and bag and followed, resigned now to the inevitable.

Alistair was right, of course: she let niggling little anxieties assume much bigger proportions than they warranted, and saw dangers where none existed. She'd always been a worrier, but since Constance was born she'd become much worse. It was the price she paid for being a mother, she supposed.

The fog this morning was just something else to fret about, a nasty, nebulous threat. But Alistair was a good driver; he wouldn't take any chances, especially with Constance in the car. And Florrie would be expecting them, and would be dreadfully disappointed if they didn't turn up.

Ever since he had managed to get things changed for the better at Catcombe, Alistair and Jessica had driven over on a Sunday morning to attend the service that was held in the asylum chapel for those inmates who wished to go and were deemed fit enough – Florrie among them. Afterwards Jessica could sit for a while chatting to her sister over a cup of tea and a plate of biscuits, time they both enjoyed spending together. Since she and Alistair had married and moved into their newly built house in Hillsbridge, Jessica had been unable to visit Florrie as often as when she had lived just a couple of miles away, in Easterton; now she was dependent on Alistair to take her.

The Sunday morning trip had become something of a ritual,

and the arrival of Constance had done nothing to change that – they simply took her with them. There were those who thought it highly unsuitable for a young child to be visiting a lunatic asylum, but both Jessica and Alistair were agreed: it was good for her to grow up seeing the mentally ill not as monsters of some kind, locked away out of sight for fear of frightening the horses, but as human beings who were ill and needed to be looked after.

Constance would never see any of the worst cases, of course – the violent or the truly deranged. Those poor souls would gain nothing from attending the service in the chapel, and would only disrupt it. Just occasionally one of the congregation would begin shouting, but would be quickly led out, and once, when a patient had suffered an epileptic fit, Jessica had quickly explained to Constance that the poor man was unwell and that was the reason Daddy had had to go and attend to him. To her relief, Constance had seemed more interested than alarmed.

When Jessica had been growing up, there had been a woman in Easterton who was epileptic; Jessica's mother had always crossed the street if she saw her coming for fear she might have a fit there on the pavement in front of her, which in turn had made Jessica and Florrie nervous of meeting her. Jessica didn't want Constance to grow up feeling that fear. She wanted her to accept people with any kind of disability as normal, and show compassion towards them.

Besides, Constance's own aunt was locked away. Jessica didn't want Constance to grow up ashamed of her. Nor did she want either of them to miss out, Constance on all the love her aunt had to give her, Florrie on seeing her little niece grow up. Family was so important, and there was no doubt Florrie adored Constance and looked forward to her weekly visits.

Much to Jessica's relief, the journey to Catcombe passed

without incident. The fog was quite thick over the Mendips, but Alistair drove slowly, his eyes narrowed and watchful. Straining her own eyes in an attempt to see through it, Jessica felt a throbbing beginning in her temple, but as they began the descent towards Catcombe, the fog cleared and her incipient headache disappeared with it as if by magic.

'See? I told you we'd be fine,' Alistair said as he turned the Model T Ford into the drive of the asylum.

'We've still got to get home again,' Jessica pointed out.

'And by that time the fog will be gone,' Alistair assured her.

He parked the motor outside the main doors, lifted Constance down and handed Jessica out on to the drive. Then, with Constance toddling between them, holding their hands, they went into the asylum.

The chapel was housed in one of the downstairs rooms in the central block that divided the two wings. Rows of upright chairs faced a large table, which had been laid out as an altar with an impressive gold crucifix – donated by Sir Oswald Whittingly Challis – and candles in gold candlesticks arranged on a white linen altar cloth. To the right of the altar, beneath a foot-high statue of the Virgin Mary, a votive with a basket of small candles on a ledge close by was a nod towards any Catholics or High Church Anglicans amongst the worshippers, though the service was usually taken by a minister from one of the Nonconformist churches in the town or, if necessary, from further afield.

Today it seemed the Reverend Carpenter would be officiating. Jessica's heart sank as she saw him tottering round the altar making minute and totally unnecessary adjustments. The Reverend Carpenter had long since retired from active ministry in the Baptist Church, and the service, when he was taking it, always took longer than it should. He spoke so slowly, and frequently had to find his place in the prayer book when he forgot the words of the time-honoured litany, and he moved at a snail's pace between altar and lectern and back again. On more than one occasion she'd seen restive patients being led out while the Reverend Carpenter waffled, and she was glad she'd put some sweets and some toy farm animals into her bag. Hopefully the sweets would keep Constance quiet and the little toys stop her from becoming too bored.

Some of the seats were already occupied – Jessica recognised the back of Florrie's head as one of those in the front row, and as the family slid into a row further back with a slight scraping of the chair legs against the polished board floor, Florrie turned around and the two sisters nodded a greeting to one another.

One of the women Florrie was sitting with turned round too – it was that poor girl who'd been sent here because she'd had an illegitimate baby, Jessica realised – but the third member of their little group sat staring straight ahead.

'That's Stella Swift, if I'm not mistaken,' Alistair whispered. 'At least that means she's well enough today to come to chapel.'

'Oh good, let's hope she's on the mend,' Jessica whispered back.

'I'll go up to the nursery and check on her baby when the service is over . . .'

Alistair broke off as a shuffling of feet and some incoherent mumbling announced the arrival of a small procession of inmates, shepherded by two or three nurses. They moved into the row in front of Jessica and Alistair with a great deal of scraping of chairs, and one, a boy in his late teens with learning difficulties, sat down so clumsily that his chair cannoned backwards into Constance's plump little legs. She began to cry, and Alistair hastily hoisted her on to his lap while Jessica fumbled in her bag for one of the jelly babies she'd intended to keep for later.

More shuffling, more commotion, and a further crocodile of inmates moved into the row behind them.

'We should have sat at the back as we usually do,' Jessica whispered to Alistair as she handed Constance a pink jelly baby.

Reverend Carpenter had straightened his stole and moved to take centre stage, where he was thumbing through his prayer book to find the appropriate page.

'Dearly beloved,' he began in his slow, measured, but surprisingly powerful voice, 'we are gathered here together in God's presence to witness . . .'

He stopped, seeming to realise his mistake, and from the row behind Alistair and Jessica came a hastily stifled giggle as someone realised the poor man had been reading from the introduction to the marriage ceremony. There was another long pause while the Reverend Carpenter turned the pages of his prayer book again and adjusted his spectacles on his fleshy nose. Once more his voice rumbled through the room, booming and ponderous.

The service had begun.

When it was over, Jessica took Constance into the small anteroom – where tea and biscuits were served just as if the service had been held in a village church rather than the asylum chapel – to wait for Florrie.

It took a little longer than usual for her to appear, and when she did, she explained she'd had to see the two women she'd been sitting with back to the day room. Evidently she had been entrusted with their care for the duration of the service.

Jessica felt a quick stab of pride. Florrie might be a patient herself, but she was treated almost as if she was a member of the staff, what with working in the nursery, and now this. There was a contented glow about Florrie these days that pleased Jessica enormously, since it was doubtful her sister would ever be released.

'Alistair said one of the women you were with is the patient he had to bring in a couple of weeks ago,' she said, sipping her tea.

'You mean Stella?' Florrie dunked her Marie biscuit in her tea and offered it to Constance, who was sitting between the two sisters, her legs dangling over the seat of the chair.

'Yes, that's right.' Jessica was frowning a little as she watched her daughter stuffing the soggy side of the biscuit into her mouth. 'I'm not sure she should be having tea at her age, Florrie.'

'It won't do her any harm, and it'll help her get used to the taste for when you want to get her off milk.'

For emphasis, she took the dry half of the biscuit from Constance and dunked that too before handing it back to her.

'Well, just be careful she doesn't get it on her Sunday-best coat,' Jessica warned. 'It's nearly new, and we don't want tea stains all down the front.'

Florrie took a large white handkerchief from the pocket of her asylum-issue smock and wound it round beneath Constance's chin.

'There you are. What's wrong with that?' She smiled triumphantly, very much the old Florrie who had always taken charge when they were growing up. 'Now, you were asking about Stella. She's one of Alistair's patients, you say?'

'Yes. The whole family are. Alistair delivered her baby – well, he didn't deliver it exactly; the midwife did that, of course, but he did go in afterwards to check them both over. He's a bit worried he might have missed something, I think.'

'There's nothing wrong with the baby that I can see,' Florrie said, dunking another biscuit, this time for herself. 'He's a bit underweight, but that's only to be expected if he hasn't been getting all the nourishment he needs. We'll soon put that right, never fear. This business of him not sleeping and that – it's all in the mother's mind. She's the one to worry about. She's in a dream most of the time, and we still can't get her to feed little Will herself.'

'Oh dear,' Jessica said, genuinely concerned. 'Alistair will be sorry to hear that. Has she rejected the baby, do you think?'

Florrie frowned. 'I wouldn't say that. She'll sit by his crib for hours if we let her, just gazing at him. And she gets in a bit of a state when they're separated. She'll cuddle him even, just as long as he's quiet. But if he starts to cry, or if we try to get him on to her breast, then . . . well, all hell breaks loose. I don't know what's going on in her head, and that's the truth. In fact, I do sometimes wonder . . .' She hesitated.

'What?' Jessica asked.

'If she makes him cry on purpose. Sometimes, when she puts him back in his crib, he starts up for no apparent reason.'

'Perhaps he just doesn't want to be put down,' Jessica suggested.

'Or perhaps she's given him a good hard pinch when nobody's looking.' Florrie shook her head. 'Oh, don't look at me like that. You never can tell. Folk do funny things sometimes, even them that are sane. In here, well, it goes without saying . . .'

'Let's just hope they can get to the bottom of it before too long,' Jessica said.

'Amen to that.' Florrie might still have been in chapel. 'Poor little chap's in need of some real mother love, not that blooming pap boat. And it's upsetting for Rose, too. You know – I told you about her. Whittingly Challis's maid, the one he had put away because she was in the family way, and her with no husband.'

'That was her sitting with you in chapel?' Jessica asked.

'That was her, poor lamb. The man ought to be lynched, if you ask me. She dotes on that baby. Nearly lost him – he was born before he should have been, all down to the stress of it, I shouldn't wonder. Rose did everything in her power to make sure he pulled through, and thank the Lord he did. But all that just to lose him all over again, and for good. He'll be adopted as soon as he's fit enough; there's new parents fixed up for him, and a wet nurse and all, so Cissie Whitcombe says. She won't let on who they are – maybe doesn't know herself – though Whittingly Challis has had a hand in it if I'm not much mistaken. She'll never see that little mite again, nor know what's become of him. It's going to break her heart. And it's all the worse for her seeing Stella Swift behaving the way she does.'

At last she paused for breath and a quick slurp of tea, and if she hadn't been so appalled by the sorry tale, Jessica would have been amused to see that her sister could still talk for England, even though she was incarcerated in this place.

'Awful,' she murmured.

'Mabel Cummings is getting fed up with her, I can tell you.' Florrie resumed her narrative with gusto.

'Mabel Cummings?' It wasn't a name Jessica knew.

'Night nurse,' Florrie said shortly. 'She's been brought in from downstairs to replace the one before, who wasn't really up to it. She's already given poor Stella a piece of her mind, and you don't want to get on the wrong side of Mabel, let me tell you. She's good at hiding what she's like when Matron or Dr Kirkwood are around, but she can be very unkind when there's no one there to see. The only one she's got any patience with is Rose Gooding. Rose's mother is her sister, and blood is thicker than water when all's said and done. It's why she was willing to change from day to night duty, I reckon, so she could work in the nursery and keep an eye on her niece.'

Constance was beginning to get restless, wriggling about on her chair and almost falling off.

'I think I'd better take her outside for a bit of a walk,' Jessica said.

'In this weather? She'll catch her death. I've got a much better idea. Would you like to see the babies, my cherub?' she asked Constance. 'After all, you're going to have one of your own at home come the summer, aren't you?'

Constance was nodding eagerly.

'Come on then, and we'll find your daddy at the same time.' Florrie lifted Constance down and took her niece's hand, leading her out of the anteroom and towards the stairs.

Shaking her head and smiling to herself, Jessica followed. Florrie certainly seemed to have found her niche, and she was probably better off here than living with that philanderer and general good-for-nothing Bert Carter.

Sometimes fate worked in the strangest ways, she thought. She only hoped it would be kind to Stella Swift and Rose Gooding.

'So how is Baby Swift doing?' Alistair asked Cissie Whitcombe as they stood at the nurses' station at the opposite end of the nursery to the row of cribs where Stella and Rose sat nursing their babies.

Cissie smoothed her apron over her broad hips. She had no concern that her voice might carry down the nursery.

'As well as can be expected, Doctor. He was certainly underweight when he came in, but not that much, and he's put on a couple of pounds already. I think we're doing a good job with him.'

Alistair nodded. 'I'm sure you are.'

'We do our best,' Cissie said proudly. 'Just look at how we

managed to pull Baby Gooding through, and him born long before he should have been. The pity of it is, all we're doing is hastening the day he'll be ready for adoption.' She sighed, shaking her head and throwing a quick glance in Rose's direction.

'And Mrs Swift?' Alistair was anxious to get this conversation back on track. Sorry as he felt for Rose Gooding, she wasn't his patient. It was Stella and baby William who were his concern. 'Has she shown any signs of improvement?' he asked, keeping his voice low even though he thought both Stella and Rose were out of earshot.

'Not so as you'd notice.' This time Cissie lowered her voice to match his. 'Why don't you have a word with her and see for yourself?'

'That's my intention. And to examine William,' Alistair said, a trifle frostily. 'I simply wanted your professional opinion first. Perhaps you could ask Miss Gooding if she could sit down here for a bit so as to give us some privacy.'

'Of course, Doctor.'

Cissie bustled the length of the nursery and spoke to Rose, who quickly got up and moved to the nurses' station, her baby still in her arms. As she passed Alistair, she gave him a sheepish glance, as if she'd been caught doing something she shouldn't.

'You can go back as soon as I've finished with my patient and her baby,' he said, hoping to set her at her ease.

Poor girl, he was thinking. She's had all the stuffing knocked out of her. Then he turned his attention to Stella.

'Mrs Swift,' he greeted her, taking the seat Rose had vacated.

For just a moment her eyes flicked in his direction, and he thought he saw a flash of recognition before the shutters came down once more. But she was cradling William close to her heart. That had to be a good sign, surely?

'And how's Baby?' he asked, hoping this might elicit a response, but still Stella refused to look at him, only clutching Will more tightly than ever.

'Would it be all right if I took a wee look at him?'

Still nothing.

'I just want to make sure he's well and healthy. Can you give him to me?'

Stella's eyes came up to meet his gaze; this time he could see they were full of terror.

'Don't worry, I'm not going to take him away. He'll be right here in his crib where you can see him,' Alistair said soothingly, and to his relief, as he gently took William from her arms, she put up no resistance.

He laid the baby in his crib, taking care to stand to one side so that Stella would not lose sight of him and panic, and unwound the swaddling, which was nowhere near as tight as Cissie liked it to be. Stella had loosened it, he guessed. Some mothers hated their babies to be wrapped up like little mummies, unable to wave a tiny fist or grasp a proffered finger.

William had been fast asleep in Stella's arms; now he gazed up into Alistair's face, blinking a little so that his long lashes feathered against his soft pink cheeks, and Alistair felt almost guilty for disturbing him. He pulled his stethoscope from his pocket and draped it around his neck.

'Sorry, little man,' he said softly as he loosened the swaddling still further, exposing the baby's shoulders and arms and a small rounded body wearing only a knitted vest and a napkin.

Suddenly, to his astonishment, the small face crumpled, the tiny hands tightened into fists, which juddered alarmingly, and William began to cry lustily.

Stella was on her feet in an instant; the catatonic state erupted into anguish.

'No! No! I can't bear it! Stop him! Stop him!'

At the uproar, Cissie Whitcombe came running.

'Stella, quiet now, there's a good girl. And for goodness' sake, Doctor, whatever are you doing to William? He'll set all the others off.'

'I haven't so much as touched him yet, but I need to listen to his heart.' Alistair attached his stethoscope to his ears and hovered it over William's chest, thinking that this was useless unless the baby quietened.

'That's the cause of his distress, you see!' Cissie announced triumphantly. 'You've laid him bare, and he likes to be swaddled nice and tight, don't you, my love?' She reached into the crib, lifted Will and began to wind the swaddling binder round him.

'Nurse Whitcombe! How can I listen to his heart and his chest with that . . .'

He broke off. Miraculously, William had stopped yelling, and his eyes were closing, as if he was about to go off to sleep again.

An idea had begun to form in Alistair's mind. When held upright, William wanted to fall asleep. At home he had cried every time he was placed in his crib, whilst here in the asylum nursery he did not. Was the difference what he was beginning to think it might be? That Cissie Whitcombe favoured tight swaddling whilst Stella resisted it? Could it be that lying down without support of some kind, the baby was in pain?

'Unwrap him again, please, Nurse.'

Cissie pulled a disapproving face, but did as she was told.

'Now hold him upright against your shoulder.'

Cissie's disapproval turned to bewilderment, but again she obeyed. After all, Alistair was the doctor. She was just a humble nurse.

William nestled into her, quiet as a lamb.

'Now lie him in his crib. No – without the swaddling.'

For perhaps a minute William remained quiet and sleepy. Then suddenly the yelling began again, the clenched fists, all the signs of distress, and Alistair knew he had hit on the cause of the trouble.

'All right, Nurse, swaddle him again.'

He was remembering now that the midwife who had delivered William had reported that he had been born with the cord wound around his neck. 'Gave me quite a fright, I can tell you,' she had said. 'I had to whip him out and it took me a minute or two to get him breathing.'

Alistair had complimented her on a job well done and forgotten all about it. Now he found himself wondering if it was possible William had sustained some kind of injury as a result of that twisted cord. Had a small bone been dislocated by his violent delivery? The more he thought about it, the more likely it seemed.

But what to do? There was no way he could confirm it. But William seemed perfectly comfortable when he was supported, either upright or with the tight swaddling holding everything in place. Hopefully, in time, whatever was wrong would right itself. In the meantime . . .

'Will you please ensure Baby is kept tightly swaddled at all times?' he said to Cissie.

'Of course, Doctor. You know that's my way.'

'But in this case it may be important.' He turned to Stella. 'You mustn't remove William's swaddling again. Do you understand?'

Stella nodded.

'Good . . .' Alistair returned the stethoscope to his pocket.

'What about examining him, Doctor?' Cissie asked.

'I won't disturb him again. I think he's perfectly healthy apart from whatever it is that's causing him discomfort, and the swaddling will take care of that.'

The door to the nursery opened and Jessica and Florrie came in with Constance trotting eagerly beside them.

'She wants to see the babies,' Florrie explained.

Alistair stifled a smile.

'Will that be all right, Nurse Whitcombe?'

'Just as long as she doesn't wake them up.'

'Quickly then, and then we're going home.'

As Constance peered eagerly into the cots, Alistair turned to Stella.

'I'll be back to see you and Baby, Mrs Swift,' he said. 'But I think I can assure you there's nothing to worry about. William is going to be fine, and so are you. Just rest now and everything will work out, you'll see.'

He hoped very much that his confidence was not misplaced. He was right about William, he was sure of it. As for Stella, only time would tell.

# Chapter Seven

Sunday afternoon, and Grace was alone in the house in Dunderwick Road, where she still felt something of an intruder.

Tom had taken the children to visit his parents, who lived on the other side of Hillsbridge, Emily in the pushchair and the two boys competing to see who could kick a small stone the furthest as they set off along the road. Really, Emily was far too big now for the pushchair, but Stella had hung on to it as the walk to their grandparents' home was quite a long one, and when William was on the way she was glad that she had. Now Tom too was glad of it. Without it he'd have had to carry Emily on his shoulders for much of the way, and she was getting too big for that as well.

He'd suggested that perhaps Grace might like to go to Shillingford to see her own parents – he'd pay for Fred Carson to take her in his pony and trap – but Grace had refused the offer. For one thing, she knew Tom could ill afford it, and she certainly couldn't; for another, she really didn't want to spend the afternoon fielding what she knew would be a barrage of questions about Stella to which as yet she had no answers.

Now, however, alone once again in the house where she felt so utterly out of place, Grace was almost wishing she'd taken advantage of Tom's offer. If the weather wasn't so miserable, she'd have gone for a walk herself, but as it was, the prospect was far from inviting. At least it was nice and warm by the fire. The trouble was, it gave her too much opportunity for thinking about Stella, and what the future might hold.

A knock at the door interrupted her reverie, though at first she thought she must have imagined it. She couldn't think who would be calling on a Sunday afternoon. Most people were only too glad to have a good rest and relax in the comfort of their homes. But when it came again, there was no mistaking it – unlikely as it seemed, someone was at the door, and they weren't going to go away.

Grace got up from the fireside chair and went to see who it was that was calling.

She didn't recognise the tall, rangy, sandy-haired man on the doorstep, nor did she notice the motor parked on the road outside the gate. She couldn't imagine that he was a neighbour. He looked too . . . she searched for the right word . . . posh. Nice coat, no flat cap, a face that somehow didn't quite fit the image of an off-duty miner or farmhand.

'Yes?' she said, a little awkwardly.

'Ah, you must be Stella's sister.' He didn't sound local, either, though for the moment Grace couldn't place the strange lilting accent. But obviously he knew who she was, and something about their situation.

'Yes,' she said again. 'I'm Grace Baker. But I'm sorry, Stella's not here.'

The man smiled. It was a nice smile, somewhat apologetic.

'I know. I'm Dr Mackay. Stella is my patient.'

'Oh!' Grace's stomach fell away; for a moment, she feared the worst. What would bring Stella's doctor to her door on a Sunday afternoon? Especially since he knew she wasn't here . . .

The doctor smiled again. 'Dinna look so worried. It's not bad news. Quite the opposite, actually. Is Mr Swift at home?'

'No – he's gone to see his mother and father and taken the children with him.'

'Then perhaps I could have a word with you?'

'Oh . . . yes.' Grace opened the door wide, all too aware that curtains would be twitching at the neighbours' windows. 'Would you like to come in?'

In the living room, Dr Mackay took a chair, for all the world as if he were at home here. More at home than she felt, Grace thought, sitting down opposite him, knees pressed tightly together, hands knotted in the folds of her skirt.

'I called in to see Stella and Baby today,' the doctor began.

On a Sunday? He must be concerned about them, Grace thought, but she remained silent, still apprehensive in spite of his assurances.

'I'm afraid Stella still seems lost in a world of her own,' he went on, 'but I think I may have stumbled upon the reason for William's problems. I'm of the opinion he may have suffered some kind of dislocation of the neck or shoulder when he was born. That's the reason he's uncomfortable when he's lying down, and why he's been crying so much. And then, of course, the moment he *is* comfortable, he falls asleep because he's tired out.'

'Oh!' Grace's apprehension crystallised into a knot of alarm somewhere beneath her breastbone. 'That sounds awful. Is it serious?'

'I hope not.' Again Dr Mackay spoke reassuringly. 'I think it will right itself in time. And now we've established that his neck needs to be supported at all times, it should put an end to the cycle that's been so distressing for Stella. When he's able to sleep when he needs to, and feed normally, I hope she'll gain confidence and return to her old self.'

'Oh, let's hope so!' Grace said with feeling.

'I came over straight away to tell Mr Swift my conclusions. I know how anxious he is and I thought I'd catch him here on a Sunday afternoon.'

'That's very kind of you, Doctor,' Grace said. 'He'll be grateful for your trouble.'

'All this must be hard for him.' His eyes narrowed sympathetically as he looked at Grace, sitting there bolt upright, her hands still knotted in the folds of her skirt, a picture of tense anxiety. 'For all of you,' he added.

'Yes. It's come as an awful shock. And the children are missing their mother.'

'That's only natural. But they're very lucky you were able to drop everything and step into the breach.'

'What else would I do? She's my sister.' Suddenly, belatedly, Grace remembered her manners. 'Would you like a cup of tea, Doctor?'

'Thank you, but no.' Dr Mackay unfolded his lanky body and stood up. 'I must be getting home. I have a little girl, and she likes me to play with her on Sundays. Would you believe, her favourite game at the moment is sitting under the table, supposedly hiding, and I have to pretend to look for her.' He smiled. 'My wife is expecting another baby, and crawling around on all fours is not really good for her.'

Grace smiled too. 'No, I don't suppose it is.' She followed him to the door. 'Thanks again, Doctor.'

'And you'll be sure to tell Mr Swift that I called when he gets home?'

'Of course.'

As she stood at the door, watching him walk down the path and carefully close the gate behind him, she saw Fluffy slinking along beneath the shadow of the garden wall. It was unusual for the cat to be out at the front of the house. Generally he made his way down across the fields at the back, hunting for mice and – much to Stella's dismay – sometimes bringing them home as trophies, though he hadn't done that since Grace had been staying here, thank goodness!

She could hear Dr Mackay cranking the engine of his motor, and it suddenly occurred to her that he would be turning around to go back the way he had come. Suppose Fluffy chose that very moment to decide to cross the road? Motors were rare, and Fluffy wouldn't have any sense of danger. If he was to get run over when she was in charge, it would be terrible. Well, terrible at any time, but on her watch . . . Whatever would she tell Tom and the children?

Grace scurried down the path; predictably, Fluffy turned and went the other way.

'Fluffy!' she called. 'Fish!'

Not that she had any to give him, and he seemed to know it. He threw her one disdainful glance and slithered beneath the laurel hedge that separated Stella's garden from the one next door, where Francie Newman and her family lived. And their house had no gate of any kind – not that Stella's would have stopped Fluffy. Like most cats, he did as he liked, and went where he wanted.

It wasn't like Grace to panic, but the events of the last days had set her nerves on edge. Dr Mackay had got the engine going now; she could hear the throaty thrum. She hurried towards the road, thinking that at least she could warn him to watch out for Fluffy, but at the gate she stopped, feeling foolish. She couldn't start shouting warnings about a cat that might not even be there, and the doctor might well be offended that she should think him incapable of noticing if it was. She stood on the path in an agony of indecision.

The motor pulled away in a wide sweeping arc, then drew up at the gate.

'Did you want me for something?' Dr Mackay called. He had obviously seen her on the path and assumed she was trying to catch him.

'No . . . no, I'm just chasing Stella's cat,' Grace called back, feeling utterly foolish.

'Well, good luck with that!'

He pulled away again. To Grace's enormous relief, there was no sudden screech of brakes, and the motor continued on its way and was gone. She turned back towards the house, and there was Fluffy, standing expectantly by the front door, tail arched, watching her disdainfully.

'All right, I'm coming . . .'

She broke off as she became aware of a commotion coming from the house next door – Francie Newman's house. A man's voice raised in anger. A crash as if someone had thrown a piece of crockery against a wall and smashed it. More shouts – this time a woman as well as a man – followed by what sounded like a scream. Grace stood on the path, momentarily rooted to the spot. What in the world was going on? She'd never heard the like before.

More shouts and screams, then a thud as something – or someone – collided with the front door so heavily that the brass knocker and letter box jangled. Grace pressed her hands to her mouth in horror, torn between retreating hastily into her own house in case the front door should open and the Newmans see her standing there, and wondering if she should do something.

But what could she do? She scarcely knew Francie Newman, and she didn't know her husband at all – presumably the man's voice belonged to her husband – though she had seen him briefly in his back yard yesterday when she'd been riddling cinders at the end of the garden. Besides, in situations such as this, anyone interfering was likely only to make things worse, or end up being turned upon by both warring parties. But all the same . . .

She wished Tom hadn't gone out. He'd know whether this was usual, and whether it was serious. To her it had sounded as if someone was being killed – or at the very least badly beaten – but perhaps they made a habit of this sort of thing.

Back indoors, she kept listening out for any more sounds of aggression coming from the other side of the dividing wall, but there were none. Fluffy had made himself comfortable in front of the fire and Grace told herself to forget all about it, but somehow she couldn't. It had shocked her so. She kept replaying it over in her head, the shouts, the crash, the thud and then the silence; kept seeing rosy-cheeked Francie Newman sitting at the kitchen table with her, kept thinking about the children, who must have seen and heard what was going on. How awful was that? Oh, she knew there were men who knocked their wives about, but to do it in front of the children . . . That just made it all the more unforgivable. If she was this upset at simply hearing the row from outside, how frightened they must be with it all going on in their home. And what effect would it have on them in the future?

Stop it! Grace told herself. It's none of your business. Concentrate on what Dr Mackay had to say about Stella and William. But somehow that was of little comfort either. Oh, it had been kind of the doctor to call on a Sunday afternoon simply to keep Tom informed about the situation, and she supposed it was good he'd come up with a reason for Will's fretfulness. But in spite of his reassurances, she didn't like the sound of some sort of dislocation in the baby's neck. The poor mite must be in agony, and who knew where it would end?

As for Stella, Grace had hoped there might be some

improvement in her condition by now, with the weight of responsibility lifted from her shoulders. But then again, being locked away with a lot of funny folk – she caught herself, feeling a little ashamed that she could think of them in that way – might not be doing her any good at all. It couldn't be a happy place. Grace thought she might well go funny herself if she was incarcerated there, and this time she didn't even feel the need to scold herself for the expression. She only hoped that the really mad ones were kept well away from the likes of Stella. She'd heard such awful things about asylums, though how much of it was true she didn't know. The constant din of demented shouting and screaming, straitjackets and padded cells for those who might harm themselves or others, the ice-cold baths, the violence that increased with the full moon. She'd seen an etching once of patients in an asylum, wild-haired and wild-eyed, shackled like dangerous criminals, wailing their torment at the bars that held them prisoner. She hoped that things were better nowadays, but she didn't suppose the worst afflicted were much different. Madness was madness, a hundred years ago or now, in 1911.

Determined to chase away her gloomy thoughts, Grace went into the kitchen and began assembling flour, butter and dried fruit. She'd make some rock cakes for tea. Unused as she was to baking in any kitchen but her own, surely she couldn't go far wrong with rock cakes! She found a mixing bowl and baking tray and set to work. As she stirred milk vigorously into the mixture, she felt her mood lightening, and by the time she slid the tray bearing the dozen rocky mounds into the oven, she was actually singing to herself: 'Ta-ra-ra-boom-de-ay, ta-ra-ra-boom-de-ay.'

She washed up the mixing bowl, spoons and knife she had used, left them to dry on the drainer beside the big stone sink and went back into the living room so that she could keep an eye on the cakes as they baked. But the heat of the fire was making her drowsy. She closed her eyes and began to drift . . .

'Hey, something smells good!'

Tom's voice brought her sharply awake. He was standing in the doorway, holding Emily in his arms, and the two boys came scooting past him, diving head-first on to the sofa in a game of rough and tumble.

'My cakes!' Grace rushed to the oven, startling Fluffy, who leapt up and streaked off upstairs. 'Oh my goodness, I hope they're not burnt!'

They weren't; apart from a few exposed sultanas, they were cooked to a lovely golden brown.

'I can't believe I fell asleep!' she said to Tom. 'What a good job you came in when you did, or they'd have been fit for nothing but the dustbin.'

'We could just do with a rock cake, couldn't we, boys?' Tom was taking off his coat. 'Nothing like a good walk to give you an appetite. Well done, Grace! You have been busy.'

The two boys had heard the magic words, and they abandoned their play fight and crowded round Grace, reaching out for a cake.

'No!' she warned them. 'They're still too hot. You'll have to wait a bit.'

She went into the kitchen and offloaded the cakes on to a cooling tray she had set ready on the oilcloth-covered cupboard, lifting each one with a clean tea cloth.

When she went back into the living room, Tom had taken off Emily's coat and the little girl had curled up on the sofa with Aggie, her favourite rag doll. Whilst the boys had returned from their walk hungry and invigorated, she was obviously missing the afternoon nap she still sometimes had at home and every day at school. Whether the enforced lie-down was for the benefit of the children or their teacher, she didn't know, Stella had told Grace, laughing. That had been in the days before the depression had claimed her, and she had been the old Stella, the cheerful, amusing woman Grace knew and loved.

'So what have you been up to other than baking?' Tom asked Grace.

'Well, it's been all go here, actually. The doctor called . . .'

A quick flash of alarm crossed Tom's rugged features.

'It's all right,' Grace hastened to reassure him. 'It's not bad news.'

'So why . . . ?'

'Mainly he wanted to let you know he thinks he's got to the bottom of Will's restlessness.'

She went on to relate what Dr Mackay had said.

'I see.' Tom paused, thinking. 'I do remember the midwife saying she'd had a bit of trouble with the cord being round his neck, but he seemed fine by the time I saw him and I thought no more of it. It does seem feasible, though. And Dr Mackay thinks it'll put itself right?'

'That's what he said. As long as he's kept wrapped up to support it.'

'And Stella?' Tom asked. 'Did he say anything about her?'

'No change as yet. But at least she's no worse, and if they can get her to start feeding Will again without him falling asleep all the time . . .' She broke off, not wanting to burden Tom with the dark thoughts she'd had about what sort of effect being in Catcombe might have on Grace, nor even to think them herself. 'I expect you'd like a cup of tea. And those rock cakes should be cool enough to eat by the time it's brewed.'

'I could do with one, yes.'

He gave her a smile, but she could hear the strained tone in his voice, see the deep furrows in his brow and the anxiety in his eyes, and her heart bled for him. Tom wasn't a man to put his emotions on display, but that didn't mean he didn't feel things deeply. This whole awful situation, coming out of the blue as it had, must have shaken him to the core, and she only wished she'd had better news for him.

She was anxious to tell him about the disturbance next door, too, but she wasn't sure this was the moment. Quite apart from anything else, it didn't seem right to mention it in front of the children. She'd wait until they were in bed. All was quiet now. There was no urgency.

She set the kettle on the hob, spread a tablecloth over the dining table, laid out crockery and poured a cup of milk for Emily. Then she went into the kitchen and slid the rock cakes from the cooling tray on to a plate.

'Here you are, children,' she said as she placed it in the centre of the table. 'Come and sit up. And no fighting over the cakes,' she added as Oliver and Alec barged into one another in their eagerness to help themselves. 'There are plenty to go round.'

'And give your sister a chance too,' Tom warned.

Emily had followed the two boys, still hugging her rag doll. Tom took it from her gently and lifted her up on to a chair.

Across the table his eyes met Grace's; he gave a slight shake of his head and smiled. 'Children!' that look seemed to say. But for a brief moment he seemed like the old Tom, the Tom without a care in the world, and quite unexpectedly, Grace found herself remembering another occasion, long ago, when he had made exactly the same face, a mixture of amusement and resignation. That had been over a child's behaviour too – though not his own, of course.

It was the day of the annual miners' gala back home in Shillingford. She and Tom had gone together; he'd called to collect her and they'd walked down the lane to the glebe field where the gala was held.

She'd been wearing a new pink blouse, Grace remembered, and she'd made a tiny corsage of pink and white roses that grew wild in the hedgerow that bordered their garden, and pinned it on her shoulder. She'd also been wearing her new straw hat, trimmed with pink ribbons – whatever had happened to that hat?

She'd been feeling happy and optimistic that day. She and Tom hadn't been walking out for long, and the frustration and heartache he would eventually cause her was way in the future. She'd felt proud, too, walking hand in hand with him. He was so good-looking, quite the best-looking boy in the village – or for miles around, for that matter – and she knew she was the envy of her friends and probably every other girl who clapped eyes on him.

The sound of music coming from behind them made them stop and turn; it was the local silver band leading the procession to the glebe field. Grace and Tom stood on the pavement to watch it pass by. The cornets, drums, and the low harrumphing of a trombone seemed to make the very air vibrate; behind them came decorated carts and children in fancy dress, some skipping excitedly, others being dragged along by older siblings. They were followed by groups of men representative of every local organisation. Some wore chains of office, some a strip of medals – won in the Boer Wars, Grace assumed – some simply had a flower in their buttonhole. The crowd lining the road clapped and cheered as they passed by. Bringing up the rear was the village fire engine with a full complement of retained firemen aboard. They waved and smiled, even though they must have been very tired – they'd been called out in the middle of the night to a rick fire, and had been there long after dawn damping down the still-smouldering hay.

When they had all assembled in the field, the fete was declared open by Royston Wilton, owner of the local brewery. Grace and Tom made a beeline for the swing boats and were almost first in the queue. Grace remembered squealing in delight as Tom pulled on the rope, taking them higher and higher, and she'd had to hold on to her hat to stop the wind from blowing it away.

They'd gone to watch the judging of the fancy dress competition then, and the children's races – a three-legged race, an egg-and-spoon race, when one little girl kept dropping her egg and finished far behind the others, and a sack race when the same poor child had toppled over and not finished at all.

'Can we go on the swing boats again?' Grace had pleaded.

'If you're up for it.'

They joined the queue, much longer this time, but Grace didn't mind waiting. She was far too happy standing there in the warm sunshine with Tom's arm about her waist.

They'd just reached the head of the queue when a child nearby started wailing loudly. 'I want to go *now*, Mammy!'

The mother tried to hush her, telling her she must wait her turn, but the child took no notice.

'Want to go *now*! My knee hurts. The swings will make it better!'

It was the little girl who'd had one disaster after another in the children's races.

'Aw!' Grace said, feeling sympathy for the child. She'd never been any good when it came to races either.

'She can ride with us if she likes,' Tom said to the agitated mother.

'Oh! That's kind, but are you sure?' The mother looked undecided.

'Yeah, course we are. You'll hold on to her, won't you, Grace?'

99

The little girl was tugging at her mother's hand, still teary, a mulish expression on her small face.

'No! Don't want to go with them! I want to go with you, Mammy!'

The child was clearly on the point of throwing a tantrum.

'Look – take our place,' Tom said. 'We can wait, can't we, Grace?'

Secretly Grace was none too pleased. They'd already waited some time, and behind them the queue was stretching back a long way and getting longer by the minute, and they'd have to go to the back of it. But she was impressed by Tom's kindness all the same.

The swing boat came to a stop, the couple inside got out, and the little girl ran up the steps and climbed in without so much as a backward glance or a thank-you. And that was when Grace had seen *that* look, the same one he'd exchanged with her now over the plate of rock cakes. The slight raise of the eyebrows, the indulgent, resigned smile.

'If she'd moved that fast before, she'd have won all the races,' Tom had said with a dry chuckle. 'Come on, we'd better go to the back of the queue before we get lynched for letting her go in front of them.'

Now, in the living room of the home he had built with Stella, Grace looked at him and remembered that Tom – kind, generous, even if he had been a bit of a Jack the Lad. That was all behind him now, and the good qualities that had always been there beneath the youthful sowing of wild oats had made him a wonderful husband and father.

Something sharp, sweet and painful quirked inside her, and she stood, one hand on the plate of rock cakes, the other pressed to her chest. In that moment she was seventeen again, desperately, crazily in love. She could remember exactly the way it had felt – warm, heady, as if she were standing on a mountain ledge with the whole world spread out beneath her. And not just remember it . . . she was feeling it now.

Tom took a rock cake, putting it on Emily's plate, and Grace snapped out of her reverie abruptly.

She'd been so sure that all they had once shared had been consigned to the past. But for a fleeting moment, when he'd given her that look, the years had melted away and she had felt that spark of the same attraction that had held her in thrall when she was seventeen years old, and it shocked her to the core.

She bent over the teapot, hoping it was dim enough in the room that Tom wouldn't see the colour that had risen in her cheeks.

Stupid, stupid, stupid! she scolded herself. The girl and boy who had ridden in the swing boats were long gone. Tom was her brother-in-law; Stella's husband, the father of her children. And as far as Grace was concerned, simply a good friend. To give even a moment's leeway to memories of the past when he had been so much more was dangerous folly. She must not think about them again.

But in those few moments of remembering, Grace had realised it was not quite that simple. For all that she'd convinced herself otherwise, it was not over for her, and probably never would be.

# Chapter Eight

In the dimly lit asylum nursery, three mothers were giving their babies their last feed of the day. Marie Mears was humming softly to herself – following the evening meal tonight, there had been some entertainment in the social room: a man with a piano accordion had come in to play for the patients. He'd got them singing along to some of the old favourites, and now one of the catchy music-hall tunes was going around and around in her head.

Marie, who had been admitted with puerperal fever, was recovering nicely, and would soon be discharged along with her baby, Gwen.

Louie Hillman, a young girl with learning difficulties who had been taken advantage of by a man old enough to be her father, would probably never be allowed back into the community, as it was considered highly likely that the same thing would happen again, but she was happy enough. She'd found herself a boyfriend amongst the male patients who had the same condition as herself, and Dr Kirkwood and Matron Carey had decided the relationship was good for them, provided a close eye was kept on them when they were together.

Now, under the supervision of Florrie Carter, Louie cooed contentedly as her baby, Billy, nestled against her breast, blissfully unaware that he'd be taken from her as soon as he was weaned.

But the third mother, Rose Gooding, knew all too well that her time with her beloved Wallace would be coming to an end when it was judged he'd made enough progress to be handed over to a wet nurse. That bastard Whittingly Challis had adoptive parents lined up and waiting – a well-to-do couple with no children of their own.

'Your baby will want for nothing,' she'd been told. 'It's for the best.'

The best for who? Rose had wanted to ask. Not for her – it would break her heart – and not for her baby. Oh, he might grow up with more advantages than she could give him, but all the riches in the world could never replace his birth mother's love, the love she felt for him with every fibre of her being. No, it was all to suit bloody Whittingly Challis. That was who it was best for – to make sure there was no gossip to rear its ugly head, no stain on his family's sainted reputation.

Tears pricked her eyes so that Wallace's darling face blurred, and her whole body ached with despair. She couldn't bear the thought of it – not seeing him grow and thrive, not being able to pick him up and give him a cuddle when he fell over and skinned his knees, or nurse him when he was sick. Missing him starting school, his birthdays, watching him open his stocking on Christmas Day. Seeing him fall in love, comforting him if things went wrong, as they were sure to do at least once or twice; being there when he made his marriage vows to the right girl. A whole lifetime of the happy and the sad, and she would miss it all.

Why was life so unfair? Why was this happening to her, when that woman Stella didn't even want her baby enough to feed him? The nurses hadn't bothered to bring her up to the nursery tonight. Cissie Whitcombe had fed him with the pap boat.

But she knew the reason. Unlike Stella, Rose didn't have a husband. She was a fallen woman, a potential embarrassment to the Whittingly Challises. And she'd brought this tragedy on herself for being so gullible, so ready to believe she was special, when all the time she'd just been used and thrown away like an old plaything.

And yet at the same time, she couldn't regret it altogether. If she'd never allowed her lover the liberties she had, there would be no Wallace. This perfect little human being wouldn't exist. Even when he'd been born too early, so small, even as she'd wept and prayed for him to survive, she'd somehow known that he would pull through. He had this sort of wiry strength; you could see it in the determined set of his small mouth, the way his tiny fists would clench and unclench and hold so tight to her finger she'd have had difficulty prising it away even if she'd wanted to.

Yes, Wallace was going to be an exceptional child, and a young man to be proud of as well as love. Except that she wouldn't be there to see it.

The nursery door opened and closed; hearing it, Rose glanced up and saw that Mabel Cummings – Aunt Mabel – had arrived to take over for the night shift. She stopped at the nurses' station to speak to Cissie Whitcombe, then made her way down the ward.

'Right, mothers, are we done here?' Cissie asked. She'd been asked to see them safely downstairs tonight when she went home, leaving Mabel to take over responsibility for the nursery. 'Let's get the babies settled.'

With some reluctance, Marie Mears did as she was told, laying little Gwen in her crib and tucking a shawl around her. Florrie had to repeat the instruction to Louie Hillman before she obeyed, and even then she went on fussing over Billy so that Cissie became a bit impatient.

'Come on, Louie, I haven't got all night. I've got a home and a bed waiting for me.'

Rose, however, remained where she was. 'Can't I stay for a bit?' she pleaded.

Cissie hesitated, glancing towards the nurses' station. She felt very sorry for Rose, and, after all, Mabel Cummings was her aunt.

'Well, it's up to Nurse Cummings,' she said. 'Mabel!' she called, and Mabel came bustling down the ward. 'Your Rose wants to know if she can stay for a while.'

'Please, Aunt Mabel!' Rose begged, and Cissie took the opportunity to head off to the nurses' station and collect her things. She didn't want to get involved. Mabel was notoriously prickly, especially where her niece was concerned.

Marie Mears followed her, with Florrie shepherding Louie, and when the two of them were alone, Rose once again appealed to her aunt.

'I don't know how much more time I'm going to have to spend with him, and every moment is precious.'

'It's not up to me.' Besides being angry with Rose for the embarrassment she had caused her, with all her colleagues knowing her niece was no better than she should be, Mabel was also a stickler for protocol. 'The night staff will be waiting to lock up down there.'

'But—'

'You made your bed, my girl, and you just have to lie in it,' she stated harshly.

Resigned to the inevitable, Rose reluctantly got up, kissed Wallace's head – still bare of anything but the lightest feathering of down, so sparse it resembled the skin of a peach – and laid him in his crib. Tears were sparkling in her eyes.

'I can't bear it, Aunt Mabel,' she whispered, straightening up.

Mabel hardened her heart. 'Goodnight, Rose.'

'Goodnight, Auntie . . .' The tears were spilling into Rose's voice, making it thick and breathy.

Then she turned and went to join the others, who were waiting for her.

Mabel Cummings sighed and shook her head as the door closed behind them. Her niece should know better than to expect special treatment just because they were related. Mabel wouldn't have allowed any of the others to stay when the duty nurse was waiting downstairs to escort them to the women's bungalow for the night, and she couldn't – wouldn't – make an exception for Rose. But underneath her outward display of cold indifference, she was boiling with anger towards the man who was responsible for Rose being incarcerated here.

Bloody Whittingly Challis! Nothing could surprise her about the bastard – she knew him of old – but how dare he treat her niece this way, as if she were a piece of dirt under his well-polished boot? Grinding her into the ground for his own ends. Threatening her that if she ever revealed who had got her into this mess, her own father would be out of a job and lose his house too. Even going so far as to arrange for the inconvenient baby to be adopted – brushed under the carpet.

It would be a few weeks yet before Wallace was deemed ready to be taken from his mother. Mabel was determined to make sure the separation was delayed as long as possible, and she knew Cissie felt the same way. But they couldn't stop it happening, any more than King Canute had been able to hold back the tide.

She looked down at the little scrap sleeping peacefully in his crib and felt her anger ratchet up a notch. Whether she liked it or not, he was her flesh and blood, no matter that Whittingly

Challis blood ran in his veins too. Her niece's son, her sister's grandchild. And Rose wasn't the only one who was in a state about losing him. Olive, her mother, was in a terrible way about it too. Only yesterday, when Mabel had called in on her for a cup of tea, Olive had been in tears over it.

'It's just awful,' she'd wept. 'I can't bear the thought of him being brought up by strangers. Who knows what they're like if they're friends of that monster? There'll be a nanny for sure, and he'll be packed off to boarding school when he's still young enough to need his mother. That's what he did with his own boys, if you remember. No more than seven or eight years old, they were, and breaking their little hearts. I saw it with my own eyes.'

Before she'd been married, Olive, like her daughter after her, had been a maid at Easterton Manor, and afterwards she'd been called on occasionally when extra help was needed. A grand dinner party to which the high sheriff of the county had been invited had been arranged for the evening of the very same day when the elder boy, Rupert, had been packed off to boarding school, and Whittingly Challis and his wife had been more concerned with the preparations for that than they had been with their own son. Olive had been polishing the crystal glasses in the banqueting room when the poor child had left with only Sir Oswald's man, Farthing, to accompany him. She'd seen it all from the window, the little boy crying, kicking and struggling as Farthing lifted him into the carriage, and she had been outraged by the casual cruelty of it. My, but the upper classes had something to answer for. Quarry workers and farm labourers the families she knew might be, but they would never dream of treating their children with such careless callousness.

Now, the thought of her own grandson being brought up that way cut her to the quick.

'Our Rose might not be able to give him what those folk can, but at least he'd be with his own family. And I'd do what I could to support her. It would cause talk to begin with, but it would all blow over in time. She's not the first girl to land herself in trouble, and she won't be the last. Surely there must be something we can do to make sure we don't lose little Wallace for good.'

'I don't see what,' Mabel had said. 'If Whittingly Challis wants to make sure this doesn't come back to bite him on the backside, he's got all the cards in his hand. Just look at the way he had our Rose committed before you could say Jack Robinson.'

That had started Olive crying again.

'Wicked, that's what it is. "Moral delinquent" indeed! If anyone is a moral delinquent it's him! Oh, our Rose might have let herself down, but she's a good girl really. None of this would have happened if she hadn't had her head turned. It's that family that ought to be locked away, not her. Thank goodness she's got you there, Mabel, that's all I can say. But I dread to think what's going to happen to her when they take Wallace away from her. She won't be up in the nursery then where you can keep an eye on her, will she? She'll be stuck with the lunatics, day in, day out.'

'They won't keep her in for ever,' Mabel said, trying to console her sister. 'Dr Kirkwood wouldn't stand for it. Once they're sure she isn't going to cause trouble for the Whittingly Challises, the two doctors who signed her in will sign her out again, or Dr Kirkwood will get another to second him in saying she's fit for release.'

'But she won't be the same Rose that went in,' Olive said. Tears were still streaming down her cheeks; she mopped at them with her handkerchief. 'Not after all that. And not knowing what's happened to Wallace. Isn't there anything you can do,

Mabel? Have a word with Dr Kirkwood, perhaps? All the years you've worked there, wouldn't he listen to you?'

'If Rose doesn't get released, then maybe. But there's nothing I can do to stop the adoption, Olive. Even Dr Kirkwood wouldn't have any say in that. It's all down to Whittingly Challis and his cronies.'

'Bloody Whittingly Challis!'

Mabel had never heard her sister swear before; it was a measure of just how upset she was. Now, standing beside Wallace's crib, looking down at his perfect little face, she found herself echoing Olive's sentiments, and acknowledging that she had her own reasons for hating the man.

Why should the Whittingly Challises of this world have everything their own way? Who did they think they were, playing God with the lives of those beneath them? She'd like nothing better than to be able to blast a hole through that bastard's carefully laid plans. But as she'd said to Olive, she couldn't see that there was anything she could do, and that in itself made her burn with suppressed fury.

Mabel Cummings didn't like anyone to get the better of her, especially Oswald Whittingly Challis. He'd done it once before, when she was young and naïve, and it rankled that he should do it again. Ever since then, she'd made sure she was top dog – one of the reasons it suited her to work as a nurse at the asylum, where she had authority over the patients. Too often, all the bitterness that was bottled up inside her came bubbling out in the form of sharp invective or even downright bullying. But she was crafty too, always careful to hide her petty cruelties, which was how she'd managed to keep her job when Dr Kirkwood had brought the practices at Catcombe into the twentieth century.

Still seething, Mabel moved along the row of cribs, checking on the babies. The name tag of one – Baby Hillman – was hanging loose. His idiot mother, Louie, had been messing about with it, no doubt. Impatiently Mabel fixed it back in place, then stopped suddenly as the germ of an idea struck her, an idea so preposterous she almost discounted it.

But as she went back to the nurses' station, it was still there, niggling at the corners of her mind. Could it work? It was dangerous, and it would take a lot of planning, but during the quiet hours of the night shifts, she'd have plenty of time to mull it over. And if it did work, it would not only ensure that she knew the whereabouts of Rose's baby, but also go some way to settling her own old scores. To finally get the better of Whittingly Challis would be well worth the risks involved.

Mabel's mouth set in a hard line. Besides being crafty and mean, she also had a ruthless streak that few people had ever seen. When her mind was made up, she'd stop at nothing to achieve her objective.

Deep in thought, she returned to the nurses' station.

In her narrow bed in the women's bungalow, Stella lay staring into the darkness that was broken only by a small night light in the corner of the room, kept burning so that the night nurse could periodically check on the occupants without disturbing them. She should have been fast asleep hours ago, but she'd managed to slip her nightly sleeping pill into the pocket of her smock when no one was looking. She hated the way the medication made her feel thick and stupid, which was almost worse than the terrible depression. In fact it didn't seem to make her any less depressed, just woolly and sleepy as well.

It would in time, though, Dr Kirkwood had said. Her body just had to get used to it.

Tonight Stella couldn't stop thinking about Will, and what a terrible mother she was to him. She hadn't even been allowed up to the nursery today. Someone else must be feeding him, changing him, doing all the things she should be doing, and for some reason it hurt, even though the thought of putting him to her breast still filled her with panic.

She'd missed him, she realised, missed nursing him in the crook of her arm, his firm little body nestled close to her heart; missed the baby smell of him, soap and talcum powder and milk and that other scent that she couldn't identify but which all young babies had. It would go soon enough as he grew. She remembered with her other three suddenly noticing one day that they no longer smelled newborn and feeling a sense of loss. They grew up so fast! Oliver and Alec, even little Emily, all at school now, smelling of ink and chalk dust and sometimes gobstoppers instead of baby.

A feeling of urgency prickled in Stella's veins. She couldn't afford to waste these precious months. Perhaps she should try to overcome her panic at the thought of feeding Will. If only she could, they might let her go home again, and she wanted that so much. Wanted Tom's arms around her, wanted to lay her head against his broad chest and feel the tickle of hair that feathered it. Wanted to hear the children's laughter and chatter, to look in on them, sleeping and angelic.

But what if it all started again? Will's constant crying, his refusal to stay awake and feed? The very thought made her tremble; not just her limbs, but the very core of her. I can't stand it! she thought, the panic beginning to build again. At least here he seemed settled and content.

But oh, she did miss him so!

The door opened quietly, just the smallest squeak of the hinges and a click as it was closed again, and she saw the figure of the night nurse, a dark shadow against all the other shadows. Then the night light was moving, a will o' the wisp in the darkness, coming closer as the nurse moved among the beds, checking on the occupants.

Stella waited until it hovered beside her bed, and then spoke softly.

'Nurse?'

'Mrs Swift? What are you doing awake?' the nurse whispered.

'I want my baby.' Stella's voice was a little thick; though she hadn't taken her sleeping pill, the other drugs she'd been given during the day were still having an effect.

'He'll be asleep. And so should you be.'

'Can I go up and see him? Please?'

'Certainly not.' Though she was still whispering, there was no mistaking the sternness of the nurse's tone.

'But I miss him! And he'll be missing me.'

'It's the middle of the night, Mrs Swift. We can't have you wandering about at this hour. Just go to sleep like a good girl, and perhaps you'll see him tomorrow.'

'Promise?' Stella was vaguely aware that she sounded like one of the children, but she couldn't help herself. This was suddenly so desperately important.

'I can't promise anything, Mrs Swift. It's not up to me.'

Stella turned her face into the pillow, twisting her head this way and that, and kicking out so hard that the sheet and coverlet came untucked. A long, heartfelt wail escaped her. She sounded, thought Betty Hillier, the night nurse, like a cow whose calf had been taken away, baying at the moon.

'Hush now! You'll wake the others!'

Another wail, but softer, as if on some level Stella had understood.

'I'll fetch you another sleeping tablet.'

The light bobbed away, then returned.

'Open your mouth.'

Stella turned her head away again, pursing her lips tight. But Betty was having none of her nonsense. She pinched Stella's nostrils closed, and Stella was forced to open her mouth or suffocate. Betty popped the sleeping pill in, then released the pressure on Stella's nose, instead clamping her jaw tight. She raised Stella's head and put a glass of water to her lips.

'Come on now, Stella, or I'll have to call Dr Kirkwood to do it another way, and he won't be best pleased to be disturbed, let me tell you.'

Defeated, Stella swallowed.

At least if she was asleep, she wouldn't be pining for Will. For Tom and the children.

She closed her eyes, only dimly aware that Betty Hillier remained at her side until she fell asleep.

Thank goodness she hadn't wakened any of the other patients, Betty thought as she drew the covers back over Stella and watched her eyes close. She could well have sparked a full-scale riot, and that was the last thing Betty wanted. She wondered why Stella's earlier sleeping pill hadn't worked, but perhaps she'd spat it out. The patients could be crafty like that. You had to watch them like hawks.

At least Dr Kirkwood's plan seemed to be working. She'd read up about it in her notes after she'd come on duty. Dr Kirkwood had reasoned that if Stella was kept from her baby, it would light the spark of natural maternal love that she undoubtedly felt for William. When she was continually forced to try and feed him, her negative emotions took over and she rebelled. Prevent her from so much as seeing him, and it might have the opposite effect.

Like all the nurses, Betty Hillier had the utmost respect for Dr Kirkwood. Not only was he humane, treating the patients as if their illness was much the same as a physical one, and not something they could help, but his methods had brought about some startling successes.

There was some way to go yet, no doubt about it, but Betty hoped very much that poor Stella would be one of them before long.

# Chapter Nine

Monday, wash day. It was a ritual for every housewife Grace knew. She'd never stuck to it herself, though she had tried in the early days of her marriage to Cliff. After he was killed, however, she'd changed her ways. For one thing, she was working in the village shop and had to be there by nine o'clock to open up. For another, when it was just her, there was less than half the laundry. No filthy vests and shirts, no rushyduck trousers full of coal dust, no grimy towels, no soiled sheets. Just her blouses, underwear and aprons, and an occasional change of bedding and towels, which hardly needed washing anyway. Her job was a clean one and there were no children to mess up her clothes as well as their own.

Grace had taken to letting the laundry basket fill up and waiting for a fine day to tackle it. And if that happened to be on a Sunday, so be it. Personally she'd never seen why it was considered such an outrage to have washing blowing on the line on the Sabbath, and the cottage where she and Cliff had lived didn't have any near neighbours to show their disapproval.

Then, when she'd moved back in with her mother and father, Annie had taken over the laundry. 'I might as well do your bit in with mine,' she'd said, and Grace hadn't argued.

Now, however, it was a very different kettle of fish. There

was a mound of washing to be done, and Grace couldn't put it off any longer, though the weather didn't look very conducive to getting it dried outside, and she hated the thought of having to drape it around the fire, making the kitchen damp with steam. But if Tom and the children were to have clean clothes to put on, there was nothing for it.

She filled the copper with water and lit the gas under it. Then she found a cake of soap in the cupboard beside the sink, fetched the clothes to be washed and sorted them while she waited for the water to heat up. She'd do the whites first – she'd need a blue bag for them – then the children's coloureds, and Tom's filthy pit clothes last of all.

At least it wasn't actually raining, just cold and dank, and by the time she'd dragged the mangle out into the back yard, the water was hot enough for the first load. Using a saucepan, which held more than the dipper, she ladled out enough to fill the sink and set to work, her mind wandering as she scrubbed and rinsed.

Presumably this was what Stella had to do every week, and sometimes in between, especially since Will had come along. Grace didn't envy her that – it was no wonder her hands were so rough and red, with long cracks around her fingernails that sometimes bled. But she did envy her her family. The children – they were a delight, if a handful at times – the baby, and Tom . . .

Grace caught herself. She was still shocked by the way her old feelings for him had been suddenly resurrected yesterday. She'd been so sure she was over all that long ago, that she thought of him only as a friend – and her brother-in-law. The rush of tenderness and the ache of longing had taken her completely by surprise, and left her not only disconcerted, but guilty. She couldn't shake the feeling that to entertain such

116

thoughts for even a moment was a betrayal of Stella, who was locked away in that awful place.

Just stop it! she told herself angrily. You're here to do a job, and as soon as Stella is well, you'll be going back to your old life.

But somehow the thought of it was a depressing one. Busy as she kept herself, working long hours in the shop and helping her mother out as much as she could in the evenings, there was still an emptiness in her life that she'd refused to recognise until now. She'd thought she'd come to terms with her lot; now, in the space of less than a week, she'd realised just what she was missing.

It wasn't as if her parents were scintillating company. Her poor dad had always been a quiet one, only speaking when he had something to say; now, laid low by silicosis, he rarely spoke at all, sitting silently in his chair – well, silent except for the rattling breath and the bouts of coughing – and staring into space.

'Are you all right, Amos?' her mother would ask

'Yes . . . yes, m'dear.'

'You're very quiet.' As if that was unusual.

'I just don't want to be no trouble, m'dear.' And then he would relapse into silence.

Annie, her mother, on the other hand, rarely stopped talking these days. It was as if she was determined to make up for Amos's silence. She talked about the weather, she related every detail of her day, she recalled things from long ago and told the same stories over and over again.

'The day of your Grampy's funeral, it never stopped raining. I had new shoes, lovely they were, and the churchyard was a mud bath. Those shoes were never the same again. And the grave was filling up with water like it were a sink. The coffin went down in it with an awful plonk – truth to tell, I think the bearers nearly dropped it, the webs were so slippery with the wet. And your Aunt Tilda got soaked, and caught her death. Not three weeks later and we were burying her . . .'

There was no stopping Annie when she got into her story. You could tell her yes, you knew, you'd heard it all before, but still she carried on regardless to the bitter end. Grace would try to close her ears to it, but it set her nerves on edge.

Then there were the routines, set in stone. Annie was a creature of habit and she believed her ways were the right ways. The washing-up had to be done in a particular order: glassware first, then the cleaner crockery and cutlery, then the plates soiled with gravy or custard – custard first, of course – and lastly the saucepans and frying pan. If Grace inadvertently got it wrong, Annie would chastise her. 'Look what you've done! Now that water is fit for nothing!' Although Grace knew it made sense, she couldn't help but be irritated at having it pointed out to her.

The cinders had to be riddled on to the same patch of garden for so many days before moving on to another patch. The washing had to be pegged out just so; if Grace had swilled out a few of her own things and hung them on the line, she'd see Annie rearranging it all. Even the cleaning had to be done starting in the far corner of the room and working around methodically.

And: 'Why do you cut the potatoes up so small?' Annie would criticise if Grace was doing the vegetables.

'They'll cook quicker.'

'Go to smack, more likely. Here, let me show you . . .' She would take the knife from Grace and demonstrate the size and shape she liked them cut.

Added to all this, Annie had developed a habit of always

looking on the black side of everything and seeming to take a perverse pleasure in wallowing when things went wrong.

Grace loved her mother dearly and was grateful she'd opened her door to her when she'd been forced to vacate the cottage that had been tied to Cliff's job as a miner. Sir Percy Wills, the colliery owner, was, unlike so many others, a kindly man and had allowed her to stay in her home for longer than he was obliged to, but in the end he'd needed it for another family and Annie had immediately insisted Grace should come home. 'Where else would you go, you silly girl?' she'd scolded when Grace had demurred, and in reality Grace had had very little option. But she'd often thought she'd like to try and get a place of her own, though she had no idea how she'd ever be able to afford it.

Now, after experiencing just a few days running Stella's home with no one to carp or criticise, the thought of returning to her old life was less appealing than ever. She might still feel like an intruder here, but at least she was left to her own devices.

She pulled the plug out of the sink, let the still warm water run away, and filled it with cold. As she dunked the blue bag, being careful to keep it away from Tom's best white shirt – he wouldn't thank her if she got a blue stain down the front of it – she saw Francie Newman crossing the yard and heading for the long strip of garden with a basket balanced on her hip. She was going to hang her washing out and take a chance on the weather, then. But it was the fracas of yesterday, not how likely the washing was to dry, that was uppermost in Grace's mind.

She'd mentioned it to Tom last night once the children were in bed, but he hadn't seemed unduly surprised or concerned.

'Oh, they're always having a bit of a ding-dong,' he'd said. 'They've both got tempers. The best thing is to shut your ears to it.'

Perhaps she had overreacted, Grace had thought. She just wasn't used to that sort of thing. She'd let the subject drop; she didn't want Tom to think she was a gossipmonger or a nosy parker. But now, watching Francie make her way up the garden path, she couldn't help noticing that she seemed to be walking gingerly, as if something was hurting her. And when, a few minutes later, she went out to put her own first load of washing through the mangle, she got the impression Francie was none too pleased to see her.

'Oh – hello,' she replied when Grace called out a greeting, but she was not at all the friendly soul who had knocked on the door on Grace's first day in Hillsbridge and shared a cup of tea. She didn't seem to want to talk, and she was keeping her face turned away from Grace, even re-pegging some of her washing in what seemed to Grace to be an effort to delay having to walk past her.

Eventually she could put it off no longer. She hurried towards her back door with her head down and a quick: 'I don't think it's going to dry much today, but at least it'll have a bit of a blow,' and Grace was sure she was indeed limping. Worse still, she caught sight of a nasty bruise on Francie's cheek.

So she'd been right! It hadn't just been a shouting match. There had been real violence involved. The thought of it made her feel quite sick.

How come Tom had dismissed it so lightly? Was yesterday the first time their 'ding-dong' had come to blows? Or did it happen so regularly that the neighbours didn't take any notice any more? But she couldn't imagine Tom condoning something like that. The Tom she knew would abhor the very idea of a man hitting a woman, his wife or otherwise.

Poor Francie! She certainly didn't deserve that sort of treatment.

Grace put the last pillowcase through the mangle and carried the load of washing down the garden. Like Francie, she didn't think it was going to dry much, but it always smelled nicer if it had been out in the fresh air.

She glanced at the kitchen window of the house next door as she crossed the yard to go back inside. But of Francie there was no sign.

And really, she reminded herself, it was none of her business.

Francie Newman closed the back door after her and leaned against it, covering her poor bruised face with her hands and flinching as her fingers touched the tender swelling. But painful as it was, she minded it far less than the shame and degradation that was flooding through her in hot waves.

Whatever must Stella's sister think of her? She'd seen, Francie was sure. How could she have missed it? Francie wished she could just curl up and die.

It was all her own fault, of course. It always was. She should have known to keep back dinner until later; it was the third Sunday in the month, and Noel always called in to see his sister on the third Sunday after the pubs turned out. She *had* thought actually, when it was too late and she was dishing up. But the children were hungry and so was she, and if she left the meat in the oven any longer it would be all dried up, and that would be sure to set him off.

So she'd put his dinner on a plate, covered it with another and set it over a pan of water on the hob to keep warm. She'd done that before when he was late and it had been all right.

Yesterday, though, it had not been all right. It was halfway through the afternoon by the time Noel got home. He'd had too much to drink, any fool could see that, and he demanded straight away to know why they hadn't waited for him. Then, when she put the plate of food on the table in front of him and he'd seen the congealed gravy and the skin that had formed over the potatoes, he'd erupted.

'What the hell is this?'

He'd picked up the plate and thrown it against the wall. The plate smashed to smithereens, cabbage and mutton and boiled potatoes sat in soggy lumps on the floor, gravy dripped like old brown blood down the cream-distempered wall.

She should have known better than to react, of course. The minute they'd seen their father and what sort of mood he was in, the children had had the sense to skedaddle. But not her, oh no, not her. Seeing the dinner she'd slaved over half the morning lying there like a great pile of vomit on her clean floor, her temper had risen too.

'Now look what you've done!' she shouted at him. 'Why couldn't you come home at a decent time instead of sitting in the boozer until they threw you out?'

'I'll do as I bloody well like. I bring the money into this house. It's your job to put food on the table.' He was shouting too. 'Food that's a bloody sight better than that rubbish. You wouldn't give slop like that to Sam Leary's pigs.'

And so it had gone on, Noel bellowing, Francie's tone getting louder and shriller, until it ended as it always did. Noel had hit her full in the face with the back of his hand. She'd staggered out into the hall and he had followed.

'Bastard!' she'd screamed. 'You bleedin' bastard!'

He'd really seen red then. Roaring like an enraged bull, he'd pushed her so hard that she'd crashed backwards into the front door, her head cracking against the solid wood. Then, as she slid down into a heap on the floor, he'd kicked out at her, the toe of his boot catching her squarely in the ribs.

'Let that be a lesson to you,' he'd snarled, towering over her, his fists clenched threateningly, before he'd turned and headed back into the living room.

Half stunned, Francie had remained where she was for a few minutes, slumped against the door. Her head was ringing, and as the initial numbness wore off, it began to throb horribly. Her face too was stinging, and the pain from the kick in the ribs almost took her breath away. Then she picked herself up and, holding on to the wall, stumbled into the living room after him.

'What are you going to get me to eat then?' Noel asked, still sounding annoyed, but almost normal, as if the beating had never happened.

Without another word, Francie had fetched bread and cheese from the larder and cut a couple of slices of mutton off the remains of the joint. Whilst Noel sat at the table to eat it, she got down on her hands and knees and cleared up the mess that should have been his dinner. Then and only then did she soak a flannel in cold water and hold it over her throbbing cheek in the hope that she might be able to stop it from swelling too much.

It was too late for that, of course. This morning she looked a real sight, with the bruise turning shades of purple, plum and green. She'd done her best to cover it with talcum powder, but she knew it was still visible.

The children must have noticed it, she knew, but although they kept casting sidelong glances at her, none of them had mentioned it. They'd seen it all before, of course, and they knew better than to draw attention to it. Tonight, when he got home from work, Noel wouldn't mention it either. But he would be nice to her. He might even bring her a miniature of gin from the pub when he went there this evening, as a peace offering. He'd be sorry, though he wouldn't say so; he'd try to make it up to her in a dozen little ways and it would all be forgotten. Until the next time. And there would be a next time, not a doubt of it.

When he'd had too much to drink. When she was stupid enough to do something to upset him. Or both.

She didn't blame him. She really didn't. Furious as she always was at the time, the minute she cooled down, she could understand. If she was a better wife and mother, if she didn't do so many stupid things, if she could only bring herself to accept his justifiable criticisms straight away instead of arguing, he wouldn't do what he did. He loved her, she was sure he did, and she was grateful for that. She hadn't been the prettiest girl around, far from it. She'd always been too plump, and the best that could be said for her face was that it was pleasant. And when she'd been young and hoping to attract a sweetheart, pleasant wasn't what most young men were interested in.

Noel had been her first and only lover, and she'd been terrified he would leave her for some other girl who was better-looking than she was. Cheekier. A flirt. Francie was none of those things. All she had ever wanted was to get married and settle down with a home of her own and children. When she'd found herself in the family way, she'd been scared to death that Noel would abandon her. But he hadn't. He'd stood by her, saved her good name, married her. He'd never actually said he loved her, not once in all these years, but he must do, mustn't he? If he didn't, he'd have done a runner. Instead he was still here, providing for all of them as best he knew how.

No one could argue that he wasn't a good father. He thought the world of the children, though he could be strict. She hated it when he gave one of the boys a hiding, even intervening sometimes, but he said he only did it for their own good, and because they deserved it. As a result, they were usually well-behaved and eager to please, and for that too she was grateful.

No, the fault was all hers. She should have learned by now to be more conciliatory and not make him angry or challenge his authority. He was only keeping her in line as he did the children.

Yet for all that, she couldn't help being ashamed. She tried to hide her bruises when Noel was rash enough to strike her where it showed – mostly he made sure the kicks and blows were to her body – and if he'd gripped her too tightly by the arms, she could always keep them covered with the sleeves of her blouse. She didn't want anybody knowing what went on behind closed doors any more than he did.

But yesterday had been a disaster. There was no way she could hide the bruised cheek. And now Stella's sister had caught a glimpse. Would she tell Tom and Stella? Friendly as they were, she didn't think Stella had any idea just how badly she was sometimes hurting as they sat together over a cup of tea, and she didn't want her to know either. Didn't want her and Tom to think badly of Noel. Didn't want them to see her for the useless lummox she was.

Perhaps the best thing would be to go next door and front it out. Make up some story to explain the damage to her face. Yes, that was what she'd do.

As she did her next load of washing, she watched out for Grace, and when she saw her at the mangle again, she hastily pushed the washing, half rinsed as it was, into the laundry basket and went out herself.

'I expect you think I look a bit of a sight,' she said conversationally, though she was shaking inside.

'Oh, I hadn't noticed,' Grace said awkwardly, but Francie could tell she was lying.

'I opened the cupboard door straight into my face yesterday,' she went on. 'Don't know what I was thinking. Anyone would reckon I'd been at the brandy bottle, but I hadn't, of course. Clumsy as a carthorse, that's me.'

'Oh dear. It must be painful,' Grace said.

'Not too bad. It looks worse than it is.'

'Well, you take care.'

'How's Stella?' Francie felt bound to enquire.

'Not much change. But Will is doing well. The doctor came yesterday to give us an update.'

'On a Sunday? That was good of him.'

'It was, wasn't it? He seems really nice.'

'I expect he is. He's not our doctor, though. Right, I'd better get on . . .' Francie headed for the clothes line, glad to escape.

She'd done her best; she could do no more.

She only hoped Grace believed her.

Grace, of course, didn't believe a word. Opened a cupboard door into her face! A likely story.

But she wouldn't let on to Francie that she knew different. Bad enough that her husband had given her a hiding; on top of that she must feel so awkward and ashamed.

She wouldn't mention it to anyone, not even Tom, she decided. It wasn't her place. But she would keep her eyes and ears open, and if she heard anything going on again . . . What? What would she do? She didn't have the faintest idea. But she hoped that if the occasion arose, she would think of something.

# Chapter Ten

March had come in like a lion and looked set to go out like a lamb. The gales had seen off the murky weather that had preceded them, and now, though it was still bitterly cold, a pale sun shone in a clean-washed blue sky and there were signs of spring everywhere. Catkins hung like tassels from hazel trees, the soft grey pads of pussy willow had appeared, and crocuses made patches of yellow and purple in the grass beneath. Birds sang in the chorus to the dawn and collected fallen twigs and moss to build nests, and the vista from the windows of the houses in Dunderwick Road was fast turning from sludgy brown to vibrant green.

Grace was still there, caring for Tom and the children, but everything came much easier to her now than it had done in the beginning. She no longer felt like an intruder, as she once had. She knew where everything was, she'd grown used to roasting and baking in what had been a strange oven, and learned what meals were the family's favourites and which to avoid.

Tom loved liver and bacon, though the children turned their noses up at it if it was red and raw in the middle the way he liked it, so she'd take the biggest slice out of the pan and keep it warm while she cooked theirs almost to a cinder. It was the same with a bit of beef steak or a mutton chop. The slightest hint of blood was enough to make them pull faces and push it around their plates, while Tom liked nothing better. At least they all enjoyed tripe and onions in a thick milky sauce, and when she managed to get hold of a nice boiling fowl, her chicken pie was an enormous success.

'You're not half a good cook, Grace,' Tom had said, and she'd flushed with pleasure.

'It's nice to have somebody to cook for,' she'd replied, and it was no more than the truth. She'd always taken pleasure in cooking for Cliff – he'd liked his food too – but when she'd lost him, she couldn't be bothered taking the trouble just for herself, and since she'd moved back in with her mother and father, she'd scarcely been allowed in the kitchen.

It was nice too to have company other than her silent dad and loquacious mam. She'd made friends with several of the neighbours, and they'd stop for a chinwag if she met them on her way to the shops. Sometimes they'd pop in for a brew, or to borrow a cup of sugar or flour or a jug of milk. Mostly they were older than she was, but they were still friendly, and much to her relief, she and Francie had overcome the awkwardness between them that had begun with the beating and the black eye.

Neither of them had ever mentioned it again, and to Grace's knowledge there had been no more violent rows and no more visible injuries. She was so glad of that, not just for Francie's sake, but for her own too. She liked Francie a lot, and being closer in age than any of the other neighbours, they had a lot to talk about. But in the first days after that horrible incident, it had been the elephant in the room, spoiling things between them, besides which she'd been really worried as to what she would say or do if it happened again. Now she felt she had a real friend just the other side of the garden wall.

Best of all, she loved the evenings, when the children were in bed and she and Tom were alone. She would tell him about her day and what the children had been up to, making him laugh sometimes when she related their antics or repeated something Emily had said. She was such an old-fashioned little soul, and she had a way of coming out with expressions she'd heard grown-ups use, as serious as an old lady. Sometimes they'd have a game of cards or dominoes, sitting at the dining table with the oil lamps casting a rosy glow, the only sounds a coal settling or sparking in the grate and the click of the dominoes or the soft plop of the cards. Sometimes Tom would doze off in the easy chair, his sock-clad feet stretched out to the warmth of the fire, with Fluffy curled up between them, and Grace would attack a pile of darning, glancing up from time to time to watch him as he slept. Often they would both have a hot drink, cocoa usually, before going to bed.

She loved him. She'd come to accept that now. There was no other word to describe her feelings for him – the tenderness that welled in her, the ache of longing, the occasional spark of desire if his hand brushed hers. Perhaps she'd never stopped loving him. She'd thought the fire that had burned so fiercely within her when she was young had long since been quenched by her eventual anger at the way he'd treated her; she'd honestly believed she'd come to see him as just a friend and her brother-in-law. But perhaps all the time that had been an act of denial, and underneath the embers had still smouldered.

She knew, of course, that there could never again be anything between them, that she must keep her feelings tightly under control. She'd never countenance doing or saying anything that might hurt her sister or threaten her marriage. She'd had her chance long ago, and thrown it away because she could no longer put up with Tom's behaviour. If she'd held her tongue and bided her time, maybe they would have been together in the end. Maybe it would have been her he'd married, not Stella, and this would be her life, not her sister's.

And then again, maybe not. Perhaps he just hadn't felt about her the way she felt about him, and never would have. But she couldn't help wondering all the same if he sometimes remembered the times they'd shared, and if so, if he remembered them fondly.

But it was all water under the bridge. None of it mattered now. He was Stella's husband, the father of her children. And in any case, it wouldn't be long before Stella came home and this whole unreal interlude came to an end.

Dr Mackay had been very positive when he'd called this week to update them on progress.

William, he had said, was thriving. He was much more settled, with or without the tight binding, and the doctor was confident that if something had been out of place, it had righted itself. And within the last couple of weeks, Stella had been persuaded to feed him. She was being allowed to spend a great deal more time in the nursery, changing him and generally caring for him, and Dr Mackay thought he would soon be able to recommend that mother and baby were ready to come home.

'Perhaps you would be willing to stay on here for a bit until we're sure Stella is able to cope,' he'd suggested, and Grace had agreed readily. Of course she was happy to do whatever he thought was necessary, she'd said. And so she was, although 'happy' was not quite the right word. She wasn't at all sure how she'd feel when Stella was there – probably like an intruder once again. Whilst still having to keep an eye on her sister, she'd be handing back all responsibility for day-to-day decisions, from what food should be put on the table to when the bed sheets needed changing. This was Stella's house, and naturally she wouldn't want Grace running it.

She wouldn't feel able to discipline the children, either. And worst of all, when she went to bed at night in Emily's room, Stella would be sharing a bed with Tom. Though that was as it should be, Grace knew that it would hurt all the same. With all her heart she would wish that it was her curling up close to his sleeping body, feeling his loving touch in the night. And whilst she hated herself for such treacherous thoughts, she could no longer deny them.

She envied her sister. She wasn't proud of it, but she couldn't help it. And having to witness Tom's delight at having Stella home once more, and the closeness between the two of them, would be the hardest thing she would ever have to do.

'That's wonderful news, Doctor,' Tom had said. And Grace had echoed him.

She was glad, of course she was, glad that her beloved sister was recovering from the awful depression that had claimed her. But at the same time, she felt as if her own heart was breaking.

The telephone call that Sir Oswald Whittingly Challis had been waiting for came halfway through a Wednesday morning towards the end of March. It was Dr Kirkwood, to tell him that the baby was now strong enough to be separated from his mother and taken away for adoption.

He'd taken the call in his study on the first floor of the mansion that was Easterton Manor, sitting at his big oak desk set in the bay window, from where he could look out over the lawns dotted with stone statues, and the pond where water gushed constantly from yet another stone effigy. The house was set in a valley, and beyond its grounds the Mendip Hills rose above a swathe of woodland, just visible from his vantage point.

The conversation with Kirkwood was short and to the point, as all exchanges between the two men were. Perhaps Sir Oswald would be so kind as to contact the prospective adoptive parents and arrange for the baby to be collected on Friday of this week.

Sir Oswald and Dr Kirkwood had never seen eye to eye, and Sir Oswald knew that the doctor disapproved of the way he was dealing with this 'domestic problem', as he liked to refer to it. But disapproval had never been of much concern to Sir Oswald. He took pride in his reputation for being a hard man – 'the only way to run a profitable business', he told anyone who dared criticise his callous treatment of the workers who toiled in his quarries. 'Give them an inch and they'd take a mile.'

To him, Dr Kirkwood was just another employee, appointed to his position by the board of trustees on which Sir Oswald sat. From the outset he'd been suspicious of the doctor and his soft new-fangled methods, but he'd been outvoted, his a lone voice in the wilderness. Nevertheless, the fact remained that he had a certain power over the superintendent, especially as the years passed and he gained seniority on the board. Let the good doctor step out of line and Sir Oswald would make his position untenable. The unspoken threat hung over Dr Kirkwood, who knew he had no option but to go along with the quarry owner's plans, little as he liked them.

'Very well,' Sir Oswald barked, curt as he always was when speaking to Kirkwood. 'I'll get on to the prospective parents right away. When would be a suitable time for them to collect the baby?'

There was a short pause while Dr Kirkwood considered.

'As early as possible in the morning,' he said at last.

'Nine – ten o'clock?'

'No, much earlier. Rose is likely to become very distressed and I don't want the other patients upset. It's not good for them.'

'Can't you lock her away to ensure that doesn't happen?'

Dr Kirkwood chose not to answer that. He didn't like anyone

to be 'locked away' unless it was absolutely necessary, and Rose was perfectly sane.

'Breakfast is at seven thirty,' he said instead. 'If the baby is removed while all the patients are in the dining room, there's far less chance of a disturbance.'

'The family have to get to you from Gloucestershire,' Sir Oswald objected.

'Then I suggest they find overnight lodging somewhere close by,' Dr Kirkwood replied staunchly, and annoyed though he was at failing to get his own way, Sir Oswald had decided that on this occasion it would be politic to concede the point.

If there was trouble at the asylum over the baby's removal, it would draw attention to Rose's situation and the arrangements he had in place to take care of the problem. He didn't want that, especially if it reached the ears of the other board members.

'Very well, I'll see what I can do,' he agreed with bad grace.

As soon as the call was ended, he picked up the heavy brass receiver again and called the operator at the local telephone exchange, who connected him to the number of the friend who was to adopt Rose's baby.

Winston Donaghue was a well-respected solicitor with offices in a country town that nestled in the Cotswold hills. He and Sir Oswald had been at Eton together, and once a year the old boys from their form met up for a reunion, a boozy weekend when they could relive memories of school and catch up on the details of the different paths their lives had taken. At one of these events Winston, somewhat the worse for wear after consuming copious amounts of whisky, claret, port and brandy, had confided that for all their efforts, his wife, Miranda, had failed to conceive a child.

For his part, Winston was indifferent to the failure. His first wife, Elizabeth, had provided him with two fine healthy sons, both now grown up, before succumbing to the tuberculosis that had eventually claimed her life. But Miranda, still a young woman, was growing increasingly despondent that she seemed unable to fall pregnant. 'She can think and talk of nothing else,' he'd said. 'Frankly, I'm worried for her state of mind.'

When the problem of Rose's pregnancy had reared its ugly head, Sir Oswald had immediately thought of his friend. If he and his wife would be willing to adopt the baby, it would be the ideal solution; Dursley was far enough away from Easterton that no one would ever make the connection. He'd contacted Winston, who, after he'd put it to Miranda, had come back to him to say they would be only too delighted to take on the child. Now all that was left for Oswald to do was let Winston know that the baby could be collected from Catcombe on Friday morning.

After a series of crackles on the line, the telephone in Winston's office was answered by his receptionist, and Sir Oswald was just about to ask to be put through to his friend when the door of his study opened and Rupert, his elder son, came in, a pile of paperwork in his hand.

'I'll call back later,' Sir Oswald said hastily, replacing the receiver on the antler-shaped brass stand. He didn't want to have this conversation in front of Rupert. Just how much his son knew of the situation Sir Oswald wasn't sure – it had never been discussed openly – but Rupert was no fool, and neither was his younger son, George, who, thankfully, was training at Sandhurst and well out of the way. But the less Rupert knew the better, and there was no sense making him party to this latest development.

'What do you want?' he demanded testily, annoyed at the interruption and concerned that Rupert might wonder why he had ended his call so abruptly.

'This contract with the new hauliers requires your signature.' Rupert showed no signs of curiosity, but Oswald knew that his elder son could be every bit as secretive as he could.

'Very well, leave it on my desk and I'll look at it later,' Sir Oswald said shortly, and knowing he'd been dismissed, Rupert left the room.

As soon as the door had closed behind him, Sir Oswald picked up the telephone again and redialled the operator. This time his call went through uninterrupted.

'The day after tomorrow, seven thirty,' he said when Winston came on the line, choosing his words carefully to give nothing away in case that nosy woman at the telephone exchange in the front room of her cottage should be listening in.

Winston understood the somewhat cryptic message as Sir Oswald had known he would.

'The day after tomorrow – Friday. We'll be there. And thank you, Oswald. I can't tell you what this means to Miranda.'

'My pleasure. Say no more about it,' Sir Oswald added, fearful that in his gratitude Winston might give something away.

The call ended, he replaced the receiver and sat back in his leather captain's chair, steepling his fleshy hands beneath the folds of his double chin. Thank God this whole unfortunate business was coming to an end. He still had to decide what was to be done about Rose Gooding, but that could wait. At least her brat would be safely out of the picture.

Early in the day as it was, he decided this warranted something to celebrate. He rose, crossed to the leather-topped occasional table that bore a tray with a crystal decanter and glasses, and poured a good measure of single malt whisky. Then he returned to his chair, swirled the amber liquid in the glass, and raised it so that it caught a shaft of spring sunlight that streamed in through the window.

'To a problem solved,' he said aloud, and smiling in satisfaction, he tossed back the whisky in one swallow.

At Catcombe, Dr Kirkwood was making arrangements to ensure that the handover of the baby would proceed as smoothly as possible. He didn't like it; didn't like anything about what Sir Oswald Whittingly Challis had done to brush the whole business of Rose Gooding's inconvenient pregnancy under the carpet, but with two highly respected physicians signing her into the asylum, there had been nothing he could do about it. As for this adoption, taking a baby from its mother against her will was, in his opinion, nothing short of criminal. But again his hands were tied; it fell well outside his jurisdiction. The only thing he could do was to press for Rose's release, but he wasn't even sure how much good that would do. If Whittingly Challis wanted her kept out of the way for the foreseeable future, he'd make sure the same two doctors who had signed her in were still on his side. And in any case, it would be too late for her to be reunited with her baby. He only hoped the trauma of it didn't impact on her mental state to the extent that there would be real reason to keep her incarcerated.

With a heavy heart he went to Matron Carey's office.

'Baby Gooding's adoptive parents will be coming for him on Friday morning,' he told her. 'I've asked that they take him away while the patients are at breakfast; I'm hoping that will avert too much trouble. The nursery nurse can feed the babies as and when they wake, and there will be no need for any of the mothers to go up there until it's all over. Will you alert Nurse Whitcombe and Nurse Cummings so that they can make the necessary preparations?'

Since Dr Kirkwood had decided Nurse Dando was more interested in reading her halfpenny periodicals than looking after the babies, Mabel's position as night nursery nurse had been confirmed.

'Of course.'

'And please ask them not to mention it to anyone else. The fewer people who know what's about to happen, the better.'

'What about Rose?' Matron asked. 'Will she be allowed to say goodbye to her baby?'

'I don't think that's advisable. She knows the adoption is imminent, but she's likely to become very upset when the time comes, and may well cause a commotion. That wouldn't be good for the other babies, or the patients, for that matter. It sounds harsh, I know, but I think it's for the best. I have to look at the bigger picture.'

'Very well,' Matron sighed. 'I know you're not in agreement with any of this, Hubert, but the baby will be going to a good home, and will have far more advantages in life than if Rose was allowed to keep him.'

Dr Kirkwood said nothing. Privately he thought that none of that was as important as the love of his real mother.

'When do you want me to tell Nurses Whitcombe and Cummings? Do we leave it until the last minute so as to minimise the risk of it getting out?' Matron asked.

'Surely we can rely on their discretion? I think they should be told at once so that they can ensure everything is ready. Nurse Whitcombe is on duty now, isn't she – have a word with her as soon as you have a chance. And speak to Nurse Cummings when she comes on duty tonight.'

'What about Florrie?'

Dr Kirkwood considered. He'd forgotten about Florrie.

'Is she trustworthy?' he asked.

'I believe so.'

'Then perhaps it would be a good idea to put her in the

picture too. It might be best for the regular nurses to have some support in case there is any unforeseen trouble.'

'There won't be. I'll make sure of that.'

Dr Kirkwood crossed to the door, opening it and checking that there was no one in the vicinity who might have overheard their conversation. The corridor was empty.

'I know I can depend on you, Maude,' he said.

But as he returned to his own office, he found himself wishing he could be so sure. If word of this got out there could well be trouble.

# Chapter Eleven

Grace came in from the coal house with a scuttleful of coal and placed it on the hearth ready to make up the fire later. It was getting dark, the scuttle had been empty, and she hadn't wanted to have to refill it when she couldn't see her nose in front of her face.

It was a job Tom usually attended to, but he wasn't here. Dr Mackay had called while they were having their tea, saying he thought Stella was ready now to have visitors, and if Tom liked, he would run him over to Catcombe to see her. Understandably, Tom had jumped at the chance. Until now, it had been considered best if Stella was left to settle into life at the asylum without distractions or reminders of home. He'd left what remained of his tea, fetched his coat, and left with Dr Mackay without giving the empty coal scuttle a thought. And nor should he have, Grace thought. Stella was far more important.

The development had affected the children, however, the mention of their mother unsettling them.

'Can't we come too?' Alec had demanded.

'Yes, and me!' Emily had echoed.

'I'm sorry, but you can't,' Tom had told them. 'Maybe next time.'

'Oh . . . why not?'

'It's the asylum,' Oliver had said flatly. 'You can't go there. Children aren't allowed.'

'Why not?' Emily had asked.

'Because there's all sorts of funny people there.' Oliver had pointed at her with his fork. 'You wouldn't like it. They're all mad.'

'Where did you get that from?' demanded Tom, buttoning his coat, his tone unusually sharp.

'Go on, Tom – you go. I'll deal with it,' Grace had said.

And so she had. As she'd guessed, some of the children at school had been taunting Oliver with talk of 'mad people'.

'Your mammy is not mad. She's just not well,' she'd explained. 'And if anyone tells you different, just ignore them.'

'Okay.'

Oliver was not one to think too deeply about things, but Emily was a different matter. Grace could see she was upset, and when she was clearing the tea things, Emily followed her into the kitchen and tugged at her sleeve.

'Will Mammy be coming home soon?'

'I hope so, darling. Why don't you go and play with Raggy Aggie for a bit? She's probably missing your mammy too.'

Emily had trotted off and Grace had hoped the doll would help to take her mind off her mother.

Now, however, as she straightened up from the hearth, she saw that Emily had curled herself into a ball on the sofa, thumb in her mouth, tears rolling down her cheeks.

'Emily – what's wrong, darling?' Grace sat down beside the little girl and put her arm round her.

'They took Raggy Aggie,' Emily wailed.

'Oliver did?'

'And Alec. They've run off with her and I don't like it. They might tear her dress . . .'

'Oh, the naughty boys!' Grace went to the foot of the stairs and called up. 'You two – get down here with Emily's doll at once!'

They came, a little shamefaced, but also defiant.

'It was only a game.'

'It's not a game to Emily,' Grace scolded. 'You should know better than to upset your sister, and at bedtime too. Any more of this behaviour, and your father will hear about it.'

For a while, peace reigned, then the two boys began squabbling among themselves over a model train they'd been building out of matchboxes.

'All right, that's it,' Grace said. 'You're going to bed.'

'Aw! Can't we wait for Dad to get home?'

'Are you sure you want to? He's not going to be best pleased when I tell him how you've been behaving.'

The boys looked at one another, still scowling, but deciding discretion should be the better part of valour. Grace heated some water and put it in a tin bowl in the sink. Then she washed Emily's face and hands, and left the boys to do their own.

She lit the oil lamp in the bedroom and tucked Emily into bed. The little girl was still upset, so Grace sat with her for a few minutes, singing softly, and at last her eyes closed.

'Right, you two,' she said, going back downstairs. 'It's time you were off as well. I've left the lamp on, so you can take a book each and read for a bit until you're sleepy. But whatever you do, don't wake Emily.'

'Night, Auntie Grace,' they chorused.

'Night night. And mind what I say.'

They scampered off, and thankfully all was quiet. At least

she was not afraid to discipline them any more, Grace thought. She'd fallen into the role of surrogate mother quite comfortably now.

She settled herself in the fireside chair, wondering how Tom was getting on with Stella. She must be improving if Dr Mackay thought she was fit for visitors. Grace wondered how long it would be before she was able to come home. It might be quite soon, and glad as she was for her sister and for Tom, she couldn't help feeling a nugget of regret that her time here was coming to an end. She'd miss it – she'd miss them all. And the thought of returning to her old life was not a happy one.

She reached for Stella's knitting bag, in the corner between her chair and the wall. It had been almost empty when Grace had arrived on the scene, just oddments of wool left over from matinee jackets and bonnets Stella had been making for Will during her pregnancy, along with some patterns and needles, scissors and a tape measure. Since he'd been born, there'd been no time for such things.

Grace had decided she'd make something for him too. She'd bought some new wool and Tom had helped her wind it into a ball by holding the skein over his outstretched hands. It was years since she had done any knitting, and she'd even had to think about how to cast on, let alone work the stitches detailed in the pattern. But after a while it had all come back to her, and now she found it relaxing as well as satisfying as she watched the little garment take shape.

For half an hour or so she worked in a silence broken only by the click of her needles and the occasional settling of a burning coal. Then Fluffy got up from where he had been lying stretched out in front of the fire, went to the back door and began scratching at it.

'Why don't you use the cat flap, you silly creature?' Grace said aloud as she went to open the door for him before he damaged the paintwork. 'You come in through it. Why not go out through it too?'

It was as she watched him walk purposefully off along the path that she heard raised voices coming from next door. Her heart sank. Noel and Francie were at it again, and from the sound of it, things were escalating.

She couldn't make out the words, but there was no mistaking Noel's furious roar or Francie's shrill tones, which were cut off in mid flow by a sharp gasping scream. Grace's hands flew to her mouth. Her neighbour was taking a beating again, she was sure of it. For a long moment she stood there, undecided. She couldn't interfere, but she couldn't just do nothing either. Perhaps she could distract Noel in some way . . .

She crept along the path to the neighbouring door and rapped on it sharply before scuttling back again. Perhaps if he thought there was someone on the doorstep, Noel would desist from whatever punishment he was meting out, but she had no intention of letting him catch her there. For a few minutes she stood inside her own half-open door, waiting and listening. Just as she had hoped, the kerfuffle seemed to have stopped. Perhaps she had done some good. But poor Francie! What bruises would she be hiding tomorrow?

Eventually she went back inside and sat down again, but she couldn't concentrate on her knitting, getting up every so often to go to the door. To her enormous relief, everything seemed to have gone quiet.

She was still jittery, though, and was very glad when she heard the front door open and Tom call: 'It's only me. I'm home.'

She wouldn't tell him about the commotion next door, she decided. And certainly not about the way she'd scuttled along the path, banged on the door and run away like a young varmint playing knock-down ginger.

'How did you get on?' she asked as he came into the living room.

'Well, she certainly seems more like her old self.' Tom was taking his coat off. 'She's still a bit withdrawn, but who wouldn't be in that place? But she asked after you and the children, and sent her love.' He smiled and added: 'Said she hoped I was treating you right.'

'That certainly sounds more like her,' Grace said. 'What about Will?'

'Doing fine. But Dr Mackay thinks it's as well to keep him in so he can be with Stella. If she wasn't showing any signs of improvement he might think about sending him home – apparently he could be fed on Bengers; that's a milk food – but as things stand, it's probably best for both him and Stella that he stays with her.'

'I expect it is,' Grace said. 'I'm not at all sure how I'd manage if I had to look after him.'

'You'd do it,' Tom said. 'You've been a brick, Grace, and you've made a wonderful job of keeping things going here. I don't know what I'd have done without you, and I don't think I tell you often enough how grateful I am.'

'You don't have to. I'm only doing what anyone in my position would.'

'You are doing much, much more. You're a very special lady, Grace.'

There was warmth in his tone and in his eyes as he looked at her, and Grace felt hot colour rising in her cheeks. He didn't mean anything by it, of course. It was her own guilt at her secret feelings for him that made her read something into his words that surely wasn't there. But all the same . . .

Something sharp and sweet twisted deep inside Grace. If only . . . if only . . . Angry with herself, she pushed the treacherous thought away.

'Are you ready for a cup of cocoa?' she asked, changing the subject.

'I'll make it if you like,' he offered.

'No, you sit down. I'll do it.'

She fetched a pan of milk and set it on the hob, then spooned cocoa into two earthenware mugs. And all the while . . .

Was it her imagination, or were his eyes on her? It was as if she could feel him following her every move.

Don't be so silly, she scolded herself.

But the warmth was back in her cheeks. And in a secret place close to her heart.

In the palatial dining room at Easterton Manor, Sir Oswald Whittingly Challis was tucking into a hearty breakfast. Bacon, kidneys, mushrooms and griddled tomatoes sat in silver chafing dishes on the long, highly polished sideboard, and as was his practice, Sir Oswald had helped himself to generous portions of all of them. He liked his food almost as much as he liked his cognac and single malt whisky, and it showed. His watch chain strained across a well-rounded belly, and his bulbous red-veined nose sat between flabby cheeks that overlapped flabby jowls. But this morning he was enjoying his breakfast more than he'd felt able to for some time. The problem that had been disturbing his peace of mind since last summer was about to be solved. Tomorrow, the arrangements he'd made for the adoption of Rose Gooding's baby would come to fruition, and that, he hoped, would be the end of the matter.

Rupert had not yet put in an appearance, but at the other end of the dining table, Lady Cecelia, his wife, toyed with a fillet of finnan haddock and regarded her husband critically from behind her wire-rimmed spectacles.

'You seem to be in remarkably good spirits this morning, Oswald.'

'With reason. A small but troublesome matter is about to be resolved.'

'Ah. The one we don't discuss, I imagine.'

'Quite.'

There was no way Lady Cecelia could have remained in ignorance about what was going on, but she refused to lower herself to talk about it even if Oswald had wanted to. He was dealing with it; more than that, she had no desire to know. It was a measure of the coldness that existed within their marriage. But he knew she was glad that the unfortunate affair was reaching a conclusion and the chance of it being made public was receding. Lady Cecelia valued her standing in the community and had no wish for the members of the ladies' committees on which she served to be acquainted with the sordid details of her family business.

Sir Oswald stuffed the last forkful of bacon into his mouth, dabbed at his chin with his napkin, and wiped his hands to remove an imaginary splatter of grease. Then he reached for the silver salver bearing a small pile of mail that Cyril, the footman, had brought in. Anything that was obviously business correspondence would have been filtered out and taken directly to his office, but he liked to open personal letters over a cup of strong sweet coffee.

Now he rifled through the pile, extracted an envelope and tossed it down the table to Lady Cecelia.

'This is of more interest to you than me, I expect,' he said gruffly. 'From your son, by the look of it.'

'He is your son too . . .'

Sir Oswald merely snorted derisively and continued looking through the mail.

Lady Cecelia gave a small, impatient shake of her head and reached for a dessert knife to slit open the envelope. The letter clearly was from George; the writing was his, and the Berkshire postmark confirmed it. He was at Sandhurst, as a gentleman cadet, training to become an army officer, and was now midway through the year-long course that had begun in September.

The letter would be brief, Lady Cecelia knew. While Rupert, his brother, had shone academically, George had never had much time for his studies, and had much preferred being out in the open air, riding, shooting, or swimming in the lake that marked the boundary of the estate. A thin smile lifted Lady Cecelia's lips as she remembered the fuss he used to make when required to write thank-you notes for Christmas or birthday presents. No, it wouldn't be a long letter, but short and to the point.

She was right. There were two pages inside the envelope, but the writing was so large and untidy that if Rupert had been the author, he would have fitted everything on to one. It had been scrawled in great haste, Lady Cecelia guessed.

She adjusted her spectacles and set about deciphering the words.

'Well?' Sir Oswald demanded, more interested than he was prepared to let on. 'What's the boy got to say for himself?'

'It seems his company is the Champion Company at Arms for the second term running,' Lady Cecelia reported. 'And George played a big part in them winning the honour.'

'Well, he would, wouldn't he?' Sir Oswald scoffed. 'He's always been better at playing games than using what's between his ears.'

The Champion Company at Arms was decided each term by a competition that consisted of military and athletic exercises and gave the winners the honour of taking the right flank in the battalion for the following term. Sports and athletics had always been George's forte; at school, he had captained both the rugby and cricket teams, and he was the holder of numerous records for various field and track events. All very laudable, but not of any use in managing the quarries and the estate, in Sir Oswald's opinion. Which was the reason a career in the military had been decided upon.

'Anything else?' Sir Oswald barked.

'Yes, actually. Apparently he's going to be in Wiltshire in a couple of weeks' time. Salisbury Plain. His company are being sent there for field training and manoeuvres, and he hopes to be able to get over for a flying visit while he's there.'

Sir Oswald snorted. 'Oh he does, does he? That's got to be the best part of a hundred-mile round trip, and God knows how long it would take on that motorcycle of his. I'll believe it when I see it.'

'I'm simply telling you what he says.' Lady Cecelia's tone was slightly acid.

'What George says and what he does are two different things. As you should well know. The boy is nothing but a liability, and always has been. Let's just hope this army training can make something of him. God knows it's costing me enough. Tuition, boarding fees, uniforms, books and all the rest.'

'Money well spent if it keeps him out of trouble.'

'Keeps who out of trouble?' Rupert had entered the room. He was, as usual, smartly dressed; his hair, slightly longer than his father would have liked, and still damp from his morning bath, curled over the stiff collar of his shirt.

'Your brother. Who else?'

'What's he done now?' Rupert asked laconically, helping himself to eggs and bacon.

'Nothing, as far as I'm aware. But it seems we may have the pleasure of his company in a few weeks' time.' Sir Oswald poured himself more coffee, added milk and sugar and took a sip. 'This coffee's cold, dammit. Ring for Cyril, will you, Rupert, there's a good chap. You'll be wanting some too. He can bring us a fresh pot.'

'So, my little brother is going to pay us a visit,' Rupert said, tugging on the bell rope and then taking his place at the table. 'When he didn't come home for Christmas, I thought perhaps he had some filly tucked away in a love nest in Wokingham.'

'Don't be ridiculous, Rupert,' Lady Cecelia retorted sharply. 'The allowance your father gives him would never stretch to such a thing . . .' She broke off as Cyril came in answer to the bell to ask him to bring fresh coffee. Then, as if the interruption had never been, she continued: 'Besides, you know very well the reason George didn't come home was because he was invited to spend Christmas with the Willoughby Browns, so that he could improve his French by conversing with their Parisian ladies' maid.'

French was one of the languages that was studied at Sandhurst, along with Hindustani for those cadets bound for the Indian Army, and it was highly likely George would be struggling with it as he did with all academic subjects.

Rupert chortled. 'I wonder what else Mademoiselle taught him beside the lingo?'

'Don't be coarse, Rupert,' Lady Cecelia reprimanded him.

'Well, you know their reputation . . . ooh-la-la and all that—'

'That will do, Rupert.'

For a few minutes silence reigned at the table as Rupert tucked into his bacon, Sir Oswald flipped through the rest of the post and scanned the freshly ironed front page of *The Times* and Lady Cecelia reread George's letter.

As he swallowed the last bit of bacon, Rupert laid down his knife and fork and pointed in the direction of the letter.

'If he comes home, I suppose he's going to find out . . .'

Sir Oswald abruptly lowered the newspaper, glowering at his son over the top of it. 'Find out what exactly?'

'Oh, I think you know what I'm talking about.'

'There are some things, Rupert, that are not discussed in polite company. I hope I make my meaning clear?'

Rupert's lip curled. 'Have it your own way.'

At that moment the door opened and Cyril returned bearing a fresh pot of coffee.

'Thank you, Cyril.' But Sir Oswald's eyes, narrow with an unspoken threat, never left his son's face, and as the footman retired again, Rupert pushed back his chair and stood up.

'I'll be in my office if you want me.'

'Aren't you going to have coffee, Rupert?' Lady Cecelia enquired.

Still standing, he poured himself a cup. 'I'll take it with me.'

As Rupert left the room, Lady Cecelia raised a delicately arched brow in the direction of her husband.

'Oh dear,' she said pointedly. 'I do hope the boy isn't going to make trouble.'

Sir Oswald's mouth was set in a hard line, annoyance spoiling his previous good mood.

'You can leave him to me. I think you'll discover he knows which side his bread is buttered.'

Lady Cecelia smiled thinly.

'Yes, my dear, I expect you are right,' was all she said.


Grace was concerned about Francie. She hadn't come to her door to wave her children off to school, nor had Grace seen her go out to the coal house or even the privy. She might have missed her, of course – she hadn't spent the entire morning watching for her out of the window – but all the same . . . She kept remembering the awful row of the night before and really wanted to see Francie to make sure she was all right.

When she'd finished the daily chores, she decided she had to set her mind at rest. She'd go next door and ask to borrow a cup of sugar. Though she and Francie had become quite friendly, it didn't extend to her knocking on the door without a good excuse. She'd always left it to Francie to make the overture.

She put on a clean apron and fetched a cup from the kitchen cupboard, then, feeling a bit awkward and nervous, she walked along the path at the back of the houses, worried that Francie might realise she had heard the commotion and was just being nosy.

She knocked on the door, blushing a little as she remembered how she'd knocked last night and then scuttled away like a naughty child. At first there was no response and no sounds of life from within, and she wondered if Francie wasn't going to answer it. Perhaps she had another black eye she didn't want anyone to see, or worse, was so badly hurt that she had taken to her bed.

Then, taking her by surprise, the door opened and Francie stood there wearing her bedroom slippers. No wonder Grace hadn't heard her footsteps on the tiled floor. And there was no sign of a black eye that she could see.

'Oh – hello!' Francie sounded perfectly normal too.

'I'm really sorry to bother you, but I wondered if I could borrow a cup of sugar . . .' Grace held out the cup as if proof were needed.

'Course you can.' Francie opened the door wider. 'Are you coming in?'

'Well . . . if you're not too busy . . .'

'I'm never too busy for a cup of tea. The kettle's on the hob.'

Grace went into the kitchen. In layout it was much the same as in Stella's house: the big stone sink under the window, the free-standing cupboards along one wall, a heavy old table against another. The table was covered now by an ironing blanket, and a pile of freshly laundered bed linen was stacked on a chair, lending the kitchen a clean, soapy smell.

'Come on in.' Francie led the way into the living room, again of similar shape and size to Stella's. 'Sit down.'

Grace took a chair at the oilcloth-covered dining table and Francie busied herself with the teapot.

'Mrs Plumley's canary went missing again this morning,' she said conversationally as she poured milk into cups and set the teapot on a trivet in the centre of the table.

'Oh, did he?'

'Didn't you hear her running up and down the rank calling for him?'

'No, I didn't.' She must have been upstairs making the beds, Grace thought. 'Has she found him?'

'I expect so. Like I told you before, mostly he just flies off upstairs. But one of these days the door or window will be open and he really will be gone.' Francie sat down at right angles to Grace. 'How's Stella?'

'Getting better, we hope. Tom went to see her last night, and he said she was almost back to her old self. With any luck she'll be able to come home soon.'

'That will be a relief for all of you.'

'It certainly will.'

Grace was beginning to think she'd got into a panic last night about nothing. Francie seemed perfectly fine. Perhaps she and Noel did have shouting matches that amounted to nothing, and she'd blown the whole thing up, letting her imagination get the better of her.

Then, as Francie reached for the sugar bowl, her sleeve caught on the edge of the oilcloth, and as it rucked up, a series of livid bruises encircling her arm was clearly visible.

Unable to tear her eyes away, Grace stared in horror at what were evidently finger marks, and Francie, realising the bruises were on show, hastily pulled down her sleeve to cover them.

'Caught my arm when I was turning the mattress . . . Blooming clumsy, I am. Always doing something.' She gave a forced laugh.

'You ought to be more careful.' It wasn't at all what Grace wanted to say. She wanted to ask Francie if she was really all right, but she couldn't do that, couldn't let on that she knew this was no accident, when Francie was clearly ashamed and wanted to keep it quiet.

She and Francie drank their tea, chatting, but there was an awkwardness between them that hadn't been there before, a forced cheerfulness. She knows I know, Grace thought. The poor woman!

'I'd better be going,' she said at last, getting up.

'Don't forget your sugar.'

'Oh . . . no.' She had forgotten.

Francie tipped some sugar into the cup Grace had brought with her; Grace thanked her, and left. But she couldn't stop thinking about the neighbour who had to put up with such treatment from her husband and was too ashamed, or too afraid, to do anything about it.

# *Chapter Twelve*

Miranda Donaghue adjusted the already perfectly arranged ruffles that framed the wicker crib and straightened the already smooth silk coverlet. She'd done it at least a dozen times since Winston, her husband, had told her the baby they were to adopt was ready to be separated from his mother, just as she'd shaken out and refolded the layette and checked once again that everything he'd need was ready for him. The porcelain bath and fluffy white towels, gentle soap and talcum powder and a cream specially formulated in case of nappy rash, even a soft hairbrush. The food and feeding equipment were downstairs, of course, in a specially cleared-out cupboard in the larder, but she checked those frequently too, leaving nothing to chance. And although they'd been told he could be fed now on Bengers, they'd engaged a wet nurse who would also act as a nanny.

She'd dispense with her services, though, as soon as she could, Miranda had decided. She wanted to care for the baby herself. After the years of longing, of hope and despair, she had not the slightest intention of taking a back seat and letting a stranger perform the tasks she had yearned for. She would lavish all her love on this baby, the love that had never yet had an outlet.

It was five years since she had married Winston, five barren years when she had grown increasingly despondent. But the longing for a child of her own went back much further than that. Even as a little girl, she had loved babies, loved helping Mama with her younger brother and sister, pushing them out in their perambulator as soon as she was able to reach the handles and strong enough to stop it from running away on the gentle slope outside their house. 'Little mother', they had called her, and she'd been proud and satisfied with the description.

When she'd left school, she'd found employment as a nanny, against the wishes of her father, a respected businessman, who considered such a position beneath her. They had been happy years caring for two little boys and watching them grow from babies to toddlers to children. But she'd hated it when she had to hand them back to their mother, and been dreadfully upset when first one, then the other was sent away to boarding school and her services were no longer required. They'd been upset, too – far more upset than they were about leaving their mother; after all, Miranda had done more for them than their mother ever had, and the bond between her and the boys was strong. It was one of the reasons she was determined to dispense with the nanny as soon as she could. She didn't want this baby to be closer to another woman than he was to her.

She had been in her mid twenties when she had been introduced to Winston, and beginning to fear she was never going to be a wife, let alone a mother. She was both flattered and relieved by his interest in her. Winston was a widower and much older than her, but he was still an attractive man who hadn't let himself run to paunchy fat as so many men of his age and standing in the community had done. There was grey in his hair and whiskers, but it made him look distinguished rather than old. And he was well set up financially, a partner in a firm of solicitors with a big house sitting in its own grounds on the outskirts of town.

She wasn't in love with him but he had seemed to offer all

she wanted from life – a ring on her finger, a home of her own, and the prospect of the children she so longed for. When he'd asked for her hand in marriage, her father, relieved that she wouldn't be left on the shelf, had readily agreed, and Miranda herself had raised no objection. Overnight she had become stepmother to two young men to whom she was closer in age than she was to their father, but that hadn't troubled her, nor them. They'd accepted her into the family, and she enjoyed their company. What was more, they were living proof that Winston was capable of fathering children, and Miranda had no doubt that soon she would have a baby of her own.

But the months and then the years had gone by, and when it hadn't happened, she'd grown more and more desperate. It was her fault, it must be. She began to dread the time of the month when her courses were due: the breathless waiting, the hope if she was a few days late, the despair when the niggly ache began deep inside her and she discovered blood on her drawers, the emptiness that came from knowing that once again she had failed to fall pregnant. She'd hated herself for becoming so obsessed by it that she feared she was failing Winston too, but she simply couldn't help herself. She'd seen doctors; they'd told her to relax and stop worrying, but how could she do that? Her whole world had come to revolve around her desperate longing, the feeling of failure, and the awful fear that she was barren. Day by day, week by week, month by month, she slipped deeper and deeper into depression.

And then Winston had told her he'd been contacted by an old friend who was looking for adoptive parents for a baby one of his maids was carrying out of wedlock. How would she feel about taking it on?

From the outset, Miranda had not entertained a moment's doubt. The baby might not be her own, but she knew from the feelings she'd had for the two boys she'd nursemaided that it wasn't necessary to have given birth to a child to love it. She'd agreed without hesitation, and her mood had instantly lifted from bleak despair to excited anticipation.

She'd known at once which room she wanted to be the nursery – the one she'd picked out when she'd first married Winston and come to live at Stoneleigh House, full of hope for the future. A room on the upper floor, small but sunny, with views across the Cotswolds – it would be perfect. To Winston's amusement, she had immediately set about making it ready, having it repainted in sunshine yellow and ordering new curtains patterned with spring flowers. She'd got rid of the hard, narrow bed with its heavy candlewick bedspread, but kept the marble-topped washstand and the tallboy, although she had had the tallboy stripped of its dark varnish and painted white. She'd bought a crib – the most beautiful and most expensive in the shop – and a rocking chair with a padded seat. She'd purchased a big shiny baby carriage, pillows, bedding and a quilted silk coverlet. Winston had indulged her, never once complaining about the amount of money she was spending. He was only glad to see her so happy.

There had been worrying times when the baby – a boy – had been born far sooner than he should have been, and his life hung in the balance. Miranda had spent a great deal of time on her knees praying for him, and her prayers had been answered. The baby had lived, though the setback had meant she would have to wait a little longer to hold him in her arms.

'We should think about a name for him,' Winston had said one day when they knew the child was going to survive.

'What does his mother call him?' Miranda had asked.

'I've no idea,' Winston had confessed.

'Can you find out?'

'I suppose so. Why?'

'Because I think we should keep that. It's the only thing he can bring with him.'

'What if it's something totally unsuitable?' Winston had objected.

'Then I suppose we'd have to think again. But let's hope not.'

It had been a relief to discover the mother had named her baby Wallace.

'I like it,' Miranda had said. 'It makes me think of that Scottish knight who led his armies into battle against the English.'

'Wallace was his surname. He was William Wallace,' Winston had pointed out.

'That doesn't matter, does it? Whichever, it has a nice ring to it.'

From that moment on, they had come to refer to the baby as Wallace, even though they had yet to meet him.

Now Miranda sat down in the rocking chair, reaching out to run her fingers along the edge of the crib and smiling to herself.

Soon – very soon – Wallace would be here, and she could scarcely believe it. Soon her life would be complete. No more empty arms. No more aching heart. This baby would be the most wanted, the most loved, in the whole of England.

Tyres crunched on the gravel drive beneath the window. Miranda got up and looked out to see Winston's motor pulling up beside the front door. Goodness, was it that time already? Winston always came home from his office for luncheon.

She got up and went to greet her husband.

He smiled indulgently at her as she came down the stairs into the generously proportioned hall.

'Been up in the nursery again? No, don't try to deny it. I saw you at the window.'

'I have been, yes,' she confessed. 'I'm just so excited! And I want everything to be perfect.'

'It will be.'

'I've been thinking . . .'

Miranda hesitated. She'd intended to leave what she had to say until later, when Winston had had his meal and perhaps a glass or two of wine. But this seemed as good a time as any, and besides, she'd started now.

'I'd like to come with you when you collect Wallace,' she said.

Winston, who had been hanging his coat on the antler stand, swung round abruptly.

'Why?' His tone was sharp; he was no longer smiling.

'Because I can't wait to meet him! And I want to be the first one to hold him, not Nanny Tyler.' It had been arranged that the nanny would go with Winston to collect the baby. 'Please, Winston!'

'I don't think that's a good idea.' He spoke decisively, in the voice he used when advising some headstrong client that the course of action he wanted to take would not be in his best interests.

'Why not?' Miranda asked, looking a little crestfallen.

Winston hesitated. He had no intention of letting her find out that the baby had been born in a lunatic asylum where his mother was incarcerated.

'It's a long journey,' he said, 'and you know long journeys don't suit you.'

'I'd be fine!' Miranda argued.

'That's a matter of opinion. And besides, we're staying overnight in a local tavern, and I have only Oswald's word for it that it's respectable. For all I know it could be very run-down, damp and none too clean, with unaired sheets. There could even be bed bugs! No, my dear, it's much better you stay here so you'll be rested and fit to take charge of your new son, not tired out and possibly sickening for some ailment you might have picked up.' He touched her arm. 'Now, shall we go into luncheon? I'm hungry, and I'm sure you must be too. You hardly ate a thing at breakfast.'

It was true. Miranda was far too excited to eat, and she didn't suppose luncheon would be any different, no matter what delicacy their housekeeper had prepared. But despite her disappointment, she could see there was no point in arguing. Winston's mind was clearly made up. She'd just have to curb her impatience and wait for him to return with baby Wallace. And that was something well worth waiting for.

'I expect you're right,' she said meekly, and followed her husband into the dining room.

At nine o'clock that evening, the social room at the asylum was full to overflowing. The man with the piano accordion was there again to entertain the patients, and those who were allowed to attend were making the most of it. Some sang along; others were dancing in the centre of the room where the carpet had been rolled back, Louie Hillman and her boyfriend Silas amongst them. Even the nurse supervisors were joining in, tapping their feet and clapping their hands in time to the music.

But Rose Gooding sat quietly in a corner, her hands twisted tightly together in her lap, her face wet with tears. Earlier on, when she'd been up to the nursery to feed her baby, Florrie Carter had let slip that Wallace was to be taken away tomorrow. And though she had known it must be imminent, the news had come as a terrible shock to Rose. Foolish though she'd known such a notion was, she'd clung to the desperate hope that somehow this terrible thing could be averted; that when the time came, someone would step in and put a stop to it. Or – even more far-fetched – that a thunderbolt would strike the asylum, and in the chaos that would follow she'd be able to take Wallace and run away with him and never look back!

Now she knew that nothing was going to happen to stop her losing her precious baby, and she didn't know how she could bear it. She wasn't even going to be allowed to see him again! When she had discovered that Rose had found out that Wallace would be taken tomorrow, Cissie Whitcombe had informed her it had been decided that a clean break would be for the best.

'I think you should say goodbye to him now,' she had told her. 'Florrie shouldn't have told you – Dr Kirkwood and Matron don't want the other patients or their babies upset, and if there's a commotion, they'll have my guts for garters.'

'I won't make a fuss, I promise!' Rose vowed, but Cissie was insistent. Little as she liked it, orders were orders. She'd gently prised Wallace from Rose's arms and placed him in his crib.

Rose hadn't put up a fight, and she'd somehow managed to keep her emotions under control. She didn't want to frighten Wallace or upset him in any way, and she knew that Florrie was already in serious trouble for letting the secret slip. Things would be all the worse for her if Rose made a scene; she might even be barred from the nursery duty that meant so much to her. She'd be devastated, and it would be a great loss to the mothers and babies.

In any case, what was the use? Wallace's adoption was inevitable; Rose had to let him go. Perhaps when Aunt Mabel came on duty later she would allow her to spend a little precious time with him; it was her last hope. So she'd kept quiet, leaned over the crib to smooth his peachy cheek and kiss him one last time, and walked out with her head held high.

Later, however, the reality of it had hit her full force, and when she'd been taken to the recreation room with the others, the music and the gaiety had somehow heightened all her emotions, imbuing them with a nightmarish quality. She'd taken a seat in a far corner of the room, where the shadows were deepest, and hoped no one would notice how upset she was.

Someone had noticed, though. And that someone was Stella.

Since she had begun feeding Will again, she and Rose had become friends. Rose's resentment of her had faded away as she'd come to accept that Stella had been ill, and that was the reason for her rejection of her baby. For her part, besides feeling dreadfully sorry for Rose, Stella had grown very fond of the girl who had been treated so disgracefully.

She didn't know the full details of how her friend had come to find herself in this awful situation – Rose never talked about it – but she couldn't find it in herself to blame her in any way for what had happened. Perhaps she'd been coerced into making free with her favours – Stella had heard that sometimes lascivious employers took advantage of a pretty maid, and with the threat of dismissal hanging over their heads the girls were afraid to protest. Or perhaps she'd been infatuated with the father of her baby and unable to resist his advances. Stella knew the temptations; she well remembered occasions when she and Tom had been courting and things had come close to getting out of hand. Fortunately she'd always managed to keep her impulses in check and draw back, and Tom had respected her determination to save lovemaking for their wedding night. But it would have been easy, so easy, to give in to the powerful urges that had made her ache with desire.

But whatever the reason, it was terribly wrong for Sir Oswald Whittingly Challis to have Rose committed to the asylum, and downright wicked to arrange an adoption of the poor little baby without her consent.

Now, as she saw Rose sitting all alone and wretched, a rush of sympathy made her cross the room and sit down beside her.

'Rose? Are you all right?'

For a moment Rose didn't answer. Her head was bent, her chin resting on her chest, eyes squeezed tight shut. Then she swallowed hard and glanced at Stella, her face a mask of misery.

'Tomorrow,' she whispered. 'They're taking my baby tomorrow.'

'Oh Rose!' Stella felt tears pricking at her eyes. 'I'm so sorry.'

'They won't even let me see him again.'

Stella was lost for words. Nothing she could say would be of any comfort to Rose, and she couldn't even begin to contemplate what the poor young woman must be going through. She simply reached over and covered one of Rose's hands with her own, a small gesture of solidarity.

For a while they sat in silence, each with their own thoughts, then suddenly Rose started.

'Aunt Mabel!'

Stella followed her gaze and saw Mabel Cummings standing in the doorway, looking around the room as if searching for someone.

'She's in early tonight . . .' she began, but Rose was hastily getting to her feet.

'I have to speak to her! She might let me go up and see Wallace when Nurse Whitcombe leaves.'

'Rose . . .'

But Rose was hurrying across the room, making her way towards Mabel Cummings, and Stella could only hope the sour nurse would be able to offer her niece the comfort that she herself could not.

'Auntie Mabel! Thank goodness you're here! They're taking Wallace away tomorrow and Nurse Whitcombe won't let me see him! Please – please – will you take me up to the nursery? Tell her—'

'I'm sorry, Rose,' Mabel interrupted her niece's tearful flow. 'I came in early so as to spend some time with you both, but it seems Dr Kirkwood has said you are to have no more contact with Wallace. I can't go against him.'

Rose pressed her hands to her mouth; above it her agonised eyes were fixed on Mabel's face.

'Oh please! There must be something you can do!'

Mabel caught her by the arm, looking around to reassure herself that no one had noticed the state Rose was working herself up into. If they did, she'd be taken away and locked up for her own safety, and then heaven only knew when she'd get out of this place. Besides which, Mabel didn't want attention to be drawn to the fact that she was a witness to her niece's acute distress. It could upset her carefully laid plans. But mercifully the music and the general hubbub were drowning out Rose's anguished pleas, and everyone else was enjoying themselves too much to be aware of the scene taking place in the doorway.

'Calm yourself, Rose, or it'll be the worse for you,' Mabel warned, and added in a low tone: 'Everything is going to be all right, I promise you.'

'How can it be?' Rose sobbed.

'You just have to trust me, Rose. Now go back inside, there's a good girl.'

To her enormous relief, Rose did as she was told.

'Tom . . . I know you think I'm making something of nothing, but I'm really worried about Francie,' Grace said.

The children were in bed and she had decided she really couldn't keep her concerns about the goings-on next door to herself any longer.

Tom looked up from the *Evening Chronicle*; he'd bought it on his way home from work, but this was the first chance he'd had to read it.

'Why?'

'There was another to-do last night.'

'That's not unusual. I did warn you that sometimes they go at it hammer and tongs.'

'But it's more than that, Tom. He knocks her about.'

Tom flattened the newspaper in his lap.

'Where d'you get that from? He's a nice chap.'

'He might seem that way to you, but I don't think he's all that nice behind closed doors. Her face was in an awful state the last time – that Sunday when you were out with the children – and today I saw bruises on her arm. She tried to hide them, and then she made some excuse about catching her arm when she was making a bed or something, but she was just trying to cover it up, Tom. Those bruises were finger marks, I'm sure of it.'

Tom folded the newspaper with a sigh. 'If Noel was hitting Francie about I'd have thought Stella would know about it, but she's never mentioned it to me.'

'That's as maybe,' Grace persisted. 'I'm simply telling you what I've seen and heard with my own eyes and ears.'

Tom shook his head. 'I'm sorry, I just can't believe it. You've got hold of the wrong end of the stick. And even if you haven't, I don't know what you expect me to do about it. I can hardly go knocking on their door and tell him he's out of order.'

Grace was getting annoyed with Tom for the first time since she'd been here.

'So you think it's all right for a man to beat his wife black and blue, do you?' she flared.

'Of course I don't. But I don't think for one minute that's what Noel is doing, and I'm not about to stir up trouble with the neighbours. We have to live next door to them, remember.'

It was useless, Grace could see. She only hoped Tom wouldn't one day have to eat his words. How could men be so blind when it came to other men?

She retrieved her knitting, clacking the needles crossly as she began a new row, and Tom, seemingly unperturbed, went back to his newspaper.

Once she had watched Rose return and take her seat in the corner beside Stella Swift, Mabel Cummings went to the main door and let herself out into the garden. It was a cold night, but clear, and she wanted a few minutes alone, away from the racket that had been blasting out from the communal room. She needed to run over her plan one last time to make sure she had every eventuality covered – and she also wanted a cigarette to calm her nerves.

She pulled the packet from her bag and extracted one, then attempted to light it, but a sudden breeze blew the match out. She struck another, shielding it with her hand, which she noticed was shaking a little, and cautioned herself to calm down. Later, when she'd carried out the first part of her plan, it wouldn't matter if she showed signs of being upset. For the moment it was imperative that she appear her usual self. She could do this, and she would. For her sister Olive; for Rose, her niece; for Wallace, her great-nephew.

And to finally get her own back on that bastard Whittingly Challis for what he'd done to her. This was the first chance she'd had. Even if he didn't know it, she would know, and after all this time, revenge would be sweet indeed.

By the time she'd smoked the cigarette and ground it out under her heel, she was calmer, and all her resolve had returned. She went back inside and climbed the stairs to the nursery. Cissie was at the nurses' station, Florrie just settling a baby after changing him. As Mabel came in, Cissie looked up from the desk, her pen still poised over some paperwork.

'You saw Rose, did you? How's she taking it?'

'Hard. As you'd expect. But I've explained the situation to her and I think I've calmed her down.'

'Well, if you can't, I don't suppose anybody can.' Cissie shook her head. 'I'm just making up Wallace's notes now.'

'You may as well go on home, Cissie, seeing as I'm here,' Mabel said, and there was no hint of a tremor in her voice. 'I can finish the notes.'

'Are you sure?' Cissie felt a little guilty to be leaving before the end of her shift, but at least Mabel had Florrie to help her. It had been a long day and the thought of her warm kitchen, a cup of cocoa and bed was a tempting one. She didn't like what she was having to do either, preparing for the baby's adoption. She'd be only too glad to leave it to Mabel, though how she could bear to do it given that the baby was her own flesh and blood, Cissie didn't know. As for tomorrow morning, when they came to take him away . . . She only hoped that by the time she arrived for her shift, it would all be over.

'Yes, you go on. No sense two of us being here,' Mabel said.

'Well, all right then. Thanks.'

Cissie capped her pen and got up, leaving the notes on the desk. She fetched her coat and put it on, and picked up her bag.

Florrie was still at the far end of the nursery, bending over one of the cribs.

'Goodnight, Florrie,' she called. She nodded at Mabel. 'Goodnight, Mabel. And thanks again.'

As she headed for the stairs, Mabel took a deep breath.

It was now or never.

# Chapter Thirteen

'Matron! Matron!'

Florrie Carter came bursting into Matron Carey's office without stopping to knock first.

Matron looked up, startled, from the paperwork she had been updating, and which had kept her at her desk later than usual. It was nine thirty, and she liked to be back in her comfortable quarters with a cup of Ovaltine by this time of night, relaxing after another busy day, but the extra work generated by the adoption tomorrow of Rose Gooding's baby had taken longer than she'd anticipated.

'Florrie! Whatever—'

She got no further.

'It's Nurse Whitcombe! She's fallen down the stairs.'

Florrie was breathless, her voice panicky, her expression too, and Matron Carey couldn't help but be alarmed.

'Fallen down the stairs?' she repeated. 'What stairs?'

'The stairs from the nursery. Nurse Cummings had just relieved her and she was on her way home . . .'

Matron Carey put down her pen and rose quickly from her chair. 'Is she hurt?'

'She's out cold. We've made her as comfortable as we can, but Nurse Cummings thinks you ought to call the doctor.'

Matron Carey hesitated. She didn't want to disturb Dr Mackay at this time of night if it could be avoided.

'We'll get Dr Kirkwood to have a look at her first,' she decided.

'But he's a psychiatric doctor,' Florrie objected.

'He has a certain amount of medical training too. He'll be able to assess the seriousness of the situation, and if necessary have Nurse Whitcombe taken to the cottage hospital. I'll call him now, tell him what's happened. You get back to the nursery. Is there anyone with the babies?'

'No, the mothers are all at the sing-song. We've fed the babies. Nurse Whitcombe said she thought it was best, as Rose isn't allowed up there tonight. She thought it wouldn't be as obvious as if she was the only one who—'

Matron raised a hand to put a stop to Florrie's flow.

'Never mind all that now. Run along, and tell Nurse Cummings Dr Kirkwood will be there shortly.'

Florrie went, still looking seriously shaken up, and Matron hurried across the corridor to Dr Kirkwood's office, hoping that he too was working late. He usually was; his entire life revolved around the asylum and his patients. Though outwardly calm, her thoughts were racing. She had the most awful feeling that this was serious. It wasn't like Florrie to panic. Since she had been allowed to work in the nursery, she'd become one of the most stable of the inmates. Once, when she'd been left alone there for a few minutes, a mother had had a fit whilst feeding her baby, and it had been Florrie who had stepped in and administered first aid until the duty nurse returned and took over.

As Matron had hoped, Dr Kirkwood was indeed still at his desk, deeply immersed in a psychiatric journal.

'Matron! I thought you'd have gone off duty by now,' he greeted her.

'I'm afraid we have an incident, Doctor. Nurse Whitcombe has had a fall, a bad one, from what Florrie tells me. She's knocked herself unconscious, and whether or not she has broken bones besides, I don't know. Could you come and take a look at her? Decide what's to be done? I didn't want to call Dr Mackay out without you seeing her first.'

'Of course.'

He put the journal to one side and slipped out from behind his desk, and the two of them made their way towards the nursery.

Cissie Whitcombe lay in a heap at the foot of the steep flight of stairs, her bag, which she had dropped as she fell, spilling its contents on to the floor a few feet in front of her. One leg was twisted awkwardly beneath her not inconsiderable frame, but she was unmoving and seemingly unaware of what had happened.

Mabel Cummings was sitting on the bottom stair holding Cissie's unresponsive hand, while Florrie watched from the top, one hand pressed against her mouth, the other gripping the handrail as if she was afraid she too might go tumbling down.

Dr Kirkwood did a cursory examination and called Cissie's name to no avail.

'I think her leg is broken,' he said at last, straightening up. 'But that's the least of our worries. It would seem she's taken a nasty blow to the head, and as you know, there's no telling where that will lead. She needs to be in the cottage hospital, and the sooner the better. If we can get a porter and a stretcher, I'll take her there myself.'

Matron met Mabel's eyes and, with a nod of her head and a flick of her eyebrows, issued a silent instruction. Mabel hurried off in search of the help Dr Kirkwood had requested.

'Well, this is a pretty state of affairs,' Matron said.

Dr Kirkwood was looking at the motionless Cissie, shaking his head sorrowfully.

'These stairs are a danger to anyone who has to go up and down them. Something should have been done about them long ago. But with the nursery where it is . . .'

'Don't go blaming yourself, Hubert.' When they were alone, Matron and Dr Kirkwood often addressed one another by their Christian names. 'Those who use the stairs regularly are quite used to them. And they should know to take care.'

'A new mother might not realise . . .'

'But Cissie should. Goodness knows, she's worked here long enough.'

'Ah – poor Cissie.' Dr Kirkwood sighed deeply.

'Yes, poor Cissie,' Matron agreed.

A porter and a male nurse arrived with a stretcher, Mabel trailing behind them. Following Dr Kirkwood's precise instructions they lifted Cissie on to it with the greatest of care.

Dr Kirkwood addressed the porter. 'You'd better come with us, Franklin. I'm taking Nurse Whitcombe to the cottage hospital in our ambulance, and I could do with your assistance at the other end.'

When they had gone, Matron heaved a silent sigh of relief. Cissie was someone else's problem now and she could turn her attention to her remit – the running of the hospital.

'It's time Florrie went to her quarters,' she said briskly, and called up the stairs to the young woman, who was still standing there watching the action. 'Off you go now, Florrie. The staff will be waiting to lock up for the night.'

Somewhat reluctantly, Florrie went.

'So tell me again exactly what happened,' Matron said when she and Mabel were alone. 'Did she catch her foot? Or is it

171

possible she fainted, or even had a stroke, before she fell? How did she seem in herself when you relieved her?'

Mabel hesitated. Then: 'As far as I could tell, she was quite all right.'

'No sign at all that she might be unwell?'

'No. But . . .' Again she hesitated, as if unwilling to go on.

'What?' Matron asked sharply.

'Do you think we could go upstairs, where it's more private?' Mabel asked.

'Well, yes – if you like.' When they'd climbed the stairs to the nursery, Matron turned to Mabel. 'Go on, Nurse. What is it that you have to say?'

Mabel swallowed hard, then met Matron's eyes.

'There's something you should know. I don't like telling tales, but this is too serious to keep to myself. I think Florrie pushed her.'

'*Pushed* her?' Matron repeated, flabbergasted.

'I was down at the other end of the nursery, but Florrie was right behind her at the top of the stairs. And I'd swear on my life she gave her a shove.'

'Surely not!' Matron was horrified. 'Why would she do that?'

'You know the patients can be unpredictable, especially when there's a full moon. And she and Cissie had been having some kind of set-to – I'd come in early, hoping to spend some time with little Wallace before he's taken away for adoption, and I could hear it going on as I came up the stairs. When she realised I was there, Cissie told Florrie she'd say no more about it – whatever "it" was – but I could see Florrie was in a proper temper, banging things about, with a face like thunder.'

'That doesn't sound like Florrie,' Matron ventured.

'She's been acting very peculiar lately,' Mabel said. 'Getting things wrong, and then flying off the handle when she's told about it. I expect it was something like that set her off tonight. Cissie was reprimanding her, and she didn't like it. Thought maybe she'd lose her position up here if Cissie was to come to you about her behaviour.'

'And she should have done, of course. And so should you. We need to know these things.'

Mabel hung her head. 'Well, I can see that now. But Cissie has a soft heart; she knows how much it means to Florrie working up here, and I expect she thought it was just a phase she was going through. I thought the same. But now . . . well, I only wish I'd reported what was going on. If I had, poor Cissie wouldn't be on her way to hospital. And the babies . . . well, you can't have someone taking care of them who could do something like that, can you?'

'That should have been obvious to both you and Cissie,' Matron said sternly. 'I shall report all this to Dr Kirkwood and he will deal with it as he thinks fit. But as you so rightly say, there is no way Florrie can be allowed to continue working in the nursery.'

'So what's going to happen tomorrow, with neither Cissie nor Florrie here?' Mabel asked. 'I could stay on a bit beyond my shift if that would help, but . . .'

'I'd be grateful if you would, Nurse Cummings. Just until I can arrange for one of the other nurses to cover for Cissie. At this moment I'm not sure who that will be, but I shall be looking for a suitably qualified nursery nurse to take over for the foreseeable future. I think it's going to be some time before poor Cissie is able to resume her duties – if ever she is.'

'That's the trouble with the older ones,' Mabel remarked. 'Recovery time is so much longer when anything goes wrong. And to be honest, I've wondered for some time if Cissie is really up to what has to be done. It might be a good thing if she took retirement and you employed someone younger in her place.'

'That, Nurse Cummings, is for me to worry about,' Matron said crisply. 'Now, perhaps you can carry on with your duties, and we'll hope for a quiet night from now on.'

'Let's hope so,' Mabel agreed.

A quiet night, when she would be undisturbed, was exactly what she was hoping for. There was still a great deal to do before the adoptive parents arrived to take the baby away.

Making sure the coast was clear and Matron had actually gone, Mabel returned to the nursery and approached the cribs. Being careful not to disturb the babies, she removed the ankle tags from both Wallace and William Swift and swapped them over. Then she gently placed the infants in each other's cribs. She was confident no one would notice they had been moved. Florrie would have, of course, but Florrie was no longer a threat. Mabel had taken care of that. By pushing Cissie down the stairs and then throwing the blame on to Florrie, she had effectively killed two birds with one stone. As for Stella, when she said the baby she'd been given to feed wasn't hers, nobody would believe her. They'd just think she had suffered a relapse. Now all that remained was to make the necessary alterations to the babies' records.

So far everything had gone according to plan. There were elements that were outside her immediate control – a part of her scheme that she'd had to delegate to Frank Gooding, her brother-in-law – and she wasn't going to count her chickens just yet. But she had every hope that things would work out as she'd planned.

A satisfied smile twisted Mabel's mouth to think that not only would she know the whereabouts of Rose's baby, but at the same time she had managed to get the better of that bastard Sir Oswald Whittingly Challis.

* * *

'Auntie Grace . . .'

Grace emerged reluctantly through layers of sleep to feel a little hand shaking her arm. It had taken her a long time to drop off last night; her emotions had been churning again, and all because of Tom.

She'd been very quiet after the conversation she'd had with him about her suspicions as to what was going on next door, annoyed with him for making light of what she saw as a very serious situation, and after a while he'd noticed.

'You're not still stewing about Francie and Noel, are you?' he'd asked when she'd handed him his nightly cup of cocoa without a word.

She'd sat down in the easy chair on the opposite side of the fire to his, cradling her own cup between her hands.

'I can't help worrying about her,' she'd said defensively.

'You know your trouble, Grace? You've got too kind a heart. Sometimes it seems you're carrying all the troubles of the world on your shoulders.'

'How can anyone not care about others?' she'd demanded.

'But you care too much. You can't solve everyone's problems, my love, and sometimes you just have to accept that.'

'I know. And I know it's not our place to interfere . . .' Her cheeks were burning suddenly. He'd called her 'my love'. And he was looking at her the same way he'd looked at her yesterday evening, with that warmth in his eyes that set her pulses racing, made that nerve deep inside her twist and tingle.

The moment had passed so quickly that she told herself she must have imagined it. But in the solitude of Emily's room, when she'd gone to bed, it kept playing and replaying, over and over, in her mind. His words. That look. She really didn't think she had imagined it, and though a treacherous part of her delighted in it, it also frightened her.

Something was being rekindled between her and Tom, and it mustn't happen. It would only lead to trouble and heartbreak. As long as it was only her revisiting the feelings she'd had for him all those years ago, it wasn't so bad. She could control that. But if Tom was feeling the same way . . .

She'd heard the mantel clock downstairs chime eleven, and then midnight, before at last sleep claimed her. But even then he'd been there in her dreams. They were at the fair, in the swing boats, happy and laughing, and then quite suddenly she was afraid. 'Stop it, Tom!' she'd said. 'You'll tip us over!' But he hadn't taken any notice and they'd swung higher and higher while the fields and the sky turned crazy somersaults and she clung on with all her might, because if she didn't, something awful was going to happen . . .

'Auntie Grace!' The whisper came again.

Grace opened her eyes, and by the light of the full moon streaming in through the half-open curtains she saw Emily beside the bed.

Somehow she shook off the dream and the echoes of all the thoughts she'd been having before she finally fell asleep.

'What's wrong, Emily?'

'I'm scared. I had a bad dream.'

You and me both, Grace thought.

'And there's a monster in the room.'

'Of course there's not, darling!'

'There is! He was sitting on the end of my bed! Please – can I come in with you?'

Grace only hesitated for a moment. 'Just as long as you don't make a habit of it.'

'I won't. Just tonight. Until the monster goes away.'

Grace turned back the covers and the little girl clambered in and snuggled down beside her.

'Go back to sleep now.'

In no time at all, it seemed, Emily's breathing grew slow and even and she was asleep again, her thumb in her mouth, her head tucked into Grace's shoulder.

If only everything could be taken care of so easily! Grace thought.

But there was a warmth spreading through her that didn't just come from Emily's firm little body curled around hers. Emily had come to her when she was frightened. She hadn't gone to her father, or wakened her brothers. If Stella was here, it would have been her she turned to, but Stella wasn't here, and so Emily had come to Grace. She'd been fully accepted as a surrogate mother, and it made her happier and more proud than she could have imagined.

If only it could last for ever! she thought. And hated herself for thinking it for even one moment.

Matron Carey was still in her office when she heard the asylum ambulance crunch along the gravel on the drive outside her window. She'd gone to her quarters, made a cup of Ovaltine and brought it back with her, but it hadn't tasted as good as it did in the comfort of her own armchair, perhaps because of the bad taste her conversation with Mabel Cummings had left in her mouth. She'd pushed the cup to one side, and now it sat on her desk, the top and sides congealed with cold scum, as repellent as what Mabel had told her.

Bad enough that poor Cissie should have had such a dreadful accident, if an accident it had been, but to think it could have been the result of Florrie Carter deliberately pushing her was infinitely worse. She'd trusted Florrie, believed that when she had abducted that baby all those years ago she had been suffering from puerperal fever, and was now as sane as anyone else; she had persuaded Dr Kirkwood to allow her to work in the nursery. How could she have been so wrong? And how had they all missed the signs that Florrie possessed such a violent streak?

There was no way now that she would be able to concentrate on the reports she'd been working on when Florrie had come bursting into her office; they'd have to wait until morning. She stacked them up neatly at the back of her desk and sat massaging her left temple, where a headache had begun to throb, while she waited for Dr Kirkwood to return.

Now, as she heard the ambulance on the drive, she got up and went out to meet him.

'How are things?' she asked as he came in.

'Not good. As I suspected, her leg is broken, rather badly, and as far as I'm aware, she hasn't regained consciousness. The doctor at the cottage hospital felt she needed more specialist care than they can offer, and she's been transferred to the Royal United Hospital in Bath.' He turned to the porter who had accompanied him. 'Thank you, Franklin. That will be all.'

'Dear, dear, dear.' Matron shook her head, her face grim.

'As I said, not good. But there was no need for you to have waited up, Maude. There's nothing you – or any of us – can do. Why don't you get off to your bed now?'

He looked tired out, she thought, and worried, and she wished she didn't have to make things worse for him.

'I'm afraid I need to talk to you, Hubert. There's been a development. Can we go into your office?'

His eyes narrowed.

'Yes, yes, of course.'

He took off his coat and hung it on the back of the door, then sat in his captain's chair while Matron took a seat opposite him. As she told him everything Mabel had said, she saw the lines around his mouth deepen.

'And Nurse Cummings is certain about this, is she?'

'As certain as she can be. Florrie has been behaving erratically for some time, she said, but she hadn't said anything about it because she believed it was just a phase that would pass. We should have been told, of course, but nevertheless, I blame myself. I've not watched her as closely as I should have done. She's still a patient, when all's said and done.'

'You're not to blame, Maude. As you say, she is a patient, and ultimately my responsibility. I'll see her tomorrow – there's nothing more that can be done tonight. But clearly she can't be allowed in the nursery again until we are quite satisfied that she is fit to be there. Perhaps you'd have a word with the night staff and ask them to also pass it on to the day nurses when they come on duty. Under no circumstances is Florrie to be allowed anywhere near the babies. And they should ensure that there is a male nurse or orderly on hand in case she becomes violent again. When you've done that, I suggest you try to get some rest.'

Matron left to do as Dr Kirkwood had asked. Her headache was worsening by the minute and she felt old, leaden and bone tired. But somehow she thought it would be a long time before she was able to sleep.

'What in the world . . . ?'

As the sound of a loud explosion rattled the windows and echoed through the house, Jessica woke abruptly from a light doze – the baby she was carrying had been pressing on a nerve, making her restless. Beside her, Alistair, always a heavy sleeper, was still snoring gently.

At first she thought she must have been dreaming. But a strange flickering light was coming through the slight gap in the curtains and intermittently lighting up the dark bedroom.

Puzzled, she slid out from beneath the covers and padded to the window. Another bang, and another – not as loud as the one that had woken her, but enough to make her really alarmed – rocked the night. She pulled the curtains aside and gasped in horror. The road was almost obscured by thick black smoke shot through with bursts of vermilion and orange flame, which seemed to be coming from a spot on the kerb just outside the house.

It took a moment for her fuzzy brain to realise – that was where Alistair parked his motor! And she could just make out the shape of it in the centre of the inferno.

'Alistair!' She rushed to the bed, almost tripping over the rag rug in her haste, and shook her husband by the shoulder. 'Alistair! Wake up!'

Alistair came to with a start.

'What . . . ?'

'The motor's on fire! Wake up! Wake up!'

Still half asleep, Alistair stumbled out of bed and followed her to the window. The sight that met his eyes quickly shook off the last vestiges of sleep.

'Oh dear God!'

There was a telephone on the bedside table, installed so that he could be called to patients who might need him during the night. He hurried to pick it up, dialling the number of the police station by feeling for the numbered buttons in the flickering darkness. It would be up to the sergeant or constable on night duty to summon the men who made up the retained fire brigade.

Jessica stood transfixed with horror, her hand pressed to her mouth. Sparks and bits of burning material were being blown about by the stiff wind. Suppose one of them flew on to the roof and set it alight? Her heart was thudding and she was shaking with the shock of being awakened to this living nightmare.

Alistair finished his telephone call and grabbed his trousers from the chair beside the bed where he had left them when he had come in last night, too exhausted from treating a desperately ill patient to do anything but fall into bed and sleep.

'What are you doing?' Jessica's voice was shrill with panic – she had visions of him trying to put out the fire himself. 'Wait for the fire brigade!'

'I can hardly go out and meet them in my nightshirt, can I?' He was stuffing his feet into his shoes now.

'Just don't do anything silly.'

'Don't worry, I won't. And you'd better put some clothes on too. You'll catch your death.'

It was true, she was shivering violently, and not just from shock and fear. She fetched her warm woollen dressing gown from its hook on the bedroom door and wrapped herself up in it, tying the cord securely about her rounded waistline.

Now fully clothed, Alistair headed for the door.

'Put the kettle on and make a good strong cup of tea,' he instructed her.

Then he was gone, and Jessica found herself drawn back to the window as if by a giant magnet. She saw Alistair emerge on to the path, a spectral shape against the billowing smoke and the flames that still danced fiercely. Her heart thudded in her throat again, but he did not go any closer, simply stood there watching what was left of his beloved car burn.

With an effort, Jessica wrenched herself away from the window and went downstairs to stir the living room fire to reluctant light and set the kettle on the hob to heat the water for the tea.

\* \* \*

As a pink and grey dawn lightened the sky, the two of them sat glumly at the dining table with yet more cups of tea within easy reach. It had seemed an age before the fire brigade had arrived, bell clanging, though in fact they had made miraculously good time given that all the volunteer firemen had had to be roused from their beds and make their way to the fire station. It had been far too late, however, to do anything to save the motor, which was now just a sad skeleton, dripping water on to the road from the bare bones of the chassis.

'How on earth did it happen?' Jessica asked.

Alistair shook his head. 'Who knows? A mechanical fault, perhaps? But there was no sign of anything wrong when I got home just before midnight, and it was about two, wasn't it, when you woke me? I'd have thought it would have caught fire much sooner than that, while the engine was still hot.'

'You weren't having a pipe on the way home, were you?'

'I did have a smoke, yes.' Alistair was fond of his pipe, especially when he'd been dealing with a difficult case. It helped him to relax, he had found.

'Might you have dropped some hot ash? It could have smouldered for ages if you did.'

Alistair thought about it. 'Possible, I suppose. But highly unlikely.'

'If you were tired, it could have happened without you noticing. Or what about the match you lit it with?'

'I would have put that in the ashtray.'

'If there was fluff in the ashtray, or a scrap of paper, and the match wasn't properly out . . .'

'I'd have smelled it.'

'Then what?'

'I don't know, Jessica, and it's a waste of time conjecturing. More to the point, how am I going to manage without the motor?

I'll have to see about getting another, but it might take a while to find anything suitable and within our budget. In the meantime, I've got to get to patients all over the district, some miles out in the country. Mrs Sobey, for one.' Mrs Sobey was the woman he'd been attending until late last night. 'I promised to call back today, but there's no way I can do it on Shanks's pony.'

'There's your bicycle.'

'I haven't ridden it for years. The tyres will be flat, and it's probably all rusted up.'

'Mine then.' Jessica had used her bicycle for getting around Hillsbridge right up until Constance was born, and even after-wards when Alistair was at home to look after the little girl. 'And it's got the basket. You could balance your medical bag on that.'

'I don't suppose I've got much choice. But what are people going to think? The doctor arriving on a ladies' bike, wobbling about as he tries to balance his medical bag in front of him? Bit of a come-down, isn't it?'

A giggle she was unable to suppress began in Jessica's throat as she pictured it.

'Oh Alistair . . .'

'I'm glad you think it's funny.'

But he was laughing too. Reaction to the events of the night had set in and resulted in uncontrollable mirth. For a few min-utes they laughed together; as one stopped, the other set them off again. By the time they were sober again, neither really knew what it had all been about. Only that if they hadn't laughed, they would have cried.

Alistair's beloved motor, of which he was so proud, had been reduced to a heap of scrap metal, and it was going to be very difficult for him to do his job. It was really no laughing matter at all.

# *Chapter Fourteen*

'Florrie Carter! Where do you think you're going?'

Mabel Cummings was at the head of the nursery staircase, arms akimbo, her bulky form blocking Florrie's way.

The nurse who had come to unlock the women's bungalow and supervise the patients while they washed and dressed had somehow missed the instruction that Florrie was not to go to the nursery this morning, and had raised no objection to her leaving as she always did to go and help with the early feeds.

Florrie frowned, confused.

'What do you mean? To the nursery, of course.'

'Oh no you're not. Haven't you been told? You're not to come up here again.'

'What? But why?' Florrie's expression of surprise and puzzlement turned to one of dismay.

'I think you know very well. But it's not up to me to tell you. Matron will do that. Mark my words, my girl, she'll be wanting a word with you when she comes in.'

'But I don't understand . . .'

'Just go back to the bungalow. I won't tell you again.'

Puzzled, indignant and upset, Florrie had no choice but to do as she was told.

What was Nurse Cummings talking about? She hadn't done

anything wrong that she could think of. But if she wasn't to be allowed to work in the nursery any more . . . Tears of shock and anxiety sprang to Florrie's eyes. Helping to look after the babies was her whole world. If that was taken away from her, life wouldn't be worth living.

Sick at heart and trembling with suppressed emotion, Rose followed the other women into the dining hall for breakfast. Not that she would be able to eat a thing. Her stomach was churning and her mouth dry. Although she'd known this day must come, now that it had, it felt as if she was living a nightmare. Wallace was going to be taken away – heaven only knew where – and she would never see him again. She hadn't slept a wink for thinking about it, and Aunt Mabel's vague assurances that everything would be all right had done nothing to comfort her. They had just been placatory, she felt sure, simply words to calm her down. There was nothing Aunt Mabel or anyone else could do to stop this happening, and Rose felt her heart was breaking.

Ahead of her in the queue to collect their porridge was Daisy Spiller, who continually brushed herself down and raked her fingers through her hair, convinced she was covered in downy feathers, as if she'd been plucking a chicken, or her pillow had burst. This morning, as her elbow jabbed repeatedly into Rose's ribs, Rose wanted to scream.

'Stop it, Daisy!' she hissed, grabbing the offending elbow, but Daisy only jerked it away and began the repetitive motion all over again.

'Got to get rid of them!' she hissed back.

When Rose reached the head of the queue, the orderly manning the serving station flopped a dollop of porridge into her bowl, almost missing the target as she watched a disturbance that had begun on the far side of the dining room. The crazy old man who sometimes got it into his head that he was being poisoned had begun throwing his food about, splattering other patients, and all the nurses had hurried to contain the situation. If they keep me here much longer, I'll be as mad as them, Rose thought wretchedly.

It was as she was walking back to take her place at the long table that she saw it. A big chauffeur-driven motor drawn up outside the main entrance, its doors standing open. Her heart leapt into her throat. No, surely not – they wouldn't be here already to take Wallace away, would they?

But as she stood staring in horror, three figures emerged from the doorway – a smartly dressed gentleman carrying a cane, a middle-aged woman in a dark coat buttoned tightly around her plump form, and following them, Auntie Mabel with baby Wallace in her arms. The gentleman helped the woman into the motor and stood aside while Aunt Mabel approached with the baby.

She was going to hand him over to the woman! Rose could scarcely believe it.

A cry escaped her, and the self-control she'd been so determined to exert snapped like an elastic band. The breakfast tray clattered to the floor and Rose ran towards the door, unguarded because all the nurses were dealing with the rumpus the old man was kicking up. Alerted by the crash of the falling tray, one of them started in her direction, but Rose was too quick for him. She pushed past Daisy, darted around the long table, and was out in the hallway before anyone could stop her. A nurse coming in the opposite direction tried to bar her path, but a desperate Rose gave her a quick hard shove, and as the nurse staggered against the wall, she raced on, into the central entrance hall and out of the front door.

Only to see the motor pulling away.

'Stop!' she cried. 'Stop! Stop!'

'Rose!' Aunt Mabel, who was standing at the foot of the steps, caught at her arm, but Rose shook her off, running after the departing motor as fast as her legs would carry her. Yet however hard she ran, there was no way she could catch it. It was gathering speed now as it headed towards the road. Her boot skidded on a patch of loose gravel, and unable to save herself, she fell headlong on the drive, before staggering to her feet again, almost hysterical, as the motor turned out between the stone gate pillars and was lost to sight.

She covered her face with her hands, breathless and sobbing. Her palms were skinned, and beneath her muddied skirts her knee was dripping blood down her shin, but she scarcely noticed. There was only one thought in her mind. Her baby. They had taken her baby.

'Rose.' Aunt Mabel was beside her, putting an arm around her shaking shoulders. 'Oh Rose, my dear, look at the state of you!'

Rose couldn't speak. She stood staring at the empty driveway, tears pouring down her cheeks.

'You shouldn't have seen that. Come on, let's get you back inside.'

Only then did Rose look at her aunt, raising anguished, tear-filled eyes to her face.

'How could you hand him over?'

'I told you, Rose. It's going to be all right. I've taken care of everything.' Mabel's voice was low and urgent, but Rose still stared at her, unhearing, uncomprehending.

Then two other nurses appeared in the doorway, one a burly male nurse, who came hurrying down the steps and took Rose's arm.

'Let's be having you, miss,' he said, firmly but kindly, and there was nothing Rose could do but allow herself to be led back inside.

Mabel followed, wishing she could have told Rose what she had done. But there had been no opportunity, and in any case, it was too dangerous. She needed Rose to continue to behave as if her son really had gone to unknown adoptive parents, so that when questions arose, as they inevitably would, there would be nothing in her demeanour to arouse suspicion. She'd know soon enough, when she was signed out of the asylum, as Mabel was confident she would be once Sir Oswald Whittingly Challis was sure she could cause him no more trouble. For the moment, though, she had to be kept in the dark.

As she went back upstairs to the nursery, Mabel allowed herself a moment's grim satisfaction. So far everything had gone according to plan. She'd taken care of everything at this end; she only hoped Frank, Rose's father, had been able to do his part and disable Dr Mackay's motor. The doctor was someone else who must be kept away from the nursery at all costs, and without his motor he'd be very unlikely to make the journey to Catcombe. A doctor from the immediate surrounding area would have to take over any medical matters for the foreseeable future, a doctor who was unfamiliar with the mothers and babies. How long it would be before Dr Mackay found himself alternative transport she didn't know, but she hoped it would be long enough for him to have forgotten what Baby Swift looked like. They grew so quickly, babies, changing all the time.

What would they all say if they knew what she'd done? she wondered, and allowed herself a small twisted smile. She could pretend to herself for all she was worth that she had done this for her sister and her niece, but the truth was she'd enjoyed it.

Enjoyed putting one over on all of them. And especially that bastard Whittingly Challis.

She'd waited a long time for her revenge, but it was all the sweeter for that.

'Florrie Carter – you're wanted in Matron's office.'

One of the male nurses had come into the sewing room where Florrie had been put to work stitching pillowcases, a job she knew she was going to hate. Sewing had never come easily to her – 'All you're fit for is a long stitch and a lie flat,' her mother used to say, describing her untidy efforts. And working on a machine was just as bad. The nurse in charge had had to show her how to thread it several times, and still she wasn't sure she'd be able to manage it when the time came to change the cotton. She couldn't seem to keep the fabric straight either; it kept rucking up and getting caught in the bobbin. So it came almost as a relief to be summoned to Matron's office, not only a respite but a chance to plead her case and find out why she'd been barred from the nursery. It must be a mistake, she felt sure, an order issued when Matron had been worried about Cissie and didn't know whether she was coming or going.

How was Cissie? she wondered as the male nurse escorted her along the corridor. She hoped it wasn't as serious as it had looked from her viewpoint at the top of the stairs. She liked Cissie, who had always been kind to her, and she didn't like to think she might be badly hurt.

The male nurse knocked on the door of Matron's office and opened it when bidden, and as he ushered her inside, Florrie was surprised to see Dr Kirkwood there too, leaning against a big filing cabinet. Matron's chair was swivelled in his direction, and Florrie guessed they had been having a serious discussion about something.

'Come in, Florrie. Sit down,' Matron said, and to the nurse: 'Thank you, Simkins, that will be all.'

The nurse left, closing the door behind him, and Florrie felt two pairs of eyes trained on her face. She glanced from Matron to Dr Kirkwood; both were wearing grim expressions.

'Is Cissie . . . ?' She had begun to feel very apprehensive.

Her question was ignored.

'Perhaps you would like to tell us in your own words what happened last night,' Matron said. Her tone was stern, making Florrie feel very uncomfortable.

'Well, Cissie – Nurse Whitcombe – fell down the stairs. That's all I know.'

'I'm sure you can do better than that.'

Florrie shook her head. 'I'm sorry, I can't. I was down the other end of the nursery with the babies. I just heard a commotion, that's all.'

Matron glanced at Dr Kirkwood. Her mouth was set in a grim line, her eyebrows slightly raised.

Dr Kirkwood straightened up. 'A very serious allegation has been made, Florrie. Matron and I would like to hear your side of it.'

'An allegation?' Florrie repeated, puzzled. 'Who by?'

'Never mind that for the moment. I'll ask you again – where were you when Nurse Whitcombe fell?'

'I told you – seeing to the babies.' Florrie was beginning to feel alarmed as well as puzzled. 'I didn't see anything.'

Dr Kirkwood moved to Matron's desk, placed both hands on the corner and leaned forward so that his eyes were level with Florrie's.

'Nurse Cummings has told us that it was she who was attending to the babies and that you were at the nurses' station, arguing with Nurse Whitcombe. She'd also heard you having a disagreement when she arrived, and presumed you were taking it up again with Nurse Whitcombe before she left. Now, in the light of that, would you like to change your story?'

Florrie's mouth had fallen open and her eyes had gone wide.

'But that's not true! There was no disagreement between me and Cissie, and I *was* down the other end of the nursery like I told you.'

'So you are denying that you pushed Nurse Whitcombe down the stairs?'

'What?' Florrie half rose from her chair, her knuckles white as she gripped the edge of the desk.

'Sit down, please, Florrie, and reconsider what you have told us. If you are truthful, it will be all the better for you. Accepting responsibility for your actions is a big step in the right direction.'

'Listen to what Dr Kirkwood says,' Matron advised grimly.

'But I didn't . . . I was nowhere near Nurse Whitcombe when she fell. Why would Nurse Cummings say such a thing?'

Dr Kirkwood sighed. 'Why indeed?' He turned to Matron. 'Sadly it seems you were right, Matron, to remove Florrie from her nursery duties.'

'But . . .' Florrie was shaking now from head to foot. 'I didn't do anything of the sort! I didn't—'

'Until you are able to face up to what you did, Florrie, I'm afraid we are going to have you restrained. We can't have you putting the other patients at risk.' The superintendent crossed to the door, and called to the male nurse, who had been waiting outside. 'Simkins, would you escort Florrie to the secure rooms? And make sure there is nothing in her possession with which she could harm herself or anyone else.'

'Yes, sir. Very good, sir.'

He put a big hand under Florrie's elbow, easing her away from the desk and towards the door.

'We'll talk again very soon, Florrie,' Dr Kirkwood said. 'In the meantime, I suggest you do some serious thinking. To say I'm disappointed in you would be to understate my feelings at this moment. I only hope you will be ready soon to admit both to yourself and to me what you did, and then we can begin to put things right again.'

Dazed, indignant and horrified, Florrie had no choice but to let the nurse lead her away.

Mabel Cummings had stayed on duty until one of the day shift was sent to relieve her. She had said she was willing to do so to ensure the smooth running of the hospital, but in fact she was anxious to make sure that Florrie would not be allowed to return to the nursery. She was fairly sure that given her accusation, that would not happen, but in her opinion Dr Kirkwood was often far too soft where the patients were concerned, and for her own peace of mind she needed to know that he had not overruled Matron's order. Once she was satisfied that this hadn't happened, she had left the nursery, retrieved her bicycle and ridden away.

It had been a long night and Mabel would be glad to fall into bed – the bed that had been hers alone since her husband had died many years ago. But there was one more thing she needed to do before she could sleep easy – call on her sister to reassure herself that Frank had done what she'd asked him to do. Their cottage was on her way home, and though Frank would be at work, Olive would know if he'd carried out his part of her scheme.

When she'd knocked at the door, then walked in, calling out: 'It's only me!' she'd found Olive on her knees sweeping down the stairs.

'Well?' she asked without preamble. 'Did everything go off as planned?'

'Yes, thank the Lord.' Olive got up, the dustpan and brush in her hands. 'I was glad when he got home, though. He was gone a long time, and I was thinking all sorts. What if he'd been stopped by a bobby? How would he explain a can of petrol? Or if it had gone up too quick and he'd got burned?'

'Well, he didn't, did he?'

'No, but it was an awful risk to take.'

'Worth it, though.'

'That's easy for you to say. I haven't got your nerve, Mabel. Never did have.'

'It's a good thing, then, that one of us is blessed that way.'

'I suppose . . .'

Olive had a conscience where Mabel did not. Distraught as she was at the thought of losing her first grandchild, she had been reluctant to go along with what Mabel had suggested. Too many people were going to get hurt for her liking. But Frank had taken Mabel's side, arguing that the only one that mattered was Rose, and eventually she'd gone along with it, even though she suspected Mabel was driven as much by a desire for revenge for what had happened long ago as she was by consideration for Rose and herself.

Now she could barely bring herself to look at her sister.

'You'd better get off to bed or you won't be fit to go to work tonight,' she said.

'As long as you're sure . . .'

'I'm sure. He was tired out after riding his bike all that way, and he stank of petrol.'

'That's all right then. We aren't out of the woods yet, but we're well on the way.' Mabel opened the front door. 'I'll be off now, but I'll keep you posted.'

As she remounted her bicycle, she allowed herself a small smirk. Who did that Dr Mackay think he was anyway, riding about in a bloomin' motor! And always knowing better than anybody else what was wrong with the babies, as if she and the other nurses were stupid. She'd been caring for babies when he was still in short trousers!

Satisfied with herself, Mabel pedalled off in the direction of her own cottage.

Miranda Donaghue was at her bedroom window when the motor pulled into the drive. She'd been watching for its arrival for the past hour or more, unable to settle to anything. Now she ran down the stairs so quickly that she tripped on the bottom riser and almost fell, but managed to save herself just in time by grabbing the banister. As she opened the front door, her pretty face was alive with eagerness.

Winston, her husband, was first out of the motor, and Madge Tyler, the woman they had taken on as the baby's nanny, handed him a bundle wrapped in the blue blanket Miranda had chosen. She ran down the steps, unable to wait a moment longer.

'Go back inside,' Winston instructed her. 'It's a cold wind, and we don't want the baby taking a chill.'

All of a flutter, Miranda did as she was told, and Winston walked briskly towards the house, carrying the baby. He looked quite comfortable with it already! Miranda thought, pleased, but all she really wanted was to see the new arrival and hold him herself.

'Here you are then,' Winston said, smiling at her eagerness. 'The new little son you've been longing for.'

He placed the baby in her waiting arms, and Miranda felt a thrill of happiness as she looked down for the first time into the perfect little face nestling between the folds of the blanket. His eyes were closed – the motion of the motor had sent him to sleep – and a fringe of thick dark lashes lay on his peachy cheek.

'Oh, he's so beautiful!' she gasped, tears of joy springing to her eyes.

'Let's go in, then,' Winston said. 'If you sit down, you'll be able to nurse him properly.'

The nanny had joined them now, and she too was smiling with satisfaction.

'He's a bonny little lad, isn't he?'

'Oh he is! He is!' Still staring into the baby's face, Miranda walked carefully into the drawing room and sat down in one of the heavily brocaded armchairs, where she proceeded to unwrap the blanket, the better to see the longed-for arrival.

'Just one thing,' Madge Tyler cautioned. 'The nurse said to keep him tightly swaddled when he's asleep.'

'Oh!' Miranda glanced up at her. 'Why?'

'That's the way he likes it, she said.'

Winston sat down on the arm of the chair and put his arm around Miranda's shoulders.

'Happy, my love?'

'Oh Winston, yes! Thank you so much.' Her eyes were still brimming with happy tears.

'What for?' he asked, smiling.

'For arranging all this, of course! For being prepared to take on a baby that's not your own. For . . . well, for everything. We're a proper family at last!'

'If you're happy, Miranda, then so am I.'

'If you'll excuse me, I'll just check that everything's fine and dandy in the nursery,' Madge bustled out, giving the new parents some privacy to enjoy the first moments with the much longed-for baby.

It was past noon when a nurse came to collect the mothers to go up to the nursery to feed their babies.

Stella went eagerly; she couldn't understand why they hadn't been called before and had been feeling very anxious. There were whispers that something terrible had happened during the night, and although the grapevine said it was Nurse Whitcombe who had been hurt, she couldn't help worrying that something had happened to one of the babies.

When she entered the nursery, she was surprised to see that the chairs had been arranged in a semicircle near the nurses' station, rather than along the row of cribs as they usually were. Presumably the nurse who was covering for Nurse Whitcombe had her own ideas about the best way of running the feeding session.

Stella took a seat between Marie Mears and Louie Hillman, and Joanie Fry, the relief nurse, began bringing the babies to their mothers. Stella waited impatiently; her breasts felt heavy and full, and she was aching for Will. At last Nurse Fry headed in her direction and placed the tightly wrapped bundle in her arms.

Stella loosened the swaddling a little to give Will some freedom – whatever had been troubling him in the early weeks seemed much better now, and he no longer fell asleep the minute he was at her breast. Then, as she looked down into his face, she frowned.

'Nurse!' she called.

Joanie Fry was on her way back with little Gwen Mears. 'What is it?' she asked.

'You've given me the wrong baby.'

Joanie placed Gwen in Marie's lap and turned to Stella, wondering if she had made a mistake. This was, after all, her first day on duty in the nursery. She unwrapped the baby fully and looked at the name tag that was fixed around his ankle.

'No, this is your baby, Mrs Swift.'

'It's not!' Stella insisted. 'Do you think I don't know my own son?'

'See for yourself.' Joanie indicated the name tag.

Stella stared at it in disbelief. 'There must be some mistake. This isn't Will, I tell you.'

'And I'm telling you, I got this baby out of the cot with your name on it, and his name tag is right there on his ankle. Now, are you going to feed him or not?'

'No!' Stella was becoming extremely agitated. She pushed the baby away from her, forcing Joanie to take him or risk him falling to the floor. 'I'm not feeding *him*. He's not my baby.' She got up, barging into Joanie and heading down the nursery in the direction of the cribs. 'Where's my Will?'

This was fast becoming a situation that was too much for Joanie to handle alone. She crossed to the head of the stairs and pulled on the bell rope to summon assistance.

Stella had checked the cribs and was trying to look at the faces of each of the feeding babies when help arrived in the form of a male nurse and an orderly.

'I can't control her,' Joanie told them. 'She's refusing to feed her baby, says he's not hers, and she's disturbing all the other mothers. Can you get her out of here, please?'

The male nurse took Stella's arm, pulling her away from the mothers and babies.

'Come on, missus. We can't have this now, can we?'

By this time Stella was almost hysterical. 'I can't find my baby! Where is he? What have you done with him?'

Joanie and the male nurse exchanged a look. What a morning this was turning out to be!

'Don't worry, we'll handle her,' the male nurse said. 'We'll take her downstairs, out of your way, and give her something to calm her down until Dr Kirkwood has a chance to look at her.'

Between them, he and the orderly marched Stella to the stairs. That was when she began to scream.

'Dear, dear, dear,' the orderly said once they had manhandled her to a secure room. 'And she was supposed to be better, and due to go home soon too.'

'Doesn't look as if that's going to happen any time soon,' the male nurse replied.

# Chapter Fifteen

'You'm quiet today, Tom.'

The gang of colliers and a carting boy who had been hard at work since the crack of dawn had stopped for a drink of tea and a bite of breakfast. They crouched side by side in the dimly lit passageway close to the coal face and far beneath the green fields of Somerset, each clutching a bottle of tea and their snap, in most cases a hunk of bread and jam, though Danny Barton, the miner who had spoken, was tucking into the wedge of cheese that was meant for his dinner.

'He ain't never got much to say for himself,' Jimmy Wheeler, the carting boy, remarked breezily.

'Don't you be so cheeky,' Walter Wheeler, his father, reprimanded him. 'And leave the bloke alone, can't you? He's got a lot on his plate, worrying about his wife.'

'Ah, sorry, mate.' Jimmy tossed a crumb of bread in the direction of a mouse that had scented food and crept out from somewhere.

'Don't encourage the blighter,' Danny warned him, though he was as bad as the others for feeding the mice.

'How's she doing, Tom?' Walter asked.

'Improving, according to the doctor,' Tom replied. 'He seems to think she'll be fit to come home soon.'

He unstoppered his bottle, took a swig of tea and fell silent again.

As Jimmy had observed, Tom was always a man of few words, but even if he had been the chatty sort, he wouldn't have come clean about the real reason he was even less communicative than usual today, or that it wasn't his wife that was preoccupying him, but Grace.

He couldn't get her out of his head, darn it. Couldn't stop thinking about her. God only knew he'd tried, but still she sneaked back into his thoughts. He wasn't sure when it had started, but certainly when he'd asked her to come and help out with the children while Stella was in hospital, it had never occurred to him that she might have this effect on him. If it had, he'd have looked for some other way to manage, though he didn't know what. This resurrection of his old feelings for her had crept up on him and caught him unawares.

Perhaps it was gratitude for all she was doing that was making him feel this way. She'd been an absolute treasure, cleaning, washing, putting meals on the table, and she was brilliant with the children. It was clear she loved them and they loved her.

Perhaps it was her kindness, always thinking of others.

But in his heart he knew it was more than that.

When he looked at her, he was seeing the girl she had once been, the girl he had fallen in love with and been too stupid to realise it until it was too late. He'd been young and a bit wild, enjoyed playing the field, not thought twice about two-timing her. He'd have his fun and she would still be there, the one he always came back to. When she'd finally ended things between them, it had come as a shock; he'd never expected that. And it had been a shock too how much it had hurt. Only when it was too late had he realised just how much she meant to him and he'd resolved to win her back. But then she'd started walking out with Cliff Baker and never given him the opportunity to make things up.

Then one day he'd looked around – and there was Stella. All grown up, pretty as a picture, full of fun and laughter. Dear Stella, his much-loved wife and the mother of his children. Only now, as he looked at Grace and felt himself drawn inexorably to her, did he wonder. Had he fallen for Stella because she was Grace's sister? Because she was like her in so many ways? Had it always been Grace for him? He'd been so sure he was over her; now the way he was feeling had made him wonder.

Tom wasn't used to emotional upheaval. He was confused as well as horrified by the turbulent feelings that he'd only just begun to acknowledge. The times when their eyes met and he was jolted back to shared memories of long ago. When a strand of hair escaped her comb and he had to stop himself brushing it off her cheek as he used to do. And, as had happened last night when she'd been so concerned for Francie next door, the moments when he looked at her and felt tenderness. The strength of his feeling had shaken him to the core.

Now, as he finished his snap in the dark passageway, he couldn't get it out of his head. He'd never do anything to hurt Stella, never be unfaithful to her, but just the thoughts he was having felt like a betrayal. Thank the Lord that Stella would soon be coming home; Grace would return to Shillingford, and temptation and turmoil would recede like the tide at Weston-super-Mare. Until that happened the best diversion was hard physical work.

Tom hauled himself to his feet, hitched up his rushy-duck trousers and collected his pick and went back to the coal face.

\* \* \*

Francie Newman stood, her hand on the latch of her kitchen door, undecided as to whether to call round to see Grace. She knew Grace had seen the bruises on her arms yesterday, and she'd been worried about it ever since. The last thing she wanted was for anyone to know Noel knocked her about, and perhaps the best way to allay any suspicions Grace might have was to act normally.

Quite apart from the shame of it, she felt curiously protective towards Noel. It was her fault, not his, and she didn't want the neighbours thinking badly of him. He'd been really nice to her since the latest episode, which, like all the others, had been entirely her fault. She should have known better than to remonstrate with him when he'd come clomping in from the garden without taking off his muddy boots, but she'd been too annoyed at the mess he'd made on her clean floor to think twice.

'Can't a man get a jibble to go with his bread and cheese?' he'd demanded. Jibble was the local word for spring onions.

'Yeah, but you don't have to traipse mud in, do you?' she'd complained. 'Just look at that!'

'There you go – at it again. Always finding summat to moan about. I'm bloody fed up with it.'

'Maybe I'm fed up too, having to clean up after you as well as the children. Well, this time you can do it yourself.'

'You think so? I'll soon show you different.'

He'd grabbed her by the wrists and propelled her into the scullery. Hoisting the tin pail up into the big stone sink, he'd filled it with water and thrown in a cake of soap and the floor cloth.

'There. Now get on with it.'

'Like I said – do it yourself.'

Furious now, Noel caught her by the shoulder and the back

of her neck and thrust her face down into the brimming pail. She struggled, her hands on the sink, trying to push herself free, to no avail. Panic filled her as he held her face under the water for what seemed like an eternity, then released her, gasping and coughing.

'Are you going to do it, or do you want some more of the same?'

'You bastard,' she managed, but she lifted the heavy pail and struggled with it into the living room. He stood over her as she did her best to clean up the mud with the cold water. Her eyes and throat were stinging, and water dripped from her hair down her neck.

'That suit you?' she asked, still defiant, when she'd finished.

'Why d'you make me do these things?' he asked, sounding more regretful than angry now.

'I'm sorry . . .'

'Not as sorry as I am. But you've got to be kept in line, Francie.' As she struggled to her feet and went to lift the pail, he took it from her. 'Go and wash your face. You're a sight.'

As far as he was concerned, that was the end of it. But Francie couldn't forget so easily. She continued to berate herself for being confrontational and losing her temper, and felt guilty for the upset she had caused, besides being mortified at the thought that Stella's sister had seen her bruises, even if she hadn't heard the shouting the night before.

Strange, really, she never felt this way with Stella. She supposed it must be because they'd been neighbours for so long. If Stella guessed what went on, she'd never mentioned it, and she knew that Noel was a good man. There'd never been any trouble between the families all the time they'd lived next door to one another. But Grace wouldn't have all their history to call on; she might get hold of the wrong end of the stick and blame

Noel. Go to the town bobby, even, and report him. No, somehow Francie had to get Grace on side.

Making up her mind, she opened the back door and made her way along the path between the houses, but there was no response to her knock, and when she tried the door, it wouldn't open. Grace must have gone on to do some shopping after taking the children to school, and unlike Stella, had locked up after her. It just went to show that she wasn't comfortable with the neighbours as Stella was, and might indeed think badly of her and Noel.

Well, hopefully she wouldn't be here much longer. And Francie, for one, would be very glad when Stella was back where she belonged.

Jessica was finding everything a dreadful struggle this morning. The broken night, the rude awakening, and the shock and horror of watching the flames consume Alistair's motor had all combined to unnerve her, and made the baby she was carrying restless too. With her stomach churning and her nerves on edge, the punches and kicks from tiny hands and feet that she usually relished as signs that he – or she – was alive and well seemed today only a further discomfort.

Unusually, Constance was playing up too – perhaps she had been unsettled by the tense atmosphere – and it was mid morning before Jessica was able to get her settled at the kitchen table with some paper and coloured pencils and go upstairs to make the beds.

As she drew back the curtains in the front bedroom, the sight of the wrecked motor made her feel sick all over again, and she turned away hastily, not wanting to look at it.

When the doorbell rang, it made her jump almost out of her skin, so on edge was she. Wondering who it could be, she hurried downstairs. Constance had heard it too, and abandoned her drawing to run into the hall. 'Someone at the door, Mammy!' she announced importantly.

Jessica opened the door and was surprised to see the uniformed figure of Sergeant Love standing there.

'Morning, Mrs Mackay. You've had a bit of trouble, I understand. And now that I'm here, I can see it for myself.' He nodded in the direction of the road.

'Oh, yes. Did my husband report it to you?' Jessica caught Constance by the arm; the little girl was about to slip past her into the garden, and she didn't want her anywhere near the shell of the motor.

'He did pop in, yes. But we'd already heard. Reg Box has put in a report.' Reg was the chief fireman. 'He's of the opinion there's something fishy about it.'

'Fishy?' Jessica repeated.

'As to what caused it. He doesn't think it combusted all by itself.' Sergeant Love looked pleased with himself at his use of the long word. 'And he thought I should investigate the matter.'

'Oh.' Jessica was momentarily speechless as she remembered the conversation she'd had with Alistair about his pipe. 'I'm sure Alistair didn't do anything to cause it,' she said hastily. 'He loves that motor, and he's always really careful.'

'I'm not thinking for a minute that the doctor had anything to do with it,' the sergeant assured her. 'Can I come in? Have a bit of a chat? And I'll need to take a statement. It was you that discovered the fire, I understand.'

'Oh yes, please do.' She opened the door wider and stood aside, still holding on to Constance's hand. But the little girl seemed mesmerised now by the policeman's uniform, and breaking free, she ran after him along the hall and into the living room, where she pushed the sheet of paper she'd been drawing on across the table towards him.

'Ah, we've got an artist in the making here, have we?' he asked jovially, before taking a seat, getting out his notebook and resuming his previously solemn demeanour.

'So, Mrs Mackay, if you could just tell me in your own words . . .'

'It was awful,' Jessica said. 'We were in bed asleep, and something woke me up and I could see the flicker of the flames . . .' She broke off.

'So it was well alight by then?'

'Oh yes. It was just a ball of flame.'

Talking about it was making it all real again rather than the shadow of a nightmare, and Jessica wrapped her arms around the swell of her stomach.

'Did you see anybody?' Sergeant Love asked.

Jessica shook her head. 'The street was deserted. It was the middle of the night.'

'Nobody lurking nearby?'

'No – why would there be?'

The sergeant fixed her with a straight gaze. 'I'm thinking this was started deliberately, and if it was, the fire raiser might have hung around to watch his handiwork.'

Jessica stared back at him aghast. 'You think it was deliberate? But why would someone do that?'

'There's some funny folk about, Mrs Mackay, that get their kicks from that sort of thing.'

'That's awful!'

'Yes. But I have to ask you . . . is there anybody you can think of that might have a grudge against the doctor? A patient, perhaps?'

'Certainly not!' Jessica was affronted by the very idea.

'Alistair is a very good doctor. He goes out of his way for his patients. They're more likely to leave a rabbit or a pheasant on the doorstep by way of saying thank you than they are to set his motor on fire.'

Sergeant Love sighed. He snapped his notebook shut and slotted it into the breast pocket of his uniform.

'Well, that'll be all for now, Mrs Mackay, but perhaps you could call into the station when you're in town and we can take a formal statement. Your husband will be doing the same when he's finished his surgery. And I'd advise you to keep an eye out, and if you see anyone acting suspicious like, give us a call straight away.'

'Yes, of course,' Jessica said, shaken by the suggestion that they might be in danger from some unknown enemy.

In the doorway, the sergeant paused. 'You'll have to arrange for something to be done with what's left of the motor,' he said, a trifle officiously. 'It can't stay there.'

'I'm sure Alistair will take care of that.'

'And while you're about it, tell him to make sure that bike he's riding is safe,' he added. 'It didn't look roadworthy to me.'

'How else is he supposed to get to see his patients?' Jessica asked, a little annoyed by the sergeant's tone. 'It's my bike, and I haven't ridden it for years, but I'm sure Alistair will be taking care on it.'

'I hope so. We don't want him knocking down some pedestrian because the brakes don't work.'

Jessica said nothing, but she hoped so too. Alistair had looked very unsteady when he'd wobbled off earlier.

The sergeant retrieved his own bicycle and rode off, and Jessica went back inside. If she had been feeling upset before the policeman's visit, now her stomach was churning afresh. The thought that someone might have deliberately set fire to the motor was a frightening one, and she wished fervently that she was back in the cottage where she'd grown up, with near neighbours on either side always ready to keep an eye out for one another. A detached villa in the grand part of town was all very well, but at times like this she missed the easy camaraderie she'd grown up with.

'Mammy?' Constance was tugging at her skirts, looking up at her anxiously, and with an effort Jessica pulled herself together.

'Come on, Constance, why don't we go and do some more drawing?'

The little girl trotted enthusiastically back along the hallway, and by the time Jessica joined her, she was once more engrossed in her composition – some stick people that Jessica thought were meant to be herself and Alistair, a lopsided house and a bright yellow sun.

She wasn't going to let Constance out of her sight today, she decided, drawing up a chair beside her. The beds and the rest of the housework could wait. All that mattered was making sure that her daughter was safe.

Sir Oswald Whittingly Challis was at his desk in his study when the call he had been waiting for finally came.

'Winston here, Oswald.'

'Winston. Good to hear from you. How did things go?'

'Without a hitch. And Miranda could not be happier. She's with him now—'

'Enough said, my friend.' Sir Oswald cut him off, concerned that the person who had connected the call might be listening in. If the woman who manned their own local exchange was anything to go by, they probably were. 'But thank you for letting me know.'

'I can't tell you how grateful I am to you, Oswald.'

'It was to our mutual benefit.' It was not in Sir Oswald's nature to voice his own gratitude in so many words. 'I hope everything will work out satisfactorily.'

'I'm sure it will. Would you like me to keep you informed as to how things are progressing?'

'That won't be necessary.' As far as Sir Oswald was concerned, the transaction had been completed. Now all that remained was to deal with Rose as he thought fit and he would be able to draw a line under the whole unfortunate episode.

He was fairly sure his threats to sack her father if she ever told anyone the truth of her baby's paternity would be sufficient to keep her quiet, but he would feel safer if she was as far away as possible from the vicinity.

When he'd bidden Winston good day, he drew a sheet of writing paper from the top drawer of his desk, uncapped his fountain pen, and began to write.

My dear Alfred,

I am wondering if you could offer a position to a former employee of mine? She is a young woman who found herself in the unfortunate position of bearing a child out of wedlock. The baby has been taken for adoption, but the shame still haunts her and I know she would feel far more comfortable if she could find employment in new surroundings where no one is aware of her fall from grace. I can vouch for the fact that her work is faultless, and I think it very unlikely she will ever make the same mistake again. It would please me enormously to know that she could make a fresh start in life. As a man of God, I feel sure you will be willing to help her to do so.

I remain, your affectionate cousin,
Oswald

Satisfied, he found an envelope and addressed it to the Right Reverend Alfred Whittingly Challis.

He hoped his cousin would take the bait, and rather thought he would. The old fool liked nothing better than doing good works, and Sir Oswald was confident that saving the soul of a fallen woman would appeal to him.

If not, he would have to think again. But for the present he was satisfied things were progressing as he had intended.

Once he'd made the necessary arrangements, he'd get her discharged from Catcombe, and hopefully that would be the end of the wretched affair.

# Chapter Sixteen

'I thought I might go over to see Stella this afternoon, if that's all right with you,' Tom said.

It was Saturday, a fine, bright day when it was beginning to look as if spring really was just around the corner. As he always did on a Saturday, he had ridden his bicycle into Hillsbridge and met his workmates in the Miners' Arms to share out their earnings. They'd have a pint or two of beer as they counted the money, and Danny Barton would place a bet on a horse that was running in the afternoon's races by writing his selection on a scrap of paper and handing it, together with however much money he was prepared to risk, to the young lad who hung about on the steps outside the pub to run it to the bookie's. Jimmy Wheeler liked a flutter too, if he could get away with it without his father seeing. He'd been caught nicely today, and earned the length of Walter's tongue: 'You daft lad, don't you know the bookie always wins?'

Tom hadn't waited to hear the ensuing exchange; he'd already decided he'd go and visit Stella and was anxious to get away. He hadn't seen her since the evening Dr Mackay had driven him to Catcombe, and it had somehow become imperative that he should, if only to banish the churned-up emotions he'd been experiencing about Grace. If Stella was so much better, she'd probably be glad to see him too, and she was certain to be anxious for news of the children. He'd said his goodbyes and ridden home, where Grace had his dinner waiting.

'Of course it's all right with me,' she said as she dished up plates of mutton stew. 'But it's a long way . . .'

'Nothing I can't manage. I couldn't have done it when the weather was bad, but it's a nice day today. And the fresh air will do me good.'

'Well, it's up to you. I'm sure Stella will be pleased.'

As soon as they'd finished eating, he left Grace to do the washing-up and set off. As she had said, it was a long haul to Catcombe across the Mendips, and it was only as he was coasting down the long last hill that it occurred to him that his visit might not be allowed. He'd arrived unannounced last time, but he'd been with Dr Mackay. If he simply turned up alone, it might well be a very different kettle of fish.

It was too late to worry about that now, though. He might as well carry on now that he'd got this far.

The gates at the end of the drive were open. He rode down to the main entrance, propped his bicycle up against the wall and rang the bell. It was answered by a uniformed nurse, who seemed uncertain when he asked if he could see Stella.

'I'll have to ask Matron,' she said, and closed the door again, leaving Tom standing on the step.

He took off his cap and twisted it between his hands as he waited, cursing himself for not having realised that a visit might need to be arranged. It was some minutes before the nurse was back, but to his relief she stood aside, gesturing for him to come in.

'I can see her then?' he asked.

'I'm not sure. Matron didn't say. But Dr Kirkwood wants to talk to you.'

'Oh, right.'

Tom wasn't sure whether this was a good thing or not, but ever the optimist, he hoped that perhaps the superintendent was going to tell him that Grace was fit to come home. He followed the nurse along the corridor, wrinkling his nose at the mingled smells of disinfectant and boiled cabbage, and disturbed by the sound of a woman shouting behind one of the closed doors. The sooner Grace could get out of this awful place, the better.

The door to Dr Kirkwood's office, adorned with a brass plate bearing his name, stood ajar. The nurse tapped on it.

'Come in.'

Tom entered and, very conscious of being in surroundings that were totally alien to him, approached the desk behind which a middle-aged man wearing wire-rimmed spectacles and a white coat was sitting. He rose, holding out his hand, and Tom was surprised by how small and wiry he was. Somehow he had expected the superintendent of a lunatic asylum to be a big man, though he didn't know what had given him that idea. But his handshake was firm, and when he spoke, it was with an air of authority.

'Mr Swift. You're here to see your wife, I'm told.'

'That's what I was hoping. I should have telephoned yesterday from work, asked if it would be all right, but I didn't think.'

'Never mind. I'm glad to have this opportunity to speak to you. Won't you take a seat?'

Tom sat down, still twisting his cap between his hands as it lay in his lap.

'I'm hoping you're going to tell me Stella's ready to come home,' he said. 'From what Dr Mackay said.'

Dr Kirkwood removed his spectacles and swung them by the arm between finger and thumb. His expression was serious.

'I'm afraid Dr Mackay isn't au fait with the latest development,' he said. 'Stella was showing a marked improvement, yes. But unfortunately she seems to have suffered a relapse.'

'A relapse?' Tom's heart sank. 'What do you mean?'

'She's once more refusing to feed Baby.'

'Oh no!' Tom groaned. 'When did this happen?'

'Just yesterday. She was taken up to the nursery as usual and went quite willingly. But when Baby was put in her arms, she became hysterical, as she did in the early days.'

'But why would that be?' Tom was struggling to make head or tail of this devastating news.

'Unfortunately, I don't have the answer to that, Mr Swift. But she is delusional. For some unfathomable reason, she is insisting that Baby isn't hers.'

'Oh . . .' Tom was lost for words.

'It's a very worrying development, and at the moment we have no idea what has triggered it,' Dr Kirkwood continued, 'But I'm afraid it means she is in no fit state to be discharged. I'm hopeful it will prove to be nothing more than a blip; the next few days will tell. But if it continues, I think we must consider sending Baby home. Do you have anyone who could care for him? A female relative, perhaps?'

Tom's head was spinning. 'Stella's sister is staying with us, looking after the children when I'm at work. But . . . oh, I don't know. I'd have to talk it over with her.'

'Of course. There's no immediate urgency. The nursery nurses are feeding him again, since Stella has refused to. But it really would be in his best interests to be in a normal home environment as soon as possible. We don't want him to become institutionalised.'

'No. We don't want that.'

'Now, you'd like to see Stella, I understand. You can have a chat with her here, in my office. It's possible that seeing you will calm her, and we can take her up to the nursery and encourage her to at least hold Baby. How does that sound to you?'

'Whatever you think is best, Doctor.'

Dr Kirkwood went in search of Stella. Left alone, Tom paced the office. He could scarcely believe what he'd been told. Why would Stella suddenly be denying that Will was hers? He'd firmly believed that it was the constant crying and refusal to feed that had tipped her over the edge. But if that was no longer happening, she should have continued recovering, not got worse again.

His train of anxious thought was interrupted as Dr Kirkwood returned with Stella, and at once Tom was dismayed at the change in her since he had last visited. She'd appeared to him then to be more or less completely back to normal. Now she looked ravaged again, her eyes red-rimmed and wild, with dark circles beneath them, and her hair untidy with loose strands falling about her face and some bits sticking up as if she'd been distractedly running her fingers through it.

As soon as she saw Tom, she ran to him, clutching at his hands.

'Tom! Oh Tom, thank goodness!'

All Tom wanted to do was to take her in his arms and hold her close, but he hesitated, all too conscious of the superintendent standing right behind her, and unsure whether he would approve.

As if he had read Tom's mind, Dr Kirkwood caught his eye and nodded.

Tom put his arms round Stella, pulling her towards him, and was shocked at how thin she was. All the weight she'd gained over successive pregnancies had melted away; he could have counted each and every one of her ribs, and she felt fragile, almost birdlike. She was trembling, too, her whole frame shaking with tiny convulsive movements.

'Oh Stella,' he murmured against her hair. 'What have they done to you, my love?'

She raised her head, which had been buried in his chest, and looked up at him with those anguished eyes, dark pools in the tight-drawn skin of her pale face.

'Will!' she said urgently. 'I don't know what they've done with Will!'

It was really no answer to Tom's question. Dr Kirkwood had said it was only in the last couple of days that Stella had been rejecting her baby, and she couldn't have lost so much weight in that time. That must have happened over a matter of weeks, though he hadn't noticed it the last time he'd visited her. But he hadn't had her in his arms then; they'd been in what he'd assumed to be a recreation room, surrounded by nurses and other patients, and he'd simply sat beside her, holding her hand. He supposed the loose asylum smock had hidden her thinness, the result of being here in this awful place. She needed to be at home, where an atmosphere of normality and some good food would put some flesh back on those bird bones. But that wasn't going to happen if she persisted with this idea she'd got in her head that Will wasn't her baby.

'William is safe upstairs in the nursery,' Dr Kirkwood said, moving round so that he could see her face. 'You know that, Stella.' His tone was low and soothing, but Stella shook her head violently.

'That baby they gave me isn't Will!' she insisted tearfully. 'Why are you making out it is?'

Dr Kirkwood caught Tom's eye and gave a tiny shake of his head, as if to say: Do you see what we're dealing with here?

Aloud, he said: 'I'll have one of the nurses fetch William,

and the three of you can spend some time together.' Clearly he was hoping that Tom could convince Stella that the baby was indeed hers.

Once he had left the office, Stella spoke urgently. 'You've got to do something, Tom. You've got to find Will!'

'Stop fretting, love. Everything is going to be all right,' Tom said, trying to comfort her but at a loss to know how to combat this disturbing turn of events. He simply couldn't understand why Stella should have suffered such a setback, and so suddenly.

Dr Kirkwood was soon back. 'A nurse is fetching William,' he said, arranging two chairs side by side against the wall, facing shelves bearing a whole collection of leather-bound psychology books. 'Why don't you sit down? You'll be more comfortable, and so will Baby.'

'Come on, Stella, let's sit down like the doctor says.' Tom urged her gently towards the chairs, and when they were seated, he took her hand in his. 'You've got to beat this, Stella. We need you home. The children miss you. *I* miss you.'

'And I miss you.'

'There you are, then. Just put all these silly ideas out of your head and we'll all be together again.'

Tears filled her eyes; she raised a hand to brush them away. 'I wish I could, Tom. But . . .'

A nurse appeared in the doorway, carrying a baby wrapped in a blue blanket. 'Here we are! And isn't he looking bonny?'

She crossed to Stella and made to lay the baby in her lap. For a moment it seemed as if Stella was going to accept him, but as she looked down into his face, she pushed him away.

'That is not Will! Why do you keep giving me someone else's baby?'

'It *is* Will, Stella. Look . . .' The nurse folded back the blanket and exposed a little foot with a name tag round the ankle. 'See? It says here – William Swift.'

'But it's not Will,' Stella insisted, and turned to Tom, her eyes full of pleading. 'Tell them, Tom! Perhaps they'll believe you.'

Tom shook his head. It was more than a month now since he'd last seen his son, and in that time he would have grown and changed. And little as he liked to admit it, all babies looked much the same to him, even his own. Will hadn't had any hair when he'd been admitted to Catcombe along with Stella; now his head was covered with a dark silky fuzz. That surprised Tom a little, as both he and Stella were fair. But it didn't necessarily mean it wasn't Will. Babies could inherit colouring from much further back in the family tree, as his mother had told him once, long ago, when he'd asked why an uncle was a carrot-top when none of his brothers and sisters were. And there was no disputing the name tag around the baby's ankle.

'It must be Will, Stella,' he said, trying to reassure both her and himself. 'They wouldn't make a mistake like that.'

'It's not, I tell you! I don't know who he is, but that baby is not my Will!'

Stella was becoming increasingly distressed, and Dr Kirkwood stepped forward and gestured to the nurse to take the baby away again.

'It's all right, Stella,' he said soothingly, and to Tom: 'I'll get something to calm her.'

He left the office and Stella turned furiously on Tom.

'Why didn't you tell them – that isn't Will.'

'Oh Stella,' Tom groaned, reaching for her hand. She tore it away.

'You don't want him, do you? You never wanted him.'

'That's not true, and you know it,' Tom said, trying to be

reasonable. 'I always said four was a good number. You were the one who didn't want any more children.'

'That was only in the beginning. Of course I want him. He's my baby. My baby! And I don't know where he is!'

Dr Kirkwood was back with the medication. 'Take this, Stella, and you'll feel much better.'

But Stella pushed him away. 'I don't want it! I want my baby!'

Dr Kirkwood turned to Tom. 'I think it would be best if we terminated this visit, Mr Swift. I think Stella needs to be quiet for a bit.'

'Yes . . . yes, of course.' Tom stood up. He hated leaving Stella, but he hated seeing her like this too.

He went to try to give her a kiss, but she turned her face away from him so his lips touched only her ear.

'I'll be back soon, love . . .' Choked, he turned away.

Dr Kirkwood followed him out into the corridor, pulling the door half closed behind him.

'I'm sorry about this, Mr Swift. As you can see—'

'Yeah, I can see all right.'

'Perhaps you could give some thought as to whether you would be able to take William home. I really think that would be for the best unless Stella shows some marked improvement.'

'I'll see what I can do.'

Tom's thoughts were whirling as he got on his bicycle and rode away down the drive. Never in a million years had he imagined that Stella could have taken such a turn for the worse. All his hopes of having her home had been dashed, and on top of that, he had to find some way of caring for William.

Normally Tom was the most pragmatic of men, but this time he was well and truly rattled.

* * *

The table was laid for tea when Tom eventually arrived home, a typical Saturday tea – slices of bread and butter, jam, and a freshly made fruit cake, with a dish of cockles and the vinegar pot in front of his plate. He liked his cockles on a Saturday, and Grace had bought a quarter of a pound of them in the fish shop when she went to market. Oliver was sitting on the padded fire box toasting crumpets, shifting the fork from hand to hand when one began to get too hot for comfort. Grace was buttering them and placing them in a pile on a plate on the hearth beside the fire to keep warm. The melted butter pooled on the china beneath them.

She looked up as Tom came in, tired out and looking worried.

'How was she?'

'I'll tell you later.'

Grace's heart sank. She could tell from both his weary tone and the look of him that the news was not going to be good.

'Well, sit down and let's have tea,' she said, deliberately cheerful. 'Come on, children, let's eat these crumpets before they get cold.'

'This is the last one.' Oliver held the toasting fork out to her, and she pulled the crumpet off the prongs, buttered it and added it to the pile before setting the plate on the table.

The children began to tuck in eagerly; they all loved crumpets. But Grace's eyes were on Tom.

'You look done in,' she said.

'It's a long ride.'

'I did warn you.'

He didn't answer, pouring vinegar over his cockles.

'We've had a busy afternoon, haven't we, children?' Grace said brightly. 'Emily helped me make the cake.'

'And we helped with the washing-up,' Alec added.

'Well, you certainly scraped the mixing bowl clean. Though a lot of it ended up on your faces.'

But her smile didn't reach her eyes. She was wondering what on earth was making Tom look so despondent, and what it was he didn't want to tell her in front of the children.

Never had the hours between tea and their bedtime seemed so long. Never had she wanted the children out of the way so much. She busied herself with the clearing-up, and then Oliver and Alec were clamouring for a game of Snap. Grace had never felt less like playing cards.

'Why don't the three of you have a game on your own?' she suggested, but they insisted she play too, and help Emily.

'She's too little. She never gets it right,' Oliver stated baldly.

It was true. When Emily played, she often dropped her cards and was either too slow spotting the connection between Mr Bunn the Baker and his daughter, Miss Bunn, or too ready to shout 'Snap!' where there was no connection at all. The boys inevitably got impatient with her, and she became upset that their piles of cards grew bigger while hers got progressively smaller, until the game ended in tears.

Reluctantly Grace drew up a chair and settled Emily on her knee.

'Dad, you come and play too!' Alec said, but Tom simply replied: 'Not tonight,' and disappeared out of the back door.

Grace presumed he was going for a walk, or a potter down the garden, to give him a chance to think things over uninterrupted. He'd done that a lot in the early days before they'd settled into a routine, even though it had been cold, dark and sometimes wet. Whatever had happened had upset him badly if he was back to wanting to spend time on his own, away from the family.

They'd played three or four games of Snap before he came back.

'Isn't it your bedtime?' he said to the children.

'Oh no! And I was winning too!' Oliver groaned.

'No you weren't! I was!' Alec claimed, and a fierce argument began.

'Your father's right. It's bedtime, and we've played for long enough.' Grace gathered up the cards. 'Upstairs and get undressed, and I'll bring your milk up to you.'

Though the boys both drank tea now, Stella always insisted they have a cup of warm milk at bedtime. It was good for them, and it helped them sleep, she said.

At long last they were all tucked up in bed, though there were the usual pleas from the boys to keep the light on for a bit, which Grace refused as Emily was sharing their bedroom and needed to go to sleep straight away. Heaving a sigh of relief, she pulled the door closed behind her and headed down the stairs.

Tom was sitting in his favourite chair, staring into space.

'So what is it?' Grace took the chair opposite him, sitting forward on the edge of the seat instead of sinking back against the cushion as she usually did for a few minutes' relaxation when the chores of the day were finished.

Tom told her, and Grace listened aghast.

'But why?' she asked, the frustration spilling into her voice. 'Why on earth would she get it into her head that Will's not her baby?'

'Part of the illness, I suppose,' Tom said resignedly.

'But she was getting better! It doesn't make sense.'

'It's no good asking me,' he said wearily.

'Then I'll ask the doctor.'

'You can't bother Dr Mackay,' Tom said. 'Stella's not his problem any more.'

'Then I'll go to Catcombe and speak to Dr Kirkwood. I'd like to see Stella, in any case. Maybe she'll talk to me.'

'I doubt it. And anyway, how are you going to get there?'

'I'll hire the pony and trap. Or the taxi cab. There's one in Hillsbridge now, I think. And before you ask how I'm going to pay for it, I've got a bit of money that I was saving up to try and get a place of my own. I brought it with me in case I needed anything while I was here, but I haven't had to touch it.'

'Don't talk silly, Grace. If you want to go and see Stella, I'll pay for the taxi. It's the least I can do after all you've done for us.'

'I don't want repaying – I'm just glad I can do my bit to help out. And how much have you got to spare? The boys will be wanting new boots soon, and Emily's shooting up fast too. I wouldn't dream of letting you pay for a taxi cab. Stella is my sister, after all.'

'Well, we'll argue about that later,' Tom said. 'There's something else I've got to talk to you about, and I hardly like to ask. You've been so good already.'

'Go on, ask. You know I'll do whatever needs to be done.'

Still Tom hesitated.

'What is it, Tom?' Grace prompted him.

Tom drew in a deep breath. 'Dr Kirkwood thinks that if Stella doesn't soon show signs of improvement, we ought to bring Will home anyway. He thinks he'd be better off here than stuck in the nursery there all the time.'

'Oh!' Grace was startled. It was a possibility she'd considered in the early days, but since Stella had seemed to be getting better, she'd thought no more about it.

'The thing is, I think he's right,' Tom said. 'It's no place for a baby to grow up, but . . . I don't know how you'd feel about it.'

'You mean because I'd have to look after him?'

'I can't think of any other solution. I've been racking my brains. But I can't afford to pay somebody to do it, and—'

'Don't give it a second thought,' Grace said emphatically. 'Of course I'll look after Will while Stella's too ill to do it herself. And I agree, he shouldn't be stuck in that nursery. He needs to be here, getting to know his brothers and sister, getting used to normal life. I just wish it didn't have to be this way.'

It was no more than the truth. She hated to think of her sister incarcerated in that awful place, once more losing touch with reality. What must she be going through? Grace's heart bled for her. And yet a tiny treacherous part of her couldn't help but be glad that she had a reprieve. That she didn't yet have to go back to the lonely life she had led since Cliff had been killed.

'Me too,' Tom said with feeling. But his worried expression had turned to one of relief, and he sat forward in his chair, reaching for her hand. 'I don't know what we'd do without you, Grace.'

The frisson that ran through her veins was electric; she could feel it prickling hot on her skin, spreading from where his fingers touched. Then, as if perhaps he was aware of it too, he drew back sharply and the moment had passed.

'Let's have a cup of tea,' Grace said, wanting to deny it had ever been. She reached for the kettle, lifting it from its trivet on the hearth and shaking it. 'I think it needs filling . . .'

Gratefully she escaped to the kitchen. Her cheeks felt hot, and a flurry of mixed emotions were making it difficult to think straight.

What was happening here? Everything was spinning out of control. Little by little, driven by events, she seemed to be taking over her sister's life. And the awful thing was, she could no longer deny that deep down it was what she wanted. A home of her own. A family of growing children. And Tom. Yes, most of all, Tom.

Consumed with guilt, not wanting to return to the living room, where she would have to face him, Grace took as long as she could to fill the kettle.

Thank God for Grace. Gratitude and warmth surged through Tom's veins. And at the same time, the sharp stab of guilt at the way his feelings for her were deepening far more than they should. He'd thought that Stella would be coming home soon and things would get back to normal. Grace would leave and there would be no more temptation. But now it looked as though that was not going to happen.

Worse, he didn't want her to leave.

He sighed and buried his face in his hands, while the conflicting emotions raged in his head and his heart.

Mabel was a little concerned. When she'd come on duty, the day nurse had told her that Dr Kirkwood had talked to Tom Swift about the possibility of baby William going home. She'd thought she'd dealt with the danger of Dr Mackay going into the nursery and realising that the baby in William Swift's crib was not the one he'd diagnosed with a dislocation in his neck or shoulder. But if the baby was going home to Hillsbridge, there was always the possibility that the doctor might visit.

Unlikely, she told herself. Unless he was called out, he wouldn't be doing many home visits on Shanks's pony. She'd do her best to delay the baby's departure as long as possible, so as to lengthen the odds on the chances of him remembering exactly what he had looked like, and presumably he would have seen a great many other babies in the meantime.

But she wished all the same that this hadn't cropped up so soon. It wasn't just knowing the whereabouts of Rose's baby that was at stake now, nor even her satisfaction in giving Sir

Oswald his comeuppance. It was her whole life. Her job. Her reputation. Perhaps even her liberty.

*Don't trouble trouble till trouble troubles you.* It had been one of her mother's sayings, and for some reason it lifted her spirits now. So far everything had gone according to plan. The rest she'd worry about when the time came. And if she thought it had become necessary to do something to prevent 'Baby Swift' going home, then she would not hesitate to do it.

# Chapter Seventeen

Breakfast on a Sunday was always a feast. In fact, on a Sunday all the meals seemed to be a celebration of the day of rest and a stoking-up of resources for the hard work of the week to come. As if the bacon, eggs, sausages and fried bread wasn't enough, dinner would be a joint of roasted meat with potatoes and cabbage from their own garden, followed by bottled fruit and custard or an apple pie, and tea would be bread, butter and jam, cake, and the remains of the bottled fruit if there was any. And somehow Tom and Grace would still find room for supper: more bread, cheese and pickled onions or gherkins.

Usually when breakfast was over, Tom would potter a bit in the garden, then sit down with the *News of the World*, which was delivered by Ferdie Newman, who did a paper round on his bicycle.

Today, however, when he had dug some potatoes, cut a cabbage and delivered them to the kitchen, he announced that he was going to take the children to visit his parents this morning, rather than leaving it until the afternoon, when rain was forecast.

Grace was relieved. The conversation they'd had last evening had been playing on her mind along with the guilt she felt at the way she seemed to be taking over her sister's life.

Of course she would care for William if it was best for him to be at home. She would actually enjoy doing it. But that was just the trouble. Like all the other duties she'd taken on, she would enjoy it too much. It should be Stella looking after Will and the others. She was missing out on so much. Besides which, Grace knew that the more involved she became, the harder it would be to return to her old life.

As for the way she was feeling about Tom . . . the less she saw of him, the better. She was beginning to be seriously disturbed about her turbulent emotions. Not that they were much calmer when she wasn't with him. Even when she was thinking of other things, he was there constantly, like a warm blanket wrapped around her but with an air of suppressed excitement that made her breathless, a feeling of something momentous just around the corner. It was dangerous, that excitement. However things turned out, it could only end in tears.

The guilt and the shame were never far away either. She loved her sister dearly. Wanted nothing more than for her to recover. Would never do anything to hurt her. And yet wasn't she already betraying her by having these thoughts, these feelings?

She was dreadfully worried too about what Stella's relapse might mean in terms of her sister's future – another cloud from which there was no escape hanging over her. What could have caused it, when she had seemed to be on the road to recovery? She must be mistaken, surely, that the baby she was being given wasn't Will? How could it not be him when, besides the label posted above his crib, he had a name tag fastened around his ankle? Grace could only think that something in Stella herself was making her reject him again, and that didn't bode well for the future. Supposing she never recovered? Supposing she had to spend the rest of her life in Catcombe asylum?

All these thoughts and more tormented her as she spread the joint of beef with dripping, popped it into the oven, and made a start on preparing the vegetables. She washed the dirt from the potatoes in a tin bowl and went out of the back door to empty the filthy water down the outside drain so as not to block up the outlet of the big stone sink. As she straightened up, she saw Fluffy at the end of the garden on his way back from his morning excursion. In a minute he'd be bothering to be let in.

'Come on, Fluffy,' she called, holding the back door open.

As he slowly approached, she could see that he had something in his mouth. Something yellow. Grace's heart leapt into her throat. No! Surely not!

But as he slipped past her into the kitchen, there could be no mistaking it. It was Mrs Plumley's canary, Joey. This time the bird really had escaped – and Fluffy had caught him.

'Oh my Lord!' Grace gasped. 'You bad, bad cat!'

She quickly closed the back door behind her and grabbed Fluffy by the scruff of his neck.

'Drop it! Drop it!' she commanded, as if Fluffy was a dog rather than a cat, but for a wonder, he obeyed, placing the bird carefully at her feet and looking up at her proudly. Joey fluttered weakly, and quick as a flash Grace picked him up before Fluffy's interest was rekindled and he began toying with him. She hurried through into the living room, using her shoulder to close the door after her so that the cat could not follow.

The bird was perfectly still in her hands now, and she laid him gently on the hearth, hoping the warmth of the fire might revive him. Then she stood watching, her hands pressed to her mouth, her heart beating a tattoo. Please, please let him be all right. Poor Mrs Plumley would be heartbroken if she lost her Joey for good. And if Fluffy had killed him . . . Oh my life . . .

After a minute or two, she got a grip on herself. For the

moment, there was nothing she could do. She forced herself to go back into the kitchen, where she put Fluffy outside again – just now she couldn't bear to look at him. She made a start on peeling the potatoes, but she couldn't concentrate and kept breaking off to look around the living room door to see if there were any signs of life. But there weren't. The little bird was still lying motionless where she had left him.

It was no use, she realised. Joey had probably died of fright. There was virtually no mark on him apart from a speck of blood, red against the yellow feathers, where Fluffy's teeth had punctured his skin.

Grace felt sick with anxiety. She was going to have to go and confess what had happened. Had Mrs Plumley even realised that Joey had escaped? Grace hadn't heard her going up and down the alleyway, swinging his cage and calling for him. How ironic that all the times she'd panicked about losing him he'd been flying around somewhere in the house, and this time, when he really had escaped, she hadn't noticed he was missing, and Grace dreaded telling her of his awful fate.

Oh why had Tom gone to visit his parents this morning? If only he were here! Grace chewed her lip, undecided. Should she wait for him to come home so that he could be the one to go and see Mrs Plumley? But it wasn't even eleven o'clock yet, and he wouldn't be back until getting on for one. She couldn't really leave it any longer. But never had she felt more alone.

Francie. The image of the friendly neighbour squeezed itself in between Grace's chaotic thoughts. Francie and Mrs Plumley must know one another quite well. Perhaps Francie would accompany her to break the awful news. Having a familiar face there when Grace told her what had happened might help to soften the blow.

Making sure the living room door was closed so that Fluffy

could not go in, Grace went out and along the back of the houses to knock on Francie's door.

'Something awful has happened,' she said when Francie opened it.

'Oh dear – not Stella?' Seeing the state Grace was in, Francie immediately jumped to the wrong conclusion.

'Well . . . she is poorly again,' Grace said, 'but that's not why I'm here. It's . . .'

'You'd better come in.'

Francie led Grace through the kitchen and into the living room. Of her children there was no sign – they had probably gone across the fields to play – but Noel was sitting at the table, which was covered with sheets of old newspaper, whittling a piece of wood.

'He's making a bubble pipe for Reg,' Francie said by way of introduction. 'This is Grace, Stella's sister. I don't think you two have met, have you?'

'No.' Warily Grace eyed the man she'd come to think of as a monster. But to her surprise and relief he appeared perfectly normal, harmless even. He was also quite good-looking, not at all what she'd expected.

'So, sit down and tell me what's wrong,' Francie said.

'I won't stay if you don't mind.' Grace felt more comfortable standing. 'But I wondered if you'd be good enough to help me out.'

She related what had happened, trying to quell the little shake in her voice. 'I really don't know Mrs Plumley, and I'd be so grateful if you'd come with me to break the news,' she finished.

'Well, of course I will,' Francie said at once. 'Where is Joey now?'

'In my living room. I put him by the fire to try and revive him.'

'We'd better take him to her,' Francie said. 'Have you got anything to wrap him up in, or shall I find something?'

Noel looked up from his whittling. 'I could make a bit of a box,' he said, surprising Grace yet again. 'I've got some odd bits of wood in the shed and it wouldn't take me long to knock one up.'

'Oh Noel, that would be nice. Then we could help her bury him in the garden,' Francie said. 'And I think I've got some oddments left over from the dresses I made for Gillie and Beattie's first communion. We could line it with that.'

'Thank you so much, both of you.' Grace was quite overwhelmed by their kindness.

'You go on back home and I'll pop round as soon as we've finished it,' Francie said.

Still shaky, Grace went back and continued preparing the vegetables for dinner. She should check on the joint of meat, she thought, but with Joey lying there on the hearth, she didn't want to go into the living room until she had to.

In no time at all Francie was knocking on the door, a bird-sized coffin in one hand, a shovel in the other.

'Here we are then. Do you want me to get the bird?'

Grace nodded, feeling foolish but unwilling to be the one to handle Joey. 'Would you?'

'You wait here then.' Francie propped the shovel up against the doorpost, deposited the wooden box on the kitchen worktop and went through into the living room.

A few seconds later she was back, the canary cupped between her hands.

'Well, talk about Lazarus! He was fluttering round the floor.'

'He's not dead?' Grace was astounded.

'Doesn't look like it to me. I don't know about a cat having nine lives. but I reckon Joey has.' She nodded in the direction of the box. 'We won't be needing that today.'

'Oh, I can't believe it!' Grace said. 'I'm so sorry to put you and Noel to all that trouble.'

Francie shrugged. 'We'll hang on to it. Next time he might not be so lucky. Or it'll come in handy when one of Ferdie's white mice kicks the bucket. I'll take Joey down to Mrs Plumley now and make sure she puts him in his cage and shuts the door. No need for you to come, and I won't mention what happened. I'll just say I found him on my doorstep.'

'Oh Francie, that is so kind.'

'That's what neighbours are for.'

Grace was almost in tears, so relieved was she. And so grateful to Francie and Noel for being ready to help her out of a pickle. Could she have been mistaken about Noel abusing Francie? Would such a man take the trouble to make a wooden box for Mrs Plumley to bury her canary in? Would he sit whittling a bubble pipe for his little son, for that matter?

As she checked on the meat and put the vegetables on to boil, Grace wondered if she had somehow got it all wrong.

She said as much to Tom when he returned with the children and she was telling him all about the fright she'd had.

'I told you Noel was all right,' Tom said. 'Okay, he's got a bit of a temper on him, and so has she, but they're good neighbours.'

But for all that, Grace couldn't quite forget Francie's bruises and other injuries. And she wondered if there was another side to Noel to the one he showed to the outside world, and if behind closed doors he became someone else entirely.

In the nursery of their home in Gloucestershire, Miranda Donaghue sat in the rocking chair cradling her new son in her lap. She was scarcely able to believe he was really here at last.

Holding him securely in the crook of her arm, she ran her fingers gently over the fair downy growth of hair that covered his head, taking care not to touch the soft fontanelle, and gazed in wonder and awe at the long lashes that lay on his cheeks.

'He is so beautiful!' she murmured.

'He's a fine lad, that's for sure.' Madge Tyler shifted her ample backside on the upright chair, the round seat of which was scarcely big enough to accommodate her. 'But don't be afraid to touch him. He won't break.'

Miranda flushed a little. She *was* half afraid, even of holding him, in case she dropped him or held him too tight, and she was glad that Madge was on hand to bath him, change his nappy and feed him. She wondered if she would feel this way if he were her own baby. How in the world did new mothers manage without someone experienced to advise them?

But her own flesh and blood or not, she couldn't possibly love him more. A great wave of warmth filled her as she gazed into the sweet sleeping face. All the years of longing, of aching to hold her baby in her arms, all the disappointment and despair had melted away as if by magic, and she whispered a prayer of thanks for this miracle.

How was his natural mother feeling now? she wondered. Was she missing him, weeping for him? Or was she relieved that her future, and that of her baby, had been taken care of?

Thank you, God. Her lips moved in a silent prayer. I promise little Wallace will have the most wonderful life. He couldn't be more loved, and we'll make sure he wants for nothing.

The nursery door opened and Winston stood there, smiling at the picture she made.

'Happy, my dear?'

'I couldn't be happier. Oh, thank you so much, my darling, for arranging this. I know you only did it for me.'

He crossed and laid a finger on her lips. 'If you're happy, then so am I, remember? And I will never treat Wallace any differently than I would if he was my own.'

Miranda smiled back at him. Her life was complete, as perfect as she had always dreamed it would be.

Matron Carey sat beside Cissie's hospital bed. The nurse lay with her head propped up on a pillow and her plastered leg raised in a contraption consisting of a sling and pulley. She had regained consciousness a few days ago, though at first she had not been fit to see visitors. It was a miracle she had come round at all, the doctor in charge of her care had told Dr Kirkwood, and it was only to be expected that she would remain confused for a while, besides tiring easily.

Both Matron and Dr Kirkwood had been anxious to see her, and as soon as they were given the all-clear they drove to the Royal United Hospital in Bath, where she had been taken when the local cottage hospital had decided the case was too serious for them. When they arrived, Cissie managed a surprised smile and a word of greeting. Her daughter was with her, but she willingly vacated her place at her mother's bedside, clearly overawed that Cissie's superiors should have come to visit.

'I've got to go in a minute anyway, or I'll miss my train,' she said, gathering her things together.

'You came on the train? All the way from Catcombe?' Dr Kirkwood asked. She nodded, and he went on: 'Don't even think of taking one back. We'll drive you, if you don't mind waiting.'

'Oh, thank you, but I couldn't . . .'

'Of course you could. It's no trouble at all. We shall be going back to the hospital when we've had a few minutes with Nurse Whitcombe.'

Dr Kirkwood was not a man to argue with, and, a little flustered, Cissie's daughter kissed her mother and left the ward.

Matron placed a paper bag of Cissie's favourite chocolates on her bedside cabinet.

'You may not feel like eating them yet, but they're there when you do,' she said.

'Thank you,' Cissie mumbled, as if she hadn't yet quite got used to speaking again.

'And how are you feeling?' Dr Kirkwood asked.

'Been better.' But Cissie managed a weak smile.

'I'm sure you have,' Matron said briskly. 'We've been very concerned about you. And we are so very sorry about what happened. Needless to say, Florrie has been taken off nursery duty, and we are keeping a very close eye on her.'

'Florrie's been taken off nursery duty?' Cissie looked puzzled. 'But why?'

'Perhaps you don't remember,' Dr Kirkwood said. 'Don't worry about it.'

'Remember what?' Clearly Cissie wasn't going to let it go.

'Nurse Cummings was able to explain to us how you came to fall down the stairs,' Matron said. 'It would appear that for some reason known only to her, Florrie pushed you.'

'A most unfortunate incident,' Dr Kirkwood added. 'We believed Florrie was trustworthy, but it seems we were mistaken.'

Cissie was shaking her head, bewildered. 'No . . . no . . .'

Matron and Dr Kirkwood exchanged a look.

'You mustn't worry about it,' Dr Kirkwood repeated. 'It's all been dealt with, never fear.'

'But . . . she couldn't have!' Although her voice was weak, Cissie sounded emphatic. 'She was with the babies. Down by the cribs. I called out goodnight to her.'

236

This time, neither Dr Kirkwood nor Matron contradicted her. Better to let her memory of events come back to her in the course of time; telling her she was wrong might very well upset her.

But after they had chatted to her for a while of inconsequential things, left her to rest, and driven home, dropping her daughter off at her home on Catcombe High Street, Matron raised the subject again.

'Cissie seemed very sure that her fall was an accident,' she said thoughtfully.

'The memory can play tricks, as well you know.' Dr Kirkwood slowed to turn through the gates of the asylum. 'In all probability she has no recollection of that night, and she's remembering another occasion entirely.'

'That's possible, I admit,' Matron said. 'But it's exactly what Florrie told me.'

'She's hardly likely to admit to pushing poor Nurse Whitcombe,' Dr Kirkwood pointed out.

'No, I suppose that's true.'

But Matron was still doubtful. She saw more of Mabel than Dr Kirkwood did, and she knew the nurse had a spiteful streak that she hid when the superintendent was around. So far, she'd chosen to ignore it. Mabel was a midwife as well as a nurse, and it wouldn't be easy to replace her. They were already struggling, with Cissie out of the picture for the foreseeable future, and Florrie returned to menial tasks such as sewing, housework and laundry. But now she couldn't help feeling that from what she knew of Mabel, if Florrie had done something to upset her it was perfectly possible that she'd seized the opportunity to blame the girl for something of which she was entirely innocent in order to have her taken off nursery duty.

Hopefully when she next visited Cissie she would be more

lucid. But in the meantime, she'd talk to both Mabel and Florrie again.

All she really wanted to do just at the moment was to go to her quarters, make a nice cup of Ovaltine, and rest her weary bones. But with Mabel on night duty, this would be a good time to speak to her. When Dr Kirkwood dropped her off at the door, she went straight up to the nursery.

All was quiet there, the babies sleeping and Mabel sitting at the nurses' station, a cup of tea on the desk in front of her.

'All good here?' Matron asked by way of greeting.

'As you can see,' Mabel answered, looking satisfied with herself.

'Dr Kirkwood and I have just been to visit Cissie,' Matron said, her innate dislike of the other woman making her voice sharper than she intended. With an effort she adopted a gentler tone. 'She's recovered consciousness, you'll be glad to hear, though it's going to be a very long time before she's ready to return to work, if she ever is.'

'Hardly surprising. It was a bad business.'

'It certainly was. But I need to ask you, Nurse Cummings, whether you could have been mistaken about how she came to fall down the stairs. Cissie seems to think Florrie was attending to the babies when it happened.'

Mabel's mouth hardened, whether in annoyance at having her word questioned, or for some other reason, Matron could not tell.

'I know what I saw, Matron. I was the one attending to the babies. Florrie was right there, by the top of the stairs.'

'And you actually saw her push Cissie?'

'That's what I said, isn't it?' Belligerence was creeping into her tone.

'You see, I'm struggling to understand why she would do

such a thing. In all the time she's been with us she's never shown any sign of being violent, or dangerous in any way. Quite the opposite.'

'There's no telling, though, is there? I, for one, wouldn't trust her up here with the babies again.' Mabel's shoulders had stiffened; everything about her exuded discomfort.

'But the final decision is Dr Kirkwood's.' Matron couldn't resist putting her in her place. 'Well, I'll leave you to your duties.'

She turned and went back down the stairs. But she was wondering – if Mabel had been at the other end of the nursery attending to the babies, how could she have seen Florrie push Cissie? Her back would have been to the stairwell.

No, she was beginning to be convinced that she was right and Mabel had accused Florrie out of spite. In her opinion it was much more likely that the truth lay with Cissie and Florrie's version of events – she rather thought Mabel would leave the hands-on tasks to her assistant, while she took her time over what paperwork needed to be completed, and there would have been a lot that night, since the adoptive parents were due to collect Wallace early next morning.

Matron sighed heavily, wondering how best to deal with the situation, and headed for her quarters and that much-needed cup of Ovaltine.

Shaken to the core, Mabel stared at Matron's retreating back. Surely she couldn't be seriously considering asking for Florrie to be reinstated? But Mabel hadn't liked her tone of voice at all, and it would be disastrous if Florrie was returned to nursery duty. Almost certainly she would know at once that 'William Swift' was not William at all, but Wallace Gooding, especially since she had most likely heard Stella protesting that the baby she'd been presented with was not hers. If she was to avert a catastrophe, she needed to act quickly.

She glanced at her watch, pinned to the front of her uniform. There was still almost an hour before the patients were locked up for bedtime. Perhaps she could catch Florrie and speak to her before that. It might be the only chance she would have, as she would be off duty during the day tomorrow, when most likely Florrie would be allowed back if Matron had her way.

Taking care not to do anything to disturb them, she crept to the other end of the nursery to check on the babies. All were sleeping soundly. Then she hurried downstairs in search of Florrie.

She found her in the big communal room playing a game of Sevens with another patient. None of the nurses on duty took any notice as Mabel approached the card table.

'Could I have a word with you, Florrie?'

Florrie looked up, resentful and wary. 'I'm in the middle of playing a game,' she said shortly.

'It won't take long, and you might learn something to your advantage.'

Reluctantly Florrie put down her cards and followed Mabel to a quiet corner of the room.

'Well?' she demanded, not caring that rudeness to the nurses was frowned upon.

'I've had a word with Matron, asked her to consider allowing you back to the nursery,' Mabel said in a low voice. 'I've told her we need your help and asked her to give you a second chance. She's going to speak to Dr Kirkwood, and I think he'll agree.'

'Oh!' Florrie was both surprised and delighted – she'd missed working with the babies so much – but she could scarcely believe that Mabel had spoken up on her behalf considering it was her false accusation that had seen her banned in the first place.

'But I must warn you,' Mabel went on, 'should you become aware that certain things are not as you would expect, and talk to anyone about it, you will be returned to the menial jobs you've been doing recently. I'll see to it that your banishment from the nursery is permanent. Do I make myself clear?'

'I don't understand . . .' Florrie gazed at her, puzzled and confused.

'I'm saying no more now. But make no mistake, one word out of place from you, to the day nurse or anyone else, and you'll never work in the nursery again. Now, go and finish your game of cards, and no gossiping about what I've told you.'

Before Florrie could ask any more questions, Mabel turned and strode away, back to the nursery.

She'd done what she could, she told herself. She only hoped it would be enough. But given Florrie's passion for working with the babies, she rather thought it would be.

# Chapter Eighteen

It was mid morning before Matron called Florrie into her office. Florrie had been on edge ever since Mabel had spoken to her last night, her thoughts running in crazy circles, her emotions ranging from elation at the thought of being able to return to her old duties to confusion and anxiety. She simply couldn't understand what Mabel's threat meant – it made no sense to her, but it had been real enough.

Today she'd been set to scrubbing the front steps – part of her punishment for her alleged offence was being assigned the most arduous jobs – and she was just swilling them down when a male nurse came to fetch her.

'Matron wants to see you.'

Florrie tossed the scrubbing brush into the bucket and went to pick it up.

'Leave that,' the nurse instructed her. 'You can finish up later.'

Florrie wiped her hands on her smock and followed him down the corridor to Matron's office.

'Come in,' Matron said, and to the nurse, 'You too, Jackson. I'd like you to hear what I have to say so that you can pass it on to the other staff.'

As if suspecting that some extra punishment was to be meted

out, the nurse, big and beefy as so many of them were, took hold of Florrie's arm and pushed her forward.

'That won't be necessary,' Matron said firmly, and reluctantly Jackson released her, still keeping a watchful eye in case of trouble.

Matron addressed Florrie. 'Would you like to return to nursery duty, Florrie?'

Florrie's face lit up. 'Oh yes please, Matron!'

'Dr Kirkwood and I visited Cissie last evening,' Matron continued. 'I'm glad to say she's recovered full consciousness, and she has confirmed that you were at the other end of the nursery, attending to the babies, when she fell. Dr Kirkwood and I are satisfied that Nurse Cummings must have been mistaken in thinking you were responsible for Cissie's fall. I'm sorry you've been punished for something you didn't do, and you can go back to work in the nursery if you so wish.'

'Oh I do! I do!' Florrie reiterated. 'When . . . ?'

'Right away, or as soon as you've finished whatever you were doing.'

'There's a bucket of water and a scrubbing brush that needs putting away,' Jackson said.

Matron smiled faintly. 'That shouldn't take too long. And when you've done it, Nurse Fry will be expecting you.'

Florrie couldn't stop smiling as she went back to clear up the things she'd left on the step. It was only as she was putting them away in their cupboard that it struck her. Mabel hadn't said anything about Cissie regaining consciousness and confirming that Florrie couldn't have pushed her down the stairs. She'd made it sound as if *she'd* been the one to instigate Florrie's reinstatement. But then that was Mabel all over, twisting the truth to make herself look good.

It didn't explain her mysterious warning, though. Perhaps

she really didn't want Florrie in the nursery, and would take any opportunity to get rid of her again. Well, whatever it was, Florrie would take care not to give her any excuse. Working with the babies meant too much to her.

As she went up the stairs, the familiar scents of soap and milk greeted her and she sniffed appreciatively. How she'd missed all this!

'So I've got some help then,' Joanie Fry said when she saw her, making no mention of Florrie's enforced absence. 'Just in the nick of time too. Make sure Louie Hillman disposes of the contents of her baby's nappy properly, will you? Yesterday she left it under the chair, stinking to high heaven. And after that, you can see if the baby that's crying needs changing. Oh – and you'd better put on an apron. You know where they are.'

Florrie nodded and went to find a clean apron in the linen cupboard. As she headed for the cribs, she met Louie coming the other way holding a dirty nappy at arm's length.

'What do I do with this?' she asked.

'It goes in the sluice, Louie. You know that,' Florrie said gently.

'I got in trouble yesterday.'

'So I heard.' Florrie followed the girl to make sure that the nappy was properly dealt with, then returned to the nursery to attend to the baby who was crying lustily to attract attention to his discomfort.

He was red in the face and waving his arms furiously, and Florrie recognised him as Wallace Gooding. She frowned. She thought he'd been taken for adoption – there had been the most awful scene in the dining room when Rose had seen what was happening. Had something gone wrong and he'd been returned? If he had, she didn't think Rose knew about it. Perhaps she was being kept in the dark to avoid a repetition of the upset when he was taken away again, as he surely would be.

'Come on then, Wallace, let's sort you out.'

She lifted him from his crib and began to undress him to deal with the offending nappy. As she caught a tiny foot to prevent him from kicking, the name tag on his ankle twisted and she straightened it automatically. When she saw what was written on it, her eyes widened. The tag was clearly marked 'William Swift'.

Puzzled, Florrie stared at it. She might not have been in the nursery for some days, but it wasn't long enough for her to forget what each of her charges looked like. This was definitely Wallace Gooding, so why did his ankle tag read 'William Swift'? And now that she came to look at it, so did the card above his crib.

Deep unease stirring in her stomach, Florrie quickly changed the baby's nappy and returned him to his crib. She was about to go and speak to Joanie Fry about the mistake when she froze, remembering Mabel's words.

If she should find something not as she would expect, she must not talk to anyone about it, or Mabel would see to it that she was banned from working in the nursery again – this time permanently. Could it be this she had been referring to? Her thoughts racing, Florrie checked each of the cribs, looking for the William Swift she knew. None of the babies was him.

Perhaps he had been taken home, she thought. She'd heard talk of it, but wasn't that because Stella was rejecting him again? Claiming he wasn't hers?

Florrie stopped suddenly, her hands pressed to her mouth. Was it possible that Mabel had deliberately swapped the babies for some reason? It was almost beyond belief, and yet . . .

Apart from Mabel, Cissie and Florrie were the only ones likely to know which baby was which. Mabel had been talking to Cissie at the top of the stairs just before she'd fallen – could it be that it was Mabel who had pushed her? Had she then accused Florrie in order to get them both out of the way?

'Are you all right, Florrie?' Joanie had approached her, looking concerned.

'Yes, I just stood up too quickly, I think,' Florrie managed, but she was far from all right. She felt sick, her stomach churning. 'I'm sorry . . .' Her hand still pressed to her mouth, she fled past Joanie and into the sluice, where she leaned against the sink. Her shaking legs would barely support her.

What next? She should tell someone, she knew, but if she did, who would believe her? They'd take Mabel's word over hers just as they had before, and she'd be banned from the nursery once more and returned to the most horrible menial tasks, this time for good.

'Oh dear God, what am I going to do?' Florrie whispered.

And received no answer.


Alistair Mackay received the call as he was finishing his morning surgery. It was Dr Kirkwood, asking if he knew whether arrangements had been made for Baby Swift to be taken home.

'I really couldn't say. It's the first I've heard of it,' Alistair replied. 'But then I haven't seen the Swift family lately.'

'I'd be grateful if you could find out,' Dr Kirkwood said. 'His mother has had a relapse, and it's unlikely she'll be fit to go home any time soon.'

'Oh, I'm sorry to hear that.' Alistair was shocked. He'd thought Stella was much improved the last time he'd seen her.

'It's most unfortunate,' Dr Kirkwood agreed. 'But the thing is, Baby is really of an age when he should be in a normal family environment. I have discussed it with Mr Swift, but as I've heard nothing from him since, I wondered if you could find out the lie of the land and encourage him to get the child home as soon as it's feasible to do so.'

Alistair's heart sank. Until now he had had no reason to go in the Dunderwick direction, though he had plenty of other home visits to make. Dunderwick Road was at the top of a long, steep hill, just as pretty well every destination was, since the town of Hillsbridge was surrounded by them. Already every muscle in his legs was protesting at the unaccustomed exercise that he'd been forced into with the loss of his motor, and he hoped he would be able to find a replacement soon. In the meantime, he had no means of transport but Jessica's old bicycle. But however daunting the prospect, he couldn't refuse Dr Kirkwood's request.

'I'll go when I finish afternoon surgery,' he said. 'Tom Swift will be at work all day, and early evening would be the best time to catch him.'

'Thank you. And you'll let me know the result tomorrow?'

Alistair promised that he would, and ended the phone call. Once he'd locked up the surgery, he balanced his medical bag on the bicycle basket, put on the cycle clips he'd bought because his trousers got so creased if he tucked them into his socks, and rode off to make his first home visit of the day.

Grace had just got the children's tea on the table and was about to light the copper to heat the water for Tom's bath when there was a knock at the door. Wondering who it could be, she went to answer it, and was surprised to see Mrs Plumley on the doorstep.

She was wearing a man's cap over her straggle of off-white hair, and her coat was unbuttoned over a floral wraparound apron. Grace had never met her face to face before; now, close to, she could see numerous fine lines and wrinkles forming webs across her cheeks and around her mouth, and her eyes were red as if she'd been crying. In one hand she was holding her empty birdcage; with the other she tugged her coat across her chest as if it were bitterly cold.

'Mrs Plumley . . .' Grace didn't know what else to say.

'I want a word with you.' The old woman's voice was shrill and quivering with emotion. 'It was your cat killed my Joey, wasn't it? Well, I've just come to say I hope you're pleased with yourself.'

Grace frowned, puzzled. She supposed the bird must have escaped yet again, but she couldn't understand why Mrs Plumley should think Fluffy had killed him. Yes, admittedly he'd caught Joey yesterday, but the bird had recovered. Perhaps he'd been caught this time by some other cat, and because of what had happened yesterday, Mrs Plumley was blaming Fluffy. But Grace was fairly sure he couldn't have been responsible – he'd been in since dinner time today. If there'd been a repeat of the unfortunate incident, he'd have brought the canary into the house again, proud to display his trophy, she felt sure.

'I'm really sorry if something has happened to Joey, but I don't think it can have been Fluffy,' she said.

'Well, that's what Francie Newman told me.' Mrs Plumley's lips pinched together tightly. 'And what I want to know is, what are you going to do about it?'

'Francie told you that Fluffy . . . ? But that was yesterday, and Joey . . .' Grace broke off as an awful thought entered her head.

'Yesterday, yes.' Mrs Plumley nodded her head with a quick, jerky movement. 'The Newmans brought him back in a wooden box. Very kind of them, but I don't know why you couldn't have come and owned up yourself.'

Grace was horrified. 'I thought he was alive! Francie said—'

'After your cat got him? Hardly!'

'Oh dear . . . that's awful. If I'd known . . .'

'I just wanted to let you know what I think of you.' The old woman swung the empty cage under Grace's nose, tears trickling down her wrinkled cheeks. 'My little friend, and he's gone, thanks to you.'

Then, before Grace could apologise again, or say another word, she turned and walked away.

'Auntie Grace!' Emily was behind her, tugging on her skirt. 'Alec's got the last rock cake and he won't share it. And he's had two already!'

'All right, Emily, I'm coming.'

Grace followed her niece back to the living room just in time to see Alec hastily stuffing what remained of the rock cake into his mouth.

'Alec! Are you being greedy?'

Alec's cheeks were bulging; he couldn't have replied if he'd wanted to.

'You're horrible!' Emily told him, beginning to cry. 'I wanted one!'

'You ought to eat faster then,' Alec spluttered.

'It's not fair!' Emily wept. 'The boys always get first dibs.'

'I'll find you a biscuit.' Grace was trembling, upset by the awful news about Joey and Mrs Plumley's vehement attack, and the last thing she needed was the children squabbling.

'Can I have one too?' Alec asked eagerly.

'No you can't,' she snapped. 'You've had quite enough sweet things already; any more and you'll be sick. If you're still hungry, you can have the crust of the bread. Now behave yourselves, for goodness' sake, while I get your father's bath water on, or he'll be home before it's hot.'

Still shaking, and unable to think of anything but poor Mrs

Plumley, she fetched a biscuit for Emily and lit the gas beneath the boiler. She'd believed Francie when she'd said Joey had recovered from his ordeal, but now that she came to think about it, she should have realised. He'd been still for far too long, lying there on the hearth each time she'd looked in to check on him, and when Francie had brought him out, he'd been cupped in her hands, so Grace hadn't actually seen any signs of life. She'd been so relieved she'd simply accepted what Francie had said as some kind of miracle.

Francie had lied to save her feelings, she supposed, because she could see how upset Grace was. And Noel had gone along with it. They'd meant it for the best, and that was kind of them, but unwittingly they'd simply made things worse. Although common sense told Grace she was not to blame, she felt dreadful.

Their tea finished, the children went outside to play hopscotch on the pavement outside the front gate, where they had drawn the staggered squares with a sharp fragment of chalky stone. But it wasn't long before they were back again, saying that it had started to rain, and the arguing, along with some rough and tumble, began again.

They were still at it, driving Grace mad, when Tom got home from work, black with coal dust, and went off to have his bath. Grace put his dinner to warm on a covered plate over a pan of boiling water, and was washing up the children's tea things when there was another knock, this time at the front door.

Still jumpy as a kitten, she went to answer it. To her surprise, it was Dr Mackay on the doorstep, rain dripping from the brim of his hat. Propped up against the gatepost was his bicycle.

'I hope this isn't a bad time, but I wanted a word with Mr Swift,' he said, wiping his wet face with the back of his hand.

'He's having his bath at the moment, but it never takes him long. Do come in.'

'Thank you.' He gave his coat a shake before stepping into the hallway.

Conscious of the noise the children were making in the living room, Grace opened the door of the little-used front room.

'It's probably best in here if you want to talk. There's no fire, but at least it's quiet. I'll tell Tom, and I'll bring you a cup of tea. You'd like one, I expect.'

'If it's no trouble.'

'None at all. There's one in the pot.'

She hurried out, wondering why the doctor was here, and whether he had news of Stella. In her present mood, she couldn't imagine it would be good.

Tom was just coming in from his bath, wearing the clean clothes she'd put out ready for him and towelling his wet hair.

'Dr Mackay's here,' she said.

Tom stopped rubbing his head, the towel bunched at the nape of his neck. 'Dr Mackay?' He looked alarmed.

'I've put him in the front room, and I'm going to take him a cup of tea. Do you want one?'

'If there's one going. But what can the doctor want?'

'I don't know. Only that he asked to speak to you.'

'Right.' Tom dropped the towel over the back of a chair and ran his fingers through his still-damp hair to straighten it before heading for the front room.

Grace set about pouring the tea and putting the cups on a wicker-edged tray, together with the sugar bowl. The children were still arguing about something and she snapped at them: 'Will you three play quietly? We've got a visitor and he doesn't want to hear your racket.'

She took the tea tray into the front room, set it on a side table and handed a cup each to Dr Mackay and Tom, who were sitting in the two easy chairs.

'Here we are. Help yourselves to sugar.'

The men had stopped talking as she entered the room, and she turned to leave so that they could continue their conversation, but Tom stopped her.

'Don't go, Grace. You should be in on this. The doctor has come to ask if we could bring Will home, and really it's up to you.'

'Oh!' Though they'd talked about it before, she hadn't really expected it to be so soon; had hoped that Stella's relapse was no more than a hiccup.

'Would you be willing to care for him until Stella is well again?' Dr Mackay asked.

'Well . . . yes.' She looked at Tom. 'You know I said I would. But when . . . ?'

'As soon as possible,' Dr Mackay said. 'It would be far better for William. As to how we get him here, I know you don't have any transport, and unfortunately at the moment neither do I, but I think the hospital would be willing to arrange it. Just as long as you're happy for them to do so.'

'Of course.' She could hear that another squabble had broken out in the living room. 'I need to get back to the children.'

She hurried out, leaving Tom and Dr Mackay to finalise the details. She felt as if she had the weight of the world on her shoulders, and ridiculously, she was close to tears. Looking after Oliver, Alec and Emily was one thing – though she didn't seem to be making much of a job of it today. But caring for a baby was something else entirely. What did she know about babies? Coming on top of the upset about the canary, and the turbulent and conflicting emotions she had been experiencing lately, it was the last straw.

With an effort she gulped back the tears and went into the living room.

'What's going on now?' she demanded in exasperation. 'What is wrong with you all today? Why can't you play nicely together without fighting all the time?'

Three pairs of eyes fastened on her. They weren't used to Auntie Grace losing her temper.

'You'll have to be a lot better behaved when your brother comes home,' she warned.

'Will's coming home?' Oliver picked up on it immediately, and Grace felt guilty on top of everything else. She should have left it to Tom to tell them, but somehow it had just slipped out.

'It looks like it,' she said shortly.

'And Mammy?' Emily's eyes opened wide in surprised delight.

'No, darling, not yet.' There was a lump in Grace's throat, and as she saw Emily's face fall, it grew until she felt as if it were choking her.

Hastily, before the children noticed, she gathered up the tea plates.

'Just behave now,' she managed, before escaping to the kitchen and letting the tears flow.

As soon as Tom walked into the kitchen after seeing Dr Mackay off, he could tell that Grace wasn't herself. Her head was bent low over the sink where she was washing up the tea things, her shoulders held rigid, and she didn't turn to speak to him as he would have expected.

'Grace? What's wrong?' he asked, though he thought he knew.

'Nothing.' But her voice was thick as though she'd been crying, and still she didn't turn to look at him.

'Is it because Will is coming home? I can always try to make other arrangements if . . .'

'No. I've just had a bad day. Eat your dinner before it spoils. We can talk later.'

'I'll have it out here.' Though he usually ate in the living room, he was reluctant to leave her when she was clearly upset about something.

'I don't blame you.' She laughed, a short, shaky sound. 'The children have been playing up something awful.'

'So I hear.' They were squabbling again. 'I'll soon sort them out.'

As Tom went into the room, Alec took a flying leap from the arm of one of the chairs and landed beside Oliver on the sofa. Emily stood in the middle of the floor, crying.

'What in the world is going on here?' Tom demanded.

'We're playing Off-Ground Touch.' Alec's arms windmilled as he attempted to get his balance.

'And I'm "on it" and they won't let me catch them,' Emily wailed.

'Get down from there at once!' Tom yelled at the boys. 'You'll break the springs! What is the matter with you?'

'We're bored,' Oliver said, jumping down from the sofa.

'And we can't play outside because it's raining.' That was Alec, landing with a thud on the rag rug.

'How about a game of table skittles?' Tom suggested.

'Yeah!' The boys brightened.

'Not Emily, though. She's rubbish at it.'

'Yes, Emily too,' Tom said firmly. 'She does her best, and you should be nicer to her.'

He went out to the cupboard under the stairs where the board was kept – a good solid board lined with felt that he'd got Noel to make for them one Christmas – set it on a cloth on the dining table and screwed in the pole with the pear-shaped wooden ball attached to it by a chain.

'You can get the skittles out yourselves,' he said. The polished wood skittles lived in a covered box integral to the board. 'Now behave yourselves if you don't want to feel my hand across your backsides.'

Leaving them to set up the game, he went back to the kitchen. Grace had laid a place on the oilcloth-covered kitchen table and taken his plate of beef stew and dumplings off the heat.

'Hopefully we'll get a bit of peace,' he said, pulling out a chair and sitting down. 'This looks good, Grace.'

'I hope it's all right.' She was drying the crockery now, stacking it up ready to put away.

Tom reached across and pulled out another chair, at right angles across the table to where he was sitting. 'Leave that and come and sit down for a bit while the children are quiet.'

'I'll finish this first.'

'It can wait. Come on.'

Reluctantly she put down the tea cloth and joined him at the table.

Tom loaded his fork with a piece of beef so tender it was almost falling apart and a chunk of carrot.

'So tell me what's the matter. I can see something is, and we've got to sort this out.'

Grace rubbed at a spot of spilt gravy on the oilcloth with the tip of her finger.

'It's not Will, honestly. I mean . . . I wish things were different, but I meant what I said. Of course he must come home if that's what's best for him, and of course I'll look after him.'

'But it's upsetting you.'

She stirred the spot of gravy some more, seeming to concentrate on it as if it was the most important thing in the world.

'It's so . . . final, somehow. It seems like Stella's never going to get well, never going to be able to come home.'

'We don't know that.'

'Well, no, I suppose we don't. But she's missing so much. She's the one who should be here, caring for him. And the other children. And you. It's not my place.'

'And like I said, if it's too much for you, I'll sort out something else. Please don't be afraid to say. You've already done far more than I have any right to expect.'

At last she stopped stirring the gravy spot, and her eyes, bright with unshed tears, came up to meet his.

'I do it because I want to, Tom. I'm happy here. Too happy. I'm getting to feel . . . well, too much at home. And I wish . . .'

She broke off, tore her eyes from his abruptly.

The stew was delicious, but suddenly Tom had no appetite. What Grace was saying – what she hadn't said – was too close to his own feelings for comfort. He wanted Stella well again, of course he did. He wanted her home where she belonged. And yet he didn't want this time with Grace to end either. Dangerous as it was, given his feelings for her, he couldn't bear the thought of her not being here, in his house, his home, his life. He shouldn't love her; it was all wrong. But he did. Perhaps he always had . . .

'Enough of that.' Grace interrupted his thoughts. 'It's like I said. It's been a horrible day, and hearing that Stella is no better, and that she's going to be separated from Will while I'm here taking her place . . . well, it was just the last straw.'

'So what else has gone wrong?' Tom asked, anxious to change the subject.

Grace grimaced. 'I've had Mrs Plumley here, blaming me for Fluffy killing her bird. She was in a terrible way – well, no wonder – but it was horrible. She was waving his empty cage under my nose.'

'But I thought you said he was all right?' Tom was puzzled.

'That's what Francie told me, but now that I come to think of it, it was a bit strange, the way she carried Joey out cupped in her hands and they both went off down the rank with the box Noel had made for a coffin. The only thing I can think is that they could see I was upset and thought it was for the best to keep it from me. But it was such a shock, having Mrs Plumley turn up on the doorstep shouting at me.'

The tears were gathering in her eyes again; she pressed her hand across her mouth, struggling to suppress them.

'Oh Grace . . .'

Tom put down his knife and reached over to cover her free hand with his, tenderness flooding through him. All he wanted to do was take her in his arms and comfort her. For a few moments there was silence, broken only by the clatter of falling skittles in the living room.

'I'm sorry – I'm just being silly, I know,' Grace said at last. But her fingers curled round his, holding them tightly.

'Not silly at all. I can understand why you're upset. Look – perhaps we can get her another bird. One of the men I work with breeds them.'

'Oh, I don't know . . . It's a nice thought, but I'm not sure she's capable of looking after one. Joey was always escaping, and the same thing might happen again.'

'True.'

Quite suddenly she withdrew her hand. 'Your dinner's getting cold.'

'Hang my dinner.'

'What? After all the trouble I went to to keep it warm for you?' She was smiling, if a little tremulously, trying to lighten the mood, he guessed.

'You're the only thing that matters, Grace.'

The words were out before he could stop them, and he

reached across, brushing away a tear that had escaped, then running his fingers lovingly across her cheek to tuck a stray strand of hair behind her ear as desire flooded through him.

Her eyes met his again, and he saw his own feelings reflected there.

'I mean it, Grace.' He began to move towards her.

'Daddy!'

Emily was in the doorway. Hastily he removed his hand from Grace's neck, sat back in his chair.

'What?' His voice came out rough, impatient.

'Alec won't let me have a go. He says I'm spoiling the game.'

'Oh, that boy!'

But as he went into the living room to deal with the latest kerfuffle, he could only thank his lucky stars for it. To his shame, he'd let down his guard, allowed his feelings for Grace to run away with him. If Emily hadn't interrupted, who knew where it might have led?

'Right, you two, that's enough. Pack up the skittles and get to bed, both of you, before I put you over my knee. And one more mean word to Emily and that's exactly what I'll do.'

He knew he was taking out his frustration and his disgust at his own loss of control on them and felt guilty for it. But it was a release of sorts.

He wondered wretchedly how the hell he was going to get through the weeks ahead with no prospect of Stella coming home and things getting back to normal.

Grace felt like crying again. Not because of the traumas and stresses of the day, not because of her anxiety for Stella and her worries about her ability to care for a baby who was not hers, not because of Mrs Plumley and her dead canary. But because she had glimpsed what might have been. She put her fingers to the spot on her cheek that his fingers had brushed, tucked the strand of hair behind her ear again, saw the reflection of her own feelings in his eyes. It wasn't just her. He still had feelings for her too. It could be, of course, that it was just an escape from all the stress he was under. But whatever, she'd lost her chance with him long ago. Now, they both cared for Stella too much to do anything to hurt her. What might have been theirs could never be.

# Chapter Nineteen

Next morning when she got back from taking the children to school, Grace went next door to speak to Francie.

'I thought I ought to let you know they're sending Will home sometime this week,' she said when she was seated at Francie's living room table with a cup of tea and a slice of fruit cake in front of her – Francie was nothing if not hospitable. 'Just in case you should hear a baby crying and wonder what's going on.'

'Oh – is Stella coming home too?' Francie asked, stirring a generous three spoonfuls of sugar into her own tea.

'I'm afraid not. She's rejecting him again.' Grace crumbled a bit of fruit cake between her fingers, not feeling as if she'd be able to eat it, but not wanting to offend Francie.

'Oh dear, that's awful. Then . . .'

'I'm going to look after him, and to tell you the truth, the very thought of it scares me to death,' Grace admitted.

'Well, you know where I am if you need me,' Francie said. 'I've had plenty of practice. Too much, I sometimes think! But I'm sure you'll be fine. It's not like he's a newborn any more, is it?'

'No, but all the same . . .'

'It's not fair on you really. I mean, what about your own life? Your job? Are they keeping that open for you?'

'I don't know,' Grace said. 'I shouldn't think so.'

Francie tutted. 'I don't know what Tom would have done without you, though.'

With the memory of their few moments of closeness last evening dominating her thoughts, Grace didn't want to go down that road. Especially since there was something in the way Francie was looking at her that made her wonder if the neighbour thought there might be something going on between them. It would be hardly surprising if she did – a single woman and a man deprived of his wife for all this time living under the same roof was bound to generate suspicion and gossip. The realisation made her feel grubby somehow, and was a bit too close to the truth for comfort.

'I'm only glad to do what I can,' she said, popping the morsel of fruit cake into her mouth. It felt dry on her tongue, and she took a sip of tea to help it go down.

'God knows, Stella must be going through hell,' Francie said, mercifully seeming not to notice her unease, or difficulty in swallowing the cake. 'But it must be a comfort to her knowing Tom and the children are being well looked after.'

'I'm not sure how much she's aware of,' Grace said.

'Really?' That look again. Curious. Prurient.

To change the subject, Grace said abruptly: 'I have to mention that I'm a bit puzzled about Mrs Plumley's bird. I thought you said he'd recovered when you took him back to her, but I had her at the door yesterday saying otherwise, and wanting to know why I hadn't confessed to her myself that our cat killed him.'

'Oh. Oh dear.' Francie blushed scarlet.

'I denied it at first, of course. But then . . . it was awful. Why did you tell me he was all right when he wasn't?'

'I'm so sorry. You were in such a state about it and we decided to let you think he'd recovered. We never thought you'd find out different. I mean, you don't know Mrs Plumley to speak to, do you? We never for a moment thought she'd come knocking on your door.'

'Well, she did. It was a kind thought, I suppose, but I just wish I'd known.'

'I'm sorry,' Francie apologised again. 'She was upset, of course, but we helped her bury him in her back garden in the box Noel made, and thought that was the end of it.'

'Tom wondered if it might be an idea to get her another bird to replace Joey, but I can't help thinking it's not fair to have a bird if you can't look after it properly,' Grace said.

'Exactly. The same thing might happen again.' Francie shrugged. 'You can't blame Fluffy. It's what cats do. If it hadn't been Joey, it would have been another bird, or a field mouse. Our friendly neighbourhood robin is too tame for his own good; it'll be him next, mark my words.'

Grace was a little shocked. What Francie said was no more than the truth, but how could she be so cold and matter-of-fact about it? It was a side of the woman she'd never seen before. But perhaps that was what living with a violent husband did to you. Made you hard.

Whatever, suddenly she really didn't want to be here any more. When Francie went into the kitchen to refresh the teapot, she slipped the remains of her fruit cake into the pocket of her apron, then stood up. 'I ought to be going,' she called. 'I've got a million things to do.'

'Well, pop round again when you've got a minute. And don't forget, if you're worried about Will when he comes home, you know where I am.'

'Thanks, Francie,' Grace said, and gratefully escaped to the kitchen she was beginning to think of as her own.

* * *

'I think I might have found a suitable motor,' Alistair said when he came home after finishing his afternoon surgery.

Ever since his Ford had been destroyed, he had been searching the 'For Sale' columns in the *Bath Chronicle*, and today he had spotted a likely replacement. A landowner on the outskirts of the city was advertising a two-year-old Wolseley, and Alistair had telephoned to ask for details.

The motor was bigger than his old Ford, and although he would have preferred something smaller and more economic to run, he imagined, given the status of the present owner, that it would have been well looked after, and he couldn't wait to be able to drive again rather than having to pedal to all his home visits on Jessica's old bicycle. As things were, by the end of the day he was bone tired, his legs ached unbearably, and if it was raining, he was more often than not soaked to the skin. It wasn't very dignified either, he thought ruefully. On Saturday a group of youths squatting against the wall on the bridge between the two railway lines in the centre of town had sniggered and jeered as he wobbled past, balancing his medical bag on the wicker basket between the handlebars.

'That's good news!' Jessica said.

Quite apart from worrying about Alistair's safety, she was missing the Sunday-morning trips to Catcombe for the church service, and her weekly meeting with Florrie.

'The owner is going to get his man to run it over for me to have a look at,' Alistair told her. 'The only trouble is, it won't be available for a week or so. They're waiting on a brand-new model and can't get rid of the old one until it's been delivered.'

'Oh.' Jessica's face fell. 'Well, I suppose we'll just have to hope that doesn't take too long.'

'But at least it will give me a chance to sort out the finances,' Alistair said. 'That's something else we need to talk about. It's quite a bit more than I'd planned to pay. I think it will be worth it, but it might mean we have to cut back a bit on our living expenses. How would you feel about that?'

Jessica didn't hesitate. 'You need a motor, Alistair. One that's reliable. I'm quite prepared to adjust my housekeeping budget accordingly. Just as long as you think we're not over-stretching ourselves beyond what's reasonable.'

'I think we'll be all right if we're careful.' He smiled, grateful as always for such a supportive wife. 'I'll just have to try and get a few more patients on to my books.'

'That shouldn't be difficult.' Jessica returned his smile. 'You know how often you have people wanting to transfer to your list.'

'I have to be careful not to upset the other doctors, though.'

It was true. On more than one occasion Alistair had had to refuse a patient in order to keep the peace. But perhaps this time he couldn't afford that luxury. Even leaving aside the expense of the new motor, their finances were going to be stretched with a new baby on the way. But at least now he had finished paying off the debt he'd incurred when he'd purchased the practice from the old retiring doctor.

'If I have to tread on a few toes, then so be it,' he said. 'Don't worry your head about it. We'll manage. Now, what's for tea?'

Jessica flashed him a teasing look. 'Liver and bacon. And isn't it lucky that one of your favourite meals is also one of the cheapest?'

In the nursery at Catcombe, Mabel finished feeding Wallace, changed him and stood for a few minutes cradling him in her arms before tucking him into his crib. This was the last night she'd be able to do it; tomorrow he was going to be taken to Hillsbridge, to the Swift family home.

There was a tightness in her chest as she pulled the covers up to her great-nephew's chin. She'd enjoyed being able to look after him; enjoyed even more the smug satisfaction of knowing she'd hoodwinked everyone. If ever she felt the slightest pang of guilt at what she'd done, she'd quickly suppressed it. And so caught up had she been in making her plan work, she hadn't thought beyond it, hadn't worked out where she was going to take it from here and how she was going to reunite Rose with her baby. The girl didn't even know yet what she had done. Mabel had come to work early on a few occasions, hoping to be able to have a word with her, but it hadn't happened, and as yet there was no news regarding her discharge. Sir Oswald was in no hurry to have her back in the community, she guessed, and it would be up to him when he gave the word to the two doctors who had signed her in in the first place.

Bastard! she muttered to herself, all her old hatred and sour resentment flooding through her in a rush – the hatred and resentment she'd harboured long before he'd had Rose committed and arranged for her baby to be adopted. No doubt the same treatment would have been meted out to Mabel herself if she hadn't gone along with his instructions. And she could well imagine how Rose had come to find herself in terrible trouble. Much the same had happened to her.

It hadn't been rape, any more than she supposed it had been for Rose. It had been an arrogant, lascivious gentleman taking advantage of a naïve young girl, easily flattered and with a head full of dreams. She couldn't for a moment blame Rose for having been taken in as she had been, bedazzled into believing that a rich man, a member of the aristocracy, was actually interested in her, rather than simply out to satisfy his lust and overweening vanity. To prove he could do whatever he liked, have whoever he liked, and never have to answer for it.

Mabel returned to the nurses' station, poured herself a nip of brandy from the small bottle she brought to work each night in her bag, and let the memories fuel the all-consuming anger that had driven her to do what she had done.

Unlike Rose, Mabel had never been employed at Easterton Manor. From school she had gone straight into a position at the hospital, working first as a lowly orderly, scrubbing floors, dusting down bedside cabinets, wiping patients' bottoms, sometimes even helping to lay out the dead. Menial as the tasks were, she'd carried them out gladly, determined to work her way up the pecking order, learning as she went, until she fulfilled her dream of becoming a fully fledged nurse. She hadn't had a bitter or resentful bone in her body in those days. That had come later, and it was all down to Oswald Whittingly Challis, though occasionally she admitted to herself that she hadn't been entirely blameless.

It was her older sister Olive – Rose's mother – who was employed as a parlour maid at Easterton Manor. The Whittingly Challises were great ones for entertaining, and Mabel loved to hear Olive's tales of the grand banquets attended by the great and good of the county, the elaborate summer picnics, and the shooting parties in the season, when the house would be full of guests staying for long weekends or even a whole week, with the days spent out in the rolling fields and woods of the estate, and beaters putting up the pheasants for the pleasure of the guns.

'I don't like it,' Olive had said. 'It fair gives me the creeps when I hear those guns bang-bang-banging. And those poor birds dripping blood all over the pantry floor, and the dogs with it dried round their mouths.'

'You're a big softie,' Mabel had teased her sister.

'You wouldn't like it if you saw it,' Olive had retorted. 'You're looking at it through rose-tinted glasses. It's beyond me how anybody could enjoy that sort of thing. It's cruel and horrible.'

But in a funny sort of way, Mabel could understand, perhaps a presentiment of the woman she would become. The power over life and death must be exhilarating, she thought. To shoot a bird and see it fall. There were some of her patients she wouldn't mind shooting, and that was a fact. The daft old man who exposed himself whenever she went near his bed, for instance. Or the woman who was doubly incontinent – it was Mabel's job to clean her and her bed up again.

But life at Easterton Manor was something else. Much as she'd always wanted to be a nurse, she'd give it all up, she thought, if she could live that sort of charmed existence. Not as a parlour maid, as Olive was, but as a lady of leisure, with nothing to do but enjoy the high life that the other half lived.

Nevertheless, she jumped at the chance when Olive came home on an afternoon off and told her the housekeeper was looking to take on casual staff to help out with a house party over Christmas and New Year. She really fancied seeing what went on there, and to make things easy, the hospital schedules had already been arranged. Besides having a whole day off on Boxing Day and on New Year's Eve, Mabel had been allocated day shifts for the week in between.

'I could help out when I'm not working at the hospital, if that would be any good to them,' she'd offered eagerly. 'I could do with a bit of extra money, too.'

'It wouldn't be much,' Olive warned.

'Every little helps. I've got a Christmas present to buy for you, remember.'

Not that it was the meagre wage she'd earn that Mabel was really interested in. She just wanted to be part of the festivities at the Manor. And to investigate the possible opportunity to better herself.

'I'll see what I can do,' Olive promised.

True to her word, she put Mabel's name forward, and the housekeeper, who was having trouble finding enough extra help since most likely candidates wanted to spend Christmas and New Year with their families, grabbed at the offer of an extra pair of hands.

When Mabel arrived at the Manor for her first spell of duty on Christmas Eve, she was delighted that rather than the job in the scullery that she'd been expecting, she had been assigned to help serve the food and clear away the empty plates afterwards.

'Your sister can tell you what to do,' the harassed housekeeper informed her. 'Just be sure to keep a steady hand and not spill anything. And remember to serve over the left shoulder and collect from the right. And make sure the meat, not the vegetables, is in front of them.'

In the smart black skirt and white frilled apron that had been loaned to her, Mabel knew she looked good, and she knew too that Sir Oswald had noticed her as soon as she entered the dining room with a basket of bread rolls fresh from the oven. Though she was only seventeen, two years younger than Olive, she was much more aware of such things than her sister. Olive had been walking out with Frank Gooding, who worked in the quarries, ever since they left school, but Mabel didn't think she'd so much as let him kiss her, and wouldn't until she had a ring on her finger.

Now, as she moved around the table offering her basket of rolls to the guests, she knew Sir Oswald's eyes were following her, and felt a spike of triumph. She might only be a hospital orderly, but she could attract the attention of the lord of the manor. The realisation excited her, and throughout the evening she played up to him as much as she dared, careful not to overstep the mark or make her response to his admiring glances too obvious. It was always best to let a man think he was making the running, and she didn't want Lady Cecelia, his wife, to notice either, though there was talk among the staff that they had not shared a bedroom since the birth of their younger son.

And so it went on, this private little game, as she served and cleared dishes, until the men withdrew to the smoking room for port and cigars and Mabel found herself elbow deep in soap suds at the scullery sink, washing up whilst Olive and another girl – a pudding-faced kitchen maid – dried up and put away. She was buzzing with excitement and the dreams that had begun with Sir Oswald's lingering looks.

'Do you think they'll let me serve again tomorrow?' she whispered to Olive before she left for the long walk home.

'I don't see why not. You did well,' Olive whispered back. Clearly she had not noticed the little pantomime that had been going on.

Though it was past midnight and Mabel had been on her feet all day, working her shift at the hospital before going to the Manor, she was too exhilarated to feel even a little bit tired. On the way home, she passed the church, where folk who had attended Midnight Mass were streaming out, and she called a merry greeting to the ones she knew. There were also a few drunks rolling and stumbling about, but they didn't bother her. Nothing could tonight, not even the prospect of spending Christmas Day cleaning up mess and wiping dirty bottoms at the hospital. Tomorrow evening she would be back amongst the gentry, and with any luck, enjoying Sir Oswald's attentions again. And she would be there every day until the New Year, after which the house guests would leave and her window of opportunity would close.

The next evening she was once again assigned to waiting at table as she had hoped, and things proceeded much as before. She'd seen the narrow look Sir Oswald had given her when she walked in, though he had quickly turned his attention to playing the charming host to his guests. Tonight the food was even more lavish – Mabel had sneaked a bit of crispy skin from the carving dish as Cook piled slices of succulent pink duck on to the serving platter – and the drink flowed freely, oiling the atmosphere of festive jollity.

As she stopped beside Sir Oswald, offering him the dish of roast potatoes, she felt his hand squeeze her thigh through the cotton fabric of her skirt, and he glanced up at her and gave her a surreptitious wink. Mabel lowered her eyes demurely but allowed herself a little smile that she knew would make the dimples play in her cheeks. She was enjoying herself immensely.

It was on New Year's Eve, as she was setting the table for dinner, that Sir Oswald made the first move beyond the meaningful looks and occasional furtive grope.

He and the house guests had spent the day out shooting, and hc was still wearing his tweeds when he entered the room.

'Mabel, my dear.' Approaching the table where she was polishing the crystal wine glasses, he lifted one and held it up so that the light from the overhead chandelier caught each facet and made it sparkle. 'Excellent work. You are doing a fine job, and I must say we have been fortunate indeed to have your assistance.'

A little flush coloured Mabel's cheeks.

'Thank you, sir,' she said demurely.

'I am wondering if you would consider a permanent post here at the Manor,' he went on. 'We would certainly value a young lady of your talents.'

His eyes on her face were speculative and left Mabel in no doubt as to what talents he was referring to. She was flattered, too, that he had called her a young lady, not a girl. But she was not going to accede to his offer so easily. If she was working here she would simply be another lowly member of the staff, and already she had ideas that were far more ambitious. She had heard of gentlemen setting up discreet homes for their mistresses; she didn't actually know anyone who had been so favoured, but that hadn't stopped her dreaming. A cottage on the estate, perhaps, or better still, an apartment in Bath. She'd pictured herself in fine clothes, reclining on a chaise longue, a glass of sherry on a spindle-legged table beside her. Picking at delicacies that would be delivered from Cater's, the high-end grocer's in the city. No more dirty and disgusting duties. No more having to live by her parents' strict rules. All that would be required of her would be to entertain Sir Oswald when he called on her, and she found the thought of that exciting and a little erotic.

No, accepting a post as a maid here at Easterton was not the right way to go about making her dream a reality.

'Thank you, sir, but I already have a very rewarding job,' she said primly. 'I'm working my way up, and soon I shall be a proper nurse and in a position to care for the needs of my patients, which I shall find very satisfying.'

Sir Oswald's fleshy lips curved into a half-smile.

'Quite the little Florence Nightingale! Most commendable. But others have their needs too, Mabel, that go beyond the provision of medication and fresh dressings.'

A nerve in her stomach flipped. Again his meaning was patently obvious.

'Sir . . .'

'We'll talk about this again. Perhaps after the fireworks at midnight. You will come out to see the fireworks, won't you? I make it a point that the staff should enjoy them as well as my guests.'

'Thank you, sir.'

'And please stop calling me "sir". My name is Oswald.'

Mabel's excitement knew no bounds. It was happening, just as she'd imagined. She could hardly wait for midnight.

Since it would be very late before the New Year celebrations ended, it had been decided that Mabel would stay the night at the Manor, and leave early next morning for her shift at the hospital. She was to share Olive's bed in the servants' quarters at the top of the house. It would be a tight squeeze, but it wouldn't be the first time the sisters had had to squash in together.

As midnight approached, almost everyone – except for some of the ladies, who preferred to watch the firework display from a window – went out into the garden, and Mabel followed the rest of the staff to their place on the outskirts of the small crowd.

Sir Oswald, wearing an overcoat over his dress suit, was checking his pocket watch, but in the event his timekeeping wasn't necessary. It was a clear night, and with the wind in the right direction, the chimes of the church clock at midnight carried sharply on the still air. At the first stroke, he gave the signal, and a groundsman put a lighted torch to the first of the fireworks, which exploded into a cascade of yellow.

Mabel had never seen anything quite like the display that followed. Roman candles, set up in flowerpots on a long bench, fizzed and spluttered, firecrackers went off with loud bangs, and a Catherine wheel attached to the trellis around the rose garden spun fitfully, the groundsman prodding it back to action with a garden rake when it stuttered to a stop. For ten magical minutes it continued until there was nothing left but a haze of drifting smoke and a pungent smell hovering in the air.

'They had them sent all the way from China,' Olive told Mabel as the little crowd began to disperse, heading back to the warmth of the house. But Mabel scarcely heard her. She had her eye on Sir Oswald, who was still out on the lawn, speaking to the groundsman and no doubt issuing instructions as to the clearing-up of the spent husks.

As the other staff went inside, she hung back at the foot of the steps. If he didn't take this opportunity to speak to her about whatever it was he had planned, another might not arise before she left in the morning.

At last she saw him heading in her direction.

'Mabel . . .' His hand closed over her elbow, urging her away from the light spilling out of the open doorway, and setting her pulses racing. 'Let's find somewhere quiet so we can talk.'

There was a summer house on the far side of the lawn. Mabel hadn't seen it before, as she always went in and out of the house by the trade entrance at the rear. Now it loomed against the skyline, a stone-built hexagonal structure with mullioned windows set into each of the walls and the door.

'We won't be disturbed here.'

It was bitterly cold inside the summer house, a damp chill emanating from the old stone. Mabel shivered.

'Here. Take my overcoat.'

He shrugged it off, draping it about her shoulders, and she thrilled at the courtly consideration he was extending to her. The cashmere was soft round her chin and beneath her fingers as she tugged it close, and it smelled faintly of whisky and cigars.

'Has anyone ever told you how pretty you are?' His hands were still on her upper arms, his mouth close to her ear. 'How sorely you tempt a man?'

One hand moved down beneath the coat, unbuttoning her high-necked blouse and sliding inside. At his touch, her nipples hardened and sharp little shivers ran through the deepest parts of her. He turned her towards him, breathing heavily now, and buried his face in her breasts.

The coat slid from her shoulders. He retrieved it and spread it over the stone bench that followed the contours of the walls. Then he lifted her bodily and laid her down on it, one hand rucking up her skirts.

At the time, she was lost in the moment, aware only of the sensations consuming her. It was only afterwards that she realised he had not kissed her on the lips, not once. She'd felt his mouth on her neck, his teeth on her breasts; smelled his breath, a little sour but also sickly sweet, a smell she'd never forgotten. But he had not kissed her.

It was all over so quickly; she felt cheated somehow. But he was buttoning his trousers, pulling her to her feet and reaching for his coat.

'I'll leave you to make yourself tidy before you go back inside,' he said, and there was no trace of softness in his tone now. He was the lord of the manor, she was the hired help. He had done what he wanted, and now she was of no further interest to him.

Dizzy, bewildered, she watched him walk away across the lawns and saw all her foolish dreams go with him. Then and only then did the other emotions overwhelm her. Anger at him for the way he had used her and dismissed her, and at herself for being so stupidly naïve as to think for a moment it could be any other way. Crushing disappointment. Shame. And fear.

She couldn't face sharing a narrow single bed with her sister. Didn't want her, or anyone, to know how stupid she had been. When she was a little calmer, she went back to the house, found her coat hanging on a peg in the passageway and left by the tradesmen's entrance. She saw no one but the groundsman emptying a wheelbarrow of firework cases into one of the bank of bins.

'Could you please tell my sister I've decided to go home after all?' she asked him, and fled.

Perhaps if it had all ended there she would, in time, have forgotten her humiliation. Unfortunately, it had not. Six weeks later, with an ache low in her stomach but no monthly bleed to show for it, Mabel was terribly afraid that all her worst fears had become reality and the brief encounter had had the most unwelcome consequences. Another month and more, and she was sure.

In desperation she penned a letter to Sir Oswald. Surely he would help her? Exactly how, she didn't know. But he must! He wouldn't want anyone to know he was the father of the child that was growing inside her. Perhaps he'd give her money so she could go away somewhere she wasn't known. Perhaps he'd provide for her and her baby even if he never wanted to see either of them.

Her hopes were raised two days later when, walking home from work at the hospital, she saw a carriage that she recognised as Sir Oswald's at the side of the road. As she neared it, the carriage door opened and Sir Oswald himself gestured for her to join him.

Trembling, she did so. Sir Oswald waited for the driver to climb down and walk a discreet distance away down the road before turning to her, his features stony and set.

'I understand you have a problem,' he said coldly.

*You.* Not *we.* Her heart sank, and all her carefully prepared words deserted her.

'Yes,' was all she could manage.

Sir Oswald took a folded sheet of paper from an inside pocket and handed it to her. 'Go to this address and everything will be taken care of. The woman has been paid.'

It was a clear dismissal, but for a moment Mabel didn't move, simply staring at the folded paper – thick, light grey in colour, hand-made, probably from an expensive writing set. Then she opened it out. It was blank but for a name and address; the address a cottage on the outskirts of Easterton, and the name she recognised as that of a woman with a most unsavoury reputation. She raised horrified eyes to Sir Oswald's.

'But she's . . .'

'Someone who will, as I say, take care of your problem.'

'You want me to get rid of it?' Mabel gasped. 'You want me to kill our baby?'

'There's no need for hysterics,' Sir Oswald said, his tone icy. 'It's by far the best solution.'

'No!' Mabel had begun to tremble violently. 'No! I couldn't!'

'Then you leave me with no alternative but to have you committed to the asylum as a moral delinquent and arrange for the adoption of your child. Your sister will be dismissed from my service, and her young man from my quarry, as will your father. He occupies a tied cottage, I believe – one of *my* cottages – so he will not only lose his job but your family their home. I hope I make myself clear.'

Mabel was gazing at him in utter horror, lost for words.

'The choice is yours, my dear Mabel,' he went on. 'I'll expect to hear from Mrs Lovelace that a satisfactory conclusion has been reached very soon. If not . . . you have been warned of the consequences.'

He signalled to the driver to return to the carriage and Mabel was left in no doubt that the meeting was at an end. There was nothing for it but to go home in the knowledge that the choice he had given her was, in reality, no choice at all.

The cottage was dirty, smelling of cats and stale cooking. The sheets on the bed were stained and worn. The woman, Mrs Lovelace, was grossly fat, with grime beneath her fingernails, and her eyes were hard and cruel. The pain she inflicted on Mabel with a knitting needle was unbearable. It was years before the nightmares tailed off, eventually coming less and less frequently, though to this day Mabel would sometimes wake in a cold sweat, roused by her own cries.

The legacy of the dreadful experience was that although she had married, she had never found true happiness. She'd been left frigid, which had caused tension between her and her husband, and she had never been able to bear a child. Over the years, her hatred of Sir Oswald simmered and festered.

He had callously used and abused her, threatened her family, and put her through hell to save his own reputation. The man was a monster. Afraid that the same fate might befall her niece, she'd tried to dissuade Rose from taking up the position at Easterton Manor. But without being able to give her a reason, she'd failed – no one, not even Olive, knew her secret, and after so long, she couldn't bring herself to share it.

When her worst fears had been realised – though Rose refused to name the father of her baby – Mabel was in no doubt as to who was responsible. And when her niece had been committed to the asylum, where Mabel had eventually worked her way up through the ranks to become a trusted nurse, she'd seen a way to take her revenge.

How much use it would be to Rose, she didn't yet know. What she could do to make things right for her niece was something she had to work out. But Mabel was a schemer by nature, and was confident she would think of a way to reunite Rose and her baby. And in the meantime, she had the satisfaction that came from knowing that this time she had bettered Sir Oswald. He thought the child he had fathered was far away in Gloucestershire. She knew different.

At the nurses' station, Mabel sipped her brandy and silently toasted the success of her plan. The game wasn't over yet, but before it was, she would see to it that the quarry owner paid for his cruel arrogance.

# Chapter Twenty

For the second night in a row, Florrie had scarcely slept a wink. Though she managed to drop off to begin with, a couple of hours later she would be wide awake, her thoughts racing, and from then on sleep was impossible. She was now sure the two babies had been swapped, and when Mabel Cummings had threatened to have her removed from her duties once more if she breathed a word of finding something amiss in the nursery, it must have been this she had been alluding to.

At first, however, Florrie had scarcely been able to believe that she was not mistaken. Perhaps that was what being locked away in an asylum did to you; made you lose touch with reality and imagine things. But in a quiet moment when she'd been left alone in the nursery, she'd pulled up William Swift's notes, and what she saw had left her in no doubt. The notes now filed under his name were definitely those of Wallace Gooding – a few of them were reports she'd added herself, and his early struggles due to his premature birth were clearly recorded.

Just to confirm it, if confirmation were still required, she'd discovered that the reason Stella Swift was no longer allowed in the nursery was because she was claiming the baby she had been given to nurse wasn't her William.

Florrie realised too that she'd been right in thinking it was

Mabel herself who had pushed Cissie down the stairs, in order to keep her out of the nursery, and then blamed Florrie for the same reason. She would have known they would see at once that the wrong baby had been sent for adoption and realise she must have been responsible. But why had she done it? No matter how much she puzzled over it, Florrie could not come up with any reason that made sense. She could only conclude that Mabel must be as mad as some of the patients.

But the main reason for her sleepless nights and anxiety-filled days was that she didn't know what to do about the awful thing she had discovered. She should tell someone, she knew, but she couldn't see what good it would do. It would just be her word against Mabel's, and no one would believe her any more than they believed poor Stella. Florrie's heart ached for Stella, and she wished desperately that she could make things right for her. But how could she? Mabel would deny everything, and Florrie would be banished from the nursery again.

If only Jessica would come and visit! she thought. Jessica would know what to do. But she couldn't come until Alistair got himself a new motor.

And now, just to make things worse, the baby who was supposed to be William Swift but wasn't was going home tomorrow, and all the evidence that he was the wrong baby would be going with him.

Around and around in her head went the dilemma, but it was getting her nowhere. She felt trapped and totally power-less, anxiety and guilt eating her up until she could no longer think straight. And she could see no end to the nightmare of conscience.

Tom had taken the day off work. It would mean his wages would be short at the end of the week, but he'd felt he had to be there when Will was brought home. Though Grace had told him she'd be fine dealing with it, he hadn't felt it was right to leave her to receive and settle his baby all on her own. Besides, he *wanted* to be there. He was Will's father, after all, and it seemed so long since he had seen him.

He took the children to school to save Grace having to do it; she'd have her hands full enough later on, he reasoned. But when they were safely inside, instead of going straight home, he found himself turning into a track that led off the main road and followed the course of the river through the valley.

As a boy, he'd played in these fields and along this river when he'd been sent to stay with an aunt and uncle because of his mother's ill health and her inability to care for him while his father worked long hours in the pit. Ironically, they were both dead and gone while his mother still survived, though bedridden to save her weak heart. His own home was on the other side of the valley, and his playground there had been a different one – fields that sloped down to the railway line at the front of the row of cottages where he lived, meadowland extending to the woods and lake that was part of the coal owner's estate to the rear. But he'd been in the same class at school as some of the boys who lived in this neck of the woods, and it was with them that he had explored this area, which had been new to him.

The river had been a great attraction. The boys had fished for tiddlers in the shallows and collected frog spawn and tadpoles in jam jars with perforated lids and a bit of string looped around the necks to form a handle. They'd tied a rope around a thick branch of one of the trees that lined the banks so that they could swing from one side to the other, and in summer they'd swum in the pool where a dam had been built to contain the water. There had even been slabs of stone for steps – not that the boys used them; they preferred to jump straight in – and a diving platform at one end.

His mother had been horrified when she learned he had been swimming there.

'It's right underneath the churchyard,' she'd said – the burial ground was on the hillside stretching from the church in the valley to a ridge of much higher ground. 'Goodness only knows what runs down into the water.'

'It's fine, Mam,' he'd assured her with all the breezy confidence of youth.

But that summer one of his mates had a cut on his foot turn septic after swimming in the pool. He'd been really ill, and the received wisdom was that he'd got an infection from the river water. Tom had never told his mother about it, but he had taken great care afterwards to make sure he didn't swim if he had any cuts or grazes.

They'd been great days, though, when the sun seemed always to shine, and he'd had not a care in the world beyond a niggling worry that his mother might die.

Then, when he was older, he'd walked out with girls along the river. Those banks and secluded spots among the trees had seen his first kisses and fumbling embraces.

Grace was not the first girl he'd brought here, but she was the one he remembered. He'd had a little mongrel dog named Queenie, and walking her had been his excuse to get out of an evening. Some of the girls had objected to him bringing Queenie along, but not Grace. Watching the dog race in circles through the grass or unsuccessfully chase a rabbit made her smile, and she loved sitting on the riverbank tossing pebbles into the shallows for her to run after. This was much further upstream, away from the nasty seepage from the churchyard, and she would take off her boots and dangle her toes in the water. Once, he remembered, she'd tiptoed across the stepping stones to the other side and almost fallen in. He could see her now, arms outstretched to help her keep her balance, the boots dangling one from each hand, and laughing. Always laughing.

He'd never brought Stella here, though. And never wondered why that should be. But now, even without asking himself the question, he knew.

This place belonged to Grace.

As the memories filled his senses, Tom stopped walking and stood stock still, losing himself in them, feeling what he had felt then.

And what he felt now.

Grace was not only his past, she was his present. And, fate seemed to have decreed, his future too. But not in the way he might wish. He'd let the moment when that could have been possible slip away from him long ago.

Now it was Stella he had to consider. His wife, and yet not his wife in any meaningful way at present, nor for the foreseeable future. But as long as there was breath in her body he could not, would not betray her. Somehow he had to resist his longing for Grace, put his feelings for her back in the locked box of memory where they belonged. With her there in his home, doing all the things Stella should be doing, caring for him and the children and now baby Will too, it wouldn't be easy. But Tom knew that if he let his guard down and allowed himself to give way to those feelings he wouldn't be able to live with himself. The guilt would destroy all of them.

Thrusting his hands deep into his pockets, he turned his back on the river, the past and what might have been, and set out for home.

\* \* \*

282

The sight of an ambulance driving along Dunderwick Road and stopping outside the gate of number 21 caused quite a stir amongst any neighbours who happened to see it, and when a uniformed nurse got out carrying a baby and walked up the path to the front door, even more eyebrows were raised.

Maud Button at number 25 was dusting a bedroom window-sill and its collection of green pottery rabbits, and hastily abandoned the task with the intention of running next door to ask Francie Newman if she knew what was going on – if anybody knew, it would be Francie. Old Sid Packer, who was just leaving his home on the opposite side of the road for his morning constitutional, stopped at his gate, peering at the unusual sight, which was blurred for him by his ever-worsening cataracts, and Gert Saunders, on her way home with a basket of shopping, slowed her pace until the nurse had made it up the path of number 21 for fear of appearing nosy. As she approached, however, she couldn't resist a peek. Though the front door was open, she couldn't see anything of interest, but to her shame, she realised that there was a man in the driving seat of the ambulance and he must have seen her looking in. As for Mrs Plumley, who had nothing to do these days but sit in a chair by the window, she felt a moment's spiteful satisfaction. She hoped the ambulance had come to take the lot of them away. It was no more than they deserved, with their blooming cat killing her beloved Joey.

Grace, however, was quite oblivious to all the interest that had been generated. She was far too nervous at the prospect of having to take charge of the baby in the nurse's arms. Though he was now almost five months old now, he looked so small, and she was terrified the nurse might pass him to her. Did his head still need supporting, as a new baby's did? She didn't know. And supposing she should drop him?

'Through here,' she said hastily, leading the way into the living room, where the perambulator was waiting for him, the pillowcases and coverlet freshly washed and ironed.

Tom, who had been upstairs and had started down when he heard the knock at the door, followed. He should have been the one to answer it, Grace thought. It was his house and his baby, and she really didn't know what he'd been doing up there in any case when the people from Catcombe were expected. She only knew that he was acting strangely, and had been ever since the other night, and she thought he might be avoiding her. She couldn't blame him; she felt much the same herself, awkward in his presence where before she had felt so comfortable. She just hoped it didn't mean he was going to leave everything to her where Will was concerned, because she honestly didn't feel capable of it.

Now, to her relief, he stepped forward, introducing himself to the nurse, though he made no attempt to take the baby from her. William was awake, and very alert, looking around with wide dark eyes, and as the nurse laid him in the perambulator, he opened his mouth as if to protest, but made no sound.

'You're home now,' the nurse said to him. 'You'll be picked up again soon, if I know anything about it, and have a lot more cuddles than you've been used to.'

She unhooked the handles of a hessian bag that had been hanging over her shoulder and extracted a sheet of paper.

'Now, first of all, this is a timetable to show you when Baby is used to being fed, how much he takes, and a list of what he should be having.'

'Thank you.' Grace took it, and the nurse dived into the bag again, taking out a small pile of clothing.

'And here are a few things for you to be going on with. He'll have grown quite a bit since he's been with us and you mightn't have had the chance to buy new. But we'd like them back when you've had the chance to sort out some that fit him. We need to keep a little stock so we've always got a change ready in case we have any new arrivals who haven't been properly provided for.'

'Oh yes . . . of course.' Grace was mortified that she hadn't given a thought to the fact that Will would have outgrown the layette Stella had bought – and knitted – for him. How stupid could she be?

'I'm presuming you've got everything else you'll need?' The nurse was looking at her a little sceptically. As if she knows I'm not up to this, Grace thought. She answered quickly.

'Yes, I think so.'

'Well, if you're sure you can manage, we need to be getting back,' the nurse said, and Grace experienced another moment of panic.

'I'm so glad you took the day off work today,' she said to Tom when the nurse had left.

'Well, of course I did.' He was standing beside the pcrambulator, looking down at the baby he thought was his son, and had set the knitted ball that Grace had attached to the hood swinging so as to keep him amused.

'I can't believe I never thought about him needing bigger clothes. I'll have to go into town and see if I can get some. Will you be all right to look after him while I'm gone? Let's see what time his next feed is due . . .' Grace looked at the list the nurse had left. 'Twelve. I'm not sure if I can be back by then. Perhaps I'd better leave it until this afternoon. I can go to the draper's and pick the children up from school at the same time.'

'Grace . . .' Tom touched her hand. 'Stop panicking. I've fed him before and I can feed him again if needs be. And there's no rush for new clothes. With the ones he's got on, there's enough here to last for a couple of days. And if you look in the bottom drawer in the tallboy in my bedroom, you might find some there. Stella kept the pushchair; she might have kept some of Emily's things too. Or Francie might have some she could lend us for the time being.'

'You're right.' Grace took a deep breath. She really needed to compose herself or she'd be no use to anyone. But again she thanked her lucky stars that Tom was here, strong, steady Tom, who took everything in his stride. 'I'll go and have a look now,' she said, and leaving him with Will, she went upstairs.

As a rule, she avoided going into Tom's room unless it was absolutely necessary, and when she had to change the bedding, or dust, sweep and polish, she completed the task as quickly as possible. She always felt she was invading his privacy, that she had no business being here, much the way she'd felt about the whole house in the early days. Besides which, she found it quite painful.

This wasn't just Tom's room, it was also Stella's. Her sister's toiletries on the dressing table, her soap in the dish on the marble-topped washstand beside the jug and basin, her clothes hanging in the wardrobe, untouched since the day she'd been taken to Catcombe: all were reminders of what Stella had been and what she was now, a shell of her former self.

And here was the bed she had shared with Tom, the bed where, presumably, their children had been conceived. That, Grace felt, was the worst of all. And she hated herself for the pang of envy that twisted inside her when she thought of it.

Today, as she pushed open the door and stepped inside, all those feelings were intensified, her emotions too close to the surface for comfort. Trying not to look at the bed, she went straight to the tallboy and opened the bottom drawer.

Tom was right. There were baby clothes there, little gowns

and matinee jackets, all wrapped in tissue paper. Grace was fairly sure Stella hadn't planned to have any more children after Emily; perhaps she'd kept them just in case, or perhaps she had simply been unable to bring herself to throw them away. She got them out, checking the size of each and making a pile on the floor beside her of anything that looked suitable. Certainly there should be enough here to last Will for a little while, for which she was truly grateful. The prospect of having to fit in a visit to the draper's shop today had been a daunting one.

There were other treasures in the drawer too, Grace noticed: an envelope containing a lock of ash-blonde baby hair and another with some milk teeth. Which of the children they belonged to wasn't clear, but Grace guessed it was probably Oliver – Stella would have been enthralled with the development of her firstborn. There was also a silk corsage of violets that Grace remembered Stella wearing when she'd attended her first grown-up dance, and a little ivory-covered prayer book that she had been given when she was confirmed. Grace didn't think Stella attended church nowadays any more than she herself did, but it was nice that she'd kept it. And there were what looked like the journals Stella used to keep. Grace remembered her writing in them faithfully each night in bed before going to sleep. One had been secured by a tiny padlock, but that had long since rusted, and the others were tied together with pink wool. If she had been so minded, Grace could easily have looked inside them to see what her sister had written all those years ago, but she wouldn't even think of doing that. Stella had guarded her journals jealously, and become really upset if she thought anyone had been reading them.

She replaced everything but the pile of baby clothes in the drawer and closed it. She could feel tears gathering in her eyes.

What has happened to us, she wondered, those two little girls who shared a bedroom? What would we have thought if we'd known how life was going to turn out for us? Stella, the loving wife and mother, now incarcerated in an asylum, unwilling or unable to acknowledge her own baby; Grace a childless widow hopelessly in love with a man who could now never be hers. A single tear escaped, rolling down her cheek, and she brushed it away impatiently. *Don't think about it.*

But she couldn't help her eyes being drawn to the bed that she usually tried not to look at. At the covers he'd drawn up a little untidily when he'd made the bed in haste this morning; at the dent in the pillow where his head had lain. For just a moment she was comforted by the feeling of intimacy it gave her. She had been forced into sharing his life, whether either of them wanted it or not. If that was all she could ever have, it would have to be enough.

It was almost eleven in the evening and they'd made it through the first day of caring for Will. He'd been very good, much better than Grace had expected, feeding well and scarcely crying at all. He'd been awake when the children came home from school and had seemed to respond well to Emily, who had been eager to play with him. His eyes had followed the knitted ball that dangled from the hood of the perambulator when she swung it for him, and when Grace had got him out and laid him down on the hearthrug, he'd kicked his legs and waved his arms as if delighted with the freedom. She could even have sworn he'd chuckled when Emily had tickled his tummy.

The boys had been less interested in him, but getting Emily to leave him and go to bed had been quite a tussle. Now Grace had given him one last feed, changed his nappy and put him in a clean nightgown, and it was time for all of them to retire.

'I wonder if he's sleeping through the night yet?' she said as she tidied away the baby cream and talcum powder. There had been nothing in the list of instructions the nurse had left them to indicate whether or not he was, and with her lack of experience she had no idea when it could be expected.

'We'll soon find out,' Tom said. 'But if I have him in with me, you'll be sure of getting a good night's rest.'

'But you've got to be up early to go to work tomorrow,' Grace protested.

'And you have a busy day ahead of you. Don't worry, we'll be fine.'

'Well, if you're sure . . .'

'Quite sure. If he does wake regularly during the night, we can always take turns later on, but for tonight I'd like to be the one to see to him.'

Grace was touched. She wondered how many men would be so ready to look after their baby. Most, she guessed, left it all to their womenfolk.

Tom went to the perambulator and picked up the baby, cradling him against his shoulder. 'Come on, my son. Let's make tracks.'

A lump rose in Grace's throat at the tender picture they made, the big man with the baby in his arms, Will's dark head in stark contrast to the white of the shirt Tom had put on this morning in deference to the importance of the occasion of his son's homecoming. But at the same time, something suddenly struck her as odd. Both Tom and Stella were fair-haired and blue-eyed, and Oliver, Alec and Emily all took after them. How strange, then, that Will should have hair that was almost black. And now that she came to think of it, his eyes, though still blue-tinged, were dark too, almost what she would call navy.

'Where did that come from?' she wondered aloud.

'What?' Tom shot her a puzzled glance.

'Will's colouring. You and Stella are both so fair.'

Tom shrugged slightly. 'Who knows?'

'Could it be the reason Stella thinks he's not hers? Because his colouring is so different to the others?'

'Possible, I suppose. But to be honest, I really don't know what's going on in her head any more.' He moved towards the door. 'I'm taking this little one up now. Don't stay down here doing things that will wait until tomorrow. You get to bed too.'

'I will.'

But as she finished clearing up, laying out the breakfast things, and putting Tom's tea bottle and the scarf for wrapping his snap ready for the morning rush, she was wondering. Had she hit on the reason Stella was so insistent Will wasn't her baby? And if so, what could she do or say to convince her otherwise?

# Chapter Twenty-One

Oliver and Alec were playing with Ned and Reg Newman on the path that ran between the houses, kicking a ball up against the kitchen wall and making quite a bit of noise, shouting and cheering whenever one of them hit the intended target.

Grace, who was at the sink washing up the tea things, wondered if she should go out and ask them to be a bit quieter, but decided against it. At least they weren't doing any harm, and hopefully they would work off some of their spare energy so they'd be more ready to go to bed when it was time. But when she heard a loud crash that sounded like the ball hitting the Newmans' kitchen window, she could ignore them no longer. For all she knew it could have been Oliver or Alec who was responsible.

She hurried to the door, wiping her wet hands on her apron as she went. But Noel Newman had beaten her to it, and from the sound of it, he was furious.

'What the hell do you think you're doing?' he was bellowing.

Oliver and Alec had backed away, looking nervous and sheepish, while the Newman boys were standing their ground defiantly.

'Just playing.'

'Scoring goals.'

Grace was quick to apologise for any part her charges might have played in this. 'Oh Noel, I'm so sorry! They haven't broken the window, have they?'

'They'd be getting worse than this if they had.' Noel didn't so much as glance at Grace; just grabbed his own two sons by the scruff of their necks and dragged them towards their kitchen door. 'Get inside, the pair of you. I'll teach you to play football against the windows. You'll get a good hiding for this.' Only then did he turn to Grace, his face ugly with fury. 'And you could try keeping your two under control too,' he snarled.

'I'm sorry,' Grace said again, but he had gone inside, slamming the door after him.

'Go down the garden and play quietly, or it'll be an early night for you,' she warned Oliver and Alec.

As she watched to make sure they did as they were told, she could still hear the commotion continuing inside the house – Noel shouting, the boys yelping, and Francie joining in at the top of her voice.

She didn't like the sound of it at all. Kind as Noel had been over the horrible incident with Mrs Plumley's canary, he certainly had a temper on him, and she dreaded to think what was going on next door. But as Tom had said, it really wasn't any of her business.

She went back inside, closed the door and carried on with the washing-up.

Grace was bathing baby Will. In the week that he'd been with them, she'd got into a routine that seemed to work well. She'd get the children their breakfast and feed Will while they were eating it. Then she'd put him in his pram and take him with her into Hillsbridge as she walked the children to school and did any necessary shopping. When she got home again, she'd give him his bath.

No longer afraid of dropping him, she had come to enjoy the ritual, supporting him in a sinkful of warm water with one hand while soaping him all over with the other, then letting him kick for a little while before towelling him dry on her lap. Another feed, and she'd put him down in his crib, where hopefully he would sleep for long enough for her to do the chores.

This morning she was just lathering suds over the soft dark hair that covered his well-shaped head when there was a knock at the back door. It opened a crack, and Francie's voice called: 'It's only me!'

'Come in,' Grace called back. 'I'm just bathing Will.'

'I'm in luck then.' Francie headed straight for the sink – she was besotted with the baby.

'Francie, I'm so sorry about last night,' Grace said, feeling the need to apologise for Oliver and Alec's involvement in what had happened.

'Oh, don't think anything of it. Boys will be boys.' Francie leaned over to chuck Will under the chin. 'Who's a beautiful one, eh? You're not up to any mischief yet, are you?'

'He's as good as gold,' Grace agreed.

'Aw, yes – just look at him!' Francie said, clearly entranced. Grace smiled. 'Making you broody, is he?'

'No fear!' Francie said emphatically. 'I'm done with all that, I hope. But that doesn't mean I can't enjoy a cuddle with one I can hand back.'

She gave Grace a narrow glance. 'More to the point, is he making *you* broody?'

Grace gave a short laugh. 'Don't be silly.'

But the truth was, there wasn't a moment when she didn't wish Will was hers – hers and Tom's. Sometimes when she was feeding or bathing him, she allowed herself the fantasy that this was her home, her baby, that she and Tom and the children were a family, before dragging herself back to reality and the fact that she was just a surrogate, a caretaker of sorts, until Stella was well again. Nothing could ever come of her foolish dreams, and she really didn't want it to, because Stella was her beloved sister and all this belonged to her.

'You're a natural,' Francie said. 'I can't understand why you haven't got any children of your own.'

'My husband got killed before it happened . . .' Grace lowered Will back so as to rinse the soap from his head without it getting into his eyes.

'I know, and I'm sorry,' Francie said. 'But I'd have thought you'd have got married again by now. Pretty girl like you, and still young.'

'I've never met anybody else I wanted to marry,' Grace said shortly, growing more and more uncomfortable with this conversation. 'Put the kettle on, Francie, and we'll have a cup of tea. I haven't had the chance since I got back from taking the children to school.'

'I don't think I ought to stay – I'm just on my way into town to do some shopping. But I'll put the kettle on for you if you like.'

While Francie went through to make the tea, Grace concentrated on letting Will have the kicking session that she thought of as his playtime. After a few minutes, she wrapped him in a big soft towel and took him into the living room. As she sat down on one of the dining chairs with the baby on her lap, Francie poured her a cup and set it on the table next to her.

'Thanks, Francie.' Grace took a welcome sip before patting Will dry and reaching for the talcum powder. Francie was eyeing him narrowly.

'What I can't understand is him being so dark when Stella and Tom are both fair,' she commented.

'It is strange,' Grace agreed. 'I've thought so myself. I said to Tom the other night, perhaps it's why Stella thinks he isn't hers.'

'They couldn't have made a mistake, I suppose? Got Will and another baby muddled up?' Francie suggested.

'I shouldn't think so. He had a tag with his name on it round his ankle when they brought him home.'

Grace got up and laid Will on a dry towel that she'd spread ready on the hearthrug, letting him kick again before reaching for a clean nappy.

'You never know with these places,' Francie said darkly.

'I can't see how it could happen.' Grace folded the nappy between the baby's legs. 'They'd have put the name tag on as soon as he got there.'

'I suppose . . . Right then, I ought to get going.' Francie dropped to her knees beside Grace for one last look at Will. 'Bye bye, my lovely. Auntie Francie will be back to see you soon.' She leaned over to tickle his tummy, bare above his nappy, and as she did so, the sleeve of her blouse rode up and Grace was dismayed to see a circlet of fresh bruises. Perhaps Francie had tried to defend her boys from the worst of Noel's fury last night after the incident with the football and he'd taken it out on her instead. Poor woman! she thought.

But Tom was right. It wasn't their business, and Francie clearly didn't want the neighbours knowing what went on behind closed doors.

'I'm off then,' Francie said, getting up. 'Is there anything you need that I can get while I'm at the shops?'

'No, I'm all right, but thank you all the same,' Grace said.

When Francie had left, Grace finished dressing Will, then fetched his feed and settled in the fireside chair to give it to him, her mind returning to what Francie had said about the little boy's colouring.

So she wasn't the only one to think it was odd. Was it possible there had been some mistake, as Francie had suggested? Surely not. As she'd pointed out, the name tag would have been put round the baby's ankle as soon as he'd arrived, and there had been a time when Stella had seemed to be getting better and had cared for him quite happily before rejecting him again. The only way he could have been confused with another baby would be if the name tags had been swapped deliberately, and why would anyone do such a thing?

No, it must be a fluke of nature, a flashback to a distant ancestor.

Grace finished feeding Will, put him down in his perambulator and got on with all the things she had to do before he woke again.

Sir Oswald was at his desk, the monthly figures for the stone excavated from his quarries stacked at his elbow ready for his perusal. As yet, though, he had done no more than glance at them. It was the letter from his cousin, the Right Reverend Alfred Whittingly Challis, that was engaging his attention.

His hopes had been raised when he'd recognised Alfred's spidery writing on the envelope that had arrived with the morning post, and he had opened it eagerly. But as he read the contents, he'd bristled with annoyance.

Yes, Alfred would be prepared to offer Sir Oswald's unfortunate servant a position, but not until the end of the month.

'It is fortunate indeed that your request has coincided with the departure of my maid, who is to enter the state of holy matrimony,' he had written, 'but at present she is still working out her notice, and I am sure you will understand that diocesan funds will not stretch to the remuneration of surplus staff.'

Sir Oswald, who had already spoken to the two doctors who had had Rose committed, had hoped to have her well out of the way before George came home to visit for Easter, which was fast approaching. They had signed the papers for her release, which were now lodged with Dr Kirkwood, simply waiting for Sir Oswald to give the word. Alfred's response would mean a most unwelcome delay to his plans.

Sir Oswald's hand hovered over the telephone. Perhaps if he offered to pay Rose's wages until the current maid left, Alfred might agree to take her sooner. But Alfred was a pedantic old fool who was unlikely to agree to any such arrangement, and in any case, he would wonder why Oswald was so eager to have him take the girl at once. If he suspected the truth, he might change his mind about employing her at all. No, there was nothing for it but to leave Rose where she was for the moment and hope George didn't make trouble.

Sighing deeply, he pulled the sheaf of paperwork concerning the quarry output towards him. At least the figures were good. He only hoped the quarries would remain as productive and profitable when Rupert took over their running. But he was reasonably confident that they would. Unlike George, Rupert had a steady head on his shoulders. That, at least, was something to be grateful for.


Matron Carey and Dr Kirkwood were having one of their regular meetings to review the progress of the patients in their care.

'I'm still very concerned about Stella Swift,' Matron said. 'She seems to have withdrawn into herself completely. She won't interact with anyone, not even the nurses she knows well. If she's encouraged to go to a social gathering, she simply sits in a corner, not joining in at all, and she scarcely touches her food, which means she's losing weight she can't afford to lose.'

'Is she sleeping? Or do we need to increase her medication?' Dr Kirkwood asked.

'She's sleeping all right. In the day as well as at night. The drugs certainly seem to be having the desired effect. But her mood when she is awake . . . I'm hoping you'll say there's something else we could try. Frankly, Hubert, as I said, I'm worried about her. And I've asked the nurses to keep a special eye on her.'

'You think she's suicidal?'

'I think she might be.'

Dr Kirkwood made a note on the pad in front of him. 'I'll fit in an extra session with her when we've finished here,' he said. 'It's disappointing to say the least that she's relapsed so badly after seemingly making such good progress.'

'I suppose we have to accept that she may well be beyond help,' Matron said. 'I've seen it before, and so have you. Women so damaged by childbirth that they never recover.'

'I'm not giving up hope yet.' Dr Kirkwood's tone was brisk. 'There was light at the end of the tunnel before; there may well be again. There's a new medication I'd like to try on her and it may be that she would benefit from it. Now, let's move on. Dorothy Chapman . . .'

Matron shuffled her reports and the meeting continued. The troubling case of Stella Swift had been put on the back burner for the moment at least.

'Good news, Jessica,' Alistair Mackay said as he sat down to the midday meal that was ready and waiting for him in the break between morning surgery and the home visits he needed to make. 'I heard this morning that the motor will be mine by the end of the week.'

'Oh, that is good!' Jessica settled Constance on a pile of cushions on one of the dining chairs and tied a bib over her little smock.

'It certainly is. Much as I've been grateful for your trusty old bicycle, I shall be very glad to be able to give my poor aching legs some respite.'

'And we'll be able to go to Catcombe for the Easter Sunday service, and I'll be able to see Florrie.'

Alistair smiled, cutting into a slice of cold pressed tongue.

'You're a hard-hearted woman, Jessica. All you can think of is a Sunday outing and a visit to your sister. Have you no pity for your poor husband, slogging along on his rounds?'

'None whatever. The exercise has been very good for you.' She smiled back.

'Killing me, more like.'

Jessica cut a slice of tongue into small pieces on Constance's plate. 'I don't suppose you've heard any more from the police as to what happened to the Ford?'

'Not a dicky bird. Nor am I likely to. If it was deliberate, most likely it was drunks staggering home who thought it would be fun to start a fire in a motor they'd never be able to afford.'

'A strange idea of fun!' Jessica said. 'How did they manage to do it, anyway?'

'Petrol from the tank and a box of matches? I don't know, Jessica. Arson is not something I've ever tried.'

'I'm glad to hear it. I just hope you won't have a pipe again when you're too tired to be sure you put it out properly,' she said with feeling.

Alistair forked an extra knob of butter into his baked potato.

He knew she still suspected his pipe might have been to blame, and truth to tell, he did wonder himself.

'If it was drunks, they'll never be caught,' he said, holding on to the explanation that was easier on his conscience. 'It could be anybody.'

'Let's just hope they don't try it again with your new motor when it arrives.'

Jessica sat down herself and picked up her knife and fork.

'Amen to that,' Alistair echoed.

'So, Stella, how are you feeling today?' Dr Kirkwood asked.

As soon as his meeting with Matron was over, a nurse had been asked to bring Stella to his office, where he'd seated her on the couch and turned his swivel chair to face her.

Stella's hands were knotted tightly in her lap, her head bent to stare down at them, and she made no attempt to answer him.

'Stella?' he prompted her gently. 'It really would help if you could talk to me about what it is that's troubling you.'

Her head jerked up then, her eyes burning fiercely in her pale, drawn face.

'I want my baby!'

'Stella, my dear, he's safe at home with your husband and your sister. And we want you to get well so that you can go home and be with him.'

'It's not Will!' Stella's voice was a little thick from the after-effects of her sleeping draught, but there was no mistaking the depth of her feeling.

She truly believes the baby isn't hers, Dr Kirkwood thought. In all the cases of post-natal madness he'd come across in his long career, this wasn't a reaction he'd ever encountered.

'Why do you think that, Stella?' he asked.

'You think I don't know my own baby?' For a few seconds

more her eyes blazed into his, then, as if a gas lamp had been turned off, all the life went out of them and she was staring into space, retreating once more into her own world. Talking to her would be useless. She was beyond reason.

'I'm going to prescribe you a new medication,' he said, because although he doubted she would understand what he was saying, he believed in behaving as if she could. 'It will help you feel better, I hope. You'd like to feel better, wouldn't you?'

As he'd expected, there was no response. Stella's head was bowed again; she was seeing nothing but her own hands twisted together in the folds of her smock.

Dr Kirkwood rose and went to his medicine cabinet, counting out a number of pills into a small brown glass bottle. Then he rang the bell to summon a nurse to take Stella back to the day room.

When the nurse answered his call, he handed her the bottle.

'She's to have one of these immediately, and another at bedtime,' he instructed. 'And please keep a close eye on her, as I believe Matron has already asked.'

'Yes, sir. Come along, Stella.'

The nurse took Stella's arm, pulled her to her feet and walked her out of the office, Stella moving like a woman in a dream.

As the door closed after them, Dr Kirkwood removed his spectacles and rubbed his eyes.

Perhaps Matron was right and Stella was set to become one of his failures. He sincerely hoped not. She had so much to live for. But there was only so much he could do. Some patients were beyond help, and sad as it made him, he had to accept it.

But at least Rose Gooding would be allowed to leave soon. Not that there had been anything wrong with her in the first place beyond her inability to resist the temptations of the flesh, and he thoroughly disapproved of her committal to the asylum.

He'd had no choice, however, but to go along with it. Not only did Sir Oswald Whittingly Challis sit on the board of governors, but he also owned the land on which the asylum stood. If Dr Kirkwood valued his position here, it would be most unwise to object – and he certainly did value it, and took pride in the improvements he had been able to make in the care of the patients and the conditions under which they were forced to live.

But he was very glad Rose would be going home soon, and it was enough to take some of the sting out of his failure with Stella. A little candle burning in a dark world, he thought, and turned his attention to the other cases he and Matron had discussed.

# Chapter Twenty-Two

George Whittingly Challis turned the Humber motor he had borrowed from a fellow officer cadet into the driveway of Easterton Manor and pulled up with a jerk outside the front entrance. He had intended to make the journey home on his motorcycle, but for some reason, it had failed to start. St John Stevens had offered him the use of his motor, and George had to admit it made for a much more comfortable ride.

Not that he would have come home at all but for one good reason. He had no great love for either of his parents. As a child, they had left him almost entirely in the care of a nanny before packing him off to boarding school as soon as they could, and they had little more time for him now. His mother was a cold fish who cared for nothing but her reputation for supporting good causes, and his father belittled him and made it clear he was a great disappointment to him. His brother Rupert was all right, he supposed, but the fact that he was constantly held up as a shining example of all George was not rankled and had caused a gulf to open up between them.

No, he wouldn't have come home to visit if it weren't for Rose. Pretty, soft, adorable Rose, with her jet-black hair and dark brown eyes. Lovely, loving Rose, who had shown him a warmth that had always been lacking in his life. Rose, with whom he had fallen in love last summer, and with whom he had been able to spend far too short a time before leaving for Sandhurst.

He hadn't seen her since that day, but she was never out of his thoughts. All that first term he had been looking forward to Christmas, and being with her again. But his commanding officer, Major Willoughby Brown, had had other ideas. Learning to speak French was a part of the cadet officer course, and George was struggling with it.

'I suggest you spend the Christmas break with us, Challis, and take some lessons from our French maid,' he had said. 'Unless, of course, you are prepared to risk failing your final assessment.'

It was an order rather than a suggestion, and George had had little option but to comply. His French wasn't up to scratch, he knew – he had always struggled academically. But he couldn't afford to fail the course. It would provide him with a career he knew he'd enjoy, well away from the family that had stifled him and made his life a misery. Besides which, his father would be furious and might well wash his hands of him, cut him off without a penny. Already he lost no opportunity to remind George how much it was costing him to fund the place at Sandhurst. George needed to qualify, earn some money of his own – enough to escape the jurisdiction of his father. Then he could live his life as he chose, and could make Rose his wife, just as he'd promised her during those magical stolen hours they'd spent together last summer.

It was all he wanted, all he dreamed of. Just thinking of her now made his pulse quicken and his body ache with desire. He couldn't wait to have her in his arms again. It wouldn't be easy, but he'd find a way. And it wouldn't be for long; these few days would pass by so quickly. But at least he could reassure her that their separation was almost over. A few more months and with any luck he'd be a fully qualified junior officer and would be able to take her with him wherever he was sent. They'd live together in the accommodation the army would provide for them, and the days, weeks, months of longing would be at an end.

George climbed out of the motor and reached for his bag, lying on the rear seat, his stomach churning with the anticipation of seeing Rose again as well as reluctance at being back in his parents' house, where their attitude towards him made him feel like the small, sad boy he had once been.

But he was no longer that boy, he reminded himself. He was a grown man, and well on the way to becoming an officer of the British Army.

Squaring his shoulders, he climbed the steps and went into the house.

'Where is Rose?' he enquired.

Luncheon was almost over. From the moment he'd walked in the door, he'd been watching for her, growing increasingly puzzled and anxious not to catch a single glimpse of her, while the maid who had waited on them at table was a girl he didn't know.

Could it be that she had a day off, or perhaps even the whole Easter weekend? His heart sank at the thought. If so, he might not see her after all during his visit. Throughout the meal he'd kept his concerns to himself, not wanting to betray his interest in her; but now he had felt compelled to ask the question that burned in his brain.

'Rose is no longer with us,' his mother said. Her voice, like her eyes, was cold and hard.

'What? She's left? But why?'

'It's time we had a talk, my boy.' Sir Oswald glared at George over the rim of his brandy glass and added, in the familiar tone that brooked no argument: 'Not now. In my study, when we've finished luncheon.'

George's stomach clenched, and the creamed rice he'd just eaten formed a hard lump in his gullet. It was an all-too-familiar summons. As a child, it had almost always ended with three stripes across his bare buttocks from the cane Sir Oswald kept for the purpose; since he had grown too big for corporal punishment, it was scathing words, which cut deeper than the cane ever had and stung for much longer.

He longed to face his father down, demand that he say whatever it was he had to say here and now, but he knew that argument was useless, and besides, he didn't want his brother to witness his humiliation, whatever form that might take.

Had his father discovered his affair with Rose and dismissed her for it? He'd thought they'd been discreet, but Sir Oswald's order had followed directly on his enquiry as to where she was.

At last his father balled up his napkin and rose from the table, indicating with a brusque nod of his head that George should follow him. As the study door closed after them, he turned on his son, fury darkening his drink-raddled features.

'You ask where Rose is. Well, I will tell you. She is in Catcombe asylum, incarcerated as a moral delinquent, and has been ever since I discovered she was carrying your illegitimate child.'

George's jaw dropped, his mouth opened, but no words came.

'How could you be so stupid? Didn't you stop to think of the consequences of a dalliance with one of our maids?' Sir Oswald spat out the words. 'Have you any idea of the trouble you've caused me? The shame and disgrace you have brought to our door? But I suppose I should have expected nothing less. You have never been anything other than a disappointment to me.'

George ignored his father's criticism – he was used to it. But Rose . . . 'You had her committed to Catcombe because she was pregnant?' he demanded, both startled and horrified.

'What alternative did I have?' It was a rhetorical question. 'By the time her condition became known to me, she was too far gone for the bastard to be aborted. I had the good name of this family to protect. Can you imagine the scandal it would have caused in the village if it had become known that you were the father of her brat? In Catcombe she is out of sight of prying eyes, and both she and her family have been warned what will happen if word should get out.'

'Has she had the baby?' His lips felt like rubber so that it was an effort to form the words.

'Of course she has. Unlike an elephant, a woman doesn't carry for years,' Sir Oscar retorted scathingly.

'And it's with her in the asylum?'

'Not any more. That was something else I had to take care of. The baby – a boy, if you are in any way interested – has been adopted. Fortunately I was able to place him quite readily. You don't need to know where he is, any more than you need to know where I've arranged for Rose to go when she's released from the asylum. I think we can consider the whole disgraceful episode closed. But I warn you, if ever there should be a repeat . . .'

George's shock was now giving way to anger. 'How could you not let me know about all this?'

'I saw no reason to. As I have said, I have taken care of everything.'

'To suit yourself! Have you given a single thought to Rose –

what she's going through? No, knowing you, I don't suppose you have.'

'Tch!' Sir Oswald snorted dismissively. 'A servant girl? It's you I am concerned about – you and this family. Hopefully you will have learned your lesson and can put this whole business behind you, try to make something of your worthless life. God knows, it's costing me enough to give you the chance.'

Somehow George got his anger in check.

'What you've done is despicable,' he said coldly. 'You disgust me, Father.' He pushed his chair back, struggled to his feet and started for the door.

'Where do you think you're going? I haven't finished with you yet!'

Sir Oswald's words stopped him in his tracks, and he turned back to face his father once more.

'Oh, I rather think you have. As for where I'm going, what do you think? I'm going to see Rose.'

'Don't be so bloody stupid, boy!'

'And don't call me "boy". I'm not a boy any more. I'm a man. More of a man than you'll ever be.'

Sir Oscar rose too, drawing himself up to his full height as the colour rose in his mottled cheeks. 'How dare you speak to me like that? Let me remind you—'

'Who holds the purse strings?' George shot at him contemptuously.

'Exactly. And I warn you, here and now, if you have any more contact with that little whore . . .'

'Do your damnedest.' With that George turned away again and stormed out of the room. He was shaking now, from both shock and anger, his thoughts reeling so he was scarcely able to take in what had happened.

Rose, his lovely Rose, pregnant and incarcerated in a lunatic asylum. Her baby – his baby! – taken from her. She must be in a terrible way. How could his father have behaved so callously? Though he should have expected nothing less. The man was a puppet master, pulling all their strings – a monster.

If only he'd known! If only he'd thought for a moment . . . but he'd been so sure he'd taken care that it hadn't occurred to him what might result from their liaison.

Into his mind flashed a vivid scene. His coat spread on the meadow grass. The sun splintering through the tracery of branches and leaves of the old oak, the sky beyond it unbroken blue. A gentle breeze murmuring in the long grass. The hum of a bumblebee in the clover. The scents of summer in the air and of lavender soap on the soft skin beneath his mouth. Rose, all soft sweetness, returning his kisses, stroking his neck, holding him fast, moulding her body to his.

But from all that bliss had come disaster. George's hands balled to fists; he struck the wall of the passageway so hard that his knuckles stung with the force of the blow, but he knew that the pain of it was nothing to what Rose had endured. Nothing to the pain in his own heart. He only wished his father's face had been on the receiving end of the punch, but he knew that would do no good.

He was going to see Rose, and to hell with the consequences. If his father cut him off without a penny, so be it. At least he wouldn't be beholden to the old bastard any more. Somehow he'd find a way to finish his course at Sandhurst. Somehow he'd make things right.

And he never wanted to set foot in this accursed house again.

But before leaving Easterton Manor for good, there was something he had to do. And only one person who might help him. Not his mother; she would treat his request with her customary cold disdain, and take his father's part though there was little love lost between them. His only hope was his brother, who had returned to the quarry as soon as luncheon was over.

George stormed up the stairs and retrieved his bag from beside the bed, where it was waiting for a servant to unpack it. Then he hurried back downstairs – a startled maid stood aside for him to pass – and out to the borrowed motor. He tossed his bag on to the rear seat and cranked the engine to life, then he jumped in and roared away from the house he had once called home, turning along the lane in the direction of the quarry.

Praying all the while that his brother, at least, would be prepared to help him.

Rupert's motor was parked outside the stone-built block that housed the quarry's on-site office. George drew up beside it, turned off the engine, climbed down and went inside.

His brother was on the telephone. He motioned George to take a seat, but George remained standing, pacing from wall to wall of the small office while he waited for Rupert to finish his call – to one of the hauliers they used, from what he could make out.

After seemingly endless minutes, Rupert replaced the receiver and raised a questioning eyebrow at his brother.

George was not about to mince his words.

'Did you know what has been going on?' he demanded.

'Do you mean your spot of trouble?' There was a smirk on Rupert's face that George badly wanted to wipe off. But antagonising his brother would not help matters.

'Why didn't you let me know?' he asked, struggling to keep his tone civil.

'And what good would that have done?' Rupert enquired mildly. 'You know Father when his mind's made up. Anyway, why are you so upset about it? He's saved you a whole lot of bother.'

'He's ruined Rose's life, Rupert. How could he do such a thing?'

Rupert only shrugged. 'What do you care?'

'I love her. I want her to be my wife.'

'A maid? More fool you.'

'I don't give a damn what you or anyone else thinks,' George said. 'One way or another I'm going to put things right. That's why I'm here. Father says he's had the baby adopted. Do you know who has him?'

'And if I do?'

'For the love of God, Rupert. Please. I have to know.'

'And you'll do what?'

'Never mind that. You're my brother, for God's sake. Just tell me, and I'll make sure Father never knows I heard it from you.'

'Well, little brother, I won't press you as to your intentions, but I must say you have more guts than I ever gave you credit for.'

'Tell me! Where is my son?'

Rupert picked up a paper knife lying on his desk and twirled it between his fingers, considering. George waited impatiently for him to make up his mind.

'I don't know for certain,' he said at last. 'It's never been talked about in front of me. I'm not even sure if Mother knows. But I did overhear Father on the telephone to Winston Donaghue. You know he married again after Elizabeth died? His new wife – Miranda, isn't it? – was anxious for a child, but it never happened, or so I understand. I think Father may well have arranged for them to adopt Rose's bastard.'

'And they already have him?'

'I believe so. As I said, I've not been party to any of it. I've simply put together bits and pieces of what I've overheard.'

Listening in to conversations he wasn't meant to hear or even poking into private correspondence if he thought he might learn something that might be of use to him was typical of his brother, George thought. There was a sly side to him, but on this occasion he was glad of it.

'Well, thanks anyway,' he said, turning to leave.

'George?' Rupert's voice followed him. 'You're not going to do anything stupid, are you?'

George turned back. His brother's expression was anxious now.

'The less you know about what I intend to do, the better,' he said flatly. 'But if I don't come home tonight, you can tell Mother and Father I've gone back to camp. I don't want to spend another night under their roof, and I suspect they'll be glad to see the back of me too.'

With that, he left the office, got the motor going, and headed off along the lane to Catcombe.

Though no visit had been arranged, George had no doubt that his father's standing at Catcombe would gain him entry, and he was right. He was greeted with the respect due to the son of one of the governors and the owner of the land on which the asylum stood.

'I've come to see Rose Gooding,' he said when he was shown into Dr Kirkwood's office. 'My father is concerned for her welfare.'

'Him and me both,' the superintendent said bluntly. 'This is not the place for her, and never was, in my opinion. I understand your father is hoping to secure a position for her with his cousin the bishop, and I already have the signatures of the committing doctors for her release when arrangements have been made. Perhaps you've come to give her some news of that?'

'I want to talk to her about it, yes,' George said, pleased that not only did Dr Kirkwood seem to be unaware that he was the father of Rose's illegitimate child, but also that he had inadvertently discovered where she was to be taken when she was finally discharged.

'I'll have her brought here.' Dr Kirkwood rose from his chair. 'I have my afternoon rounds to do, so you will have some privacy. I imagine half an hour will give you the time you need?'

'Yes. Thank you.' But his choice of words made George wonder if he'd been mistaken in thinking the superintendent was unaware that he was the father. No matter. The whole world could know as far as he was concerned, and would soon enough. The important thing now was that he would be able to see Rose alone.

The superintendent left, and George waited anxiously. At last he heard footsteps in the corridor outside, the door opened, and Rose stood there. A very different Rose to the girl he had loved and left last summer, thinner, paler, her hair scraped back from a face that had lost its soft roundness, and with dark shadows beneath her lovely brown eyes.

They widened with surprise as she saw him; her hand flew to her mouth.

'Rose . . .' Shocked as he was at the change in her, it was all he could say. But it was enough.

'George?' she said wonderingly, as if unable to believe her eyes.

'Oh Rose – what have they done to you?'

Her lip was trembling, but an expression of wonder and delight was spreading across her face, and happy tears were bringing back some sparkle to her dark eyes.

'George! I thought . . .'

'I didn't know, Rose. I swear I didn't know.'

She was in his arms before either of them could speak another word, her thin frame pressed against him, his lips in her hair, smelling now of carbolic soap rather than lavender, but still sweet to him for all that.

At last he held her at arm's length, looking into her face, determined to somehow make her understand that none of this was his doing.

'I am so sorry, Rose. They never told me. I've only just found out. But I promise you, I'm going to make everything right.'

Her mouth puckered again. 'It's too late. They've taken my baby. He was so beautiful, and I loved him so much. They took him away, and I'll never see him again . . .'

'You will, Rose. You will. I'll make sure of it. Just trust me.'

She clung to him, sobbing, and he felt as if his heart was being torn out of his chest.

'You should have let me know,' he said. 'Why didn't you write to me at Sandhurst?'

'I did. You never replied.'

'I never got a letter from you,' he replied truthfully, and wondered what could have happened to it. Had it been lost in the post? Or had some officer opened it, seen its contents and made sure it never reached him? Perhaps they had contacted his father and that was how Sir Oswald had found out about Rose's condition and the identity of the father of her child.

'Anyway, you never wrote to me,' she said in a whisper. 'You left without even saying goodbye.'

'There was no chance, Rose.' Those last days had been a whirl as he'd prepared to leave, and he hadn't been able to slip away to meet her. 'You'd been given time off, don't you remember? Your mother was sick with influenza, or so I understood.'

314

'Sir Oswald insisted. I thought he was being kind.'

So his father had realised what was going on between him and Rose, and deliberately got her out of the way until he'd left for Sandhurst, he thought bitterly.

'And I had no address to reach you by letter,' he went on. 'I couldn't write to you at Easterton Manor – I had to wait to hear from you.'

'I thought you didn't care,' she whispered. 'I thought I was just . . . well, a bit of fun, and you wanted to forget all about me.'

'Never, Rose! How could you think that?'

'What else was I to think?'

He pulled her towards him again and kissed her, a warm, chaste kiss on the mouth, quite unlike the passionate kisses they had shared in their stolen moments last summer, but meaning all the more for it.

'I love you, Rose. There'll never be anyone but you for me. And when you get out of here, I'll take care of you for the rest of our lives. I love you. Do you hear me?'

'And I love you. But . . .'

Footsteps in the passageway outside the door.

'I love you, Rose,' he repeated softly. 'And I'll make everything right if it's the last thing I do.'

She nodded tremulously, but he could see in her eyes she wasn't sure she believed him. She'd been through too much, had her spirit broken along with her heart. He gripped her hands, looking intently into her face.

'I swear it.'

The handle of the door began to turn, and he released her so that when Dr Kirkwood entered the room there was nothing to arouse his suspicions about this unscheduled visit.

'All done then?' the superintendent asked briskly.

'Yes, thank you, sir. For the moment.'

'Good. You may go now, Rose.'

With just one pleading glance from beneath her lowered lashes, Rose left, and George felt as if his heart was going with her.

He thanked Dr Kirkwood again, and as he returned to the borrowed motor, his mind was made up. Somehow he would keep his promise to Rose. Somehow he would make it up to her for all the pain and heartache she had been forced to endure. Somehow he would get their son back.

# Chapter Twenty-Three

Bowling along in their new motor, Jessica was smiling with delight, even though Alistair was driving a little too fast for her liking. This morning's trip to Catcombe was quite different to the last time they'd made the journey. Instead of the fog that had made her so nervous that day, the sky was clear and periwinkle blue above hedges that were burgeoning with fresh growth, and the farmland beyond them was lush and green in the warm spring sunshine. As they passed a field where lambs gambolled round the mother ewes, Jessica pointed them out to Constance, who was sitting on her lap.

'Look, darling! Aren't they the sweetest thing?'

Constance giggled, wriggling as she pointed a chubby finger.

'Sit still now,' Jessica warned. And to Alistair: 'Slow down a bit, can't you?'

Alistair cast her a smiling sideways glance. 'Just putting her through her paces. This is the first time I've had the chance to open her up and see what she'll do.'

It was true. Since the motor had been delivered to their door, he'd only driven it in and around Hillsbridge, where the winding lanes and steep hills made a good fast run impossible. Today, with the road snaking across the crest of the Mendip Hills, the temptation had been too much to resist.

They were approaching the curving descent towards Catcombe now, however, and even without Jessica's heartfelt plea, Alistair would have slowed a little for safety's sake. But it did no harm to let her think he was doing as she asked.

'Your wish is my command,' he said, applying the brakes and coasting towards the first bend. But he couldn't resist asking: 'What do you think, though? Did I do the right thing in buying this motor?'

Jessica nodded. 'I think so. It's a much more comfortable ride than poor old Lizzie.'

'So the vandals who set her on fire did us a favour, then?'

'I wouldn't go that far,' Jessica said, thinking of the juggling she was going to have to do to make her reduced housekeeping money go around. 'But I'm certainly very glad I can go and see Florrie again,' she added, not wanting to put a damper on Alistair's pleasure in his new acquisition.

'And she'll be pleased to see you. And surprised, I imagine.'

'She will be.' Jessica smiled again, picturing her sister's astonishment.

At the foot of the long hill, Alistair turned into the drive that led to the asylum and parked where he always did, near the main entrance.

A woman wearing a black silk coat and a straw hat was negotiating the steps, leaning heavily on a stick and holding on to the arm of a younger woman with her free hand. In the doorway the pair paused – presumably, in view of their slow progress, to let Jessica and Alistair pass – and Jessica was surprised when Alistair stopped to speak to the older woman.

'Nurse Whitcombe! Whatever has happened to you?'

'You may well ask, Doctor. I had a bad fall down the nursery stairs, and I've been in hospital ever since. But they let me out for Easter. Wanted my bed empty, I expect.'

'Good Lord! I had no idea,' Alistair said.

'Well, I don't suppose you would, would you, with your car catching fire the very same night – Matron told me about it when she and Dr Kirkwood came to visit me in hospital. I reckon there was an evil old witch riding about on her broomstick that night! But never mind, here I am, a bit the worse for wear, but still alive and kicking. And you've got a new motor too, I see.'

'I have indeed. Well, take care of yourself, Nurse.'

He rejoined Jessica and Constance, who were waiting for him in the entrance hall.

'What was that all about?' Jessica asked.

'That was Cissie Whitcombe. Believe it or not, she was one of the best nurses on the baby ward just a few weeks ago,' Alistair said. 'It seems she had a bad fall and has been in hospital ever since.'

'Oh dear. She looks in a bad way.'

'She does. She shouldn't be walking on that leg, in my opinion. But she'll be sorely missed on the ward, that's for sure.'

They reached the doorway of the room that served as a chapel and went inside. It was bright with posies of primroses and vases of daffodils on every available window ledge, and candles glowed on the makeshift altar. Florrie was nowhere to be seen.

A nurse who was shepherding a crocodile of patients into a row of chairs noticed Jessica looking around anxiously.

'It's Florrie's sister, isn't it?' she asked.

Jessica nodded. 'Yes. I haven't been able to come for a couple of weeks and I was hoping to see her.'

'She won't be in chapel today.' The nurse broke off to steer one of her wandering charges in the right direction. 'We're short-staffed in the nursery, and Florrie's in sole charge.'

'So I'll be able to find her there after the service?' Jessica asked.

'Since you're the doctor's wife, I'm sure that will be all right.' The nurse glanced down at Constance, who was playing her own version of hopscotch on the tiled floor. 'Would the little one like to go up to see her while you attend the service?' she suggested. 'As long as she behaves herself, of course.'

Jessica had no need to ask Constance if she would like to spend some time with the babies. She already knew the answer. And it would be good to be able to enjoy the Easter Matins without having to try to keep her little daughter amused.

'I'll take her up as soon as I've settled this lot,' the nurse said, and good as her word, when the last patient was seated on the hard upright chairs, she returned for Constance.

'You're going to see Auntie Florrie and the babies,' Jessica told her daughter, and the little girl trotted off happily, holding the nurse's hand.

Jessica settled herself as comfortably as possible on the hard chair. The baby she was carrying was pressing on a nerve, but she was determined not to let it spoil her enjoyment of the service.

And enjoy it she did. The hymns were joyful and uplifting, and Jessica was almost moved to tears when the officiating minister removed the stone from the entrance to the tomb in the Easter garden that had been laid out to one side of the makeshift altar.

The patients, too, had been infected by the joyous atmosphere, quiet during the prayers – though there was some shuffling of chairs during the short sermon – and joining in lustily, and not always tunefully, with the hymns.

When it was over, Alistair told her he was going to find Dr Kirkwood, and Jessica made her way up to the nursery, where she found Constance watching contentedly as Florrie bathed one of the babies.

Jessica dropped a kiss on her sister's head, unable to hug her as she usually did with Florrie's hands full of soapy baby.

'I'm so glad to be able to come and see you again, Florrie,' she said. 'How are you?'

Florrie glanced up at her for a moment and Jessica saw something in her eyes that disturbed her. Hesitation, indecision, even anxiety. And when she spoke, she didn't answer Jessica's question, but asked one of her own.

'Never mind me. How are you and that baby doing?'

'Well, I think. It's certainly keeping me awake at night with its kicking.'

'A boy, then? Going to play football for Hillsbridge?' Florrie lifted the baby she was bathing out of the water and on to the towel spread on her lap.

At once Constance reached out and touched the baby's hand, chuckling in delight as the small fingers curled around hers.

'You'll have a little helper when it arrives, I can tell you that for nothing,' Florrie said.

But again Jessica sensed that her sister was not her usual cheery self. She sounded stressed, her attempt at bright concentration forced. 'Are you sure you're all right?' she asked.

Florrie hesitated, concentrating on drying the baby, then seemed to make up her mind. 'I have to talk to you, Jess. I can't stay quiet any longer. If I keep it to myself, I'll go crazy.'

'What is it, Florrie?' Jessica asked, alarmed.

'Let me get this baby down first, and find something to keep Constance amused, and then I'll tell you.'

Jessica waited as she powdered the baby and dressed it in a fresh nappy and robe, her mind racing over all the possibilities. Was Florrie ill? Had they discovered something seriously wrong with her? She did look pale, as well as stressed. The awful saying popped into her head: One in, one out. She would be giving birth to a new life very soon. Surely, surely it couldn't be that Florrie . . . Oh dear God, don't let it be that!

After a few minutes that seemed like hours to Jessica, the baby Florrie had been tending was back in its cot, and Constance was settled on a pile of pillows on the chair at the nurses' station with paper and crayons to amuse her.

'What is it, Florrie?' Jessica asked anxiously. 'What's wrong?'

Florrie twisted the damp towel she was holding between her hands.

'Something terrible has happened, Jess. Something I wasn't meant to find out about. I was blamed for pushing Cissie Whitcombe down the stairs, but I know now that was just to get me out of the way so I wouldn't find out what Mabel Cummings had done. But then they let me back and I saw straight away—'

'Whoa, Florrie, slow down. You've lost me.'

Nothing her sister had said was making any sense to Jessica. She remembered that Cissie Whitcombe was the woman Alistair had spoken to in the doorway. But what on earth did that have to do with Florrie? And who was Mabel Cummings?

She leaned over and covered Florrie's hand with her own. 'Why don't you start again, and take your time. This Cissie fell down the stairs and someone said you'd pushed her. Is that right so far?'

Florrie nodded emphatically. 'Mabel Cummings said she'd seen me push her, but I think she did it herself and then blamed me to get us both out of the way so that the coast would be clear for what she planned to do. Cissie was in hospital, and I was banned from the nursery.'

'But you're here now.' Jessica was still trying to make sense of the garbled story.

'Yes, because when Cissie came round, she told Matron it couldn't have been me, so they let me come back. And I knew straight away that things weren't right. But Mabel had warned me that if I found anything amiss and told anyone, she'd have me banned again, and you know how I love working here. It's my life, Jess, and I just didn't know what to do . . .'

Tears had filled her eyes and her hand beneath Jessica's was trembling violently. Jessica longed to put her arms around her sister and comfort her. But she still didn't know what all this was about, and until she did, there was no way she could help her.

'What was it that this Mabel didn't want you to know?' she asked gently.

Florrie raised tear-filled eyes to Jessica's. 'It's awful, Jess. You'll never believe it. And I don't suppose anyone else would if I told them. It would be my word against hers.'

'I'll believe you. Of course I will! Just tell me, Florrie, please.'

'She swapped the babies . . .' Florrie's voice cracked and she began to sob, and Jessica became more confused than ever.

'What babies?' she asked.

'One belongs to her niece, Rose Gooding. She was put in here because she's an unmarried mother, hasn't even got a man friend to look out for her. And her baby was taken away for adoption, except that it wasn't him. Mabel must have changed the name tags over because it was Stella Swift's baby that was gone, and Rose's was still here.'

Jessica automatically glanced towards the cribs.

'Oh, he's not here now. They've sent Wallace – that's Rose's baby – home because Stella was insisting he wasn't hers and they thought she was rejecting him again.'

Stella Swift. Alistair's patient. Jessica remembered him mentioning that she'd had to be sectioned because she was refusing to feed her baby, but she knew he'd thought she was improving and getting back to normal.

Her mind was racing. If what Florrie said was true, perhaps Stella *had* been getting better, enough to realise that the baby they were trying to get her to bond with wasn't her own. But it was easy to see why no one would believe her.

Much harder, though, to try and understand why someone would do such a wicked thing. Even if the baby to be sent for adoption was this Mabel's own flesh and blood. What could possibly be gained from it?

Florrie was clutching her hand urgently. 'You can't tell anybody, Jess. Mabel will have me banned again, and I couldn't bear that.'

Jessica hardened her heart. 'So why did you tell me?'

'Because I couldn't keep it to myself any longer.'

'And because you knew it was the right thing to do. Think of how poor Stella must be feeling, knowing she's lost her baby and no one will believe her. We can't keep this quiet any longer, Florrie.'

'But . . . who will you tell?' Florrie's eyes were frantic. 'Not Matron?'

'I'll talk to Alistair. He'll know the best way to approach this.' Jessica thought for a moment. 'Do you know what happened to the baby that was taken away for adoption? Who the new parents are; where they live?'

Florrie shook her head. 'The records have all gone to be filed,' she said. 'I expect Dr Kirkwood has them. I'm never allowed into his office unless he's there.'

'Mammy, look!' Constance was tugging at Jessica's sleeve, holding out the picture she'd drawn for her mother's inspection. A big yellow sun, a house, and three stick figures that Jessica imagined must be her, Alistair and Constance.

'That's very nice, darling,' she said, though her mind was still elsewhere, boggling at the enormity of what Florrie had told her and anxious to share it with Alistair.

'Look, I'm going to have to go now, Florrie. But try not to worry. I'm sure Alistair will take care of everything.'

'But how?' Florrie was close to tears again.

'I don't know, but we'll work something out.'

Jessica hugged her sister, took Constance's hand and went in search of her husband.

She couldn't tell him on the way home, in front of Constance, and in any case this was something that demanded his full attention. The last thing she wanted was for him to run into a ditch as she tried to explain the complicated story Florric had told her. But fortunately the motion of the motor sent Constance to sleep, and although it was really too early for her nap, Jessica carried her in and settled her on the sofa without waking her.

'So what's wrong?' Alistair asked. 'Is it Florrie?' He had noticed Jessica's strange mood the moment he'd met up with her, but he too had decided to wait until they got home before mentioning it.

'Oh Alistair, she's in the most awful fix.' Usually, as soon as they got home from Catcombe, she would begin getting the Sunday dinner on the go, but not today. 'I think we'd better go and sit down before I tell you.'

He raised an eyebrow. 'That bad?'

'Worse. It's almost beyond belief.'

'Let me get a drink, then. Do you want one?'

Although it was contrary to habit, Jessica thought she could do with something. 'I'll have a glass of sherry. Just a small one. I don't want to get the baby tipsy.' She patted her stomach and attempted a smile.

He fetched it, and a bottle of beer for himself, which he poured into a tall glass.

'Go on then,' he said. 'Tell me the worst.'

'This is very serious indeed – if it's true,' Alistair said when she had finished.

'I'm sure it must be,' Jessica said. 'Florrie loves all those babies. Some people might struggle to tell one from the other, but not her. This Mabel must have known that, and it's the reason she accused Florrie of pushing Cissie down the stairs – to get her banned from the nursery. And she pushed Cissie herself to make sure she was out of the way too.'

'It seems a bit extreme,' Alistair mused.

'But it worked, didn't it? And now that Cissie has told them it couldn't have been Florrie and she's been allowed back in the nursery, this awful woman has threatened to have her banned again if she tells anybody what she knows.'

'I can't see what Mabel Cummings could hope to gain by swapping the babies,' Alistair argued.

'Nor me, really. But I'm certain Florrie is telling the truth. She's in a terrible way about it, Alistair.'

Alistair drained his glass and stood up. 'If there is any truth in this, the police will have to be involved. I'll get on to Hubert Kirkwood right away.'

'Alistair . . . no.' For the first time, Jessica felt a moment's doubt. Suppose Florrie had dreamed the whole thing up? Suppose she was having a funny spell again? If that proved to be the case, she would almost certainly be taken off nursery duty and returned to the treatment wards, and not being with the babies she loved so much would only worsen her condition. It was looking after them that had saved her sanity, Jessica was sure.

'There's no alternative, Jessica. This has to be investigated. We can't keep quiet about it,' Alistair said. Then, seeing her anguished expression, he relented. 'I'll tell you what I'll do. At the moment we have only Florrie's word for all this, but if I go and visit the Swift family – say I'm calling to check how William is doing – I can take a look at him for myself.'

'Would you know him?' Jessica asked.

'I would, yes. I'd probably recognise him anyway, but he has a small birthmark on his head, just above his right ear. If it's missing, it will confirm what Florrie has told you.'

Jessica frowned. 'Wouldn't the family have noticed if it had suddenly disappeared?'

'Not necessarily. His hair will have grown by now, I should think, and covered it up. But if I'm examining him and check his fontanelles, I can easily part his hair where the birthmark should be.'

It made sense, and although she felt sure in her heart that Florrie was telling the truth, it would be reassuring to have some confirmation.

'You're going there now?' she asked.

'No time like the present.'

'What about dinner?'

'Carry on with it as usual. I won't be long.'

'All right.' But Jessica didn't think she had much appetite. The very thought of food was making her feel queasy.

It was only after Alistair had left that the thought struck her.

Cissie Whitcombe had told him that she had fallen down the stairs the very same night that the motor had caught fire. And Alistair had just said that he could tell the difference between William Swift and the other baby, Mabel's great-nephew Wallace.

She caught her breath, her hand flying to her mouth. Was

there a connection? Had Alistair's motor been torched deliberately so that he would be unable to visit Catcombe, where he might see the babies? It seemed incredibly far-fetched, but then wasn't this whole business? Or was it coincidence? Jessica couldn't make up her mind.

But at least if Alistair got to see the baby the Swifts were caring for, perhaps the matter would be settled once and for all. And if Florrie was right and had uncovered a crime, then she would be rewarded, not punished. It might even lead to her release from Catcombe.

Holding on to that hope, Jessica began preparing the vegetables.

Alistair parked his new motor in Dunderwick Road, walked up the path of number 21 and knocked on the door. He could still scarcely believe the story Jessica had told him, but he knew he had to find out once and for all if there was any truth in it.

Footsteps in the hall, then the door opened and Stella's sister Grace stood there.

'Doctor!' She looked surprised to see him.

'I was passing and I thought I'd pop in to see how William is getting along now that he's home again.' Alistair was striving to come across as relaxed and casual.

'Oh, that's kind, but he's doing fine.'

'Could I see him while I'm here?'

'Well, yes, but . . .' She sounded a little hesitant, and Alistair hoped he hadn't offended her. Perhaps she thought it was her he was checking up on, wondering if she was capable of taking care of the baby. Then she stood aside.

'I'm sorry, Doctor, please do come in. It's just that Will's fast asleep, and I'd rather he didn't wake up until I've finished what I'm doing with the dinner. Tom and the children will be home soon – they've gone to visit Tom's mother – and they'll be starving.'

Alistair was not to be deterred now that he had come this far. 'I'll try not to disturb him too much.'

'No, don't take any notice of me, Doctor. I wouldn't want you to have had a wasted journey. He's in his pram in the back yard. I thought the fresh air would do him good.'

'I'm sure it will. And he's behaving himself, is he?'

'Good as gold.' Grace led the way through the house and out of the back door.

'Oh look, he's awake already! See – he hardly ever cries.' She reached into the pram and lifted the baby out. 'Hello, my sweetheart! You've got the doctor come to see you.'

Back in the living room, Alistair took a seat in one of the easy chairs and Grace handed him the baby. 'He certainly is the picture of health,' he said. But he was already uneasy. The William he remembered had had very little hair, but what there was had been fair like Stella's. This baby was altogether darker – skin, eyes and the growth of almost jet-black hair.

He made a great play of opening the baby's vest and listening to his heart and lungs before turning his attention to what he knew would be proof that this was not William Swift.

'The fontanelles,' he murmured, gently feeling for the soft membrane. 'You do know to take care with them until they close over, don't you?'

'Of course.'

Again he wondered if he had offended her, but if he had, it couldn't be helped. Turning the baby on his knee so that he had a clear view of the right side of his head, he parted the silky dark hair just above his ear. Nothing. He felt the breath catch in his chest, but continued exploring the area just to be sure.

There was definitely no birthmark, and Alistair was certain

now. This was not William Swift. The mark might have faded a little – they often did – but it wouldn't have disappeared completely in such a short space of time.

'All good,' he said, making sure he kept his voice level so that Grace would not realise something was wrong. It wasn't his place to tell her this baby was not her nephew but Wallace Gooding. That would be up to Hubert Kirkwood, and as soon as he got home he would contact him and tell him what he had found. The way the superintendent handled it from then on was for him to decide.

He returned the baby to Grace, murmured a few more platitudes and left hastily.

Back in the motor, he sat for a moment, thinking, then banged his hand hard against the steering wheel to release some of the tension he was feeling, before starting the engine. As he drove along the road towards Hillsbridge, he passed Tom Swift with his two sons, wheeling his daughter in a pushchair. He raised his hand in greeting but did not stop, really not wanting to speak to Tom now. The poor man's world had been turned upside down, and soon would be again.

The only bright spot was that it meant Stella had been right when she had protested that the child she was being handed was not hers, and was not sick again as had been assumed.

Alistair forced himself to slow down to take the bend at the top of the hill. He was driving too fast, he knew, but he was anxious to get home and call Hubert Kirkwood.

He wasn't looking forward to it, but the sooner he got it over with, the better, so that steps could be taken to put right the terrible wrong that had been perpetrated.

'Florrie was right,' was all he said to Jessica. 'I'm calling Kirkwood now.'

Without waiting for her reply, he went into the hall and picked up the telephone.

'Hubert,' he said when he had the superintendent on the line, 'I'm afraid I've got something very serious to tell you. It's about the baby who was placed for adoption recently.'

'You know something?' Dr Kirkwood sounded agitated.

'I'm afraid I do.' Alistair had not yet registered that the superintendent's response was not quite what he would have expected.

'Then out with it, man! The police have only just left – I might be able to catch them if you have something I can tell them.'

'The police?' Alistair repeated, confused now. Did Dr Kirkwood already know what he was about to tell him?

'The police, yes. They've been here to speak to the mother. A terrible business – terrible.'

'The mother? You mean Stella Swift?' Alistair asked.

'No, Rose Gooding. She's distraught, naturally. You do know, don't you, that her baby was abducted this morning? Taken from his perambulator in broad daylight from the garden of his adoptive parents' home in Gloucestershire. He has to be found, and quickly, before any harm befalls him . . .'

He broke off briefly and Alistair heard another man saying something.

'I have to go, Alistair. The policeman is back and wants to talk to me again. We'll speak again later.'

Then, before a stunned Alistair could say another word, he hung up.

331

# Chapter Twenty-Four

George Whittingly Challis drove carefully along the narrow lane. Driving carefully was something he rarely did, but today was different. He couldn't risk running into a ditch or mounting the bank, and one never knew what might be around the next bend. A horse-drawn farm vehicle, a cow, maybe even someone on a bicycle or taking a walk in the spring sunshine. He wasn't about to take a chance with a baby lying in the well between the front seat and the back.

He cast a quick glance behind him. For the moment the baby was quiet, rocked no doubt by the motion of the motor. Thank the Lord for that! George had no idea what he would do if he woke up and began to cry. He had no experience whatever of babies, and not for the first time he wondered what the hell he had done. Could he be sent to jail for stealing his own son? He couldn't see where the justice would be in that, but he might very well be thrown out of Sandhurst, whether his father continued to pay for him to be there or not.

But he had promised Rose he'd get Wallace back, and nothing on earth would make him break that promise. Her baby. *His* baby. George wasn't going to allow him to be brought up by strangers, no matter how well-to-do they might be. And from what he knew of the Donaghues, they were certainly that.

Winston Donaghue was one of his father's oldest friends, a country solicitor who had come into serious money when he'd married his first wife, Elizabeth, the daughter of a viscount. Their two sons had wanted for nothing, and George had envied them – though his own father was a wealthy man, he had always been remarkably mean when it came to Rupert and George. He preferred to splash out on lavish entertaining to impress his friends and to keep Cecelia happy – though that wasn't entirely successful, George thought bitterly – and he had considered that paying for a nanny and their boarding school fees was quite enough to fulfil his obligation to his sons.

When Elizabeth had died, Winston had married again. George couldn't imagine why he would want to start a second family at his age, but there was no accounting for people's behaviour. He knew his son would be provided with a happy childhood and a secure future with the Donaghues, but that wasn't the point. Wallace was *his* son, his and Rose's. She was grieving for him, and George himself couldn't stand the thought of losing the child who had come into the world through their love for one another.

After leaving Rose yesterday, he'd made up his mind. He'd get the baby back, and when Rose was released he'd marry her and they would be a family. He hadn't really taken the time to think things through, though; it wasn't his way. Whereas Rupert was cautious, he was impulsive, and thankful that he had the borrowed motor and not his bike, he'd driven straight to Gloucestershire.

By the time he'd arrived, of course, it was too late in the day to do anything about snatching the child, and he'd found himself lodging for the night in a country inn. This morning he'd been up with the lark – truth to tell, he'd scarcely slept – paid his bill, and set out for Stoneleigh House, still without any clear plan as to how he could achieve what he'd set out to do.

He'd parked the car on the village green, aware that if he drove right up to the house he'd draw attention to himself, then taken all his things out of his bag and put them on the back seat. He'd need the bag to conceal the baby if he was successful. Then he'd walked along the lane, past the front gate of the house, climbed a stile and made his way across the field that stretched out behind the rear garden.

From visiting as a boy, he knew the layout of the grounds quite well. There was an orchard, where he, Rupert and the Donaghue boys had feasted on ripe pears, apples and plums – Rupert had been stung on the tongue once, he remembered, when he'd bitten into a plum that a wasp had already laid claim to. Then there was the kitchen garden – that had been of little interest to the boys – and a walled garden with strawberries, raspberries, and even a peach tree trained against the sunniest wall. Beyond it was an arbour that was a suntrap, with a central fountain, and chamomile-covered seats nestled beneath over-hanging clematis and honeysuckle that buzzed with bees in summer.

That, George thought, was most likely where they'd take the baby for him to get some air: a warm, sheltered spot that wouldn't be too hot at this time of year. He wriggled under a barbed-wire fence intended to keep any livestock that might be in the field out of the orchard, and made his way to the bower, where he hid himself behind one of the low laurel hedges that bordered it.

Though the wait seemed endless, it wasn't that long before his patience was rewarded. Soon after ten by the watch he had been checking every few minutes, he saw a woman in nurse's uniform emerge from the house and walk down the crazy paving that led to the arbour, wheeling a shiny coach-built perambulator.

Triumph tingled in his veins – he'd been right, thank goodness. If the perambulator had been parked close to the conservatory that ran the length of the house, it would have been nigh on impossible for him to take the baby without being seen.

He flattened himself behind the hedge, parting the laurel leaves as much as he dared so that he was able to see the nurse push the perambulator over to one of the chamomile-covered seats. To his dismay, she sat down, jiggling the pram by its handles and singing softly a tune he recognised as Brahms's Lullaby.

Again the minutes stretched out endlessly, and more than once George had to stifle a sneeze. His eyes were beginning to itch and water too – at this time of year, when there was tree pollen in the air, he often suffered this way, although the grass and hay dust later in the year didn't seem to affect him. Was the nurse going to stay with the baby? If she did, there would be nothing he could do. Frustration burned like acid in his gut. So near, and yet so far!

Just when he thought she was going to stay there all morning, the nurse rose, straightened the covers of the perambulator and walked off towards the house. How long she'd be gone he didn't know – if she was simply going to answer a call of nature, he would have only a few minutes. The moment she was out of his sight, he crawled on his belly to the corner of the hedge, checking that the coast was clear. It was now or never. He scrambled to his feet and darted towards the perambulator, his heart hammering a tattoo against his ribs.

The baby was fast asleep. As gently as he could, so as not to wake him, George lifted him out of the pram, grabbed the shawl the nurse had straightened and dived back behind the hedge where his holdall was still hidden. He laid the baby inside and partly closed the bag, making sure his face wasn't covered. The baby was stirring, whimpering a little, and George knew he had no time to lose. If he started to cry in earnest, and anyone was about, it would be disastrous.

He hotfooted it back through the orchard, under the barbed-wire fence and across the meadow. Much to his relief, the lane leading back to the village green was deserted. He reached the motor without incident, opened the bag fully and placed it between the front and rear seats. Then he cranked the engine to life, climbed in and drove away.

Mercifully, the baby – his son! – was quiet again. Presumably he'd just been fed when the nurse had wheeled him into the garden, but George had no idea how long it would be before he was awake again, and hungry. How often were babies fed? He didn't know anything about their care.

But Rose's mother would know. She'd raised five children of her own. And it was to Rose's mother that he planned to take his son. She'd be shocked, of course, but he felt sure he could count on her to look after her grandchild until Rose was released from the asylum. After that . . . He wasn't sure yet what would come next, but he'd work something out. The hardest part, snatching the baby, had gone more smoothly than he had dared hope. If his luck held, the rest would follow. For the moment, he just had to concentrate on getting the baby away safely.

The trouble was that driving more carefully than usual meant the return journey had taken much longer than getting there had done. Now, however, he was at last on the home straight, lanes he knew well. Just a few more miles and he would reach the cottage where Rose's parents lived. Heaving a sigh of relief, George relaxed his grip on the steering wheel and flexed his aching hands. Not far now, and he would be able to hand his son over into the care of his grandparents.

He could only imagine how delighted they would be.

* * *

Miranda Donaghue, a handkerchief crumpled between her hands, her eyes red from weeping, perched on the edge of a brocaded sofa in the drawing room of Stoneleigh House. Winston was closeted in the study with a police inspector who had arrived from Swindon, but Madge Tyler was with her. Almost as distraught as Miranda herself, the nanny was nevertheless trying her best to remain calm.

'Would you like some more water, Mrs Donaghue?' she asked, filling a tumbler from a crystal decanter with hands that trembled and offering it to Miranda, who pushed it away impatiently.

'No! I don't want water! I just want Wallace back!'

Tears began to course down her cheeks again and she dabbed at them with the already sodden handkerchief.

'Where is he?' she wailed. 'Who can have taken him? How could such a thing have happened?'

The nanny shook her head, tears welling in her own eyes. 'I don't know, Mrs Donaghue. I only left him for a minute. I never would have done if I'd thought for a moment . . .'

'Please don't blame yourself, Madge.' Even in her present state Miranda found it in herself to understand how distressed the nurse must be. 'You weren't to know. But are you sure you saw no one? Nobody lurking in the garden or the orchard?'

'No one. I saw no one. It was all quiet. Wallace was asleep, and I never thought he'd come to harm in just a few minutes.'

*Come to harm.* The words jarred on Miranda's shattered nerves, made her sob aloud.

'Oh dear God, he must be safe! Please let him be safe! I'll do anything – anything! – as long as he's safe!'

'He will be,' Madge Tyler said, and knew she was attempting to reassure herself as much as Miranda. 'Whoever has taken him must want him very much. They won't hurt him, mark my words.'

'But they don't know him! They don't know his little ways!'

'And we'll have him back before they have the chance to find out.'

Again the nanny spoke with more conviction than she was feeling as she racked her brains trying to remember if anyone had taken a particular interest in the baby when she had been pushing him out. No one came to mind. Plenty of women peered into the perambulator, cooing over him, admiring his golden hair and big blue eyes fringed with long lashes, but she had seen none of them as a threat.

'Oh Madge, I just can't bear it!' Miranda sobbed.

The door opened and Winston and the police inspector came into the room. Winston was pale and drawn; the inspector wore a grim expression.

'There's little more I can do here at present, Mrs Donaghue,' he said, not mentioning that his questioning had revealed nothing, but that his suspicions still lay with the nanny. He had already questioned them all at length and learned nothing

'But you won't give up?' Miranda asked anxiously.

'Not until your son is safely returned to you. Rest assured of that. At this very moment I have men knocking on every door in the vicinity. Someone must have seen something, and no stone will be left unturned until your baby is found and the culprit is behind bars.'

As Winston was returning from seeing the inspector out, he met Miranda crossing the hallway.

'Where are you going, my love?' he asked.

'To the nursery. I just want to . . .'

'Wallace isn't there,' he said gently.

'I know, but I'll feel closer to him there.'

'Come and sit down. They'll find him, I promise you.'

But truth to tell, Winston was not sure that they would. Baby Wallace, it seemed, had vanished into thin air.

With a sigh of relief, George drew to a halt on the lane outside Rose's parents' cottage, then jumped out of the car and opened the back door. Wallace had been silent for some time now, and George was becoming anxious about him. It would almost have been a relief if he had begun to cry, though he hadn't wanted that distraction either.

He carefully lifted out his bag and opened it wide. Two blue eyes looked up at him, and the baby reached out his little arms.

Thank God! He was still alive! George lifted him out, holding him awkwardly in one arm as he unlatched the wicket gate and walked up the path edged with neat flower beds. At the front door, he knocked, and waited.

He had never actually met Rose's mother, knew her only by sight, and he wondered if she would recognise him. He didn't even know if Rose had told her about him. Perhaps she was unaware that she had a grandson. But no – she would surely have been told the reason for Rose being committed to the asylum, even if she didn't know who the baby's father was.

Footsteps sounded on the tiled floor within, and the door opened. A buxom woman wearing a wraparound house dress was standing there, a woman with Rose's dark eyes, though they were almost lost in the fleshy folds of her cheeks, and hair that would once have been as dark as Rose's, though now it was shot through with grey.

Those dark eyes were startled now; she looked from George to the baby and back again.

'What in the world . . . ?'

'I'm George Whittingly Challis,' he said. 'Rose and—'

'Oh, I know who you are all right,' she said shortly. 'The son

339

of that bastard that got our Rose put where she is. But what . . . ?'

'Please – can I come in, and I'll explain?'

Rose's mother poked her head out of the door, looking in the direction of the adjoining cottage to hers; checking that there was no sign of the neighbours, George guessed.

Then: 'I think you better had.'

She stood aside. George went in and found himself in a long, low room on to which the front door opened directly. It was neat and nicely furnished with a dining table and chairs at one end and a sofa and two easy chairs arranged around the hearth at the other. In the far corner a staircase with white-painted newel posts and banister led to the upper storey of the cottage.

A man was seated in one of the easy chairs, the Sunday newspaper spread out across his knees.

'What's going on?' he asked in a bemused tone.

'That's what I'm about to find out.' Rose's mother obviously wore the trousers in this house. 'You'd better tell me what you're doing here, *Mister* Challis,' she went on, laying heavy emphasis on the word. 'And who *this* is,' she added, jerking her double chins in the direction of the baby.

'This is your grandson,' George said. 'Rose's baby – and mine.'

'Yours?' she repeated, as if she was unable to believe what she was hearing. 'But I thought . . .'

'Yes, mine. I don't know how much you know, but he was sent for adoption to a couple in Gloucestershire – my father arranged it. I've been away and had no idea what was going on until I came home yesterday. I went to see Rose, promised her I'd get him back somehow – and here he is. But I can't look after him, and I was hoping you would, until Rose gets out, that is. Then I'll take care of them both.'

He went to hand the baby over, but Rose's mother made no

move to take him. She had remained speechless throughout his garbled explanation; now she found her voice with a vengeance.

'You bloody fool!'

'I'm sorry?' This was hardly the reception he had expected.

Olive jabbed an angry finger at the baby's chest; her lip curled and spittle flew from her mouth as she shouted: 'That's not our Rose's baby!'

'What are you talking about?' They were the only words George was capable of uttering.

'That's not Wallace, I'm telling you.'

'But it must be! He was with the Donaghues at Stoneleigh House.'

'That's as maybe, but it's not Wallace. My sister Mabel arranged it all. She didn't want him taken all that way away, wanted him somewhere Rose could at least get to see him, even if she couldn't get him back. She swapped the babies, changed their name tags, got rid of anybody who'd know the difference. She even got Frank here to set light to the doctor's motor in case he took it into his head to go to Catcombe. Isn't that right, Frank?'

'Oh, ah,' Frank confirmed, still looking completely bemused.

'You mean . . . this is somebody else's baby?' George managed.

'Too right. A woman who's in Catcombe because she refused to have anything to do with him.'

'And Wallace is still there, in the asylum?'

'No. According to Mabel, he's been sent home to what's supposed to be his family. You've landed us in a pretty mess and no mistake. You *stole* this baby, did you?'

'Yes, this morning.'

'Well, the police will be on your tail by now. They might even come knocking on our door. The whole thing's going to come out, and Lord only knows what'll happen to our Mabel.'

Mabel, George thought, was the least of his worries. The baby, whoever he was, had begun to cry, frightened, no doubt, by the angry voices.

'I don't know what you're going to do about it, but you'd better do something, and pretty damn quick,' Olive told him. 'Just get out of here and take that child with you. Go on, before I call the police myself and tell them there's a madman here turned up on my doorstep with a baby.'

She shooed him back towards the open door and gave him a push between his shoulder blades, then slammed it behind him.

For a moment George simply stood there, shaken to the core. What the hell had he done? He'd risked everything, and somehow ended up with the wrong baby. Rose couldn't have known about the switch, and he couldn't understand why her aunt Mabel hadn't told her. But he couldn't waste time worrying about that now. He had to decide what to do. The baby had begun to cry lustily – hungry, no doubt – and he had no way of feeding him. Perhaps he should take him to the nearest police station, but he didn't suppose they'd have milk or baby food there, and in any case he'd most likely be arrested on the spot.

Really there was only one place where this stranger's baby would be looked after – Catcombe asylum. He could go back into the nursery, where at least he'd be safe and cared for.

With his nerves jangling and his head spinning, George went back to the motor, replaced the screaming baby in his bag and set off towards Catcombe.

By the time he had parked outside the main entrance, George had managed to marshal his thoughts – not easy with the baby screaming blue murder – and had come up with a plan.

He lifted the holdall with the baby still inside from the motor, carried it up the steps and put it down. Then he rang the bell. The door was opened by a nurse, and George instantly pointed to the bag.

'There's a baby on your step,' he said, and if he looked upset, he certainly wasn't putting on an act.

'Lawks!' The nurse's face reflected her shock and horror, though it wasn't the first time an unwanted infant had been left there. 'Oh, the poor little mite!' She reached into the bag and lifted the baby out, cradling him comfortably in her arms, and turned to go inside. George followed her. If he left now without explaining what he was doing here, it would only arouse suspicion.

'I'm here to see Dr Kirkwood,' he said. 'It's just lucky I arrived when I did.'

'I'll say. Poor little soul's hungry by the sound of it. He looks well cared for, though.'

A small crowd was gathering, attracted by the commotion: two or three nurses and a handful of patients who had been in the day room just down the hall. Suddenly one of them pushed her way to the front, a young woman with hair like spun silk, blue eyes wide in her pale face.

She gasped, then stretched out her arms. 'Will!' she sobbed. 'It's my Will! Oh, thank God! Thank God!'

The nurse turned to her, astonished.

'Stella . . .' she cautioned.

'It is! It's my Will! He's come back to me!'

Again she reached for him, taking him from the surprised nurse before she could be stopped and holding him close.

To everyone's amazement, the baby stopped crying.

# Chapter Twenty-Five

Florrie was on her way downstairs to fetch a cup of tea for herself and Joanie Fry when the chaos erupted. She stopped short and stared in disbelief at the scene – Nurse Hilliard holding a baby, a young man she thought was one of Sir Oswald's sons looking tense and anxious, and a small crowd of onlookers. What in the world was going on? Then she saw Stella Swift rush forward and take the baby from Nurse Hilliard's arms, heard her cry that it was her William.

Florrie gasped, holding on to the handrail for support as she felt her legs threaten to give way beneath her. She couldn't see the baby's face – it was buried in Stella's breast – but knowing what she did, she had no doubt that it was indeed William. But how did he come to be here? He was supposed to be in Gloucestershire with his adoptive parents. Jessica had said she'd have to tell Alistair what Florrie had told her – had he somehow discovered where William was and brought him back? But there was no sign of either him or Jessica. And what did Sir Oswald's son have to do with any of it?

As she stood there, hanging on to the banister, Dr Kirkwood appeared, closely followed by Matron Carey.

'What's going on here?' the superintendent demanded.

'Oh Doctor, this baby's been left on our doorstep!' That was

Nurse Hilliard. 'Mr Challis was coming to see you and found him there.'

Dr Kirkwood took one look at the crowd of gaping onlookers and spoke severely to the staff members.

'Please return these patients to the day room. There's nothing here for them to see.' Then he turned to the young man. 'You found this baby on our doorstep?'

'I did. I don't know how long he'd been there, but I think he's hungry.'

'That's hardly surprising,' Dr Kirkwood said. 'I'm wondering if he might be the baby who was stolen from a perambulator this morning in Gloucestershire. Rose Gooding's baby. But who would kidnap him only to bring him here? No matter. I'll get in touch with the police immediately and tell them we have an unexplained foundling.'

Florrie's stomach clenched. She thought she was going to be sick, but she was unable to tear her eyes away from the scene.

Matron was looking now at Stella, who was holding the baby suspiciously close. 'What are you doing, Stella?'

Stella didn't reply; she was totally engrossed in the infant in her arms.

'She snatched him away from me,' Nurse Hilliard said. 'She thinks it's her baby.'

'Stop that at once!' Matron's voice was sharp, and from her vantage point on the stairs, Florrie could see that Stella had unbuttoned her smock and put the baby to her breast.

Dr Kirkwood laid a hand on Matron's arm. 'Leave her. If she still has any milk left and the baby is hungry, it will keep them both quiet for the time being until we can sort this out.' He glanced up and saw Florrie standing on the stairs. 'Ah, Florrie, will you take Stella and the baby up to the nursery and make sure he's changed and fed?'

'Yes, sir.' Somehow getting control of her shaking legs, Florrie descended to the hall and put an arm round Stella. 'Come with me, dear.'

As she led Stella up to the nursery, she heard Dr Kirkwood say: 'You'd better come to my office, Mr Challis. The police will want a statement from you.'

And Matron: 'Should I send for Rose Gooding? She'll be able to tell us if this is her missing baby.'

Florrie slowed her steps to hear Dr Kirkwood's reply.

'Not yet. Maybe not at all. The baby no longer belongs to her, remember, and we don't want her upset all over again when he is returned to his adoptive parents.'

Their voices faded as they headed up the corridor, and Florrie could hear no more.

Joanie Fry was at the top of the stairs now, probably wondering what was going on, and what had happened to her promised cup of tea.

Her voice shaking, Florrie managed a few words of explanation. Then: 'Can you take care of Stella and the baby? I don't feel very well . . .'

Without waiting for a reply, she turned and bolted down the stairs. That she didn't feel well was no lie. But most importantly, Stella was still not being believed. The time had come for Florrie to reveal what she knew – that the baby was indeed Stella's William, and that Rose's baby had been taken to the Swift family.

Shaking with terror, but no longer able to live with her guilty conscience, she hurried along the corridor to Dr Kirkwood's office.

With her hand already raised to knock, Florrie hesitated. She could hear voices; it sounded as if the Whittingly Challis boy was still with the superintendent, and she didn't want to have to make her confession in front of him. It would have been hard enough if Dr Kirkwood had been alone. But she had to do this. For Stella's sake if nothing else.

As she stood there summoning up the courage to knock, Matron Carey emerged from her own office, carrying a file of paperwork. She looked at Florrie questioningly.

'Did you want something, Florrie?'

In that moment, Florrie made up her mind. In many ways she was more frightened of Matron than she was of the superintendent; where he was gentle and understanding, she was of the old school, strict, a woman who stood no nonsense. But at least Florrie could speak to her one to one without an outsider listening to every word she said. She remembered, too, how Matron had stood up for her when Cissie Whitcombe had regained consciousness and revealed that Florrie couldn't have had anything to do with her fall. Matron had believed in her then and had her reinstated in the nursery. She could only hope that she would believe her now.

'Could I have a word with you, Matron?' she asked, her voice unsteady.

Matron raised an eyebrow.

'In private,' Florrie added.

'Very well.' Matron turned back into her office. Florrie followed her and closed the door behind her.

Matron placed the file of papers on her desk and sat down. 'Well?'

'Matron . . . that baby . . . the one that's been found on the doorstep . . . he *is* Stella's.'

Surprise flared in Matron's eyes, though her expression remained inscrutable. 'What makes you say that? Dr Kirkwood believes he could be the baby who was abducted this morning – Rose Gooding's son.'

Florrie's lip trembled. 'He's that too. Though I don't know how he got here.'

'Florrie, I haven't the faintest idea what you're talking about.' Matron was becoming impatient.

'The babies. Wallace Gooding and William Swift. Mabel Cummings swapped them. It was William that got taken away for adoption. I've known ever since you let me go back to work in the nursery, and I should have spoken out then, but Mabel said if I did she'd have me banned again, and I didn't know what to do . . .'

The tears that had been threatening spilled over, running unchecked down her cheeks, and her voice dissolved into sobs.

'You'd better sit down, Florrie,' Matron said, somehow maintaining her brisk attitude. 'Try and compose yourself. I'll fetch Dr Kirkwood and you can tell him what you have just told me. And maybe for all our sakes you can make yourself a little clearer.'

Florrie nodded, wiping her face on the sleeve of her smock. 'I'll try, Matron.'

'You'll do more than try,' Matron said sternly, and left the office.

Florrie heard her cross the corridor, knock on Dr Kirkwood's door and say: 'I'm sorry to interrupt, Doctor, but could you come to my office? I have Florrie there, and you need to hear what she has to say.'

'Matron, I am dealing with—'

'I know, Doctor, but this might well be relevant,' Matron interrupted him. 'If so, we have a very grave situation on our hands.'

'Would you excuse me, Mr Challis?' Dr Kirkwood said.

Then his door clicked shut and both he and Matron entered the office.

Florrie wiped her face on her sleeve again and sniffed hard to clear her nose. She was still shaking, but somehow it seemed the worst was over. Her awful secret was out; she'd told Jessica and she'd told Matron. Now all she had to do was tell Dr Kirkwood too.

'So what is this all about?' Dr Kirkwood asked her.

Florrie took a deep breath and began her story again.

In the superintendent's office, George was sweating profusely. So far, it seemed, his story about finding the baby on the doorstep seemed to have been believed, but if a policeman started asking questions, it might be a very different matter.

He was almost certain he hadn't been seen in Gloucestershire, but if he was asked where he'd been this morning, what could he say? Not at home. If they spoke to his father, he'd tell the truth, that George had left yesterday afternoon and not been back since. That would raise the question of where he'd spent the night. He could say that after a disagreement with his father he'd slept in the motor, and had spent the morning just driving around, but even to his own ears that sounded feeble.

What the hell had he done? he asked himself yet again. Why hadn't he thought things through? His father was right – he was an idiot. He'd ruined his chance of becoming an army officer, and for what? Even if his plan hadn't gone disastrously wrong, how could he have imagined for a moment that he, Rose and their baby would live happily ever after? Now he had no future and nothing to offer them, and their baby – his and Rose's – was still heaven knows where.

He sank his head in his hands and massaged the back of his aching neck.

Perhaps the best course now would be to come clean and admit the truth. He didn't know. He honestly didn't know, and the indecision, along with the knowledge that he'd ruined everything, was a lead weight in his heart.

Mabel Cummings hadn't long been up when she saw her brother-in-law push his bicycle past her kitchen window; in fact she was still in her nightgown, dressing gown and slippers, making herself a pot of tea before she got dressed. She was getting used to working nights now and had established a routine – breakfast when she got home from the hospital, six or seven hours' sleep, a cup of tea when she woke and a snack of bread and cheese, then a few hours to potter about before she had her main meal and went back to work again.

The teapot in her hand, she opened the back door.

'What brings you here, Frank?'

'You may well ask.' Frank looked hot and bothered, whether from the ride or something else she couldn't tell.

'Well, you'd better come in. There's a cup of tea in the pot if you want one.'

'Better not stop. Olive's in a bit of a state, and I ought to get back to her.'

'What's up then? Has she had one of her funny turns?'

Olive was prone to 'funny turns', when she fainted clean away; Mabel wondered if it might be her heart.

'No, nothing like that, at least not yet. It wouldn't surprise me if she did after what's happened.'

'Get on and tell me then,' Mabel said impatiently.

'Well . . .' Frank took off his cap and laid it on the table. 'That boy of Sir Oswald's turned up at our door – just finished dinner, we had.'

'Rupert?' Mabel asked.

'No, the other one – George, is it? And you'll never guess what he had with him.'

'So tell me.'

'He'd only been and stolen what he thought was our Rose's baby.'

'What?' Mabel was flabbergasted.

'I know. He went and took it out of its pram this morning. Brought it to us thinking Olive would look after it.'

'You mean he went to Hillsbridge, to the Swifts, and—'

'No,' Frank interrupted her. 'To Gloucestershire. To wherever it is the people who adopted him live.'

'But Wallace never went to Gloucestershire.'

'I know that, and so do you, but he didn't. And according to him, he's the baby's father.'

'What?' Mabel was flabbergasted. 'George Whittingly Challis? And our Rose?'

'That's what he said. Well, as you can guess, Olive told him to get rid of the baby quick sharp and he went off again, but she thought you ought to know about it. So you're prepared, like, in case it all comes out.'

The seat of the chair was hard against the back of Mabel's knees. She sat down, staring at Frank in horror.

'Oh my Lord! Surely that won't happen?'

'Goodness only knows,' Frank said. 'But it's a tidy kettle of fish and no mistake.'

Mabel was silent for a moment. Unlike Frank, who wasn't the sharpest knife in the box, she could think on her feet. As long as she was properly awake.

'Look – like as not he'll be taken straight back again,' she said. 'Nobody but you, me and Olive know I switched the babies. I haven't even had the chance to tell Rose.'

*Nobody except Florrie*, murmured a small voice in her head. But she didn't think Florrie would say anything. She valued her job in the nursery too highly.

'So just tell our Olive to stay calm and carry on as normal. It'll all blow over, you'll see.'

'Well, I hope you'm right,' Frank said, picking up his cap. 'If I get fingered for torching that doctor's motor . . .'

'Why would you?' Mabel blustered. 'Even if it does come out, there's nothing to tie you to that. It's me that would be left carrying the can. But I can't see that it's going to.'

When Frank had left, however, pedalling away on his bicycle, she had to admit to herself that she was worried – and puzzled, too. None of this made any sense. Sir Oswald had gone to great lengths to have his illegitimate child adopted – with her own experience to draw on, she had no doubt that he was the baby's father, though Rose had always refused, for some reason, to confirm it. So why would George have stolen the child and taken it to Olive and Frank? The only reason she could think of was that he was disgusted with his father and infatuated with Rose. Word was that he'd been to visit her in Catcombe, and he'd have realised she was heartbroken over the loss of her baby.

If only I'd been able to talk to her! Mabel thought. Reassure her that I knew exactly where he was. But she hadn't had the opportunity. By the time she arrived for night duty, Rose was back downstairs. All she'd ever been able to tell her was that she would take care of things.

And she had.

A shadow fell across the room as the sun passed behind a cloud.

Mabel sipped her tea and tried to push away the thought that she might have done for them all.

As Alistair turned into the drive of Catcombe asylum, he was surprised to see a motor he didn't recognise parked beside the front entrance.

But perhaps he shouldn't be surprised, given what was going on, he thought. The motor was new, shiny and, he guessed, expensive – not a police vehicle, unless he was very much mistaken. Could it belong to the adoptive parents of the stolen baby? That too seemed unlikely. He couldn't think of any reason why they would be here. They wouldn't yet know that a nurse on the Catcombe staff had swapped the babies and the one they had been caring for wasn't Wallace Gooding. Most likely they would be at home, waiting anxiously for news.

He parked beyond the unfamiliar vehicle and hurried into the asylum. It was imperative he wasted no more time before speaking to Dr Kirkwood and telling him what he knew.

Ever since the superintendent had ended their telephone conversation so abruptly, Alistair had been trying to call him back, but with no success. He'd even interrupted his Sunday roast several times to pick up the telephone, but the line to the asylum seemed to be permanently engaged and he had decided he had no option but to drive to Catcombe and speak to Dr Kirkwood in person.

The nurse who answered his ring on the bell was a big, beefy man whose uniform stretched so tightly over his barrel chest that the buttons looked fit to burst. Presumably he'd been deployed as gatekeeper in case of trouble.

'I'm here to see Dr Kirkwood,' Alistair said.

'Right, Doctor – go straight along. You know we've got trouble here today, do you?' the nurse asked.

'Yes,' Alistair said shortly, and thought that the trouble they'd had so far was nothing to what was in store when he dropped his bombshell.

He strode along the corridor, knocked briefly on the superintendent's office door and opened it without waiting for a reply.

Dr Kirkwood was not at his desk, but a young man was

sitting in the visitor's chair, his head in his hands. He looked up sharply as Alistair entered, leaving his short dark hair standing up in spikes where he had been running his fingers through it.

'Oh – I'm sorry. I was looking for Dr Kirkwood,' Alistair said.

'He's not here.' The voice was cultured, no hint of the local burr. Perhaps he was the owner of the motor parked outside, Alistair thought.

'So I see. Would you know where I can find him?' he asked.

'I don't know, but he went off with the matron. At least that's who I think she was.'

'Thank you.'

Alistair crossed the corridor. The door to Matron's office was closed; again he knocked and then opened it.

Dr Kirkwood was indeed there, as was Matron, but it was the third person in the room who took Alistair by surprise.

'Florrie!'

She was seated on a hard-backed chair, twisting a handkerchief between her hands, and she'd clearly been crying. She turned anguished eyes to Alistair but said nothing.

'Come in, Doctor,' the superintendent said. His expression was grim. 'Since Stella Swift is your patient, I think you need to hear what your sister-in-law has just told us.'

Alistair closed the door behind him.

'I think I already know, and it's the reason I'm here. Florrie spoke to Jessica this morning. I've been trying to reach you ever since our telephone conversation, but the line was always engaged.'

'I've left it off the hook apart from when I've wanted to make a call,' Dr Kirkwood said. 'I've had too much to deal with to have constant interruptions. Once the local papers get hold of this . . .' He shook his head. 'Anyway, I'm glad you're here, and that you already know Florrie's story. More importantly, you'll be able to confirm or deny what she has told us. A lot has happened since we spoke earlier. A baby has been found on our doorstep and Stella is claiming it's her son. If you could take a look at him . . .'

'Of course. But before I do, I should tell you I called on the Swift family as soon as Jessica relayed to me what Florrie had told her. I wanted to see the baby for myself. And there is absolutely no doubt in my mind that the child they are caring for is not William.'

Dr Kirkwood and Matron exchanged a long look. Clearly this was not the news they had been hoping for.

'It's William that was found on the doorstep.' Florrie spoke for the first time. 'Stella's right. She'd know him anywhere, and so would I.'

'But you'll take a look at the foundling anyway?' Dr Kirkwood pressed Alistair.

As they moved towards the door, Florrie got up as if to follow them.

'No, you stay here, Florrie,' Dr Kirkwood told her. Once he and Alistair were in the corridor, he whispered: 'I don't want her muddying the waters, and in any case, she's not in a fit state.'

The scene that greeted them in the nursery should on its own have been enough to convince Dr Kirkwood that the baby was indeed William. Stella radiated pure happiness as she nursed the baby on her lap, holding him tightly as if she would never let him go again. But after a few well-chosen words from Alistair, she allowed him to take the child, simply gazing adoringly as the doctor gently parted the fine golden hair and located the telltale birthmark.

He met Dr Kirkwood's eyes and nodded. 'Not a doubt of it,' he said in a low voice as he returned William to Stella.

'We need to talk.' Dr Kirkwood ushered Alistair out of the nursery, Joanie Fry's curious gaze following them. Once downstairs, he pointed the way to one of the empty treatment rooms. 'I don't want to speak in front of Florrie, and the young man who found the baby on the doorstep is in my office, waiting to give a statement to the police when they arrive,' he said by way of explanation. 'This is a bad business and no mistake.'

'What I can't understand is how William got here,' Alistair said when the door was closed and they were alone. 'Who on earth abducted him and brought him all the way here – and why?'

Dr Kirkwood spread his hands in an expression of bewilderment. 'I have no idea. I only hope the police can get to the bottom of it. But what we have to consider is what we should do now. The baby with the Swifts is Rose Gooding's son, you say?'

'I can't be sure of that. I've never seen him before. All I can tell you is that it's not William Swift. And he's very dark – hair, eyes, complexion.'

'That certainly sounds like Rose. If Florrie's story is true, and Mabel Cummings switched the babies, it would seem that he probably is Wallace Gooding. I think the only course of action is for you to fetch him and bring him here. I'll have Rose confirm it is indeed Wallace before mentioning any of this to the police.'

'You want me to go and break it to them . . . take the baby away?' Alistair shrank from the very thought of it, but he could see no alternative.

'Would you do that?'

'I suppose so. But what about William?'

'I think it's best he remain here with Stella for the time being. Once all this is resolved, hopefully she can be discharged, and the baby with her. It seems to me that what we took to be a relapse was in fact Stella behaving as any mother would when presented with a child who was not her baby.'

'Which means that at least some good will come out of all this,' Alistair said.

'Every cloud . . .' Dr Kirkwood attempted a smile.

It would indeed be good that Stella's treatment had not been a failure, as he had feared. But given the scandal that would erupt when the whole dreadful business came to light, and the damage it would do to both his reputation and that of the hospital, it was small compensation.

# Chapter Twenty-Six

As Dr Kirkwood re-entered his office, George rose impatiently from his chair.

'How much longer before I can leave?' he asked shortly. 'I have to be back at my camp on Salisbury Plain by roll-call this evening, or I'll be up on a charge.'

The superintendent, still trying to process the enormity of what Mabel Cummings had done, forced his mind back to the young man who had found baby William on the asylum steps.

'The police should have been here by now,' he said, looking at his watch. 'It's an hour or more since I telephoned the station. But I'm afraid things don't always move as quickly as they should out here in the country.'

'They've always moved sharply enough when my father has called on them for assistance,' George said.

'Yes, well . . . I suppose they would,' Dr Kirkwood agreed.

He could well imagine the police wouldn't let the grass grow under their feet where Sir Oswald was concerned. They'd be too wary of probable repercussions. But this matter wouldn't be top of their list of priorities. The kidnapping wasn't their case and they would be hoping that an officer from Gloucestershire would come down to look into this end of developments if they delayed long enough. Besides which, Constable Smart, who'd answered Dr Kirkwood's call, hardly lived up to his name. He was a slow-moving, slow-thinking man nearing retirement, who pedalled around town at a stately pace, his face red above the collar of his tunic from even that modest exertion. A solid enough policeman, but hardly dynamic. It could well be hours before he put in an appearance, if at all. And what could George tell them? Nothing more than he'd already told Dr Kirkwood.

'What was it you came to see me about anyway?' he asked. The purpose of George's visit had been completely forgotten in all that had happened since.

'I was just going to confirm that my father is arranging a position in service for Rose,' George said, uncomfortable again.

'I thought that was agreed upon.' Dr Kirkwood looked slightly irritated.

'And to make sure you have the necessary paperwork.'

'That too.'

Dr Kirkwood had had enough of this young man sitting in his office. He had things to do, and he wanted his privacy and the space to think all this through alone.

'To be truthful, I don't really feel I can keep you here any longer,' he said. 'It's not as if you have anything useful to tell the police, and if they insist on a statement, I dare say you can be contacted at your camp.'

'I'll be there until the end of next week,' George confirmed.

'In that case, you might as well be on your way,' Dr Kirkwood said. A thought struck him. 'Did you want to see Rose before you go? I seem to remember you did when you were here last.'

'No, it's all right,' George said, a little too quickly. Much as he longed to see her, he didn't think he could face her just now, when he'd made such a dreadful mess of things. Besides, he was anxious to get away from here as soon as possible – certainly before a policeman who might ask awkward questions arrived on the scene.

'Probably just as well.' Dr Kirkwood was thinking that for the moment, the less Rose knew about what was going on, the better. He offered George his hand. 'Well, goodbye, Mr Challis, and thank you again,' he said. 'I'm only sorry this has taken up so much of your time.'

'Goodbye, Doctor.' It was all George could manage as he shook the proffered hand. Then, light-headed now with relief, he left the asylum, got his borrowed motor going, and roared away as if all the hounds of hell were on his tail.

Once George had left, Dr Kirkwood seated himself at his desk, considering all the aspects of the disaster that had occurred, and how best to deal with it.

What Mabel had done was criminal; he needed to report it to the police – not the plodding Constable Smart, but the inspector at the divisional headquarters, whom he knew well and considered a friend. Gloucestershire police needed to be informed of the situation too, but he quailed at the thought of trying to explain that although the missing baby had been found, it was the wrong one. And somehow things had to be put right with the Donaghues; that, perhaps, was the most vexing thing of all. Would they be prepared to take on a different baby? Was it even legally possible? He knew nothing about where the law stood in a case such as this.

Really, he thought, he needed advice before he did anything at all.

He reached for the telephone receiver lying disconnected on his blotter, jiggled the cradle to get a line, and put in a call to his friend Cuthbert Drayton, a barrister who appeared before the circuit judges at assize and quarter sessions. If Cuthbert couldn't help him, he didn't know who could.

Half an hour later, armed with his friend's advice, he telephoned Walter Dudley, the inspector in charge of the division, who was fortunately reachable in spite of it being Easter Sunday. The inspector was shocked at what he had to say, though for the moment Dr Kirkwood had decided not to tell him the whole story, preferring to pass off the mix-up with the babies as a terrible mistake until he'd had the chance to speak to Mabel Cummings himself.

Much to his relief, Dudley agreed that he would contact the Gloucestershire police who were dealing with the abduction and let them know the missing baby had been found. He also expressed his annoyance at the seeming incompetence of the local police in the shape of Constable Smart in not following up Dr Kirkwood's call.

'It's time the man was pensioned off,' he said crossly, and Dr Kirkwood couldn't agree more.

Now the only thing left for him to do was to speak to the Donaghues. Cuthbert Drayton had assured him that there was no legislation that made it legally binding for the same child to be returned to them. In fact there was very little legislation at all on adoption, though plans for it were in the pipeline. What paperwork there was would be in the name of Wallace Gooding, and if it could be proved that another child other than the one they had cared for was in fact Wallace, that should be good enough for any court in the land.

Thinking things over, Dr Kirkwood decided to wait a while to give the Gloucestershire police a chance to explain the situation to the Donaghues before calling them himself. Far better to allow them a little time to process this startling information before he suggested they come to collect the real Wallace.

His head aching, his heart heavy, Dr Kirkwood did something

he rarely did. After removing his spectacles and massaging his eyes, he reached into the bottom drawer of his desk, took out the quarter bottle of Irish whiskey he kept there for emergencies and took a wee nip.

There was still no sign of Constable Smart, and the superintendent hoped he wouldn't put in an appearance while the whiff of whiskey was still on his breath. But knowing the plodding constable as he did, he doubted the man would even notice.

For the second time that day, Alistair drove across Hillsbridge to Dunderwick Road, this time wondering how best to break the news to Tom and Grace that the baby they were caring for was not William.

As he walked up the path, the shadows were already lengthening and the row of cottages was lit with the rosy glow of the setting sun, which warmed the old lias stone of which they were built. No doubt about it, the days were well and truly drawing out now and summer was just around the corner. The thought that Stella might soon be released from Catcombe and able to enjoy it with her family cheered him. The news he had to give the Swifts would be good, though at first it was bound to come as a terrible shock.

A black cat was sitting on the doorstep; when Grace answered his knock, it brushed past her legs and walked sedately inside.

'Doctor!' she said, the expression of concern and surprise that was always her reaction when he called crossing her face.

'I expect you're wondering why I'm here again,' he said. 'May I come in?'

'Yes. Yes, of course.'

She stood aside to let him in and closed the door behind him.

In the living room, Tom was seated in one of the easy chairs, dandling the baby on his knee. Of the other children there was no sign – they were outside playing, Alistair guessed, making the most of the warm evening. The remains of the tea they hadn't long finished lay on the table – a few slices of fruit cake, a pot of jam, a pile of plates stacked ready to be taken to the kitchen for washing.

'Please excuse the mess, Doctor,' Grace said. 'I haven't finished clearing away yet. I've been feeding Will.'

'Don't worry about it,' Alistair said.

Tom was looking at him curiously, but Alistair could see the same shadow of anxiety in his eyes as he'd seen in Grace's. Whenever he called, they expected bad news about Stella.

'May I sit down?' he asked, and took the chair opposite Tom. Grace, looking more anxious than ever, perched on the edge of one of the dining chairs.

'I'm afraid what I'm going to say is going to come as a shock to you,' he began. 'But please don't worry. Stella and William are both fine.'

Bemused, Tom glanced at the baby on his knee, and reading his expression, Alistair took his cue.

'And so is this baby. But that's the reason I'm here. I'm afraid there has been a terrible mistake. Stella was quite right in claiming that the baby she was presented with wasn't William. Somehow a mix-up occurred. This baby, the one she rejected, is in fact Wallace Gooding, the child of one of the other patients.'

Both Tom and Grace stared at him, stunned.

'How could—' Tom began.

'And where is William?' Grace cut across him.

'He's perfectly safe and well,' Alistair hastened to reassure them. 'In fact Stella is with him now, and very happy to be so. If things continue to go well, both she and William will be able to come home soon.'

'That's very good news, but . . .' Tom's relief was beginning to turn to anger. 'How could such a thing happen?' he demanded, finishing the question he had begun to ask before. 'Are you telling me Stella has been put through hell because of some *mistake*?' He laid heavy emphasis on the word, and his hands tightened on the baby, evidence that his temper was rising.

'Tom, give him to me.' Grace must have noticed, and she got up and took the child from him.

'I asked you a question, Doctor. How could this happen?' Tom repeated, his voice dangerously low.

'I don't know,' Alistair lied. It wasn't his place to tell them the whole truth. 'But let me assure you it will be fully investigated, and I'm sure you'll be kept informed of whatever comes to light.'

'And whoever made this *mistake* will get what's coming to them, I hope. I won't let this rest, Doctor, you can be sure of that.'

'I can understand that you're angry, Mr Swift,' Alistair ventured. 'I'm sure I would be in your place. And I can only apologise on behalf of the hospital. But please hold on to the fact that it means Stella wasn't delusional, and that she and William will be able to come home soon.'

'And what about this baby?' Grace asked, stroking his cheek. 'What will happen to him?'

Again Alistair avoided telling the whole truth – that Wallace was to be sent to the adoptive parents. He didn't want to tell Tom that William had been in Gloucestershire. He supposed it would all come out eventually, but now was not the time.

'I have to take him back to Catcombe,' was all he said.

'When?' Grace demanded.

'Right away, I'm afraid.'

'Oh my goodness!' Grace was horrified. 'Tonight?'

'I'm afraid so.'

'But . . .'

Alistair felt dreadful. It was obvious to him that Grace had bonded with this baby, whether he was her nephew or not.

'You've just fed him, you say?' he asked, attempting to put his personal feelings to one side and remain professional. Grace nodded. 'So he should be fine until I get him to Catcombe.'

'What about his things?' Grace said. 'I'll have to get them together.'

'But they aren't his things, are they?' Alistair said as gently as he could. 'Apart from what he was wearing when I brought him to you, they are William's, and he'll need them when he comes home.'

'I suppose so.' There were tears in her eyes.

'The doctor's right. They're Will's things.' Tom's tone was hard. It seemed he could scarcely bring himself to look at the baby he had held on his knee such a short time ago. 'When will he be coming home, Doctor?'

'When it's considered Stella is ready,' Alistair said. 'From now on she'll be allowed to spend as much time with him as she likes.'

'And so she should,' Tom said hotly.

Alistair rose and stepped towards Grace. 'Shall I take him now?' he asked gently.

Grace nodded, but the tears sparkled even more brightly in her eyes as she let Alistair remove the baby from her arms. As he made his way to the front door, she followed him like a lost soul, but Tom stayed where he was, still fuming over what had happened.

'I'll be in touch,' Alistair said, but she remained in the doorway, watching as he carefully placed Wallace in the crib the asylum nursery had equipped him with so that the baby could travel in safety.

What a complete and utter mess! he thought. Heads would roll for this. But at least now he'd done what he'd been asked to do.

Hoping he could reach Catcombe before darkness fell, he set off on the journey to the asylum.

'No! For the last time – no!' Miranda was crying again, as she had done for most of the day. 'I don't want another baby! I want Wallace!'

'But my darling, that baby wasn't Wallace,' Winston tried, for the umpteenth time, to explain. 'There was a terrible mistake. The real Wallace is waiting for us to collect him.'

Fresh tears ran down Miranda's cheeks. 'I don't want another baby, I tell you. I won't have another baby in the house. In Wallace's nursery, Wallace's perambulator . . . I won't!'

'All right, my darling. Try to calm yourself, please.' Winston was at a loss to know what more he could say. All day Miranda had been inconsolable; now she was on the verge of hysteria. He spread his hands helplessly. 'So what am I to do? Am I to refuse to accept the real Wallace?'

Shocked as he had been to receive the telephone call from Dr Kirkwood, he'd been relieved to know that the little boy who had been in their care was safe and well and back with his birth mother. He'd hoped Miranda would feel the same way, and be prepared to accept another baby in his place. Not so, it seemed.

'Yes!' she cried. 'You can tell them they can bring Wallace back to me, or no baby at all!'

'I'm sure you'd grow to love him just as much,' Winston ventured.

'And what if they took him away too? I couldn't bear it, Winston. I couldn't go through this again.'

She collapsed on to the sofa, sobbing helplessly once more, and with a heavy heart Winston picked up the telephone to call Dr Kirkwood and apprise him of the situation.

Perhaps it was for the best, he tried to console himself. The mother, after all, was locked away in an asylum. Who could say how her child would turn out? And there was one small speck of hope on the horizon.

Over the last few days, he'd noticed that Miranda was quite unwell in the mornings. He'd seen it with his first wife when she had been pregnant with their sons. Could it be that after all this time Miranda was with child? It was far too early to think such a thing, but he'd heard of cases when a seemingly barren woman who had taken on someone else's child had unexpectedly conceived herself. A release of anxiety could work miracles, his medical friends had told him. The baby had only been with them a short time, but in the weeks leading up to his arrival Miranda had been happier than he'd ever seen her. Glowing, in fact. Relaxed. Was it possible her unwilling body had at last responded? Her happiness was his sole concern, and he could only pray it might be so.

His telephone call to Catcombe was answered at last; Dr Kirkwood was on the line.

'I'm sorry,' Winston said, 'but I'm afraid at present Miranda is refusing to accept a different baby. She may change her mind, of course, and if she does, I'll get in touch with you again. But somehow I doubt it.'

'And I can only apologise for what has happened,' Dr Kirkwood said.

'Yes, well, what's done's done,' Winston said resignedly.

He hung up and went back to trying to comfort his distraught wife.

\* \* \*

'Sir Oswald, I'm afraid to say we have a problem,' Dr Kirkwood said.

Sir Oswald, already annoyed at being disturbed from the post-dinner brandy he was enjoying in his favourite wing chair, glared at the telephone as if it were the man himself in front of him.

'A problem, Kirkwood? What kind of problem?'

'Something very unfortunate has happened,' the doctor said, and went on to outline the details of the error that had occurred and the subsequent abduction. 'Both babies are now here, safe and well, and we were planning to have Wallace Gooding returned to his adoptive parents. But Mrs Donaghue is refusing to take him at the moment,' he finished.

'Hang on a minute, Kirkwood, you've lost me.' Sir Oswald, his brain already a little fuzzy from the alcohol he'd consumed, was struggling to make sense of all this. As far as he was concerned, the whole business had been settled satisfactorily. Now the doctor was telling him . . . what, exactly?

Dr Kirkwood, used to dealing with patients who were unable to make sense of the simplest communication, repeated himself patiently.

'It's just fortunate your son arrived when he did and found the baby on the doorstep,' he finished.

'My son?' An awful suspicion had begun to take shape in Sir Oswald's befuddled brain, sobering him as quickly as if he'd been drenched by a bucket of cold water. 'Which son? Do you mean George? What was he doing at Catcombe?'

'He said you'd asked him to come and see me to confirm the arrangements for Rose's release,' Dr Kirkwood replied.

'To see that wench more like,' Sir Oswald muttered, though he was suddenly sure there was a good deal more to it than that, and this whole debacle was George's doing. But disgusted and angry as he was with the son who had never failed to disappoint him, he wasn't going to say anything that might arouse Dr Kirkwood's suspicions. If it ever came to light that George had abducted the baby, it would only bring more shame to his door. Damn the boy to hell!

'So you will see to it that Rose's bastard is taken to Gloucestershire?' he said, shifting the topic of conversation.

'I'm sorry, I thought I'd explained,' Dr Kirkwood said. 'Mrs Donaghue is refusing to take a different baby just now. I'm afraid he will have to remain where he is for the moment.'

Dear God, this was a nightmare.

'Are you prepared to wait and see if Mrs Donaghue changes her mind? Or would you prefer us to try and find alternative adoptive parents?' the doctor asked.

A pain that Sir Oswald had been vaguely aware of for the last few days, and put down to indigestion, had returned, far worse than before, and a tingle was running down his arm.

'Oh, do what you like,' he snapped, and banged down the receiver without waiting for a reply.

'What's wrong, Oswald?' Lady Cecelia, with Rupert following close behind her, had entered the drawing room and overheard the last part of the conversation.

Sir Oswald reached for his brandy glass, emptied it in one gulp and refilled it from the crystal decanter.

'Bloody disaster,' he ground out. He turned furiously on Rupert. 'Did you tell your brother where to find Rose Gooding's brat?' he demanded.

Rupert blanched, and the look on his face told his father all he needed to know.

'You did, didn't you?'

As Sir Oswald continued to rage at Rupert, the pain in his chest worsened, and he covered his heart with his free hand, struggling to breathe.

'Oswald?' Alarmed, Cecelia took a step towards him.

But she was blurring before his eyes as panic gripped him.

'Oswald!' she cried again. 'Rupert – do something!'

They were the last words Oswald would ever hear. The brandy glass fell from his hand, its contents soaking the priceless Oriental rug, and a moment later he had collapsed beside it.

'What have you done?' Cecelia shot at Rupert, and dropped to her knees beside her husband's crumpled body.

Rupert, whom Sir Oswald had always considered the son he could trust, said nothing at all.

Hubert Kirkwood had made up his mind.

From the moment Rose had been committed to the asylum, he had despised the way the poor girl was being treated and wished wholeheartedly that he could do something for her. But he'd had no say in the matter. Sir Oswald and his cronies had rendered him helpless.

Now things had changed. No matter that the words 'do what you like' had been spoken in anger, the old tyrant had expressly given him permission to act as he saw fit. And what he saw fit to do was to put an end to Rose's suffering. The papers the two committing doctors had signed for her release were safely locked away in his desk, and he could see no way they could be rescinded even if Sir Oswald changed his mind. As for her baby, he would have the two of them reunited immediately, and see to it that when she went home, little Wallace would go with her.

Leaving his office, he crossed the corridor to Matron's room.

'Will you find Rose and have her taken up to the nursery?' he said.

Matron smiled, a smile of grim satisfaction. 'And not a moment too soon,' she replied.

* * *

When George got back to his camp on Salisbury Plain, his commanding officer was waiting for him.

'I'm afraid I have bad news for you, Challis,' he greeted him.

George's heart fell away. Somehow what he'd done had come to light, he guessed. Just when he'd thought he'd got away with it.

'What news, sir?' he managed.

'I've had a telephone call from your brother. It's my sad duty to have to tell you that your father has suffered a heart attack. You are to return home immediately.'

'My father?' George repeated, scarcely able to believe what he was hearing.

'Yes. I'm very sorry for your loss.'

'He's . . . dead?'

'I'm afraid so. It's a tragedy, Challis. Such a fine man. You'll have compassionate leave, of course. Cadet Officer Stevens has said he's happy for you to borrow his Humber for a few more days, so I suggest you go right away.'

George was stunned. His father . . . dead! 'Such a fine man', the CO had said. If only he knew! And what would he think if he realised that the only emotion George was feeling was relief?

Relief that what he'd done hadn't come to light – yet, at least.

And relief that his life would no longer be dominated by his cruel, arrogant, all-powerful father.

# Chapter Twenty-Seven

The moment Mabel arrived for her night duty, and before she had even had the chance to go up to the nursery, she was told Dr Kirkwood wanted to see her. With some trepidation she made her way to his office.

'Sit down, Mabel.' The superintendent's tone was stern.

She sat. 'Is something wrong?' she asked, struggling to keep her composure.

'Yes.' Dr Kirkwood wasn't in the mood to beat about the bush. 'Some very serious allegations have been made against you.'

Her heart was pounding; she felt sick. 'Allegations? What sort of allegations?'

'That after you had got Nurse Whitcombe and Florrie out of the way, you exchanged Baby Swift and Baby Gooding's name tags so that the wrong baby was sent for adoption.'

'Got Cissie and Florrie out of the way? Whatever do you mean? How am I supposed to have done that?' Mabel blustered.

'By pushing Nurse Whitcombe down the stairs and accusing Florrie of doing it.'

'She did push her! I saw it with my own eyes!' Mabel protested.

'As you know, Cissie told Matron and me that Florrie couldn't have been responsible. We then assumed it must simply have been an accident. But Matron has been to see her again this afternoon, and she agrees she did feel what felt like a push between her shoulder blades before she fell.'

'Well, there you are then! Florrie *did*—'

'Florrie tells a very different story,' Dr Kirkwood said.

'She would, wouldn't she? Are you going to believe her over me? A woman who stole a baby herself? Very likely she's the one behind snatching the adopted baby. She's done it once, she'd do it again.'

Dr Kirkwood's eyes narrowed behind his spectacles. 'Really, Nurse Cummings? And how do you know the baby was snatched this morning?'

Mabel turned cold, but a fiery flush spread up her neck. 'News travels fast. Everybody is talking about it.'

'But you only arrived for duty a few minutes ago. If there had been any talk in the corridor between the front door and my office, I would have been aware of it. I ask you again – how do you know what happened?'

'In the village. I heard about it in the village.'

'On Easter Sunday afternoon? I doubt that. Besides which, no one outside these walls, except for the police, know about it.'

'All right. I heard it from my brother-in-law, Frank. He came to see me,' Mabel admitted.

'And where did he hear it?'

'I don't know . . .'

'The stolen baby, who turned up on the doorstep here, was supposedly Rose's baby, except that it wasn't – it was William Swift. You are Rose Gooding's aunt, and in charge of the nursery. Please don't lie to me any more, Nurse Cummings. You do yourself no favours.'

Mabel was trembling now, but she remained defiant. 'What exactly are you accusing me of, Doctor?'

'I am not accusing you of anything, Nurse Cummings. I shall leave it to the police to do that. I don't pretend to understand what has happened, or why, but I have no doubt they'll get to the bottom of it.'

'You're involving the police?' Mabel gasped.

'They are already involved. And believe me, they will question you more thoroughly than I have done. I'm calling them now. Not the local constabulary, but the inspector at divisional headquarters. And you will kindly remain here, in my office, until he arrives.'

With that he reached for the telephone, and a frightened Mabel realised the dangerous game she had been playing was up.

And all because of the Whittingly Challis family. Once again, they had won. But she was damned if she would let them get away with it without revealing the secret she'd kept all these years. How a man of influence had seduced a young girl and forced her to have an abortion that had left her unable to bear another child. How his sainted son had got Rose in the family way and he'd had her locked up in Catcombe to keep it quiet. Oh, she'd see to it that the bastard's reputation was torn to shreds. That men would no longer doff their caps to him when he passed, and women drop a curtsey. Even if she couldn't prove any of it after so long, the mud would stick. And she was going to begin right here and now.

'All right,' she said. 'I did it. I swapped the babies. And if you'll give me the chance, I'll tell you why.'

As Mabel told her terrible story, Dr Kirkwood let the telephone fall back into its rest and listened intently, initial disbelief turning to shock and horror. Because of what had happened to her she was, he thought, as sick as many of his patients, and compassion for what she had endured welled in him. Though he knew he should make the telephone call to the police as he'd intended before she'd unburdened herself, he was now reluctant to do so.

What good would it do? Cissie was recovering well and was looking forward to a well-earned retirement spending more time with her family. Both babies were back with their birth mothers; Stella would be able to go home with William and Rose was united with Wallace. So good had come out of disaster. If he reported what Mabel had done, the reputation of Catcombe that he'd built up so painstakingly would be tarnished. And Mabel herself . . .

Hadn't she suffered enough? Hadn't she already served a life sentence?

Dr Kirkwood sighed deeply, replaced his spectacles and made up his mind. 'I can see, Mabel, why you would feel this way, but you must know that what you did was very wrong. You should have come and talked to me about all this, not resorted to doing what you did. But as long as Matron is in agreement with me I won't take any further action with regards to reporting the matter to the police. When you've had the chance to come to your senses, living with your conscience will be punishment enough.'

'Oh thank you, Doctor!' Mabel slumped in her chair, all the fight going out of her in a rush of relief.

'You must know, however, that I can't allow you to continue working here,' he went on severely.

Mabel stiffened again. 'But then who will look after the babies?'

'That's not something you need concern yourself with. I suggest you go home and give some very serious thought as to what the consequences would have been had I not come to this decision.' He stood, making it clear the interview was at an end.

Mabel got up and turned for the door. The slump of her shoulders and the trembling of her hand on the knob was so unlike her usual capable demeanour that the doctor felt another rush of sympathy for the woman who had been so wronged and was now her own worst enemy.

'It may be of some comfort to you to know that I shall be discharging both Rose and her baby tomorrow,' he said. 'There will be no more plans made for his adoption.'

'Oh, thank the Lord!'

But she didn't turn to face him, and he guessed that she didn't want him to see the tears he could hear in her voice.

When she had gone, and he had watched from his window as she wobbled away on her bicycle, he crossed the corridor to Matron's office, where he related Mabel's revelation and what he had decided to do about it. As he'd expected, Matron was as shocked as he was at the story, and fully agreed with the action he had decided upon.

'So we're going to be a nurse down,' she said, practical as always. 'We'll need to advertise the position as soon as possible. Unless, of course . . .' She hesitated. 'There's always Florrie.'

Dr Kirkwood considered, then made up his mind. 'You're right. It's my opinion she's as sane now as you and I. Considering she was charged with a criminal offence, I'm not sure how we would go about her release, but I think she has come to look upon Catcombe as her home, and there's nothing to say she shouldn't be treated as a member of staff rather than a patient who is a casual nursery helper. I believe I could even persuade the board to pay her a small wage.'

'A very good idea, Hubert.'

'That's decided then. I'll leave you to inform her about her change of status.'

Dr Kirkwood returned to his own office satisfied with the

outcome of all the chaotic events of the day and thinking that perhaps he'd allow himself to celebrate with another tot of the whiskey he kept hidden in his desk drawer.

He certainly thought he'd earned it.

The house in Dunderwick Road was quiet – too quiet. The children were in bed and presumably asleep, tired out from hours of boisterous outdoor play. Tom was flicking through the pages of the Sunday paper, though Grace wasn't sure he was actually reading it. Probably, like her, he was thinking about the events of the day.

Certainly Grace knew she wouldn't be able to concentrate on a single word. She was shaken to the core by what had happened – more shaken than she should have been, she acknowledged. The baby she had been caring for was not her nephew, but a dark-haired stranger, someone else's child. Hadn't she half known that all along? Hadn't she even suggested herself that there might have been some sort of mistake?

But in spite of all that, his loss was eating away at her. She missed him already. Missed feeding and cuddling him, missed those dark eyes looking up at her, his soft, sweet baby scent, the feel of him nestling against her.

Of course it was different for Tom. He wasn't the one who'd had daily care of the baby. And now, because of what had happened, his real son would be coming back to him. And so would his wife.

Tears pricked Grace's eyes. She got up abruptly and went into the kitchen, feeling the need to find something to do. She'd clean out the cupboards, wipe down the oilcloth that lined the shelves, make it all nice and clean for Stella to come home to. But as she began unloading the contents on to the worktop, she remembered how she'd felt when she'd first come here – like an intruder in her sister's house, anxious not to poke and pry. And later, a thief who had stolen Stella's life.

Now it was all coming to an end, and she didn't know how she could bear it. The baby being taken away today was just the beginning. She was about to lose everything that had come to mean so much to her in these last weeks and months. The daily routine. The feeling of being needed. The children. Tom . . .

The tears pricked her eyes again and she tried to blink them away. She had no business feeling this way. She was glad, of course she was, that Stella had seemingly recovered and the nightmare she had been living through was over. But for all that, she couldn't stem the awful feeling of loss.

'Grace? What are you doing?' Tom's voice, from the doorway.

Grace made a great show of moving things around in the cupboard. She couldn't turn to face him, couldn't let him see the tears that were threatening again.

'Just a bit of cleaning,' she said, but for all her efforts, there was a wobble in her voice.

'Grace?' he said again, anxious now.

She tried to answer, but the words caught in her throat.

'Are you crying?' He came closer, caught her arm, turning her to face him. Grace lowered her chin to her chest in another effort to hide her tears from him.

Useless, of course.

'What's wrong?' he asked, his tone concerned and tender.

'Nothing.'

'You don't cry over nothing, Grace.'

She lifted her head, attempting a weak, watery smile. 'No?'

'No. Is it because they've taken the baby?'

She snatched at the explanation; after all, it was part of the truth. 'Yes. It's horrible without him.'

'Oh Grace.'

He put his arms around her, pulling her against his broad chest, stroking her hair. The contact only made the tears start again, and she couldn't control the sobs that racked her body.

'He wasn't our baby, Grace. The real William will be coming home soon, and everything is going to be all right,' he said, trying to comfort her.

'For you, maybe.' The words, muffled, were out before she could stop them, and suddenly she could keep it to herself no longer.

She looked up at him, at the face she loved so much, had always loved, tears streaming down her cheeks.

'It's not just the baby, though I had come to love him. It's everything. Oh, I'm really glad Stella is better, of course I am. I'm glad she and William will be home soon and you can have everything back to normal. But I'm going to miss you all so much.'

'And we'll miss you.'

Not *I'll* miss you. But that look was back in his eyes, the look she'd seen on several occasions before; the look that she could almost believe meant he felt about her the way she felt about him.

'Will you?' she whispered.

'You know I will.'

His face was close to hers now, so close it was out of focus, her heart beating against his. She closed her eyes, breathing him in, and suddenly his lips were on hers, gentle at first, then harder, more urgent. The world was spinning round her so it held nothing but the two of them.

'You know I love you, Grace.' He whispered the words against her ear so softly that she thought she might have imagined them because they were the words she yearned to hear.

He kissed her again, holding her so close that she could feel every line of his lean, muscled body, and she drowned in the pleasurable sensation of their closeness. Then, as his hands went to the buttons of her blouse, reality kicked in, sobering her abruptly, and she pulled away, stilling his hand with hers.

'Tom – no!'

Instantly he too was aware of what he had been so close to doing, and the realisation shocked and horrified him.

'Grace – I am so sorry.'

'Don't be sorry,' she managed. 'I wanted it too.'

'You did?'

'More than anything. You know I did! But we can't. We mustn't. We shouldn't even talk about it.'

'You're right. We shouldn't.'

His tone was harsh. He released her, backed away, and she felt the loss of him in every fibre of her body. It was wrong, she knew, but she couldn't help herself.

'Best we forget this ever happened,' he said.

There was both regret and determination in his eyes, the eyes that had looked at her with love and desire that mirrored her own. But he had gone away from her, and not just physically. The distance between them was an arid desert with none of the closeness they had shared these last months remaining, and she wept inwardly, knowing that now nothing could ever again be the same between them. They had crossed the Rubicon, given way to their feelings, however briefly, and there was no way back.

Without another word, Tom crossed the kitchen and went out into the garden. He can't bear to look at me, Grace thought. The next week or so would be torture, being under the same roof, trying to behave as usual. And then . . .

And then Stella would be coming home with Will. Grace

would stay on a few more days if Stella needed her to. Then she would escape. Back to her mother and father's home. Back to her job in the village store – if she still had a job to return to. Back to long, lonely evenings and an empty bed. The dream she'd been living would be over, and the future looked bleak, far bleaker than it had before these last few months had happened. She'd accepted her lot then, never giving in to the vague feelings of dissatisfaction, never allowing herself to dwell on what was missing from her life.

Now she had experienced how it might have been, and she didn't know how she could bear to go on. But what choice did she have? None. This was Stella's home, Stella's children, Stella's husband. And the baby . . . the baby she'd cared for so lovingly was the only thing that didn't belong to her sister, and she'd lost him too. Suddenly Grace was longing for the feel of him in her arms, the sweet smell of him, the utter dependence of him, the innocence.

If only she had the baby, she could face the future. But just like Will, he belonged to someone else. There seemed to be no chink of light anywhere in the darkness that surrounded her.

George was back in the house he'd sworn he'd never return to.

By the time he'd arrived, the doctor had been and certified death, the undertaker and the woman who cared for the dead had attended, and Sir Oswald was laid out in a temporary coffin on trestles in the drawing room where he had breathed his last. Later, once the carpenter had made it, his body would be transferred to a casket that reflected his status: dark oak with ornate handles and the family crest engraved on a brass plate on the lid.

There was no great atmosphere of mourning in the house, though there had been recriminations.

'I hope you realise you caused your father's death,' Cecelia had said, addressing both her sons. But her face was set in hard lines; there had been, and would be, no tears shed. In some ways she felt freer than she had done for years. Everything now would pass to Rupert, and she knew she could influence and control her elder son. Though he was now the baronet, it was she who would pull the strings.

She had retired to bed now, and the brothers were alone in the library, each nursing a glass of their father's single malt.

'You realise she's right, dammit?' Rupert said. 'It's our fault his heart gave out. If I hadn't told you where the baby was, and if you hadn't snatched him—'

'And if he hadn't been so fond of the bottle,' George interrupted. 'God, Rupert, he drank enough day after day to sink a battleship. It was going to kill him sooner or later – you only had to look at him to see that. His nose was as red as a good claret. And working himself into his rages wouldn't have helped his blood pressure. Maybe between us we put the last straw on the camel's back, but really he brought it on himself.'

'Perhaps . . .' Rupert took a swig of his whisky, all too ready to absolve himself of any part in his father's death. 'And you were quite right. He shouldn't have treated Rose the way he did. But for that, none of this would have happened.'

'I'll never forgive him,' George said. 'Never, as long as I live. Getting her certified, arranging for our baby to be adopted without either of us having any say in the matter – it's unforgivable. Wicked, actually.'

'How the devil did they manage to send the wrong baby, though? That's what I can't understand.' Rupert swirled what little remained of his whisky in his glass.

'God knows. Her aunt Mabel had something to do with it,

but Rose didn't know anything about it. She was in a terrible state when I went to see her, thinking she'd never see him again. That's when I made up my mind to get him back.'

'A bloody stupid thing to do.'

'Probably,' George admitted. 'But I couldn't think of anything else.'

'Well, it's just lucky for you that it was the wrong baby,' Rupert said.

'Lucky?'

'Yes, lucky. If it had been Rose's son, he'd have been sent straight back. As it is, Mrs Donaghue is refusing to have him. So at least you know where he is, and now Father is dead . . .'

He broke off, downing the rest of his whisky and reaching for the decanter.

'Do you want another one? Because I certainly do.'

George hesitated, then drained his own glass in one gulp and held it out for Rupert to refill. 'Yes. Go on then.'

'With Father no longer here to call the shots, I'm guessing Rose will be able to keep the baby if she wants to,' Rupert said, picking up where he'd left off.

'Oh, she'll want to, that's one thing I'm sure of,' George said. 'The trouble is, if they find out it was me who abducted him, I might very well end up in jail and unable to provide for them.'

'I thought you'd got away with it?' Rupert was already making inroads into his second whisky.

'So far,' George said glumly. 'But for how long? Rose's mother and father know it was me – one word from them and I'm in the soup.'

'Surely they wouldn't put the police on to you, seeing as you and Rose . . .'

'I'm not sure if they believed me when I told them I'm the baby's father. I don't think they knew about us. They looked pretty shocked . . .' He broke off as a thought struck him. 'Rose said she wrote to me, but I never got the letter. Perhaps they had something to do with that.'

'Well, you'd better make sure they know your intentions are honourable pretty damn quick,' Rupert advised. 'It wouldn't just be a jail sentence you'd be looking at; you'd be thrown out of the army too, and have nothing to come back to.'

'I know.'

'And you were prepared to risk it anyway? Christ, George, you must really love the girl.'

'I do.'

'Well,' Rupert said, 'let's just hope you're not caught. If you are, I'll provide for Rose and the child. If not, I'll see to it that the remainder of your cadet officer training is funded, and that you have a better monthly allowance from the estate.'

His words took George by surprise. Somehow, although he knew without doubt that his father was dead, it hadn't really registered yet that his brother was now the lord of the manor and would have control over all the finances. Nor that his cadet officer training might no longer be paid for – if he wasn't booted out for what he'd done today.

'That's jolly decent of you, Rupert,' he said.

'I am your brother, goddammit! We might not always see eye to eye, but I wouldn't throw you to the wolves, however damn stupid you've been. And I wouldn't see your child raised in poverty either,' he added.

'Mother might have something to say about that,' George said.

'That doesn't mean to say I have to listen to her.'

George had never seen his brother show such determination. 'Thanks, Rupert,' he said roughly.

'Let's drink to it then.' Rupert raised his glass. 'I get to run the estate and the quarries. And you . . . well . . . I hope things turn out the way you'd like them to.'

George raised his glass too. 'I'll second that.'

Whilst his own future was still uncertain, he had a feeling that from now on, things here at home were going to be very different.

In the wee small hours of the night Mabel sat at her kitchen table, the last of endless cups of tea cold in front of her. She'd gone to bed at around eleven, but sleep had been impossible. The fact that she was used to working through the night was partly to blame, of course, but also it was that every time she closed her eyes, the events of the day ran on a hamster wheel inside her head. After an hour of tossing and turning she could stand it no longer, and she'd got up, put on her dressing gown and gone downstairs.

Depression, thick as a storm cloud, had settled over her now. At first when she'd left the asylum she'd felt nothing but relief that Dr Kirkwood wasn't going to report her to the police. Instead of going straight home, she'd cycled to Olive and Frank's cottage to tell Frank he had no need to worry about being arrested for setting fire to Dr Mackay's car, and also to give them the good news that Rose's baby was safely back with her and both of them were going to be discharged.

Frank was out – he'd gone down to his local for a pint of bitter – but Olive was immensely relieved that he was off the hook and that Mabel too would be spared a court appearance, though she was sorry that she had lost her job. But her delight at the news that Rose was going to be allowed to keep Wallace, and they would both be coming home soon, trumped that.

'It was all worth it in the end then,' she said, beaming, before her face clouded over as a thought struck her. 'I just hope Sir

Oswald won't take it out on us. There's no knowing what he might do, and if Frank lost his job . . .'

'But what's Sir Oswald going to have to say about that? I mean, I know that George said Wallace was his, but—'

'He won't be doing nothing.'

Neither Olive nor Mabel had heard Frank come in. Now they whirled round, puzzled, to see him in the doorway, grinning from ear to ear.

'What are you talking about?' Olive asked.

'Sir Oswald. He won't be doing nothing any more. Not after what happened to him tonight.'

The two sisters looked at one another, then back at Frank, both speaking at once.

'He's dead?'

'Never!'

'That's what I come home to tell you.' Frank took off his cap and placed it on the kitchen table. 'Josiah Barker's missus were sent for earlier on, and you know what she do. Laying out the dead.'

'But how do you know it was Sir Oswald?' Olive demanded.

'Josiah said, a'course. An' he wouldn'ta said it unless he were sure it were right. Heart attack by the sound of it, he said.'

'Well, it's a blessing, is all I can say.' Olive sat down heavily on a kitchen chair, but Mabel remained standing, stunned into silence.

Sir Oswald dead of a heart attack! She didn't know whether to be glad or sorry about that. Oh, the world was well rid of him; she was only sorry she hadn't had the courage to kill him herself. But ever since she'd unburdened herself to Dr Kirkwood, she'd wanted nothing but to spread her story far and wide, let everyone know what a bastard he was, destroy his reputation, make him pay with a thousand painful pricks to his ego as the gossip about him spread. That pleasure would now be denied her. She could still talk, but he would be beyond knowing or caring.

Bitterness welled up in her. He'd got away with it again. Rose might have her baby back, Frank's job and his home might be safe, but the chance for true revenge had been snatched away from her.

It was these thoughts that had kept her from sleeping, along with a sick despair for her own future.

What was she going to do with herself? Nursing was her life. It had taken the place of a happy marriage and the children she'd been unable to bear. The thought of the long, empty days was an awful one; the realisation that she would no longer have an income chilled her bones. For the first time in many years, Mabel wept, overcome with self-pity.

Dawn was breaking as the idea struck her. When Rose and baby Wallace were released from Catcombe, they would need somewhere to go. Olive and Frank had only the one spare bedroom – the one that had been Rose's – and there was scarcely enough space to swing a cat. Whereas she had plenty of room. If she took Rose in, she'd be able to share Wallace's care, something she'd really enjoy, and if George Whittingly Challis was indeed the baby's father, perhaps he would be willing to pay for their board and lodging – with a little bit extra for her help.

As her mood lightened, Mabel's proclivity to scheming began to reassert itself, albeit in a positive way.

Just one vengeful thought entered her head.

If she was partly responsible for the upbringing of Sir Oswald's grandson, then perhaps she would have the last laugh after all.

# Chapter Twenty-Eight

News of Sir Oswald's demise swept through the immediate district and beyond.

At Catcombe asylum, Dr Kirkwood and Matron publicly expressed regret whilst privately feeling relief that the overbearing lord of the manor would no longer dominate meetings of the board of trustees or hold sway over matters for which Dr Kirkwood believed he alone should be responsible.

The workers in the quarries were less reticent about displaying their delight; if it hadn't been Rupert himself who had delivered the news for the benefit of those who hadn't already heard, no doubt a cheer would have gone up. To a man, they detested Sir Oswald, and though there were those who had their doubts about Rupert's capabilities, they felt sure that working conditions could only improve under his stewardship.

And back at Easterton Manor, no tears were shed over the loss of a husband and father. Lady Cecelia, dry-eyed, presided over the arrangements for the funeral, which would be held in Wells Cathedral and attended by the Lord Lieutenant of Somerset and a host of other local dignitaries and titled gentlemen.

Rupert and George were happy to leave it all to their mother; they had quite enough to keep them occupied discussing the future of the estate and the quarries.

'Are you sure you won't come home and work with me so that we can sort it all out together?' Rupert had suggested, but George was adamant. His future lay with the army and, when the time came, with Rose.

He made only one stipulation with regard to his father's funeral – that Rose and baby Wallace should be allowed to attend.

At first Rose was unwilling.

'Why would I go to his funeral after the way he treated me?' she demanded.

'Because soon you'll be my wife and I want to show the world I'm proud of you,' he said. 'Besides, Wallace is the next generation of Whittingly Challises. If Rupert never has a son, he'll inherit the title.'

As he saw realisation dawn on her, he kissed her.

'Please, Rose. For me.'

And at last she had agreed.

By the day of the funeral, she had been released from Catcombe and was living with her aunt – Mabel's offer had been accepted, and Rupert had also agreed that when his father's financial affairs had been settled, he would see that Rose and her son were provided for until such time as George graduated as an army officer and had a salary of his own. He would also arrange to set up a trust fund for Wallace.

Apprehensive as she was about attending the funeral, Rose absolutely refused to wear black. Though she knew anything else would be frowned upon, she was determined not to go into mourning for the man who had caused her so much heartache. Eventually she settled on a new white blouse, ruffled at the neck, a dark grey silk skirt and matching hat. As the only nod towards respect for the occasion, she wore a black velvet band with a cameo pinned to it around her throat. Wallace had a new white silk gown, paid for by Rupert, which would also do service later as his christening robe.

George had a taxi collect her and Wallace to take them to Wells, and when she stepped out on to the cathedral green she was overwhelmed by the majesty of the surroundings as well as by the obvious importance of the assembled mourners in their black tail coats and dress uniforms. But she lifted her chin high as she entered the cathedral and shifted Wallace in her arms so that the emeralds in the ring George had given her caught the light from the chandeliers and sparkled defiantly. She had every right to be here, she told herself. And at least her training as a parlour maid had taught her how to behave in polite company.

It was as she slipped into the seat that George had reserved for her that her nervousness melted away as if by magic, and with it her anger and resentment towards the man who lay in the dark oak coffin at the altar steps. Sunshine was slanting in through the glorious stained glass windows and it seemed to enter her heart. The past months had been terrible ones, but they were over now. Sir Oswald could no longer hurt her. The future lay ahead brighter than she could ever have imagined.

Rose bowed her head, her chin resting against Wallace's dark downy hair and whispered a prayer of thanks to a God who, in the dark days, she had ceased to believe in.

'Oh Grace, I don't know how to thank you for all you've done.'

Stella hugged her sister as they stood at the gate waiting for the taxi cab that Tom had ordered to take Grace home.

'Don't even think about it,' Grace said, hugging her back. 'If our roles had been reversed you'd have done the same for me. And I'm just glad you're well again, out of that awful place and back with your family where you belong.'

'All the same . . . looking after them for me all that time . . . staying on to help me out until I'd settled back in . . .'

'It's been a privilege, honestly.'

'I'll miss you!'

'And I'll miss you. And the children.' *And Tom.* 'But it's time for me to go, Stella. Time for everything to get back to normal.' Grace smiled, hoping it didn't look forced. 'Emily can't wait to get back to her own room, for one thing – and the boys can't wait to be shot of her.'

It was ten days now since Stella and William had come home. Grace had stayed on to help Stella through those first difficult days while she adjusted to being back and resuming all her old duties. Considering all she had been through, she looked remarkably well, but to begin with she still tired easily, a result of the months of inaction coupled with the dreadful stress she'd endured, and she had been grateful for her sister's help and support.

For Grace, however, every waking moment had been painful. Seeing Stella with baby Will, caring for him, cradling him to her as if to never again let him go, warmed her heart, but also broke it, since she knew such joy could never be hers. To have the children rush past her to reach their mother, eyes shining, faces bright with joy at having her home again, when during the last months it had been Grace to whom they had turned, hurt her, even though she knew she had no right to be hurt. And worst of all was seeing the way Tom was with Stella – tender, caring, protective – and knowing that when the bedroom door closed after them at night, it was Stella who lay in his arms where Grace so longed to be. Though she hated herself for it, she had found it unbearable and wanted only to go home to her lonely life, where at least she could lick her wounds in relative privacy.

Understandably, the atmosphere between her and Tom had

been strained too. They skirtcd around one another, both uncomfortably aware of what had so nearly happened and determined at all costs to try to forget it.

The taxi appeared suddenly, chugging along the road.

'This is it, then,' Stella said. 'Come back and see us soon, won't you, Grace?'

'Just try to stop me.' Tears were pricking at Grace's eyes. She blinked them away, managing to smile at the children, who had all come out to wave her goodbye. 'And you three – be good for your mother, all right?'

'Yeah, we will,' they chorused.

Tom was standing on the path, Will in his arms. As Grace reached for her sister, giving her one last hug, her eyes met his over Stella's shoulder, and in them she saw for a brief moment a reflection of her own love and loss. For a fleeting second their hearts too met before Grace tore her eyes away and turned towards the taxi cab, which had pulled up at the kerb.

She climbed in, settled her bag on the seat beside her, called her last goodbyes and turned to wave as the taxi pulled away. The last sight she had of them was the boys running alongside the vehicle until their legs could no longer keep up, and Tom with one arm about Stella's waist, the other cradling Will, while Emily clutched at her mother's skirts, a picture of perfect family unity.

So this was it. The dream was over. As the cab drove along the winding lanes, Grace saw the green meadows, the golden cornfields, the burgeoning hedgerows through a haze of tears, and the coal-black batches silhouetted on the skyline reflected the dark places within her that were the vision of her future.

As usual on a Sunday, Alistair, Jessica and Constance drove to Catcombe for the morning service. When it was over, Jessica went up to the nursery in search of Florrie, taking Constance with her, while Alistair sought out Dr Kirkwood to ask about the outcome of the disturbing events of the previous week.

As they topped the staircase, Jessica could see only one person in the room – a nurse who was bending over one of the cribs at the far end. Where was Florrie? she wondered anxiously. Had things gone badly for her and she'd been banned from the nursery again?

Then the nurse straightened up and turned, and to her astonishment, Jessica saw that it was her sister.

'Florrie!' she exclaimed. 'Whatever . . . ?'

Florrie came towards her, beaming and smoothing the nurse's uniform down over her hips.

'Nicer than the smock, isn't it?' she said proudly. 'And much more convenient.'

'But . . .' Jessica was still confused.

'It's all right, I didn't steal it,' Florrie said, laughing. 'It's mine by right. I've been promoted, Jess. I'm not an inmate helper any more. I'm a proper nurse. Matron said they'd even pay me a small wage! Now what do you think of that?'

'Well! I think it's wonderful news! But are you having to cope all on your own?' Jessica asked, anxious that given Florrie's uncertain emotional stability it might prove too much for her.

'We're not busy at the moment. I've only got three babies to care for – Wallace Gooding and William Swift have both gone home, and Louie Hillman comes up to see to Billy, so really there are only the two.'

'So you didn't get into too much trouble over keeping quiet about the baby swap?' Jessica said, relieved.

'No – for a wonder! It was Mabel that got all the blame. She's been sacked, and that's why I've been made a nurse. The only difference is that I'm working days and the day nurse has been put on nights. Not that I'd have cared what shifts I took, just as long as I can be up here with the babies.'

'I'm so pleased for you . . .' Jessica broke off as a sudden pain gripped her like a girdle. 'Oh!' she gasped.

'Are you all right, Jess?' Florrie asked, alarmed.

'I'm not sure.'

Jessica had been having little aches since early this morning, but it had been nothing more than mild discomfort and she hadn't mentioned it to Alistair. She'd been afraid that if she did, he'd say they'd better not go to Catcombe, and she'd been desperate to see Florrie. But this was more, much more than mere discomfort. That painful squeezing was, she felt sure, the beginnings of labour. And this was her second child. She'd been in labour for the best part of twenty-four hours with Constance, but she knew it was likely she'd deliver this baby in a much shorter time.

'I'm sorry, Florrie, but I think I'd better find Alistair and get him to take me home,' she said. 'I think the baby may be on its way.'

'Oh my Lord, yes! You don't want it born in a lunatic asylum!'

'I must say I'd rather have it in my own bed.' Jessica gave a forced, shaky laugh. 'And I don't fancy having it in our motor either.'

'Come on,' Florrie urged her sister. 'I'll run ahead and find Alistair. You just take it steady.'

She ran off down the stairs and Jessica followed more slowly, holding on to the handrail with one hand and Constance with the other. As she reached the foot of the stairs, another pain gripped her and she stopped short, catching her breath and pressing her hand to her stomach.

Alistair and Dr Kirkwood were still deep in conversation

when Florrie came bursting in. They both looked round, startled.

'Florrie! What are you doing here? Is something wrong?' Dr Kirkwood asked sharply.

Florrie ignored him, addressing Alistair. 'You'd better come quick! It's Jess. I think she's started.'

'Where is she?' Alistair was already halfway to the door.

'On her way down from the nursery.'

Alistair hightailed it along the corridor.

Jessica was still at the foot of the stairs, grasping the banister, Constance, looking frightened, clutching at her skirts.

'We need to get home, Alistair,' she said urgently.

'Not before I've examined you and timed a few contractions.' Alistair had switched to professional mode. He turned to Dr Kirkwood, who was not far behind them. 'Is there somewhere . . . ?'

'One of the treatment rooms.' The superintendent led them to an open door, then stood aside as Alistair helped Jessica up on to the couch.

'Please!' she begged. 'Just take me home!'

But when he'd finished his examination, Alistair shook his head.

'I daren't risk it, love. The jolting of the motor might well speed things up, and we might not make it. By far the safest option is to stay here.'

'But . . .' Jessica's protest was cut short by another pain, so sharp she felt as if it was tearing her apart.

Alistair squeezed her hand. 'Just be grateful your husband is a doctor,' he said with a smile. 'Now try to relax and let nature take its course.'

Little as she wanted to, Jessica had no option but to do as she was told.

* * *

Two hours later, Sarah Mackay made her appearance into the world.

'Another girl,' Jessica whispered apologetically as she cradled the newborn to her breast. You were hoping for a boy, weren't you?'

'Next time maybe,' Alistair said. 'For now, another girl is fine by me. As long as you are both well – and you are – that's all that matters. Besides which,' he added with a smile, 'baby boys have given me enough trouble to be going on with just lately.'

When he was satisfied everything was as it should be, he drove home to Hillsbridge with an excited but tired Constance – who'd been looked after by her Aunt Florrie while her parents were otherwise occupied – leaving Jessica at Catcombe to be cared for by the nursing staff. Unsurprisingly, Jessica had raised objections, saying she felt fine and perfectly fit to travel, but Alistair had been insistent.

'You know the usual advice is not to put a foot to the ground for at least two weeks,' he told her sternly.

'I can't stay here for two weeks!' Jessica had said, horrified, and Alistair had promised that if she was still making good progress, he'd take her home in a couple of days, as long as she agreed to be carried to and from the motor. In the meantime, he would arrange for a daily woman to come in to look after Constance and make sure Jessica could rest without being disturbed.

'And how do women with large families and their husbands out at work manage?' Jessica had demanded.

'With the help of family and neighbours,' Alistair had replied. 'But we don't have any close neighbours to pop in and out, and your sister is here at Catcombe.'

'I suppose,' Jessica was forced to reply.

Florrie, of course, was only too happy to be on hand for the first days of the new baby's life, delighted that she was able to care for her in the nursery and help her sister with getting Sarah to take the breast. Not that much help was needed. Whereas Jessica had struggled initially with getting Constance to feed, from the very first Sarah fastened on at once, sucking greedily.

'This one's going to be a little tomboy, if I'm not much mistaken,' Florrie said, and Jessica smiled.

'Perhaps she'll even be up for kicking a ball around with her daddy,' she said. 'He wanted a boy, I know, but do you know what he said? "Next time maybe"! He should be so lucky! This time might have been a lot easier than last, but I'm still not sure I'm ready to go through it all again.'

'We'll see,' Florrie said with a knowing grin.

She was sad when, a few days later, Alistair took Jessica and Sarah home, Jessica with a dressing gown over her nightgown and Sarah nestled safely in her lap, but her regret lasted only a short while.

She had three other babies to care for, after all, babies for whom she was primarily responsible. That, really, was all she could wish for. All she had ever wanted.

She could scarcely believe her good fortune.


'I really think you should have the doctor pay you a visit,' Winston said, spreading marmalade on his buttered toast as his wife pushed her own breakfast around her plate without taking a single mouthful.

'There's no need for that.' Miranda was very pale; she'd been vomiting into the bathroom sink half an hour earlier, and still felt nauseous. 'I'm not ill. It's just something I ate, I expect.'

'And yesterday? And the day before?'

Miranda said nothing.

'It's morning sickness if I'm not much mistaken.' Winston looked at her over his spectacles. 'And the sooner we find out, the better.'

Miranda gazed down at her plate. The same thing had occurred to her, but she was afraid to believe it; afraid to dare to hope that after all this time she might have actually conceived. And yet she *did* hope, with little tremors of excitement she could not suppress. But she was reluctant to see a doctor. If that tiny shard of hope was dashed, she couldn't bear it. It would be like losing Wallace all over again.

'Let's wait a little longer,' she begged.

Winston sighed, then smiled at her lovingly.

'Very well, my darling, but not too much longer. I want to be sure you and the baby – if there is one – are properly cared for. I couldn't stand to lose either of you.'

She smiled back at him.

'And I couldn't stand to lose you. So just be sure you don't overindulge the way poor Oswald did, and follow him to an early grave.'

'You can rest assured that's not going to happen.' Winston scooped up the last of his toast. 'You mean too much to me for me to want to take that sort of chance. And you know I'm not a great drinker, in any case.'

He bunched his napkin, placed it on his plate and rose from the table.

'I have to go to the office now – I've an appointment with a client at nine thirty. But you take care of yourself while I'm away.' He squeezed his wife's shoulder and kissed her on the cheek before leaving the room.

Miranda crossed to the window to watch him drive away. She was very lucky, she thought, to have Winston for a husband. Her mother had been concerned about the age difference between them, but she'd been proved wrong. He was kind, caring and wise and they loved each other dearly. Really she had no business being so desperate for a baby when she already had so much. And yet . . .

The tiny shard of hope pricked her once again and she pressed both hands to her stomach, praying that there was a new life growing inside her.

It would make her life complete. She would no longer feel second best to Winston's first wife, who had given him two healthy sons. They would be a real family. And she would know the joy of a child of her own.

# Chapter Twenty-Nine

As the weeks went by, Stella gradually relaxed into her old life, happier than she could ever remember. Will was sleeping through the night, so she was no longer tired out during the day, and her relief at having him back made her appreciate every moment she spent with him. The other children seemed to be going out of their way to behave themselves, afraid, perhaps, of losing her again, and Tom was caring, loving and thoughtful. After her dreadful experiences, she took pleasure in the smallest things, and sang over the washtub and the cooking pots just as she used to do before the black depression had stifled her like a storm cloud from which there was no escape.

A warm but wet May gave way to a flaming June, when the sun shone relentlessly from the moment it peeped over the horizon in a pink and golden glow to the time it set in a blaze of scarlet, and not a breath of air stirred the leaves on the trees or whisked away the petals of the roses.

It was too hot for comfort, some said, sweating beneath their high-necked blouses and buttoned-up shirts. An elderly woman had actually collapsed and died outside the hardware shop in Hillsbridge; Dr Mackay had said her heart had given out through heatstroke. The peas, beans and cabbages in the vegetable plots and the sweet williams and stocks in the flower beds had to be watered each evening. The farmers were praying for rain.

Only the children were really enjoying the hot spell, building hideouts in the woods and copses and playing in the shade of the trees that lined the banks of the river only to be yelled at by their hot and bothered parents when they returned home with their boots and socks soaked and their legs covered with splashes of mud, their shorts yellow from the pollen of the celandines or covered with burrs and the white fluff from the dandelion clocks that dotted the meadows.

The Swift and Newman boys were no different. They could easily reach the river by cutting across the fields that sloped down to the valley below, and one evening at the end of the month, the four of them headed down to the spot where they'd fixed a rope to the branch of a tree.

For a while they had a high old time, whooping and yelling as they swung from one bank of the river to the other and back again, but inevitably an argument eventually broke out over whose turn it was next. Reg Newman tried to pull his brother away from the rope, Ned clung on, and both of them finished up in the water.

Luckily it wasn't deep – the long dry spell had reduced the flow to a trickle – but it was quite enough to soak them both to the skin, and a jagged rock had torn a hole in Reg's shorts. Just to make things worse, the cows had trampled through in search of shade, and the mud that hadn't dried up was filthy with the pancakes they'd dropped.

'You'll be for it!' Oliver warned the pair as they trudged home, still arguing and blaming one another.

And so they were.

Stella was sitting outside her back door looking at a picture book with Emily and gently rocking Will's pram. As the four boys rounded the corner, she looked up, aghast at the state of them, though she was relieved that Oliver and Alec were not as filthy as the Newman brothers.

'What in the world have you been up to?' she asked as Ned and Reg disappeared through their back door.

'They fell in the river,' Oliver said, and Alec added: 'And the cow muck.'

'I guessed that. I could smell it from here,' Stella said.

And then the ruckus began.

'Let's go in,' Stella said, anxious to get the children, especially Emily, out of earshot of the raised voices and choice swear words, but though she shut the door she couldn't bring herself to close the window, hot as it was in the kitchen, and she could still hear the commotion that seemed to be escalating.

Though it was nothing new, their neighbours' fights always upset Stella. The thought of the boys being beaten was bad enough, but even worse, she knew that more often than not it ended up with Noel turning on Francie. She'd seen the cuts and bruises her friend suffered, and hated that she was helpless to do anything about it, but Francie, who remained loyal to Noel, had begged her not to tell anyone, even Tom, and so she never had. As far as he knew, it was no more than verbal abuse, and his stance was that it was none of their business.

This evening, however, for some reason Stella felt she couldn't remain silent any longer. Perhaps because of her own recent traumatic experiences her shell was thinner than it used to be, and she was suddenly dreadfully concerned for Francie's safety.

Parking Will's pram in the living room and instructing the children to play indoors, she hurried down the garden to find Tom, who was watering the vegetables.

'Tom, we have to do something. All hell's broken out next door.'

Tom sighed, setting down his watering can and stretching his back. 'Tell me something new. You know it's been going on for years. It'll all be forgotten tomorrow.'

'But this time it sounds really bad. Like they're killing one another! I'm really worried.'

'If you interfere between husband and wife, they'll both turn on you,' Tom said. 'What started it this time anyway?'

'The boys came home sopping wet and covered in cow muck—'

'Our boys too?' Tom interrupted, his face darkening.

'No, thank goodness. Just Ned and Reg.'

'That's all right then. If it had been Oliver and Alec, they'd have felt my hand on their backsides too.'

'But it's not just the boys he beats up. It's Francie too.' Stella was too concerned about her friend to keep silent any longer. 'I've seen the bruises.'

Tom looked shocked, but he shook his head. 'If that's truc, then it's well out of order, but it doesn't change anything, Stella. What goes on behind closed doors is their business. If it's really serious, Francie should go to the police. But I doubt it is. It's mostly a lot of screaming and shouting, I expect.'

'Tom, please . . .'

He could see that Stella was upsetting herself, the last thing he wanted. 'All right,' he said reluctantly. 'If it's still going on when I've finished doing this, I'll go and knock on the door. Will that do?'

What Stella really wanted was for him to knock right now, but she guessed this was the best she was going to get. 'Thank you,' she said, and went back to the house. To her enormous relief, everything seemed to have gone quiet next door.

Tom was still working in the garden when it was time to take Will upstairs to give him his last feed and settle him for the night. From the bedroom window Stella saw Noel walk down his front path and along the road, off to the Miners' Arms, most likely. Well, at least that meant it was all over for the time being, but she only hoped he wouldn't have too much to drink and start on Francie when he got home.

Feeling desperately sorry for her poor ill-used friend, Stella settled Will, then crept quietly downstairs.

Stella was half asleep when something roused her, something that sounded like banging. Beside her, Tom was snoring gently. They'd been in bed for the best part of an hour, and she'd rolled into him, laying her head against his shoulder and fitting her body to his, hoping that he would make love to her. But as had happened too often since she had come home, he hadn't responded.

'Not tonight, my love. I'm dog tired.'

He'd kissed her, given her a hug, then rolled over and was asleep within minutes, but Stella, frustrated and aching with desire, had been unable to sleep.

It had been like this ever since she'd come home, and it was the one thing about her life that was less than perfect. Kind and caring as Tom was during the day, the regular lovemaking they'd used to share was now far less frequent, and Stella was beginning to wonder if her illness had left her less desirable to him. Did he see her now as a patient in a lunatic asylum rather than his wife and lover?

Or perhaps he was afraid she'd fall pregnant again and the resulting baby would plunge her back into the dark days of depression. Truth to tell, she was half afraid of it herself, but for all that, she longed for the closeness their union could bring.

But really the most likely explanation was that Tom *was*

tired. With the long days of backbreaking work underground, jobs around the house and garden when he came home, and three children and a baby in the house, it was no wonder he was exhausted. Besides which, she couldn't expect the frantic need for one another that had characterised their early days together to last for ever. Hadn't there been plenty of times when she herself had fallen into bed after a day of cooking, cleaning and caring for the children, too tired to want to do anything but snatch a few hours' much-needed sleep?

At last she had begun to feel drowsy, the thread of her thoughts drifting into woolly confusion before the knocking sound invaded them and she was awake again and thinking it must have been part of a dream.

And then it came again, loud and insistent, and she knew it was no dream. Someone was hammering on the back door. Puzzled and alarmed, she slipped out of bed, taking care not to wake Tom. Who on earth could it be at this time of night? Had something happened to her mother or father or Grace?

She reached for her dressing gown, pulling it on as she hurried downstairs and into the kitchen.

'All right, I'm coming!' she called out as she turned the key and fumbled the bolt open.

It wasn't a policeman come to give them bad news who stood on the doorstep, but her neighbour.

'Francie!' she exclaimed.

'Oh Stella . . .' Francie's voice was trembling and thick with tears. 'Please . . . oh please . . . can I come in?'

Stella stood aside as Francie pushed past her and collapsed on to a kitchen chair. Guessing that this had something to do with Noel, she closed the door and lit the gas mantle, but by its light she was shocked to see that one of Francie's eyes was swollen shut. Beneath it her cheek was swollen too into a lump the size of a lemon, and already discolouring. Blood ran down her chin from a badly split lip, and she was shaking from head to foot.

'Oh my God!' Stella gasped. 'Is this Noel's doing?'

Francie nodded. 'The boys upset him earlier . . .'

'Yes, I know.'

'. . . and then he went out to the pub and came home drunk and still mad as a hatter and . . .'

'And took it out on you,' Stella finished for her. 'Let's go through to the living room. You'll be more comfortable there. Don't try to talk. I'll put the kettle on. Get you cleaned up. Make a cup of tea.'

She helped her friend up, took her through and settled her in one of the easy chairs, then poked the banked-up fire to stir it to life and set the kettle on the trivet. She fetched lint and a wad of cotton wool, and a pat of butter which she would rub into Francie's bruised face. Then she drew up one of the dining chairs to sit opposite Francie so she could take a good look at the damage and do what she could to help her friend.

'I'm sorry to be so much trouble, Stella,' Francie mumbled wretchedly.

'Don't be daft. It's no trouble. And it's not your fault either.' Stella dunked the cotton wool in a basin of warm water and dabbed gingerly at Francie's split lip. Gentle as she tried to be, Francie winced and drew back.

'But it is my fault,' she whispered. 'When Noel disciplines the boys I get upset and say things I shouldn't, and it makes him angry.'

'That's no excuse,' Stella said firmly. 'He has no right to do this to you.'

'He's my husband. The children's father. And he loves us really.'

406

'Well, he's got a funny way of showing it,' Stella said shortly.

They'd had this conversation before, or one very like it. The difference this time was that this wasn't just a quick slap or a push. It showed that Noel's attacks were getting more and more violent and he was beyond caring whether there were marks to show the world what went on behind closed doors.

'This is really serious, Francie. He's getting worse, isn't he?'

Francie nodded. A tear squeezed itself out from her swollen eye and ran down her cheek.

'I don't think I can stand it any more, Stella, and I don't know what to do.' Her voice was low and trembling. 'Sometimes I just feel like ending it all.'

'Don't talk like that,' Stella said, alarmed. 'The children . . .'

'Maybe they'd be better off without me.'

A crash from the kitchen, as if someone had bumped into a chair and overturned it, made Stella start. She just had time to remember she hadn't locked the back door before Noel appeared in the doorway, clutching at the frame to steady himself and gesticulating angrily at Francie.

'I thought I'd find you here.' His words were slurred, his face red with drunken rage. 'Get back home, you bitch. Now!'

Stella's legs were unsteady from shock, but she rose and faced him defiantly. 'She's hurt, and it's your fault. Get out of my house and leave her alone.'

'Like hell! She's coming with me or she'll get more of the same.'

Noel lurched towards Francie; Stella moved to block his path.

'Get out of my way, you interfering bitch!'

He lunged round Stella, attempting to drag a struggling Francie to her feet. Stella grabbed his arm, and with a roar of fury he wheeled round, striking her full in the face. She staggered backwards, vainly trying to save herself as she collided with the dining chair, became entangled with its legs and went down like a felled tree. The back of her head cracked against the edge of the fire surround.

For a split second, brightly coloured stars flashed before her eyes. Then darkness closed in, cold and unrelenting.

'What the hell . . . ?'

Woken by the commotion downstairs, Tom had leapt out of bed and rushed down the stairs just in time to see Noel strike Stella. Without a second's thought his own fist shot out, connecting with Noel's jaw. The other man staggered, then lunged for a cowering Francie, grabbing her by the arm and dragging her towards the door.

'Help me, Tom!' Francie screamed.

But Tom had eyes only for Stella, lying motionless on the fireside rug, her head twisted at an unnatural angle.

He dropped to his knees beside her, bending double over her prone frame.

'Stella!' he gasped. No response. 'Stella! Sweetheart! Speak to me!'

Still no response. For the first time, Tom took in the serious implications of that strangely angled head.

His heart seemed to stop beating, his stomach fell away, his blood ran cold.

He bent closer, listening for the merest whisper of breath. Nothing. He felt for a pulse, first in her wrist and then at her throat. Still nothing.

'Oh my God – Stella!'

He'd lost her. He knew it without a shadow of a doubt. Desperately he smoothed her tangled hair away from her forehead and kissed it, and then her nose, her cheek, her lips.

*She wanted me to make love to her tonight and I didn't . . . couldn't . . . Why couldn't I have done that one last thing for her?*

It was a thought that was to torture him for a very long time. He'd never make love to her again. Never get the chance to make up for the wrong he'd done her, because even though he loved her, he could think of no one but Grace. Her face as she'd left haunted his every waking moment and his dreams. Her voice, soft and musical, with the hint of a laugh in it. The perfume of her hair and her skin. Grace, who, if he had not ruined everything, should have been his wife.

This is all my fault, Tom thought. If I hadn't been so eager to sow my wild oats, none of this would have happened, and Stella would still be alive.

He slid round to sit on the fire surround beside her, lifted her head and cradled it in his lap, stroking every inch of her dear face. Then he bent his head over hers and wept.

Dawn was breaking before he could bring himself to move.


As the taxi cab came to a halt in Dunderwick Road, Grace steeled herself to pay the driver, climb out and walk up the path to the front door. Her overwhelming feeling was that she was living in a nightmare from which she couldn't wake. Apart from the curtains drawn closed at all the windows, the house looked exactly as it always did, even down to Fluffy sitting on the front step waiting to be let in. But today there was something threatening about it, a dark shadow that defied the relentless glint of the sun on the window panes and highly polished brass door knocker, and heightened the sense of the macabre.

This terrible feeling that shivered in her veins and formed a leaden weight in her stomach had intensified with every mile of the journey from Shillingford to Hillsbridge. She still felt sick from the awful shock of seeing the bobby on the doorstep, and her knees, which had almost given way beneath her as he told her the dreadful news, felt weak and shaky.

Stella was dead. She could still scarcely believe it and yet she knew it was true. It had to be. No officer of the law would make up something like that. But how? Why? He'd been unable to give her any more details, simply the bare and inescapable fact that her sister had died during the night.

Had she been taken ill? Had an accident? Surely, surely she hadn't suffered a serious relapse and taken her own life? All the various scenarios played out endlessly in her head whilst she broke the news to her devastated parents and went into the village to call a taxi cab to take her to Hillsbridge.

Tom hadn't asked for her, or at least if he had, the policeman hadn't passed on the message. But Grace hadn't hesitated for a moment. She had to go to them, Tom and the children. They'd need her. And she had to go to Stella, even though her sister was beyond knowing she was there.

Now she hesitated on the doorstep of the house where she had been so happy, wondering whether she should knock or just go straight in. In the event, she settled for both, giving a brief tap on the brass knocker and then opening the door and stepping inside.

'Tom? It's me.'

As she stood uncertainly in the hall, which seemed now to smell of death as well as lavender furniture polish, Tom appeared in the living room doorway.

'Grace!'

He looked haggard, both from lack of sleep and grief, and fair stubble bristled on his unshaved face.

'Tom. I had to come. Is it true?' A stupid question, she knew, but she couldn't stop herself from asking it all the same.

'Yes, Grace, it is.' His voice was heavy, weighted down by those few words of confirmation.

'But what happened?'

'Come in. Sit down. We don't want to talk out here.'

They went into the living room, each taking one of the easy chairs that faced one another on either side of the fireplace, though both perched on the edge of their seat, ramrod straight and tense. Of the children there was no sign.

For a moment Tom was silent, staring at the floor.

'She fell,' he said at last. 'Hit her head on the fire surround.'

'Fell?' Grace echoed.

'Well, not so much fell as was pushed,' Tom said woodenly.

'Pushed?' Grace seemed incapable of anything but repeating Tom's words. 'Who by?'

'Noel Newman. I was asleep and got woken up by the commotion. I came down and found Noel and Francie struggling, and Stella . . . She was trying to intervene and he lashed out and she fell . . .' He glanced again at the spot on the hearth. 'She'd gone, Grace, before I could do anything to save her.'

Grace swallowed hard, fighting back the threatening tears. 'Oh Tom . . . How terrible!'

'I don't know what they were doing there – Francie and Noel. They'd been rowing earlier and Francie must have come round to ours to get away from him. But he followed her, was trying to drag her home when Stella got in the way. What happened after that I don't know, except that I punched him on the jaw. I was more concerned with Stella. I can only think Francie must have got away from him and run all the way down to the police station, because the next thing I knew, Sergeant Love was at the door and Francie was with him. After that . . . well, it's been all go.'

'Where are the children?' Grace asked.

'Over at Mum and Dad's. Maud Button at number twenty-five took them. I thought it best to get them out of the way.'

'And Stella?'

'In the front room.'

'Can I see her?'

Tom stood silently, moving to the door and motioning her to follow.

Stella was laid out on a trestle covered with a white sheet. Another was draped over her. Tom folded it back tenderly, and Grace gazed down at her sister. Her eyes were closed, her hair brushed tidily away from her face.

'She looks just as though she's sleeping,' she said softly, though it wasn't quite true. There were no roses in Stella's cheeks, no hint of colour in the hands that were crossed over her breast. She might have been carved out of alabaster.

She bent over and touched one of her sister's cold white hands, then kissed her forehead.

'Sweet dreams, my love,' she murmured, and the tears she'd held back for so long were there, filling her eyes, running down her face, falling like gentle rain on Stella's ivory cheeks.

It was what they used to say to one another each night in the bed they'd shared when they were young. And sometimes, giggling: 'Sleep tight, mind the fleas don't bite.' But this was no time for laughter or silly jokes.

Touching her fingers to her lips, she pressed them to Stella's and took one last loving look at her sister before leaving her alone with her grieving husband.

Francie sat at her kitchen table, her head in her hands. Her split lip was throbbing and her whole face felt tight and hot, but the physical discomfort was nothing to the turmoil churning inside her.

Noel had been arrested and taken away by the police. She didn't know what was going to happen to him, and she didn't care. She never wanted to see him again as long as she lived. Bad enough that he had abused her for years, cowed her into believing she was the one to blame and made her despise herself for it. But this . . .

Stella, her friend, was dead. Noel might not have meant to kill her; Francie didn't think for a moment that he had. But he'd done it nevertheless. Stella's only crime had been kindness and trying to help Francie. And it had cost her her life.

Francie couldn't face Tom, couldn't face Grace, couldn't face anyone ever again. She still felt she was to blame for this whole tragedy – she'd provoked Noel, and she'd run to Stella for help. But at the same time she knew she'd meant what she'd said – that she couldn't do this any more.

She had a sister who lived on the Somerset Levels. She'd go to her, take the children with her. It would be like fitting sardines into a can, but she knew Freda wouldn't turn her away. She'd understand and give them a roof over their heads until Francie could sort something out. It would mean she could leave Noel behind, along with the constant fear that came from never knowing when his temper would explode into violence. And leave behind everyone who knew her, escape the shame when it all came out.

Francie lifted her chin. It would be a new beginning.

'What are you going to do?' Grace asked.

They were sitting at the kitchen table, cups of tea in front of them.

Tom shrugged helplessly. 'I haven't had time to think.'

Grace hesitated. In the light of what had so nearly happened between them, she was unwilling to be the one to suggest she should move back in for the time being. But she could see that Tom was in no state to make any decision.

'Do you want me to stay on for a bit?' she asked tentatively.

His eyes came up to meet hers, but now there was no spark of connection in them, just gratitude and confusion.

'Would you?'

'Of course.'

He nodded, twisting the signet ring he wore on his wedding finger round and round.

'I loved her,' he said simply.

'I know you did.'

Though unspoken, the agreement was implicit between them. There could be no repeat of that last evening, nothing that would be a betrayal of Stella. Their shared grief and guilt would not allow it.

'That's one thing settled then,' Grace said shakily.

'Thank you.'

For a long time they sat in silence, lost in their memories of a beloved wife, sister and mother.

They had intended the funeral to be a simple and quite private affair. It had been decided it would be too upsetting for the children to attend, Stella's father was in no fit state, and her mother was laid low with a fluey cold, probably brought on by the shock of her daughter's death. But in the event, as Tom and Grace followed the coffin into the church, Grace realised it was almost full.

It was only to be expected, she thought as she passed the rows of pews occupied by people whose faces were no more than a blur to her. Stella had been young. She had been well known in the town, and well liked.

Throughout the service, Grace held herself erect, looking

straight ahead, shoulders stiff, hands clenched, and biting her lip to hold back the tears. If she began to cry, she knew she would be unable to stop. She did manage to soundlessly mouth a few words of the hymns, and during the prayers she bent her head, trying without success to follow the words. How could she pray to a God who could have allowed this to happen?

Then they were standing beside the open grave, watching as the simple pine coffin was lowered, hearing the splatter of dry earth on wood and the rector's voice as he intoned the words: 'Ashes to ashes. Dust to dust . . .' She saw Tom's head drop to his chest, knew that, like her, he was fighting to control his emotions. Men didn't weep. For him, pride was more important than the need to shed tears.

Instinctively she reached out and took his hand, and his fingers curled around her knuckles, gripping them tightly as they shared the awful finality of what was happening. But there was no physicality or hidden meaning in their touch, simply the sharing of comfort and support.

That, they had both accepted, was the way it had to be.

# Chapter Thirty

Christmas was fast approaching, and both Grace and Tom were dreading having to put on a show of festivity for the sake of the children when they would be feeling wretched and all too aware of the gaping hole in the family. But just a few days before, there would be another poignant occasion: Will's first birthday. And in some ways that would be even worse.

The last months, as the long hot summer cooled into autumn, the leaves fell from the trees in drifts of russet and ochre, and the days drew in for winter, had been difficult and painful ones. The joy that Grace had found in caring for the family in the spring was absent now. Though she put a brave face on it, her spirits were low and there were moments when she blamed herself for her sister's tragic and untimely death. 'Be careful what you wish for' had been one of her mother's sayings, and it played uncomfortably on her mind. Hadn't she wished for what Stella had? Envied her her home, her husband, her children? Was it possible that some higher power had engineered events to grant her wish and allow her to step into Stella's shoes? No matter how often she tried to tell herself she was being foolish, the idea was a worm of discomfort deep inside her that refused to be quietened.

Sometimes she wondered if Tom felt the same way. There

was no denying the strength of their attraction that had been reignited whilst Stella had been in hospital, or the closeness that had grown between them. Neither could she forget that last night, when they had so nearly given in to their feelings. The memory of it was as fresh in her mind as if it had been just yesterday.

But that was all it was now, all it could ever be. A memory. Stella stood between them, even more of a barrier in death than she had been in life. Though things were relatively easy when the children were around them, when they were alone, the defences came up. There were awkward silences, and the avoidance of any contact that might create a spark to light the fuse to feelings that still existed but must be denied.

The children, too, had been something of a worry. Naturally they were very upset by the loss of their mother. Whilst she had been in hospital, they had accepted Grace as a surrogate, secure in the knowledge that some day soon Stella would be back where she belonged. Now there were problems. Alec, in particular, seemed to resent Grace, and challenged her authority. 'You can't tell me what to do. You're not my mother,' he would say with a scowl. Tom had had a stern word with him and things had begun to improve a little. Oliver, who had been dry since the day he came out of nappies, had begun wetting the bed, and Grace thought that he, as the eldest, probably realised more clearly than the others that Stella was never coming back. Certainly Emily hadn't really accepted it and still asked sometimes where her mummy had gone. But she was very clingy and easily reduced to tears, as if she was afraid that Tom and Grace might also suddenly disappear, and she had been only too happy to go back to sharing a room with Oliver and Alec so that Grace could have hers.

It didn't help either that the boys no longer had the Newmans to play with. Noel had been sent to prison, found guilty of manslaughter, and as soon as he'd been charged Francie and the children had moved away. Not that she would have had any choice in the matter, since the house was a tied cottage, but she'd told Grace it was what she wanted – to make a fresh start away from all the inevitable gossip and finger-pointing.

Only Will was unaffected by the tragic events. He was the happiest of babies, always laughing and gurgling. To begin with it had felt very strange to Grace, caring for him instead of Wallace. She'd grown used to Wallace's little ways, while Will was a stranger to her. But she'd come to love him even more, if that were possible. He was, after all, her nephew, and the son of her dearly loved sister. He'd learned to crawl now, streaking across the floor on all fours at an unbelievably fast rate, and he was curious too, wanting to reach beneath the furniture and into cupboards, and stuffing anything he found into his mouth. All this activity was quite a hindrance to Grace as she tried to do the housework and cooking, but she didn't mind that. She was just happy to have him around, back where he belonged. When the weather allowed, she loved wheeling him out in his pushchair, pointing out to him anything and everything from pretty leaves and birds to a neighbour's cat or the horses in the field at the end of the road.

'We have to do something special for his birthday,' she said to Tom. 'I know we're not going to feel like it, but we've got to make the effort.'

'I'll leave it to you, Grace,' he said, and she knew he was dreading the anniversary as much as she was, a poignant reminder that Stella would not be here to see it.

She went to market and bought a wooden duck on wheels and a big colourful rattle for presents, and some balloons to decorate the living room for the birthday tea. Then she made a

Victoria sponge cake with a jam and buttercream filling and decorated it with sugar flowers, hundreds and thousands and a single candle.

When the day arrived, the children were all excited, their grief forgotten for the moment at least. They fell over one another in their eagerness to help blow up the balloons and assist Will in opening his presents, tearing off the paper before Grace could stop them, running around dragging the duck behind them and shaking the rattle in front of Will's nose until she reminded them that the toys were his, not theirs, and would they please let him play with them.

Tom was home in time for tea. Besides the birthday cake there was strawberry jelly and blancmange, bread and butter and chocolate biscuits. All was quiet while they tucked in, Grace spooning jelly and blancmange into Will's mouth but allowing him to feed himself tiny squares of buttered bread. Then she lit the candle on the cake and Oliver, Alec and Emily clustered round to help him blow it out. When tea was over and the plates were cleared away, Tom set up the table skittles and they all had a game, Tom holding Will and guiding his hand on the ball so that he could take a turn too. He gurgled with delight as the skittles tumbled noisily.

After a while, Tom sat down in the easy chair opposite Grace and set Will down on the rug. Instantly he pulled himself up by the arm of the chair, another trick he'd mastered. Usually he simply stood there before flopping down on his bottom and crawling like lightning to whatever had attracted his interest. But today it looked to Grace as if he was about to try a step.

She caught Tom's eye and drew his attention to Will with a little nod of her head, then dropped on to her knees, retrieved the rattle and held it out to the little boy.

The concentration on his face was absolute, and after a moment's hesitation he took one unsteady step towards her, and then another, before swaying perilously. Grace reached out and caught him, lifting him safely into her arms.

'You walked, Will!' she cried. 'Tom – he walked!'

'Will walked!' Emily echoed.

'Yes, he did! Can you do it again, Will?'

She turned him round and steadied him, and Tom leaned forward, spreading his arms wide.

'Go to Daddy, Will,' Grace encouraged him, and to everyone's delight, he launched himself into a few tottering steps before collapsing into Tom's outstretched arms.

'What a day!' Grace said.

The children were in bed, Tom had refilled the coal scuttle and taken out the detritus from the birthday celebrations and put it in the dustbin, and Grace had finished tidying up. Now they were having a well-earned rest. To celebrate the momentous occasion that had seen Will walk for the first time, Tom had opened a bottle of beer and Grace had allowed herself a small sweet sherry.

'Yup. This is one birthday we'll always remember, even if he can't,' Tom agreed.

'And we thought it would be memorable for quite another reason.'

The moment the words were out, Grace wished she could take them back. She didn't want to remind Tom that it should have been Stella presiding over Will's party, Stella who should have seen her son's first steps.

'I'm sorry,' she said swiftly. 'I didn't mean to put a damper on things.'

Tom was silent for a moment, taking a long pull of his beer.

Then he set the glass down on the table and raised his eyes to hers.

'Don't be silly. It's time we stopped treading on eggshells. I've been thinking about Stella all day and I wouldn't mind betting you have too.'

'I have,' Grace admitted. 'And when Will took his first steps . . .' Tears pricked her eyes.

'I know.' Tom leaned forward, covering her hand with his. It was the first deliberate contact between them since Stella's funeral, and it was all Grace could do not to draw back, unable to trust herself with what his touch would do to her long-suppressed emotions. But his hand was firm on hers, and the self-imposed distance that had been between them seemed to shrink and fade as he went on: 'We both loved her, Grace, but she's gone, and we have to carry on without her. We can't let our grief rule our lives, though. She wouldn't want that.'

'No, I suppose not. But still . . .' She blinked back the tears. 'It should have been Stella he took his first steps to.'

'But it wasn't. It was you.' Tom was looking at her steadily, and there was both sincerity and warmth in his eyes. 'You've done a wonderful job with all the children. And it wouldn't surprise me if Will's first words were to you as well as his steps. Isn't "Mama" the first word they utter?'

Grace did draw her hand away then, sharply, her fingers curling into a fist so that her nails dug into her palms.

'He mustn't call me that. I'm not his mother. Stella is and always will be.'

'Of course. But you are his second mother – the only one he knows. I can't imagine what any of us would have done without you, Grace. We owe you a debt we can never repay.'

Grace shook her head. 'I'm the lucky one. Everything I've

ever wanted is here, under this roof. And I feel so guilty for it! As if I've stolen what is rightfully Stella's.'

'If we really are what you want, then she'd be happy for you. And so grateful that you've stepped in to fill what would have been a gaping hole in our lives. That you're making us a family again. It will take time, of course. It won't happen overnight. And none of us will ever forget Stella or stop loving her. But one day, that's what we'll be. A proper family. You, me and the children.'

He reached for her hand again, and this time she didn't draw away.

'Oh Tom, do you really think so?'

'I'm sure of it. When the time is right,' he said, and the sincerity in his voice told her it was so. Then he smiled mischievously, a rare glimpse of the old Tom, released her hand and reached for his glass, raising it.

'Let's drink to Will's first steps,' he said.

Grace lifted her sherry. 'Will's first steps . . .'

They clinked glasses.

'And to Stella,' she added.

'And to Stella,' he repeated.

As they clinked glasses again, their eyes met, love and understanding passing between them.

Both knew it was a promise for the future.

# Author's Note

Language is a living thing, always changing. New words appear in the Oxford English Dictionary each year, words in common use change their meaning, others become unacceptable and are considered offensive. I can think of dozens of examples, and I'm sure you can too.

This can be a challenge when writing a book about past times, and *The Stolen Child* was no exception.

At the beginning of the book, one of my main characters, Stella Swift, is suffering from what we now call postnatal depression. In my lifetime it has been referred to as 'baby blues', though I haven't heard that expression for a long time now. But both terms would have been unheard of in 1911.

In those days I believe it was sometimes still known as 'puerperal fever', which some of my research suggests was first used by Hippocrates, to cover all aspects of problems following childbirth. Today, however, that would be taken to mean a physical condition rather than a psychological one. 'Mania' was also frequently used, as in 'acute mania'.

The same goes for other psychiatric conditions; the words used for many of them would be offensive today. The asylum to which Stella was sent was, shockingly, the home of many people who would today be cared for in the community, and painting a picture of these other patients posed a dilemma. How, for instance, could I indicate that one had Down's Syndrome when that description would have been unknown in 1911 and the term used then is certainly not acceptable today?

With the help of my wonderful editor, Kate Byrne, I hope I have managed to find a way to be true to the world as it was in 1911 without causing offence to anyone!

Read on for an exclusive early preview of the next
enthralling saga from Jennie Felton

# A MOTHER'S SACRIFICE

Coming soon from Headline

# *Prologue*

## Hillsbridge, Somerset – 1907

Sergeant Love was in bed and snoring loud enough to wake the dead when something disturbed him. He shifted restlessly, thinking that Alice, his wife, must have given him a poke in the ribs as she sometimes did to try to put a stop to the regular droning that she likened to sleeping in a farmyard.

'Leave me be, can't you?'

But now Alice's hand was on his shoulder, shaking him.

'Wake up, for goodness' sake, Will. Can't you hear there's somebody at the door?'

'What?' He rubbed his fist over his chin to wipe away the dribble that had run from his open mouth.

'Somebody's at the door!' Alice repeated impatiently, and simultaneously the knocking that had woken her came again, loud and insistent.

'Oh bugger.'

Sergeant Love struggled to a sitting position, rolled out of bed and reached for his dressing gown.

That was one of the drawbacks of living above the police station. You were always at the beck and call of anybody who wanted a policeman, whatever the time of the day or night it happened to be.

By the light of the moon that was streaming in through a gap in the curtains he could see that the hands of the bedside clock were showing twenty to three, and that surprised him. He'd have thought Constable Sparrow, who was on night duty, would have been in the office by this time, having a cup of tea and making up his notebook. The town was usually quiet at this time of night. Perhaps Sparrow was out on his bicycle making a last round – or perhaps the dozy bugger had fallen asleep at his desk. That wouldn't surprise the sergeant. Sparrow had looked even more lethargic than usual when he'd come on duty at ten.

Sergeant Love thrust his feet into his highly polished black boots, not bothering to lace them, and made his way down the stairs, through the small living room, and into the lobby. The door to the little office was open – no sign of Sparrow there – and before the sergeant could unlatch the door the hammering began again.

'All right, all right, I'm coming!' he called grumpily. If it was young tearaways having a laugh, they'd catch the rough end of his tongue.

But it wasn't young tearaways. On the doorstep, her hand raised to knock yet again, was a middle-aged woman he recognised as Martha Packer, landlady of The Three Feathers, a pub at the very outskirts of his patch. And if her insistent knocking had not told him that her reason for being here was that something very serious had occurred, her grim expression certainly did.

Sergeant Love sighed inwardly, seeing the remainder of his night's sleep disappear 'down the Swanee' as he described it, and thinking that he wouldn't mind betting that whatever Martha's problem was, it involved her son, Garth.

* * *

The Three Feathers, several miles outside Hillsbridge on the road to Bath, had been owned by the Packer family for as long as anyone could remember. Successive generations had served beer and spirits to the hardened drinkers of the nearby villages, first from what had once been the front room of their home – a sizeable house with a cottage adjoining and land that stretched to the surrounding fields and woods. Later the ground floor layout had been tinkered with so that there was a lounge as well as a public bar and a snug and Seb, Martha's husband, had built a skittle alley in one of the outbuildings at the rear of the property so that The Feathers, as it was known, could raise a team from amongst their regulars to play in the local skittles league.

Just over a year ago, Seb had died in a tragic accident that had devastated the family. His will had left everything to his three sons, Garth, Conrad and Lewis, but it was still Martha who ran the business and served behind the bar.

At fifty-four she was still a handsome woman, evidence that she'd been known for 'a stunner' when she was young. Though there were now broad streaks of silver in what had once been a fine head of coal-black hair, her face was remarkably free of lines and wrinkles, perhaps thanks to a tendency to plumpness, and her posture as upright as it had ever been, with no hint of the rounded shoulders or widow's hump that afflicted many women of her age.

As for her nature, it was ideally suited to her role as a pub landlady. Although her manner was friendly, warm and welcoming, she could also be formidable if the occasion warranted, as any customers who became rowdy or overstepped the mark soon learned to their cost. Life had dealt Martha some hard blows; besides losing her husband, she had buried four children, three who had died in infancy and one still-birth, but somehow the terrible losses had failed to break her. Instead they had made her stronger, so that now a core of steel lay beneath her generally pleasant demeanour.

This was the Martha Packer Sergeant Love knew – strong, resilient, optimistic. But now, as she stood on the doorstep of the police station, erect as ever, her face was ravaged, and her hands, tightly clasped around the bone handles of the tapestry bag she held in front of her like body armour, also spoke of something very wrong.

'What's up then, Mrs Packer?' he asked.

Her chin rose; she hesitated for only a moment.

'I need to talk to you, Sergeant.'

Another brief hesitation.

'I have just killed my son.'

# Chapter One

## St Peter's Workhouse – April 1896

'Jeannie – hush, my love. Don't cry, please!'

Eleven-year-old Ella Martin rolled as close as she could to the edge of her narrow bed and reached across to her little sister. There were eight beds in the dormitory and luckily Jeannie occupied the one next to her.

'I want Mammy!' Jeannie's voice was thick with tears.

'I know. So do I. But you mustn't cry. Miss Hopkins will hear you and then . . .' Ella broke off, not wanting to put into words what would happen if the housemother was disturbed. Children who cried at night were silenced with a rag soaked in chloroform to keep them quiet. And it did that all right. Not so long ago one girl had gone to sleep and never woken up again. Her bed, next to the door, was still empty, and Ella was terrified the same fate might befall her sister. 'You don't want to make her cross, do you?' she finished.

'N . . . no . . .' Eight-year-old Jeannie's sobs softened into hiccups and snuffles and her fingers curled round Ella's, gripping them tightly.

'You'll see Mammy soon. When she's well again,' Ella

whispered urgently, trying to ensure that Jeannie didn't start crying again in earnest.

'Really soon?'

'Yes.'

But she knew it was an empty promise. Here in the workhouse families were separated, wives from their husbands, children from their parents, boys from girls. Siblings did get to see one another for two hours each afternoon when they were taught their lessons, either by the local rector or Miss Owen, who had once run a dame school in a nearby village. But it was only on Sundays, when they attended church, that the children had any contact with their mothers and fathers, and next Sunday was a whole week away. Six long days and nights. Even then, if Lilah was still ill they wouldn't be allowed up to the infirmary where she was being looked after for fear of spreading germs. They hadn't been allowed there today, and they hadn't been allowed to visit their father when he was dying of the lung disease that had cost him his job in the pits and the house that went with it – the reason the family had ended up here in the workhouse.

Ella's greatest fear was that her mother might follow him to an early grave. She had never been in good health since giving birth to Jeannie, and Ella had only faint memories of the strong, fun-loving woman who had used to take her for long walks in the fields and woods behind their home, play hide-and-seek with her while she buried herself in the laundry basked or crouched behind the sofa, and sing her to sleep at bedtime. She'd been only three years old when Jeannie was born. But when Daddy had explained to her that Mammy wasn't well and needed help with the new baby she had been eager to do her bit.

She'd taken soiled nappies to the soaking bucket and prodded them in with the wooden spoon Lilah kept especially for the purpose, and sat beside the crib, rocking it gently until Jeannie fell asleep, however long that took. Later, as Jeannie grew, Ella had kept her entertained when Lilah was tired, or forced to take to her bed, even preparing food for them, albeit mostly jam sandwiches or bread and dripping.

As time had gone by Lilah's health had improved, but since they had been forced into the workhouse the awful conditions there had weakened her again, her reserves of strength eroded by the hard physical work, often in the laundry or the kitchens, and the cold and damp that permeated the place – even in summer the chill still emanated from the old stone walls. Ella had seen her grow thinner and paler, and during this last bitterly cold winter she'd developed a chesty cough that she couldn't seem to shake off, which had worried Ella, though Lilah tried to reassure her that it was nothing that some spring sunshine wouldn't cure.

Since the weather had taken a turn for the better this week, Ella had been in hopes that she'd see some improvement in her mother when they met in church on Sunday. But it wasn't to be. Instead she was worse, and sick enough to have been taken to the infirmary, so that Ella and Jeannie hadn't been able to see her at all.

Just to make matters worse it was Mothering Sunday. Along with the other children they had been allowed out into the meadows to pick a bunch of flowers for their mams and they had both been looking forward to giving them to her so much. No wonder Jeannie had been in tears on and off for most of the day, Ella thought. She'd felt like crying too, and still did.

But at least Jeannie was quiet now, just sniffling occasionally, and when at last the snuffles stopped and her breathing became even, Ella whispered a little prayer of gratitude that the danger of her being quietened with a chloroform-soaked rag had passed – for now, at least.

Her hand, which Jeannie had been clasping tightly, had gone through the stage of pins and needles to being completely numb, but she had been afraid to move in case she disturbed her sister and set her off again. Now, however, she inched closer to the edge of the thin straw mattress so that she could reach across with her other hand and gently prise herself free of Jeannie's fingers. Success. She rolled over on to her back, rubbing life back into her hand, then pulled the coarse blanket covering her up as far as the neck of her nightgown – any higher and it would make her throat itch – and closed her eyes. But with all her worries about Mammy churning round in her head sleep felt as far away as ever.

Would she be all right? Would she get better? Or – the thought was so terrible it ran a shiver through her body and made her feel sick – might she die as Daddy had? If she did, Ella didn't think she could bear it. And what would become of her and Jeannie? Ella felt as if all the cares of the world rested on her young shoulders.

A solitary tear escaped and rolled down her cheek and she turned her head to brush it away on the worn pillowcase. Crying would do no good. Somehow she had to be strong, for Jeannie as well as for herself. But oh – it wasn't easy! And her bitter disappointment at not seeing Mammy today, not being able to give her the wild flowers they'd picked for her, wasn't helping either.

How, she wondered miserably, could a day that had started off so well have ended so badly?

Because it was Mothering Sunday, the children were excused their morning chores for once so that they could go out to gather the wild flowers they would give to their mothers during Matins. Ella and Jeannie were both so excited that not even the icy cold water they had to wash in, stripped to the waist, for their morning ablutions, or the porridge and dry bread that made up their breakfast, could dampen their spirits, though they still sniffed enviously at the delicious aroma of crisp bacon rashers that wafted their way from the table where the staff ate. When the meal was over and they'd helped clear away the dishes they were escorted out of the workhouse grounds and across the road to the open countryside beyond.

It was a beautiful spring morning, the sky the clean-washed blue of April and scattered with fluffy white clouds, the crisp air full of the fresh sweet scent of dew-wet grass. At first, given a little freedom, the children scattered, taking the opportunity to run about in this paradise, so different to the workhouse exercise yard, where a high wire fence divided the boys' section from the girls'. Then, when Miss Sparks, the assistant mistress who had accompanied them, reminded them sharply why they were here in the meadow, they began hunting for wild flowers to make their posies.

Cowslips, buttercups and daisies nestled amid the rough tufts of meadow grass, clumps of primroses blossomed on the banks, and violets peeped out from the moss around the roots of trees. Ella picked some of each, careful not to damage the delicate stalks, and soon had enough to make a pretty posy. A little further on, in a copse that bordered the field and the river beyond, she spied a cluster of late bluebells, and was just making her way towards them when Jeannie came running up to her.

'Look, Ella! See what I found! Isn't it lovely?'

She held out a long-stemmed dandelion.

'Oh – not that one,' Ella said, wrinkling her nose.

Jeannie's face clouded. 'Why not?'

Ella realised that Jeannie had never had the chance to learn about wild flowers – or butterflies and bees, for that matter. She'd been scarcely more than a toddler when they'd been forced to come and live in the workhouse, and never roamed the fields and meadows with Mammy as Ella had.

'It's a weed. We called it a wet-the-bed,' she explained gently. 'You don't want that one.'

'But it's so pretty! It's like the sun!' Jeannie protested.

Ella shook her head, smiling, and sighed.

'Oh, go on then. If you think Mammy will like it.'

'She will! I know she will!'

Jeannie was probably right, Ella thought. She'd like anything Jeannie had picked especially for her. But wild garlic grew here beneath the trees – the air was full of the smell of it – and Ella didn't want Jeannie picking any of the pretty little white flowers because she thought they looked like stars.

'Don't touch that, Jeannie!' she cautioned as her sister made a bee-line for the plants. 'Your hands will stink all day. And so will Mammy's if you give it to her.'

'Come along now! Time to go back!' Miss Sparks was calling and clapping her hands.

Reluctantly the children abandoned their treasure hunt and headed in her direction, some – eager to please – making haste, some dawdling. But a small knot of three boys, two big and one little, ignored her all together, and it looked as if a fight was starting between the two older ones.

'Leo! Arthur! Stop that!' Miss Sparks called, but again she was ignored, and the scuffling only worsened as they fell to the ground, rolling over and over, punching and gouging.

Miss Sparks hitched up her skirts and ran towards them with surprising speed, followed by some of the boys who were eager not to miss a good fistiuffs, while the girls hung back, looking frightened. Not so Ella. Leo, one of the combatants, was her best friend in the workhouse.

# Have you met the Families of Fairley Terrace?

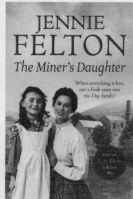

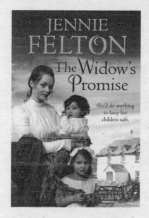

Jennie's compelling saga series is available now from Headline!

Author photograph © Will Nicol

**Jennie Felton** grew up in Somerset, and now lives in Bristol. She has written numerous short stories for magazines as well as a number of novels under a pseudonym. Her Families of Fairley Terrace Sagas is her series about the lives and loves of the residents of a Somerset village, beginning in the late nineteenth century, which started with *All The Dark Secrets*.

## Stay in touch with Jennie!

Visit her on Facebook at
www.facebook.com/JennieFeltonAuthor
for her latest news.

Or follow her on Twitter @Jennie_Felton